January 2014

Dear Friends,

It's exciting to me as an author to see these stories, written near the beginning of my career, getting a second life. *Marriage Between Friends* contains two of my early books: *White Lace and Promises* and *Friends— And Then Some*. Both were originally published in 1986—so I consider them "vintage"!

I've noticed how often we marry men who started out as friends. Over time that friendship deepens and in some cases ends in marriage, which is what happens in these two stories—as the title implies. But then, what else would you expect from an author with a romantic heart? One of the reasons I fell in love with my husband was that he could make me laugh like no one else. (Trust me, he's about the least romantic man you'll ever meet.) But Wayne can still make me laugh, and I consider him my dearest friend.

A highlight of my day is receiving reader mail. What you have to say is important to me, and I make a point of paying attention. Your opinions matter! You can reach me any number of ways: through my website at debbiemacomber.com or through Facebook. If you prefer, you can write me at P.O. Box 1458, Port Orchard, WA 98366. I look forward to hearing from you.

Warmest Regards,

Debbie Macomber

DEBBIE MACOMBER

MARRIAGE
Between Friends

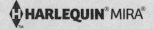

ISBN-13: 978-0-7783-1580-3

MARRIAGE BETWEEN FRIENDS

Copyright © 2014 by Harlequin Books S.A.

The publisher acknowledges the copyright holder of the individual works as follows:

WHITE LACE AND PROMISES
Copyright © 1986 by Debbie Macomber

FRIENDS—AND THEN SOME
Copyright © 1986 by Debbie Macomber

Recycling programs for this product may not exist in your area.

For questions and comments about the quality of this book, please contact us at CustomerService@Harlequin.com.

Printed in U.S.A.

Midnight Sons

VOLUME 1
(Brides for Brothers and
   The Marriage Risk)
VOLUME 2
(Daddy's Little Helper and
   Because of the Baby)
VOLUME 3
*(Falling for Him,
   Ending in Marriage* and
   Midnight Sons and Daughters)

This Matter of Marriage
Montana
Thursdays at Eight
Between Friends
Changing Habits
Married in Seattle
   (First Comes Marriage and
   Wanted: Perfect Partner)
Right Next Door
   (Father's Day and
   *The Courtship of
   Carol Sommars)*
Wyoming Brides
   (Denim and Diamonds and
   The Wyoming Kid)
Fairy Tale Weddings
   (Cindy and the Prince and
   Some Kind of Wonderful)
The Man You'll Marry
   (The First Man You Meet and
   The Man You'll Marry)

Orchard Valley Grooms
   (Valerie and *Stephanie)*
Orchard Valley Brides
   (Norah and *Lone Star Lovin')*
The Sooner the Better
An Engagement in Seattle
   (Groom Wanted and
   Bride Wanted)
Out of the Rain
   (Marriage Wanted and
   Laughter in the Rain)
Learning to Love
   (Sugar and Spice and
   Love by Degree)
You...Again
   (Baby Blessed and
   Yesterday Once More)
Three Brides, No Groom
The Unexpected Husband
   (Jury of his Peers and
   Any Sunday)
I Left My Heart
   (A Friend or Two and
   No Competition)
Love in Plain Sight
   (Love 'n' Marriage and
   Almost an Angel)

*Debbie Macomber's
   Cedar Cove Cookbook*
*Debbie Macomber's
   Christmas Cookbook*

CONTENTS

To
Robyn Carr

I always knew you'd be a superstar.
Congratulations, my friend.

WHITE LACE AND PROMISES

One

Maggie Kingsbury ground the gears of her royal-blue Mercedes and pulled to a screeching halt at the red light. Impatient, she glanced at her wristwatch and muttered silently under her breath. Once again she was late. Only this time her tardiness hadn't been intentional. The afternoon had innocently slipped away while she painted, oblivious to the world.

When Janelle had asked her to be the maid of honor for the wedding, Maggie had hesitated. As a member of the wedding party, unwelcome attention would be focused on her. It wasn't until she had learned that Glenn Lambert was going to be the best man that she'd consented. Glenn had been her friend from the time she was in grade school: her buddy, her co-conspirator, her white knight. With Glenn there everything would be perfect.

But already things were going badly. Here she was due to pick him up at San Francisco International and she was ten minutes behind schedule. In the back of her mind, Maggie realized that her tardiness was another symptom of her discontent.

The light changed and she roared across the intersection, her back tires spinning. One of these days she was going to get a well-deserved speeding ticket. But not today, she prayed, please not today.

Her painting smock was smudged with a full spectrum of rainbow colors. The thick dark strands of her chestnut hair were pinned to the back of her head, disobedient curls tumbling defiantly at her temples and across her wide brow. And she had wanted to look so good for Glenn. It had been years since she'd seen him—not since high school graduation. In the beginning they had corresponded back and forth, but soon they'd each become involved with college and had formed a new set of friends. Their texts and emails had dwindled and as often happens their communication became a chatty note on a Christmas card. Steve and Janelle had kept her updated with what had been going on in Glenn's life, and from what she understood, he was a successful stockbroker in Charleston. It sounded like a job he would manage well.

It surprised Maggie that in all those years, Glenn hadn't married. At twenty-nine and thirty they were the only two of their small high school graduation class who hadn't. Briefly she wondered what had kept Glenn away from the altar. As she recalled, he had always been easy on the eyes.

Her mind conjured up a mental picture of a young Glenn Lambert. Tall, dark, athletic, broad shouldered, thin—she smiled—he'd probably filled out over the years. He was the boy who lived next door and they had been great friends and at times the worst of enemies. Once, in the sixth grade, Glenn had stolen her diary and as a joke made copies and sold them to the boys in their class. After he found her crying, he had spent weeks trying to make it up to her. Years later his patience had gotten her a passing grade in chemistry and she had fixed him up with a date for the Junior-Senior prom.

Arriving at the airport, Maggie followed the freeway signs that directed her to the passenger-pickup area. Almost immediately she sighted Glenn standing beside his luggage, watching the traffic for a familiar face. A slow smile blossomed across her lips until it hovered at a grin. Glenn had hardly changed, and yet he was completely different. He was taller than she remembered, with those familiar broad shoulders now covered by a heather-blue blazer instead of a faded football jersey. At thirty he was a prime specimen of manhood. But behind his easy smile, Maggie recognized a maturity—one he'd fought hard for and painfully attained. Maggie studied him with fascination, amazed at his air of deliberate casualness. He knew about her inheritance. Of course he knew; Steve would have told him. Involuntarily, her fingers tightened around the steering wheel as a sense of regret settled over her. As much as she would have liked to, Maggie couldn't go back to being a carefree schoolgirl.

She eased to a stop at the curb in front of him and leaned across the seat to open the passenger door. "Hey, handsome, are you looking for a ride?"

Bending over, Glenn stuck his head inside the car. "Muffie, I should have known you'd be late."

As she climbed out of the vehicle, Maggie grimaced at the use of her nickname. Glenn had dubbed her Muffie in junior high, but it had always sounded to Maggie like the name of a poodle. The more she'd objected the more the name had stuck until her friends had picked it up. The sweet, innocent Muffie no longer existed.

After checking the side-view mirror for traffic to clear, she opened her door and stepped out. "I'm sorry I'm late, I don't know where the time went. As usual I got carried away."

Glenn chuckled and shook his head knowingly. "When haven't you gotten carried away?" He picked up his suitcase and tucked it inside the trunk Maggie had just opened. Placing his hands on her shoulders, he examined her carefully and gave her a brief hug. "You look fantastic." His dark eyes were somber and sincere.

"Me?" she choked out, feeling the warmth of many years of friendship chase away her earlier concerns. "You always could lie diplomatically." Maggie had recognized early in life that she was no raving beauty. Her eyes were probably her best feature—dark brown with small gold flecks, almond shaped and slanting upward at the corners. She was relatively tall, nearly five foot eight, with long shapely legs. Actually, the years hadn't altered her outwardly. Like Glenn's, the changes were more inward. Life's lessons had left their mark on her as well.

Looking at Glenn, Maggie couldn't hide the feeling of nostalgia she experienced. "The last time I looked this bad I was dressed as a zucchini for a fifth-grade play."

He crossed his arms and studied her. "I'd say you were wearing typical Muffie attire."

"Jeans and sneakers?"

"Seeing you again is like stepping into the past."

Not exactly. She didn't stuff tissue paper in her bra these days. Momentarily, she wondered if Glenn had ever guessed that she had. "I've got strict instructions to drop you off at Steve's. The rehearsal's scheduled at the church tonight at seven." This evening he'd have the opportunity to see just how much she had changed.

Of all the people Maggie knew, Glenn would be the one to recognize the emotional differences in her. She might have been able to disguise them from others, but not from Glenn.

"With you chauffeuring me around there's little guarantee I'll make the wedding," Glenn teased affectionately.

"You'll make it," she assured him and climbed back into the car.

Glenn joined her and snapped the seat belt into place. Thoughtfully he ran his hand along the top of the dashboard. "I heard about your inheritance and wondered if it'd made a difference in your life."

"Well, I now live in a fancy beach house, and don't plan to do anything with the rest of my life except paint." She checked his profile for a negative response and finding none, she continued. "A secretary handles the mail, an estate planner deals with the finances, and there's a housekeeper and gardener as well. I do exactly as I want."

"Must be nice."

"I heard you haven't done so shabbily yourself."

"Not bad, but I don't lounge around in a beach house." He said it without censure. "I've had dealings with a lot of wealthy people the past few years. As far as I can see, having money can be a big disappointment."

The statement was open-ended, but Maggie refused to comment. Glenn's insight surprised her. He was right. All Great-aunt Margaret's money hadn't brought Maggie or her brother happiness. Oh, at first she had been filled with wonderful illusions about her inheritance. But these days she struggled to shroud her restlessness. To anyone else her life-style was a dream come true. Only Maggie knew differently.

"Money is supposed to make everything right. Only it creates more problems than it solves," she mumbled and pulled into the flow of traffic leaving the airport. Glenn didn't respond and Maggie wasn't sure he heard her, which was just as well, because the subject was one she preferred to avoid.

"It's hard to imagine Steve and Janelle getting married after all these years." A lazy grin swept across his tanned face.

Maggie smiled, longing to keep things light. "I'd say it was about time, wouldn't you?"

"I've never known two people more right for each other. The surprising part is that everyone saw it but them."

"I'm happy for those two."

"Me, too," he added, but Maggie noted that Glenn's tone held a hint of melancholy, as if the wedding was going to be as difficult for him as it was for her. Maggie couldn't imagine why.

"Steve's divorce devastated him," Maggie continued, "and he started dating Janelle again. The next
thing I knew they decided to march up the aisle." Maggie paused and gestured expressively with her right
hand.

Glenn's eyes fell on Maggie's artistically long fingers. It surprised him that she had such beautiful
hands. They looked capable of kneading the stiffest
clay and at the same time gentle enough to soothe a
crying child. She wore no rings, nor were her well-
shaped nails painted, yet her hands were striking. He
couldn't take his eyes from them. He had known Maggie most of her life and had never appreciated her
hands.

"Are you going to invite me out to your beach
house?" he asked finally.

"I thought I might. There's a basketball hoop in
the gym and I figured I'd challenge you to a game."

"I'm not worried. As I recall the only slam dunk you
ever made was with a doughnut into a cup of coffee."

Hiding her laugh, Maggie answered threateningly,
"I'll make you pay for that remark."

Their families had shared a wide common driveway, and Maggie had passed many an hour after
school playing ball with Glenn. Janelle and Steve and
the rest of the gang from the neighborhood had hung
around together. Most of the childhood friendships remained in place. Admittedly, Maggie wasn't as trusting of people nowadays. Not since she had inherited
the money. The creeps had come crawling out of the
woodwork the minute the news of her good fortune
was out. Some were obvious gold diggers and others

weren't so transparent. Maggie had gleaned valuable lessons from Dirk Wagner and had nearly made the mistake of marrying a man who loved her money far more than he cared for her.

"I don't suppose you've got a pool in that mansion of yours?"

"Yup."

"Is there anything you haven't got?" Glenn asked suddenly serious.

Maggie didn't know where to start, the list was so long. She had lost her purpose, her ambition, her drive to succeed professionally with her art. Her roster of friends was meager and consisted mainly of people she had known most of her life. "Some things," she muttered, wanting to change the subject.

"Money can't buy everything, can it?" Glenn asked so gently that Maggie felt her throat tighten.

She'd thought it would at first, but had learned the hard way that it couldn't buy the things that mattered most: love, loyalty, respect or friendship.

"No." Her voice was barely above a whisper.

"I suppose out of respect for your millions, I should call you Margaret," Glenn suggested next. "But try as I might, you'll always be Muffie to me."

"Try Maggie. I'm not Muffie anymore." She smiled to take any sting from her voice. With his returning nod, her hand relaxed against the steering wheel.

She exited from the freeway and drove into the basement parking lot of Steve's apartment building. "Here we are," she announced, turning off the engine. "With a good three hours to spare."

While Glenn removed his suitcase from the car

trunk, Maggie dug in the bottom of her purse for the apartment key Steve had given her. "I have strict instructions to personally escort you upstairs and give you a stiff drink. You're going to need it when you hear what's scheduled."

With his suitcase in tow, Glenn followed her to the elevator. "Where's Steve?"

"Working."

"The day before his wedding?" Glenn looked astonished.

"He's been through this wedding business before," she reminded him offhandedly.

The heavy doors swished closed and Maggie leaned against the back wall and pulled the pins from her hair. It was futile to keep putting it up when it came tumbling down every time she moved her head. Stuffing the pins in her pocket, she felt Glenn's gaze studying her. Their eyes met.

"I can't believe you," he said softly.

"What?"

"You haven't changed. Time hasn't marked you in the least. You're exactly as I remember."

"You've changed." They both had.

"Don't I know it." Glenn sighed, leaned against the side of the moving elevator and pinched the bridge of his nose. "Some days I feel a hundred years old."

Maggie was mesmerized by him. He was different. The carefree, easygoing teen had been replaced by an introspective man with intense, dark eyes that revealed a weary pain. The urge to ask him what had happened burned on her lips, but she knew that if she inquired into his life, he could ask about her own. Instead she led the way out of the elevator to the apartment.

The key turned and Maggie swung open the door to the high-rise that gave a spectacular view of San Francisco Bay.

"Go ahead and plant your suitcase in the spare bedroom and I'll fix us a drink. What's your pleasure?"

"Juice if there's any."

Maggie placed both hands on the top of the bar. "I'll see what I can do." Turning, she investigated the contents of the refrigerator and brought out a small can of tomato juice. "Will this do?"

"Give it to me straight," he tossed over his shoulder as he left the living room.

By the time he returned, Maggie was standing at the window holding a martini. She watched him take the glass of juice from the bar and join her.

"Are you on the wagon?" she asked impulsively.

"Not really. It's a little too early in the afternoon for me."

Maggie nodded as a tiny smile quirked at the corners of her mouth. The first time she had ever tasted vodka had been with Glenn.

"What's so amusing?"

"Do you remember New Year's Eve the year I was sixteen?"

Glenn's brow furrowed. "No."

"Glenn!" She laughed with disbelief. "After all the trouble we got into over that, I'd think you'd never forget it."

"Was that the year we threw our own private party?"

"Remember Cindy and Earl, Janelle and Steve, you and me and...who else?"

"Brenda and Bob?"

"No...Barb and Bob."

"Right." He chuckled. "I never could keep the twins straight."

"Who could? It surprises me he didn't marry both of them."

"Whatever happened to Bob?"

Maggie took a sip of her martini before answering. "He's living in Oregon, going bald, and has four kids."

"Bob? I don't believe it."

"You weren't here for the ten-year reunion." Maggie hadn't bothered to attend either, but Janelle had filled in the details of what she'd missed.

"I'm sorry I missed it," Glenn said and moved to the bar. He lifted his drink and finished it off in two enormous swallows.

Mildly surprised at the abrupt action, Maggie took another sip of hers, moved to a deep-seated leather chair, sat and tucked her long legs under her.

Glenn took a seat across from her. "So what's been going on in your life, Maggie? Are you happy?"

She shrugged indolently. "I suppose." From anyone else she would have resented the question, but she'd always been able to talk to Glenn. A half hour after being separated for years and it was as if they'd never been apart. "I'm a wealthy woman, Glenn, and I've learned the hard way about human nature."

"What happened?"

"It's a long story."

"Didn't you just get done telling me that we had three hours before the rehearsal?"

For a moment Maggie was tempted to spill her frustrations out. To tell Glenn about the desperate pleas for money she got from people who sensed her soft heart. The ones who were looking for someone to invest in a sure thing. And the users, who pretended friendship or love in the hopes of a lucrative relationship. "You must be exhausted. I'll cry on your shoulder another time."

"I'll hold you to that." He leaned forward and reached for her hand. "We had some good times, didn't we?"

"Great times."

"Ah, the good old days." Glenn relaxed with a bittersweet sigh. "Who was it that said youth was wasted on the young?"

"Mark Twain," Maggie offered.

"No, I think it was Madonna."

They both laughed and Maggie stood, reaching for her purse. "Well, I suppose I should think about heading home and changing my clothes. Steve will be here in an hour. That'll give you time to relax." She fanned her fingers through her hair in a careless gesture. "I'll see you tonight at the rehearsal."

"Thanks for meeting me," Glenn said, coming to his feet.

"I was glad to do it." Her hand was on the doorknob.

"It's great to see you again."

The door made a clicking sound as it closed and Glenn turned to wipe a hand over his tired eyes. It was good to be with Maggie again, but frankly, he was glad she'd decided to leave. He needed a few minutes to compose his thoughts before facing Steve. The first thing his friend was bound to ask him about was Angie.

Glenn stiffened as her name sent an instant flash of pain through him. She had married Simon two months earlier, and Glenn had thought that acceptance would become easier with time. It had, but it was far more difficult than he'd expected. He had loved Angie with a reverence; eventually he had loved her enough to step aside when she wanted to marry Simon. He'd been a fool, Glenn realized. If he had acted on his instincts, he'd have had a new bride on his arm for this trip. Now he was alone, more alone than he could ever remember. The last place he wanted to be was a wedding. Every part of it would only be a reminder of what could have been his, and what he'd allowed to slip through his fingers. He didn't begrudge Steve any happiness; he just didn't want to have to stand by and smile serenely when part of him was riddled with regrets.

Maggie shifted into third gear as she rounded the curve in the highway at twenty miles above the speed limit. Deliberately she slowed down, hating the urgency that forced her to rush home. The beach house had become her gilded cage. The world outside its door had taken on a steel edge that she avoided.

Although she had joked with Glenn about not being married, the tense muscles of her stomach reminded her of how much she envied Janelle. She would smile for the wedding pictures and be awed at all the right moments, but she was going to hate every minute of it. The worst part was she was genuinely happy for Janelle and Steve. Oh, Janelle had promised that they'd continue to get together as they always had. They'd been best friends since childhood, and for a time they probably would see each other regularly. But Janelle wanted to start a family right away, and once she had a baby, Maggie thought, everything would change. It had to.

Automatically Maggie took the road that veered from the highway and a few minutes later turned onto the long circular driveway that led to her waterfront house. The huge structure loomed before her, impressive, elegant and imposing. Maggie had bought it for none of those reasons. She wasn't even sure she liked it. The two-story single-family dwelling on Eastwood Drive where she had grown up was far more appealing. Even now she couldn't bring herself to sell that house and had rented it for far less than market value to a retired couple who kept the yard and flower beds meticulously groomed. Sometimes during the darkest hour of a sleepless night, Maggie would mull over the idea of donating her money to charity. If possible, she would gladly return to the years when she had sat blissfully at her bedroom window, her chin resting on her crossed arms as she gazed into the stars and dreamed of the future. Childhood dreams that were never meant to come true.

Shaking herself from her reverie, Maggie parked the fancy sport car in front of the house. For this night she would put on her brightest smile. No one would ever know what she was feeling on the inside.

* * *

Janelle's mother looked as if she were preparing more for a funeral than a wedding. Flustered and worried, she waved her hands in five different directions, orchestrating the entourage gathered in the church vestibule.

"Girls, please, please pay attention. Darcy go right, June left and so on. Understand?"

The last time anyone had called Maggie a girl was in high school. Janelle, Maggie, the bridesmaids, the flower girl, and the ring bearer were all positioned, awaiting instructions. Maggie glanced enviously to the front of the church where Steve and Glenn were standing. It didn't seem fair that they should get off so lightly.

"Remember to count to five slowly before following the person in front of you," Janelle's mother continued.

The strains of organ music burst through the church and the first attendant, shoulders squared, stepped onto the white paper runner that flowed down the center aisle.

"I can't believe this is really happening," Janelle whispered. "Tomorrow Steve and I will be married. After all the years of loving him it's like a dream."

"I know," Maggie whispered and squeezed her friend's forearm.

"Go left, go left." Mrs. Longmier's voice drifted to them and Maggie dissolved into giggles.

"I can't believe your mother."

"The pastor assured her he'd handle everything, but she insisted on doing it herself. That's what I get for being the only girl in a family of four boys."

"In another twenty years or so you may well be doing it yourself," Maggie reminded her.

"Oops." Janelle nudged her. "Your turn. And for heaven's sake don't goof up. I'm starved and want to get out of here."

Holding a paper plate decorated with bows and ribbons from one of Janelle's five wedding showers, Maggie carefully placed one foot in front of the other in a deliberate, step-by-step march that seemed to take an eternity. The smile on her face was as brittle as old parchment.

Standing in her place at the altar, Maggie kept her head turned so she could see Janelle's approach. The happiness radiating from her friend's face produced a curious ache in Maggie's heart. If these feelings were so strong at the rehearsal, she couldn't help wondering how she'd react during the actual wedding. Maggie felt someone's eyes on her and glanced up to see Glenn's steady gaze. He smiled briefly and looked away.

The pastor moved to the front of the young couple and cracked a few old jokes. Everyone laughed politely. As the organ music filled the church, the bride and groom, hands linked, began their exit.

When it came time for Maggie to meet Glenn at the head of the aisle, he stiffly tucked her hand in the crook of his elbow.

"I never thought I'd be marching down the aisle with you," she whispered under her breath.

"It has all the makings of a nightmare," Glenn countered. "However, I'll admit you're kinda cute."

"Thanks."

"But so are lion cubs."

Maggie's fingers playfully bit into the muscles of his upper arm as she struggled not to laugh.

His hand patted hers as he whispered, "You're lovely."

"Is that so?" Maggie batted her eyes at him, blatantly flirting with him. "And available. I have a king size bed too."

They were nearing the back of the church. Glenn's dark eyes bored holes into her. "Are you looking for a lover?"

The question caught Maggie by surprise. The old Glenn would have swatted her across the rump and told her to behave. The new Glenn, the man she didn't know, was dead serious. "Not this week," she returned, deliberately flippant. "But if you're interested, I'll keep you in mind."

His gaze narrowed slightly as he tilted his head to one side. "How much have you had to drink?"

Maggie wanted to laugh and would have if not for a discouraging glare from Mrs. Longmier. "One martini."

The sound of a soft snort followed. "You've changed, Maggie." Just the way he said it indicated that he wasn't pleased with the difference.

Her spirits crashed to the floor with breakneck speed. Good grief, she thought angrily, it didn't matter what Glenn thought of her. He had made her feel like a teenager again and she'd behaved like a fool. She wasn't even sure why she was flirting with him. Probably to cover up how miserable the whole event made her.

Casually, Glenn dropped her arm as they entered

the vestibule and stepped aside to make room for the others who followed. Maggie used the time to gather her light jacket and purse. Glenn moved in the opposite direction and her troubled gaze followed him.

A flurry of instructions followed as Steve's father gave directions to the family home, where dinner was being served to the members of the wedding party.

Maggie moved outside the church. There wasn't any need for her to stay and listen. She knew how to get to the Grants' house as well as her own. Standing at the base of the church steps, Maggie was fumbling inside her purse for her keys when Glenn joined her.

"I'm supposed to ride with you."

"Don't make it sound like a fate worse than death," she bit out, furious that she couldn't do what she needed.

"Listen, Maggie, I'm sorry. Okay?"

"You?" Amazed, Maggie lowered the purse flap and slowly raised her dark eyes to his. "It's me who should apologize. I was behaving like an idiot in there, flirting with you like that."

He lifted a silken strand of hair from her shoulder. "It's rather nice to be flirted with now and then," he said with a lazy smile.

Maggie tore her gaze from his and withdrew her car keys. "Here," she said, handing the key chain to him. "I know you'll feel a whole lot safer driving yourself."

"You're right," he retorted, his mood teasing and jovial. "I still remember the day you wiped out two garbage cans and an oak tree backing out of the driveway."

"I'd just gotten my learner's permit and the gears slipped," she returned righteously.

"Unfortunately your skills haven't improved much."

"On second thought, I'll drive and you can do the praying."

Laughing, Glenn tossed an arm across her shoulders.

They chatted easily on the way to the Grants' home and parked behind Steve and Janelle in the driveway. The four car doors slammed simultaneously.

"Glad to see you still remember the way around town," Steve teased Glenn. The two men were nearly the same height, both with dark hair and brown eyes. Steve smiled lovingly at Janelle and brought her close to his side. "I hope everyone's hungry," he said, waiting for Glenn and Maggie to join them. "Mom hasn't stopped cooking in two days."

"Famished," Glenn admitted. "The last time I ate was on the plane."

"Poor starving baby," Maggie cooed.

Glenn was chuckling when the four entered the house. Immediately Janelle and Maggie offered to help Steve's mother and carried the assorted salads and platters of deli meats to the long table for the buffet. Soon the guests were mingling and helping themselves.

Maggie loaded her plate and found an empty space beside Glenn, who was kneeling in front of the coffee table with several others. He glanced up from the conversation he was having with a bridesmaid when Maggie joined them.

"Muffie, you know Darcy, don't you?" Glenn asked.

"Muffie?" Darcy repeated incredulously. "I thought your name was Maggie."

"Muffie was the name Glenn gave me in junior high. We were next-door neighbors. In fact, we lived only a few blocks from here."

"I suppose you're one of those preppy, organized types," Darcy suggested.

Glenn nearly choked on his potato salad. "Hardly."

Maggie gave him the sharp point of her elbow in his ribs. "Glenn thought he was being cute one day and dubbed me something offensive. Muffie, however, was better than Magpie—"

"She never stopped talking," Glenn inserted.

"—or Maggie the Menace."

"For obvious reasons."

"For a while it was Molasses." Maggie closed her eyes at the memory.

"Because she was forever late."

"As you may have guessed, we fought like cats and dogs," Maggie explained needlessly.

"The way a lot of brothers and sisters do," Glenn inserted.

"So where did the Muffie come in?"

"In junior high things became a bit more sophisticated. We couldn't very well call her Magpie."

Darcy nodded and sliced off a bite of ham.

"So after a while," Glenn continued, "Steve, Janelle, the whole gang of us decided to call her Muffie, simply because she talked so much we wanted to muffle her. The name stuck."

"Creative people are often subjected to this form of harrassment," Maggie informed her with a look of injured pride.

"Didn't you two...?" Darcy hesitated. "I mean Steve and Janelle obviously had something going even then."

"Us?" Maggie and Glenn shared a look of shock. "I did ask you to the Sadie Hawkins dance once."

Glenn nodded, a mischievous look in his eyes. "She'd already asked five other guys and been turned down."

"So I drastically lowered my standards and asked Glenn. It was a complete disaster. Remember?"

Their eyes met and they burst into fits of laughter, causing the conversational hum of the room to come to an abrupt halt.

"Hey you two, let me in on the joke," Darcy said. "What's so funny?"

Maggie composed herself enough to begin the story. "On the way home, Glenn's beat up car stalled. We learned later it was out of gas. Believe me, I wasn't pleased, especially since I'd sprung for new shoes and my feet were killing me."

"I don't know why you're complaining; I took you to the dance, didn't I?"

Maggie ignored him. "Since I didn't have a driver's license, Mr. Wonderful here insisted on steering while I pushed his car—uphill."

"You?" Darcy was aghast.

"Now, Maggie, to be fair, you should explain that I helped push, too."

"Some help," she grumbled. "That wasn't the worst part. It started to rain and I was in my party dress, shoving his car down the street in the dead of night."

"Maggie was complaining so loud that she woke half the neighborhood," Glenn inserted, "and someone looked out the window and thought we were stealing a car. They phoned the police and within minutes we were surrounded by three patrol cars."

"They took us downtown and phoned Glenn's dad. It was the most embarrassing moment of my life. The Girls' Club had sponsored the dance and I was expecting roses and kisses in the moonlight. Instead I got stuck pushing Glenn's car in the rain and was darn near arrested."

"Believe me, Maggie made me pay for that one." Glenn's smiling eyes met hers and Maggie felt young and carefree again. It'd been so long since she had talked and laughed like this; she could almost forget. Almost. The present, however, was abruptly brought to her attention a few minutes later when Steve's cousin approached her.

"Maggie," he asked, crowding in next to her on the floor, "I was wondering if we could have a few minutes alone? There's something I'd like to ask you."

A heavy sensation of dread moved over her. It had happened so often in the past that she knew almost before he spoke what he would say. "Sure, Sam." As of yet, she hadn't found a graceful way of excusing herself from these situations.

Rolling to her feet, she followed Sam across the room to an empty corner.

"I suppose Steve's told you about my business venture?" he began brightly with false enthusiasm.

Maggie gritted her teeth, praying for patience. "No, I can't say that he has."

"Well, my partner and I are looking for someone with a good eye for investment potential who would be willing to lend us a hundred thousand dollars. Would you happen to know anyone who might be interested?"

Maggie noticed Glenn making his way toward them. As she struggled to come up with a polite rejection to Sam, Glenn stopped next to her.

"Sam," he interrupted, taking Maggie by the arm, "excuse us for a minute, will you?" He didn't wait for a response and led her through the cluttered living room and into the kitchen.

"Where are you taking me?" Maggie asked when he opened the sliding glass door that led to the patio.

"Outside."

"That much is obvious. But why are you taking me out here?"

Glenn paused to stand under the huge maple tree and looked toward the sky. "There's only a half-moon tonight, but it'll have to do."

"Are you going to turn into a werewolf or something?" Maggie joked, pleased to be rescued from the clutches of an awkward conversation.

"Nope." He turned her in his arms, looping his hands around her narrow waist and bringing her against the hard wall of his chest. "This is something I should have done the night of the Girls' Club dance," he murmured as he looked down at her.

"What is?"

"Kiss you in the moonlight," he whispered just before his mouth claimed hers.

Two

Maggie was too amazed to respond. Glenn Lambert, the boy who had lived next door most of her life, was kissing her. And he was kissing her as if he meant to be doing exactly that. His lips moved slowly over hers, shaping and fitting his mouth to hers with a gentleness that rocked her until she was a churning mass of conflicting emotions. This was Glenn, the same Glenn who had teased her unmercifully about "going straight" while she wore braces. The Glenn who had heartlessly beaten her playing one-on-one basketball. The same Glenn who had always been her white knight. Yet it felt so right, so good to be in his arms. Hesitantly, Maggie lifted her hands, sliding them over his chest and linking her fingers at the base of his neck, clinging to him for support. Gently parting her lips, she responded to his kiss. She savored the warm taste of him, the feel of his hands against the small of her back and the tangy scent of his after-shave. It seemed right for Glenn to be holding her. More right than anything had felt in a long time.

* * *

When he lifted his head there was a moment of stunned silence while the fact registered in Glenn's bemused mind that he had just kissed Maggie. Maggie. But the vibrant woman in his arms wasn't the same girl who'd lived next door. The woman was warm and soft and incredibly feminine, and he was hungry for a woman's gentleness. Losing Angie had left him feeling cold and alone. His only desire had been to love and protect her, but she hadn't wanted him. A stinging chill ran through his blood, forcing him into the present. His hold relaxed and he dropped his arms.

"Why'd you do that?" Maggie whispered, having difficulty finding her voice. From the moment he had taken her outside, Maggie had known his intention had been to free her from the clutches of Steve's cousin— not to kiss her. At least not like that. What had started out in fun had become serious.

"I'm not sure," he answered honestly. A vague hesitancy showed in his eyes.

"Am I supposed to grade you?"

Glenn took another step backward, broadening the space between them. "Good grief, no; you're merciless."

Mentally, Maggie congratulated him for recovering faster than she. "Not always," she murmured. At his blank look, she added, "I'm not always merciless."

"That's not the way I remember it. The last time I wanted to kiss you, I got a fist in the stomach."

Maggie's brow furrowed. She couldn't remember Glenn even trying to kiss her and looked at him with surprise and doubt as she sifted through her memories. "I don't remember that."

"I'm not likely to forget it," he stated and arched one brow arrogantly. "As I recall, I was twelve and you were eleven. A couple of the guys at school had already kissed a girl and said it wasn't half-bad. There wasn't anyone I wanted to kiss, but for a girl you weren't too bad, so I offered you five of my best baseball cards if you'd let me kiss you."

Maggie gave him a wicked grin as her memory returned. "That was the greatest insult of my life. I was saving my lips for the man I planned to marry. At the time I think it was Billy Idol."

"As I recall you told me that," he replied with a low chuckle. He tucked an arm around her waist, bringing her to his side. "Talking about our one and only date tonight made me remember how much I took you for granted all those years. You were great."

"I know," she said with a complete lack of modesty.

A slow, roguish grin grew across his features. "But then there were times…"

"Don't go philosophical on me, Glenn Lambert." An unaccustomed, delicious heat was seeping into her bones. It was as if she'd been standing in a fierce winter storm and someone had invited her inside to sit by the cozy warmth of the fire.

"We've both done enough of that for one night," Glenn quipped, looking toward the bright lights of the house.

Maggie didn't want to go back inside. She felt warm and comfortable for the first time in what seemed like ages. If they returned to the house full of people, she'd be forced to paint on another plastic smile and listen to the likes of Steve's cousin.

"Do you ever wonder about the old neighborhood?"

Grinning, Glenn looked down on her. "Occasionally."

"Want to take a look?"

He glanced toward the house again, sensing her reluctance to return. The old Maggie would have faced the world head-on. The change surprised him. "Won't we be missed?"

"I doubt it."

Glenn tucked Maggie's hand in the crook of his arm. "For old times' sake."

"The rope swing in your backyard is still there."

"You're kidding!" He gave a laugh of disbelief.

"A whole new generation of kids are playing on that old swing."

"What about the tree house?"

"That, unfortunately, was the victim of a bad windstorm several years back."

His arm tightened around her waist and the fragile scent of her perfume filled his senses. She was a woman now, and something strange and inexplicable was happening between them. Glenn wasn't sure it was right to encourage it.

"How do you keep up with all this?" he asked, attempting to steer his thoughts from things he shouldn't be thinking, like how soft and sweet and wonderfully warm she felt.

"Simple," Maggie explained with a half smile. "I visit often." The happiest days of her life had been in that house in the old neighborhood. She couldn't turn back the clock, but the outward symbols of that time lived on for her to visit as often as needed. "Come on," she said brightly and took his hand. She was feeling both foolish and fanciful. "There probably won't be another chance if we don't go now."

"You'll freeze," Glenn warned, running his hands down the lengths of her bare arms and up again to cup her shoulders.

"No," she argued, not wanting anything to disturb the moment.

"I'll collect your jacket and tell Steve what we're up to," Glenn countered.

"No," she pleaded, her voice low and husky. "Don't. I'll be fine. Really."

Glenn studied her for an instant before agreeing. Maggie was frightened. The realization stunned him. His bubbly, happy-go-lucky Maggie had been reduced to an unhappy, insecure waif. The urge to take her in his arms and protect her was nearly overwhelming.

"All right," he agreed, wrapping his arms around her shoulder to lend her his warmth. If she did get chilled he could give her his own jacket.

With their arms around each other, they strolled down Ocean Avenue to the grade school, cut through the play yard and came out on Marimar near East-wood Drive.

"Everything seems the same," Glenn commented. His smile was filled with contentment.

"It is."

"How are your parents doing?" he inquired.

"They retired in Florida. I told them they ought to be more original than that, but it was something they really wanted. They can afford it, so why not? What about your folks?"

"They're in South Carolina. Dad's working for the same company. Both Eric and Dale are married and supplying them with a houseful of grandchildren."

A chill shot through Maggie and she shivered involuntarily. She was an aunt now, too, but the circumstances weren't nearly as pleasant. Her brother, Denny, had also discovered that his inheritance wasn't a hedge against unhappiness. Slowly shaking her head, Maggie spoke. "Do you realize how old that makes me feel? Dale married—I'd never have believed it. He was only ten when you moved."

"He met his wife the first year of college. They fell in love, and against everyone's advice decided not to wait to get married. They were both nineteen and had two kids by the time Dale graduated."

"And they're fine now?"

"They're going stronger than ever. The boys are in school and Cherry has gone back to college for her degree." There wasn't any disguising the pride in his voice.

"What about Eric?"

"He married a flight attendant a couple of years ago. They have a baby girl." His hand rested at the nape of her neck in a protective action. "What about your brother?"

"Denny was already married by the time you moved, wasn't he? He and Lisa have two little girls."

"Is he living in San Francisco?"

"Yes," she supplied quickly and hurried to change the subject. "The night's lovely, isn't it?"

Glenn ignored the comment. "Is Denny still working for the phone company?"

"No," she returned starkly. "I can't remember when I've seen so many stars."

They were silent for a moment while Glenn digested the information. Something had happened between Denny and Maggie that she was obviously reluctant to discuss.

"Do you realize that there's never been a divorce in either of our families?" she said softly with sudden insight. She knew what a rarity that was in this day and age. Nearly thirty percent of their high school class were on their second marriages.

"I doubt that there ever will be a divorce. Mom and Dad believe strongly in working out problems instead of running from them and that was ingrained in all three of us boys."

"We're in the minority then. I don't know how Janelle is going to adjust to Steve's children. It must be difficult."

"She loves him," Glenn countered somewhat defensively.

"I realize that," Maggie whispered, thinking out loud. "It's just that I remember when Steve married Ginny. Janelle cried for days afterward and went about doing her best to forget him. Every one of us knew that Ginny and Steve were terribly mismatched and it would only be a matter of time before they split."

"I wasn't that sure they couldn't make a go of it."

Maggie bristled. "I was, and anyone with half a brain saw it. Ginny was pregnant before the wedding and no one except Steve was convinced the baby was his."

"Steve was in a position to know."

Maggie opened her mouth to argue, glanced up to see Glenn's amused gaze and gingerly pressed her lips tightly closed. "I don't recall you being this argumentative," she said after several moments.

"When it comes to the sanctity of marriage, I am."

"For your sake, I hope you marry the right woman then."

The humor drained from his eyes and was replaced with such pain that Maggie's breath caught in her throat. "Glenn, what did I say?" she asked, concern in her voice.

"Nothing," he assured her with a half smile that disguised none of his mental anguish. "I thought I had found her."

"Oh, Glenn, I'm so sorry. Is there anything I can do? I make a great wailing wall." From the pinched lines about his mouth and eyes, Maggie knew that the woman had been someone very special. Even when Maggie had known him best, Glenn had been a discriminating male. He had dated only a few times and, as far as she could remember, had never gone steady with one girl.

The muscles of his face tightened as he debated whether to tell Maggie about Angie. He hadn't discussed her with anyone over the past couple of months and the need to purge her from his life burned in him. Perhaps someday, he thought, but not now and not with Maggie, who had enough problems of her own. "She married someone else. There's nothing more to say."

"You loved her very much, didn't you?" Whoever she was, the woman was a fool. Glenn was the steady, solid type most women sought. When he loved, it would be forever and with an intensity few men were capable of revealing.

Glenn didn't answer. Instead he regarded her with his pain-filled eyes and asked, "What about you?"

"You mean why I never married?" She gave a shrug of indifference. "The right man never came along. I thought he might have once, but I was wrong. Dirk was more interested in spending my money than loving me."

"I'm sorry." His arm tightened around her as an unreasonable anger filled him over the faceless Dirk. He had hurt Maggie, and Glenn was intimately aware of how much one person could hurt another.

"Actually, I think I was lucky to discover it when I did. But thirty is looming around the corner and the biological clock is ticking like Big Ben. I'd like to get married, but I won't lower my standards."

"What kind of man are you looking for?"

He was so utterly blasé about it that Maggie's composure slipped and she nearly dissolved into laughter. "You mean in case you happen to know someone who fits the bill?"

"I might."

"Why not?" she asked with a soft giggle. "To start off, I'd like someone financially secure."

"That shouldn't be so difficult."

He was so serious that Maggie bit into her bottom lip to hide the trembling laughter. "In addition to being on firm financial ground, he should be magnanimous."

"With you he'd have to be," Glenn said in a laughter-tinged voice.

Maggie ignored the gibe. "He'd have to love me enough to overlook my faults—few as they are—be loyal, loving, and want children."

She paused, expecting him to comment, but he nodded in agreement. "Go on," he encouraged.

"But more than simply wanting children, he'd have to take responsibility for helping me raise them into worthwhile adults. I want a man who's honest, but one who won't shout the truth in my face if it's going to hurt me. A special man to double my joys and divide my sorrows. Someone who will love me when my hair is gray and my ankles are thick." Realizing how serious she'd become, Maggie hesitated. "Know anyone like him?" Her words hung empty in the silence that followed.

"No," Glenn eventually said, and shook his head for emphasis. Those were the very things he sought in a wife. "I can't say that I do."

"From my guess, Prince Charmings are few and far between these days."

They didn't speak again until they paused in front of the fifty-year-old house that had been Glenn's childhood home. Little had altered over the years, Glenn realized. The wide front porch and large dormers that jutted out from the roof looked exactly as they had in his mind. The house had been repainted, and decorative shutters were now added to the front windows, but the same warmth and love seemed to radiate from its doors.

Maggie followed Glenn's gaze to the much-used

basketball hoop positioned above the garage door. It was slightly crooked from years of slam dunks. By the look of things, the hoop was used as much now as it had been all those years ago.

"I suppose we should think of heading back. It's going to be a long day tomorrow." Maggie's gaze fell from the house to the cracked sidewalk. It hit her suddenly that in a couple of days Glenn would be flying back to Charleston. He was here for the wedding and nothing more.

"Yes," Glenn agreed in a low, gravelly voice. "Tomorrow will be a very long day."

The vestibule was empty when Maggie entered the church forty minutes before the wedding. Out of breath and five minutes late, she paused to study the huge baskets of flowers that adorned the altar, and released an unconscious sigh at the beauty of the sight. This wedding was going to be special. Hurrying into the dressing room that was located to her right, Maggie knocked once and opened the door. The woman from The Wedding Shop was helping Janelle into her flowing lace gown. Mrs. Longmier was sitting in a chair, dabbing the corner of her eye with a tissue.

"Oh, Maggie, thank goodness you're here. I had this horrible dream that you showed up late. The wedding was in progress and you ran down the aisle screaming how dare we start without you."

"I'm here, I'm here, don't worry." Stepping back, Maggie inspected her friend and could understand Mrs. Longmier's tears. Janelle was radiant. Her wedding gown was of a lavish Victorian style that was exquisitely fashioned with ruffled tiers of Chantilly lace and countless rows of tiny pearls. "Wow," she whispered in awe. "You're going to knock Steve's eyes out."

"That's the idea," Janelle said with a nervous smile.

Another woman from the store helped Maggie don her blushing-pink gown of shimmering taffeta. Following a common theme, the maid of honor's and the bridesmaids' dresses were also Victorian in style, with sheer yokes and lace stand-up collars. Lace bishop sleeves were trimmed with dainty satin bows. The bodice fit snugly to the waist and flared at the hip. While the woman fastened the tiny buttons at the back of the gown, Maggie studied her mirrored reflection. A small smile played on her mouth as she pictured Glenn's reaction when he saw her. For years she wore tight jeans and sweatshirts. She had put on a dress for the rehearsal, but this gown would amaze him. She was a woman now and it showed.

The way her thoughts automatically flew to Glenn surprised Maggie, but she supposed it was natural after their kisses and walk in the moonlight. He had filled her dreams and she'd slept better than she had in a long while.

After their visit to the old neighborhood, Maggie's attitude toward the wedding had changed. She wouldn't be standing alone at the altar with her fears. Glenn, her friend from childhood, would be positioned beside her. Together they would lend each other the necessary strength to smile their way through the ordeal. Maggie realized her thoughts were more those of a martyr than an honored friend, but she'd dreaded the wedding for weeks. Not that she begrudged Janelle any happiness. But Maggie realized that at some time during the wedding dinner or the dance scheduled to follow, someone would comment on her single status. With Glenn at her side it wouldn't matter nearly as much.

From all the commotion going on outside the dressing room, Maggie realized the guests were beginning to arrive. Nerves attacked her stomach. This wasn't the first time she'd been in a wedding party, but it was the most elaborate wedding to date. She pressed a calming hand to her abdomen and exhaled slowly.

"Nervous?" Janelle whispered.

Maggie nodded. "What about you?"

"I'm terrified," she admitted freely. "Right now I wish Steve and I had eloped instead of going through all this." She released her breath in a slow, drawn-out sigh. "I'm convinced that halfway through the ceremony my veil's going to slip or I'll faint, or something equally disastrous."

"You won't," Maggie returned confidently. "I promise. Right now everything's overwhelming, but you won't regret a minute of this in the years to come."

"I suppose not," Janelle agreed. "This marriage is forever and I want everything right."

"I'd want everything like this, too." Maggie spoke without thinking and realized that when and if she ever married she wanted it to be exactly this way. She yearned for a flowing white dress with a long train and lifetime friends to stand with her.

Someone knocked on the door and, like an organized row of ducklings, the wedding party was led into the vestibule. Organ music vibrated through the

church and the first bridesmaid, her hands clasping
a bouquet of pink hyacinths, stepped forward with a
tall usher at her side.

Maggie watched her progress and knew again that
someday she wanted to stand in the back of a church
and look out over the seated guests who had come to
share her moment of joy. And like Janelle, Maggie
longed to feel all the love that was waiting for her as
she slowly walked to the man with whom she would
share her life. And when she repeated her vows before
God and those most important in her life she would
feel, as Janelle did, that her marriage was meant to
last for all time.

When it was her turn to step onto the trail of white
linen that ran the length of the wide aisle, Maggie
held her chin high, the adrenaline pumping through
her blood. Her smile was natural, not forced. Mentally she thanked Glenn for that and briefly allowed
her gaze to seek him out in the front of the church.
What she found nearly caused her to pause in midstep.
Glenn was standing with Steve at the side of the altar
and looking at her with such a wondrous gaze that her
heart lodged in her throat. This all-encompassing wonder was what Maggie had expected to see in Steve's
eyes when he first viewed Janelle. A look so tender it
should be reserved for the bride and groom. The moment stretched out until Maggie was convinced everyone in the church had turned to see what was keeping
her. By sheer force of will she continued with short
steps toward the front of the church. Every resound-
ing note of the organ brought her closer to Glenn.
She felt a throb of excitement as the faces of people

she'd known all her life turned to watch her progress. A heady sensation enveloped her as she imagined it was she who was the bride, she who would speak her vows, she who had found her soul mate. Until that moment Maggie hadn't realized how much she yearned for the very things she had tried to escape in life, how much she was missing by hiding in her gilded cage, behind her money.

As they'd practiced the night before, Maggie moved to the left and waited for Janelle and Steve to meet at center front. At that point she would join her friend and stand at Janelle's side.

With the organ music pulsating in her ear, Maggie strained to catch Steve's look when he first glimpsed Janelle. She turned her head slightly, and paused. Her gaze refused to move beyond Glenn who was standing with Steve near the front of the altar. Even when Janelle placed her hand in Steve's, Maggie couldn't tear her eyes from Glenn. The pastor moved to the front of the church and the four gathered before him. Together they lifted their faces to the man of God who had come to unite Steve and Janelle.

The sensations that came at Glenn were equally disturbing. The minute Maggie had started down the aisle it had taken everything within him not to step away from Steve, meet her and take her in his arms. He had never experienced any sensation more strongly. He wanted to hold her, protect her, bring the shine back to her eyes and teach her to trust again. When she had met him at the airport he'd been struck by how lovely she'd become. Now he recognized her vulnerability, and she was breathtaking. He had never seen a more beautiful woman. She was everything he'd ever wanted—warm, vibrant, alive and standing so close that all he had to do was reach out and touch her. He felt like a blind man who had miraculously and unexpectedly been gifted with sight. Maggie needed him. Charleston, with all its painful memories, lay on the other side of the world.

"Dearly beloved, we are called here today to witness the vows between Janelle and Stephen."

The rush of emotion that assaulted Maggie was unlike anything she'd every known. She couldn't keep her eyes from Glenn, who seemed to magnetically compel her gaze to meet his. Their eyes locked and held as the pastor continued speaking. There was no exchange of smiles, no winks, nothing cute or frivolous, but a solemn mood that made that instant, that moment, the most monumental of their lives. Maggie felt a breathless urgency come over her, and an emotion so powerful, so real that it brought brimming tears that filled her vision. In order to keep her makeup from streaking, she held one finger under each eye a hand at a time and took in several deep breaths to forestall the ready flow. The void, the emptiness in her life wasn't entirely due to her money. What she needed was someone to love and who would love her. Desperately, Maggie realized how much she wanted to be needed. Several seconds passed before she regained her composure. The tightening lessened in her chest and she breathed freely once again.

When the pastor asked Steve and Janelle to repeat

their vows, Maggie's gaze was again drawn to Glenn's. He didn't speak, nor did Maggie, but together, in unison, each syllable, each word was repeated in their hearts as they issued the same vows as their friends. When the pastor pronounced them man and wife, Maggie raised stricken eyes to the man of God who had uttered the words, needing the reassurance about whom he had meant. It was as if he had been speaking to Glenn and her, as well, and as if the formal pronouncement included them.

The organ burst into the traditional wedding march and Steve and Janelle turned to face the congregation, their faces radiant with happiness. As the newly wedded couple moved down the aisle, Glenn's arm reached for Maggie's, prepared to escort her. At the touch of his hand at her elbow, Maggie felt a series of indescribable sensations race through her: wonder, surprise, joy. Their eyes met and for the first time that day, he smiled. An incredible, dazzling smile that all but blinded her. Their march down the aisle, her arm on his elbow, added to the growing feeling that that day, that moment was meant for them as well.

Family and friends gathered outside the church doors, spilling onto the steps, giving hearty applause as Steve turned Janelle into his arms and kissed her. A festive mood reigned as Janelle was joyously hugged and Steve's hand was pumped countless times. The photographer was busily snapping pictures, ordering the wedding party to pose one way and then another.

For a brief second the fantasy faded enough to frighten Maggie. What game was Glenn playing with her? No. She'd seen the sincerity in his eyes. But pretending was dangerous, far too dangerous.

"Are you all right?" Glenn whispered in her ear.

Maggie didn't have the opportunity to answer. As it was, she wasn't sure how to respond. Under other circumstances, she would have asked him to drive her to the hospital emergency room. Her daydreams were overpowering reality. This wasn't her wedding, nor was the man at her side her husband. She had no right to feel sensations like these.

The next thing she knew, Glenn had disappeared. Maggie hardly had time to miss him when a shiny new Cadillac pulled to the curb. Just Married was painted on the back window. Glenn jumped out and opened both doors on the passenger side. Then, racing up the church stairs, he took Maggie by the hand and following on the heels of Steve and Janelle, pulled her through a spray of rice and laughter as he whisked her toward the car.

Amidst hoots and more laughter, Glenn helped her gather her full-length skirt inside the automobile before closing the door and running around the front to climb in beside her.

Maggie was still breathless with laughter when he flashed her another of his dazzling smiles and started the engine. A sea of happy faces was gazing in at them. Turning her head to look out the side window, Maggie was greeted with the well-wishes of several boys and girls—children of their friends—standing on the sidewalk and waving with all their might. Glenn checked the rearview mirror and pulled into the steady flow of street traffic.

"Maggie, it was just as wonderful as you claimed it would be," Janelle said softly from the back seat.

"Did you doubt?" Steve questioned, his voice thick with emotion.

"I'll have you know, Mr. Grant, that I nearly backed out of this wedding at the very last minute. The only thing that stopped me was Maggie. Somehow she convinced me everything was going to work out. And it did."

"Janelle, I hardly said anything," Maggie countered, shocked by her friend's admission.

"You said just enough."

"I'm eternally grateful," Steve murmured and from the sounds coming from the back seat he was showing Janelle just how grateful he was that she was his bride.

Glenn's hand reached for Maggie's and squeezed it gently. "You look stunning." He wanted to say so much more and discovered he couldn't. For weeks he had dreaded the wedding and having to stand at the altar with his friend when it should have been his own wedding. The day had been completely unlike anything he'd expected. Maggie alone had made the difference.

"You make a striking figure yourself," she said, needing to place their conversation on an even keel.

Glenn unfastened the top button of the ruffled shirt and released the tie. "I feel like a penguin."

Laughter bubbled up in Maggie. She felt happy, really happy for the first time in a long while. When Glenn held out his arms, she scooted across the seat so that they were as close as possible within the confines of the vehicle.

The sounds of smothered giggles from the back seat assured Maggie that things were very fine indeed. They stopped at a light and Glenn's gaze wandered to her for a brief, glittering second, then back to the road. "Thank you for today," he said, just low enough for her to hear. "You made our friends' wedding the most special day of my life."

"I...felt the same way about you," she whispered, wanting him to kiss her so badly she could almost taste his mouth over hers.

"Maggie," Janelle called from the back seat. "Will you check this veil? I can't walk into the dinner with it all askew. People will know exactly what kind of man I married."

"Oh, they will, will they?" Steve said teasingly, and kissed her soundly.

Maggie turned and glanced over her shoulder. "Everything looks fine. The veil's not even crooked, although from the sound of things back there it should be inside out and backward."

"Maggie," Steve said in a low and somewhat surprised tone as he studied her, "I expected Janelle's mother to cry, even my own. But I was shocked to see you were the one with tears in your eyes."

"You were shocked?" she tossed back nonchalantly. "Believe me, they were just as much of a surprise to me. Tears were the last thing I expected."

"Count your blessings, you two," Glenn said, tossing a glance over his shoulder. "Knowing Muffie, you should be grateful she didn't burst into fits of hysterical laughter." He glanced over to her and leaned close and whispered, "Actually, they should thank me. It took everything in me not to break rank and reach for you." Glenn hadn't meant to tell her that, but those tears had nearly been his undoing. He had known when he'd seen her eyes bright with unshed tears that what was happening to him was affecting Maggie just as deeply. He had come so close to happiness once, and like a fool, he'd let it slip away. It wouldn't happen again; he wouldn't allow it.

Everything was happening so quickly that Maggie didn't have time to react. Glenn's breath fanned her temple and a shiver of apprehension raced up her spine. They were playing a dangerous game. All that talk in the moonlight about the sanctity of marriage had affected their brain cells and they were daydreaming. No…pretending that this moment, this happiness, this love, was theirs. Only it wasn't, and Maggie had to give herself a hard mental shake to dislodge the illusion.

A long string of cars followed closely behind as the other members of the wedding party caught up with the Cadillac. Watching Glenn weave in and out of traffic, Maggie was impressed with his driving skill. However, everything about Glenn had impressed her today. Fleetingly, she allowed her mind to wander to what would happen when he left on Monday. She didn't want this weekend to be the end, but a beginning. He lived in Charleston, she in San Francisco. The whole country separated them, but they were only hours apart by plane and seconds by phone.

When he turned and caught her studying him, Maggie guiltily shifted her attention out the side window.

The way her heart was hammering, one would think she was the bride. She struggled for composure.

Janelle's family had rented a huge Victorian hall for the dinner and dance. Maggie had no idea that there was such a special place in San Francisco and was assessing the wraparound porch and second-floor veranda when the remainder of the wedding party disembarked from the long row of cars that paraded behind the Cadillac. Wordlessly, Glenn took her by the elbow and led her up the front stairs.

Everything inside the huge hall was lushly decorated in antiques. Round tables with starched white tablecloths were set up to serve groups of eight. In the center of each table was a bowl of white gardenias. A winding stairway with a polished mahogany banister led to the dance floor upstairs.

Being seated at the same table as Steve and Janelle added to the continuing illusion. Somehow Maggie made it through the main course of veal cordon bleu, wild rice and tender asparagus spears. Her appetite was nonexistent and every bite had the taste and the feel of cotton. Although Glenn was at her side, they didn't speak, but the communication between them was louder than words. Twice she stopped herself from asking him what was happening to them, convinced he had no answers and the question would only confuse him further.

When Janelle cut the wedding cake and hand-fed the first bite to Steve, the happy applause vibrated around the room. The sound of it helped shake Maggie from her musings and she forced down another bite of her entrée. The caterers delivered the cake to the wedding guests with astonishing speed so that all the guests were served in a matter of minutes.

Glenn's eyes darkened thoughtfully as he dipped his fork into the white cake and paused to study Maggie. He prayed she wasn't as confused as he. He didn't know what was happening, but was powerless to change anything. He wasn't even convinced he wanted anything different. It was as if they were in a protective bubble, cut off from the outside world. And although they sat in a room full of people, they were alone. Not knowing what made him do anything so crazy, Glenn lifted his fork to her mouth and offered Maggie the first sample of wedding cake. His eyes held her immobile as she opened her mouth and accepted his offering. Ever so lightly he ran his thumb along her chin as his dark, penetrating eyes bored into hers. By the time she finished swallowing, Glenn's hand was trembling and he lowered it.

Promptly Maggie placed her clenched fingers in her lap. A few minutes later she took a sip of champagne, her first that day, although she knew that enough was happening to her equilibrium without adding expensive champagne to wreak more damage.

The first muted strains of a Vienna waltz drifted from the upstairs dance floor. Maggie took another sip of champagne before standing.

Together, Steve and Janelle led their family and friends up the polished stairway to the dance floor.

When he saw the bride and groom, the orchestra leader stepped forward and announced: "Ladies and gentlemen, I give you Mr. and Mrs. Stephen Grant."

Steve took Janelle in his arms and swung his young bride around the room in wide fanciful steps. Pausing briefly, he gestured to Glenn, who swung Maggie into his arms.

Again the announcer stepped to the microphone and introduced them as the maid of honor and best man. All the while, the soft music continued its soothing chords and they were joined by each bridesmaid and usher couple until the entire wedding party was on the dance floor.

As Glenn held Maggie in his arms, their feet made little more than tiny, shuffling movements that gave the pretense of dancing. All the while Glenn's serious, dark eyes held Maggie's. It was as though they were the only two in the room and the orchestra was playing solely for them. Try as she might, Maggie couldn't pull her gaze away.

"I've been wanting to do something from the moment I first saw you walk down the aisle."

"What?" she asked, surprised at how weak her voice sounded. She thought that if he didn't kiss her soon she was going to die.

Glenn glanced around him to the wide double doors that led to the veranda. He took her by the hand and led her through the crowd and out the curtained glass doors.

Maggie walked to the edge of the veranda and curled her fingers over the railing. Dusk had already settled over the city and lights from the bay flickered in the distance. Glenn joined her and slipped his arms around her waist, burying his face in her hair. Turning her in his arms, he closed his eyes and touched his forehead to hers. He took in several breaths before speaking.

"Are you feeling the same things I am?" he asked.

"Yes." Her heart was hammering so loud, Maggie was convinced he'd hear it.

"Is it the champagne?"

"I had two sips."

"I didn't have any," he countered. "See?" He placed the palm of her hand over his heart so she could feel its quickened beat. "From the moment I saw you in the church it's been like this."

"Me too," she whispered. "What's happening to us?"

Slowly, he shook his head. "I wish I knew."

"It's happening to me, too." She took his hand and placed it over her heart. "Can you feel it?"

"Yes," he whispered.

"Maggie, listen, this is going to sound crazy." He dropped his hands as if he needed to put some distance between them and took several steps back.

"What is?"

Glenn jerked his hand through his hair and hesitated. "Do you want to make this real?"

Three

"Make this real?" Maggie echoed. "What do you mean?"

Glenn couldn't believe the ideas that were racing at laser speed through his mind. Maggie would burst into peals of laughter and he wouldn't blame her. But even that wasn't enough to turn the course of his thoughts. He had this compulsion, this urgency to speak as if something were driving him to say the words. "Steve and Janelle are going to make this marriage a good one."

"Yes," Maggie agreed. "I believe they will."

The look she gave him was filled with questions. Surely she realized he hadn't asked her onto the veranda to discuss Steve and Janelle. After Angie, Glenn hadn't expected to feel this deep an emotion again. And so soon was another shock. Yet when he'd seen Maggie that first moment in the church the impact had been so great it was as though someone had physically assaulted him. She was lovely, possessing a rare beauty that had escaped his notice when they were younger. No longer had he been standing witness to his best friends' wedding, but he'd participated in a ceremony with a woman who could stand at his side for a lifetime. Maggie had felt it, too; he had seen it in her eyes. The identical emotion had moved her to tears.

"Glenn, you wanted to say something?" She coaxed him gently, her mind pleading with him to explain. He couldn't possible mean what she thought.

Remembering the look Maggie had given him when Steve and Janelle exchanged vows gave Glenn the courage to continue. "Marriage between friends is the best kind, don't you think?"

"Yes," she answered, unable to bring her voice above a husky whisper. "Friends generally know everything about each other, whether good or bad, and then still choose to remain friends."

They stood for a breathless moment, transfixed, studying each other, hesitant and unsure. "I'd always believed," Glenn murmured, his voice low and seductive, "that it would be impossible for me to share my life with anyone I didn't know extremely well."

"I agree." Maggie's mind was formulating impossible thoughts. Glenn was leading this conversation down meandering paths she'd never dreamed of traveling with him.

"We're friends," he offered next.

"Good friends," she agreed, nodding.

"I know you as well as my own brothers."

"We lived next door to each other for fifteen years," she added, her heart increasing its tempo to a slow drumroll.

"I want a home and children."

"I've always loved children." There hadn't been a time in her life when the pull was stronger toward a husband and family than it was that very moment.

"Maggie," he said, taking a step toward her, but still not touching her, "you've become an extremely beautiful woman."

Her lashes fluttered against her cheek as she lowered her gaze. Maggie didn't think of herself as beautiful. For Glen to say this to her, sent her heart racing. She hardly knew how to respond and finally managed a weak. "Thank you."

"Any man would be proud to have you for his wife."

The sensations that raced through her were all too welcome and exciting. "I…I was just thinking that a woman…any woman would be extremely fortunate to have you for a husband."

"Would you?"

Her heart fluttered wildly, rocketed to her throat and then promptly plummeted to her stomach. Yet she didn't hesitate. "I'd be honored and proud."

Neither said anything for a timeless second while their minds assimilated what had just transpired, or what they thought had.

"Glenn?"

"Yes."

Her throat felt swollen and constricted, her chest suddenly tight as if tears were brewing just beneath the surface. "Did I understand you right? Did you— just now—suggest that you and me—the two of us— get married?"

"That's exactly what I'm suggesting." Glenn didn't hesitate. He'd never been more sure of anything in his life. He had lost one woman; he wasn't going to lose Maggie. He would bind her to him and eliminate the possibility of someone else stepping in at the last moment. This woman was his and he was claiming her before something happened to drive her from his arms.

"When?"

"Tonight."

She blinked twice, convinced she hadn't heard him right. "But the license, and…"

"We can fly to Reno." Already his mind was working out the details. He didn't like the idea of a quickie wedding, but it would serve the purpose. After what they had shared earlier they didn't need anything more than a document to make it legal.

Stillness surrounded them. Even the night had gone silent. No cars, no horns, no crickets, no sounds of the night—only silence.

"I want to think about it," she murmured. Glenn was crazy. They both were. Talking about marriage, running away this very night to Reno. None of it made sense, but nothing in all her life had sounded more exciting, more wonderful, more right.

"How long do you want to think this over?" A thread of doubt caused him to ask. Perhaps rushing her wasn't the best way to proceed, but waiting felt equally impossible.

A fleeting smile touched and lifted Maggie's mouth. They didn't dare tell someone they would do anything so ludicrous. She didn't need time, not really. She knew what she wanted: she wanted Glenn.

"An hour," she said, hoping that within that time frame nothing would change.

The strains of another waltz drifted onto the veranda and wordlessly he led her back to the dance floor. When he reached for her, Maggie went willingly into his arms. His hold felt as natural as breathing, and she was drawn into his warmth. The past two days with Glenn had been the happiest, most exciting in years. Who would have thought that Glenn Lambert would make her pulse pound like a jackhammer and place her head in the clouds where the air was thin and clear thought was impossible? Twenty-four hours after his arrival, and they were planning the most incredible scheme. Their very best scheme, crazy as it sounded.

"This feeling reminds me of the night we stole out of the house to smoke our first cigarette," Glenn whispered in her ear. "Are we as daring and defiant now as we were at fourteen?"

"Worse," she answered. "But I don't care as long as you're with me."

"Oh, Maggie." He sighed her name with a wealth of emotion.

Her hands tightened around his neck as she fit her body more intimately to the contour of his. Her breasts were flattened to his broad chest; and they were melded together, thigh to thigh, hip to hip, as close as humanly possible under the guise of dancing.

Every breath produced an incredible range of new sensations. Maggie felt drugged and delirious, daring and darling, bold and extraordinarily shy. Every second in his arms brought her more strength of conviction. This night, in less than an hour she was going to walk out of this room with Glenn Lambert. Together they would fly to Reno and she would link her life with his. There was nothing to stop her. Not her money. Not her pride. Not her fears. Glenn Lambert was her friend. Tonight he would become her lover as well.

Unable to wait, Maggie rained a long series of kisses over the line of his jaw. The need to experience his touch flowered deep within her.

Glenn's hold at her waist tightened and he inhaled sharply. "Maggie, don't tease me."

"Who's teasing?" They'd known each other all these years and in that time he had only kissed her once. But it was enough, more than enough to know that the loving between them would be exquisite.

Without her even being aware, Glenn had maneuvered her into a darkened corner of the dance floor where the lighting was the dimmest. His eyes told her he was about to kiss her and hers told him she was eager for him to do exactly that. Unhurriedly, Glenn lowered his mouth to hers with an agonizing slowness. His kiss was warm and tender and lingering, as if this were a moment and place out of time meant for them alone. Her soft mouth parted with only the slightest urging and her arms tightened around his neck. Trembling in his embrace, Maggie drew in a long unsteady breath. Glenn's kisses had been filled with such aching tenderness, such sweet torment that Maggie felt tears stinging for release. Tears for a happiness she had never hoped to find. At least not with Glenn. This was a wondrous surprise. A gift. A miracle so unexpected it would take a lifetime to fully appreciate.

"I want you," he whispered, his voice hoarse with desire. His breath warmed her lips.

"Yes" she returned, vaguely dazed. "I want you, too."

His arms tightened and Maggie felt the shudder that rocked him until her ribs ached. Gradually his hold relaxed as his gaze polarized hers. "Let's get out of here."

"Should...should we tell anyone?" *No*, her mind shouted. Someone might try to talk them out of this and she didn't want that to happen. She yearned for everything that Glenn suggested.

"Do you want to tell Steve and Janelle?" Glenn asked.

"No."

Tenderly he brushed his lips across her forehead. "Neither do I. They'll find out soon enough."

"It'll be our surprise." She smiled at him, the warm happy smile of someone about to embark on the most exciting adventure of her life. And Maggie felt like an adventurer, daring and audacious, dauntless and intrepid, reckless and carefree. There'd be problems; she realized that. But tonight with Glenn at her side there wasn't anything she couldn't conquer.

Glenn raised her fingertips to his lips and kissed each one. "I'm not letting you out of my sight. We're going directly to the airport."

"Fine." She had no desire to be separated from him, either.

"I'll call a taxi."

"I'll get my purse."

The night air brought a chill to her arms, but it didn't sharpen any need to analyze what they were doing. If Glenn expected her to have second thoughts as they breezed through the streets of San Francisco, she found none. Even the busy airport, with its crowded concourses and people who stared at their unusual dress, wasn't enough to cause her to doubt.

Glenn bought their airline tickets, and she found a seat while he used his cell to make hotel reservations. When he returned, the broad smile reached his eyes. Maggie was struck anew with the wonder of what was happening.

"Well?"

"Everything's been taken care of."

"Everything?" It seemed paramount that they get married tonight. If they were forced to wait until morning there could be second thoughts.

"The Chapel of Love is one block from city hall and they're going to arrange for the marriage license." He glanced at his watch and hesitated. "The plane lands at ten-thirty and the ceremony is scheduled for eleven-fifteen." He sat in the seat beside her and reached for her hand. "You're cold."

"A little." Despite her nerves she managed to keep her voice even. She didn't doubt they were doing the right thing and wanted to reassure Glenn. "I'm fine. Don't worry about me."

Rising to his feet, Glenn stripped the tuxedo jacket from his arms and draped it over her shoulders. "Here. We'll be boarding in a few minutes and I'll get you a blanket from the flight attendants." His dark eyes were full of warmth and he was smiling at her as if they'd been sitting in airports, waiting for planes to fly them to weddings every day.

His strong fingers closed over hers and for the first time she admired how large his hands were. The fingers were long and tapered and looked capable of carving an empire or soothing a crying child. "Are you—" Maggie swallowed convulsively, almost afraid to ask "—are you having any second thoughts?"

"No," he answered quickly. "What about you?"

"None." She was never so positive of anything in her life.

"I'll be a good husband."

"I know." She placed her free hand over the back of his. "And I'll be a good wife."

His returning smile, filled with warmth and incredible wonder, could have melted a glacier.

"My parents are going to be ecstatic." Shocked too, her mind added, but that didn't matter.

"Mine will be pleased as well," Glenn assured her. "They've always liked you."

He bent his head toward her and Maggie shyly lifted her face and met him halfway. His kiss was filled with soft exploration, and they parted with the assurance that everything was perfect.

"After we're married, will you want me to move to Charleston?" Maggie ventured.

"No," he said on a somber note. "I'll move to San Francisco." The time had come to leave Charleston. Glenn wanted to bury the unhappiness that surrounded him there. The brief visit to San Francisco had felt like coming home. With Maggie at his side he'd build a new life in San Francisco. Together they'd raise their family and live in blissful happiness. No longer would he allow the memory of another woman to haunt him.

Maggie felt simultaneously relieved and confused. Her career in art made it possible for her to work anywhere. For Glenn to move to San Francisco would mean giving up his Charleston clientele and building up a new one on the West Coast. It didn't make sense. "I don't mind moving, really. It would be easier for me to make the change. You've got your career."

He slid his hand from her arm to her elbow, tightening his hold. "I'll transfer out here." Turning his wrist he glanced at his watch, but Maggie had the feeling he wasn't looking at the time. "I'm ready for a change," he murmured after a while. "You don't mind, do you?"

Did she? No, Maggie decided, she loved California. "No, that'll be fine. You'll like the beach house."

"I don't doubt that I will."

Their flight number was announced and Maggie returned Glenn's tuxedo jacket before they boarded the plane. The flight attendant came by a few minutes later, after they were comfortably seated, to check their seat belts. She paused and commented that they both looked as if they were on their way to a wedding. Glenn and Maggie smiled politely, but neither of them opted to inform the young woman that it was exactly what they were doing. Maggie feared that if they let someone in on their plan it would somehow shatter the dream. Briefly she wondered if Glenn shared her fears.

The flight touched down on the Reno runway precisely on schedule. With no luggage to collect, Glenn and Maggie walked straight through the airport and outside, where a taxi was parked and waiting.

"You two on your way to a wedding?" the cabdriver asked with a loud belly laugh as he held the door open for Maggie.

"Yes," Maggie answered shyly, dismissing her earlier fears.

"Ours," Glenn added, sliding into the seat next to Maggie and reaching for her hand.

The heavyset cabbie closed the door and walked around to the driver's side. He checked the rearview mirror and merged with the traffic. "Lots of people come to Reno to get married, but then a lot of folks come here to get unmarried, too."

A thundering silence echoed through the close confines of the taxi. "There won't be any divorce for us," Glenn informed him.

The driver tipped back the rim of his cap with his index finger. "Lot of folks say that, too." He paused at the first red light, placed his arm along the back of the seat and turned to look at Glenn. "Where was it you said you wanted to go?"

"Chapel of Love," Glenn said firmly and glanced over to Maggie. "Unless you want to change your mind?" he whispered.

"You're not backing out of your proposal, are you?" The words nearly stuck in her throat.

"No."

"Then we're getting married," she murmured, more determined than ever. "I didn't come this far in a shimmering pink taffeta gown to play the slot machines."

"Good."

"Very good," she murmured, unwilling to let anyone or anything ruin this night.

A half hour later, after arriving at the chapel, Maggie had freshened her makeup and done what she could with her hair. They stood now before the proprietor of the wedding chapel.

"Organ music is fifteen dollars extra," Glenn told her as he reached for his back pocket.

Her hand stopped him. "I don't need it," she assured him with perfect serenity. "I'm still hearing the music from the church."

The impatience drained from his eyes and the look he gave her was so profound that it seemed the most natural thing in the world to lean forward and press her lips to his.

The justice of the peace cleared his throat. "If you're ready we can start the ceremony."

"Are you ready?" Glenn asked with smiling eyes.

"I've been ready for this all night," she answered, linking her arm with his.

The service was shockingly short and sterile. They stood before the justice and repeated the words that had already been spoken in their hearts. The stark ceremony wasn't what Maggie would have preferred, but it didn't diminish any of her joy. This wedding was necessary for legal reasons; their real vows had already been exchanged earlier that day as they stood witnesses for Steve and Janelle. Those few moments in the church had been so intense that from then on every moment of her life would be measured against them. Maggie yearned to explain that to Glenn, but mere words felt inadequate. He, too, had experienced it, she realized, and without analyzing it, he had understood.

Their room at the hotel was ready when they arrived. With the key jingling in Glenn's pocket they rode the elevator to the tenth floor.

"Are you going to carry me over the threshold, Mr. Lambert?" Maggie whispered happily and nuzzled his ear. She felt a free-flowing elation unlike anything she'd ever experienced. That night and every night for the rest of her life would be spent in Glenn's arms.

"I'll see what I can manage," Glenn stated seriously as he backed her into the corner of the elevator and kissed the side of her neck.

Maggie shot him a dubious look. "I'm not that heavy, you know."

"What I suggest we do," he murmured as he nibbled on her earlobe, "is have me lift one of your legs and you can hop over the threshold."

"Glenn," she muttered, breaking free. "That's crazy."

Chuckling, he ignored the question. "On second thought I could probably manage to haul you piggy-back."

Deftly her fingers opened his tie and she teased his throat with the moist tip of her tongue. If he was going to joke with her then she'd tease him as well. "Never mind," she whispered. "I'll carry you."

The elevator came to a grinding halt and the doors swished open. Glenn glanced around him, kissed Maggie soundly and with a mighty heave-ho, hauled her over his shoulder fireman fashion.

"Glenn…" she whispered fiercely, stunned into momentary speechlessness. "Put me down this instant."

Chuckling, he slowly rubbed his hand over her prominently extended derriere. "You said you wanted me to carry you over the threshold. Only I can't very well manage you, the key and the door all at once."

Using her arms against his shoulders for leverage, Maggie attempted to straighten. "Glenn, please," she begged, laughing until it was difficult to speak and probably just as impossible to be understood.

He shifted her weight when he fidgeted with the key card. Maggie couldn't see what was happening, but the sound of the door opening assured her all was well. Her eyes studied the same door as it closed and the narrow entryway as he carried her halfway into the room. The next thing Maggie knew, she was falling through space. She gave a frightened cry until the soft cushion of the mattress broke her rapid descent.

Panting and breathless with laughter, Maggie lay sprawled across the bed. She smiled up at Glenn playfully and raised her arms to her husband of fifteen minutes. Glenn knelt beside her, his eyes alive with passion as he lowered his mouth to hers in a deep kiss that sent her world into a crazy tailspin. She clung to him, her fingers ruffling the thick, dark hair that grew at his nape. Wildly, she returned his kiss, on fire for him, luxuriating in the feel of his body over hers. Unexpectedly, he tore his mouth from hers and lifted his head. Without a word, he brushed the soft wisps of hair from her temple and dipped his head a second time to sample her mouth. When he broke away and moved to the long dresser that dominated one side of the hotel room, Maggie felt a sudden chill and rose to a sitting position.

A bottle of champagne was resting in a bed of crushed ice. With his back to her, Glenn peeled off the foil covering and removed the cork. He ached with the need to take her physically, but feared his building passion would frighten her. Silently, Glenn cursed himself for not having approached the subject sooner. He wanted her, but did he dare take her so soon?

The dresser mirror revealed Glenn's troubled frown and Maggie felt a brooding anxiety settle over her. For the first time she could see doubt in his eyes. The breath jammed in her lungs. No, not doubt, but apprehension, even foreboding. Maggie was feeling it, too. Maybe advancing from friends to lovers in the space of a few hours wasn't right for them. Maybe they should think it through very carefully before proceeding with what was paramount on both their minds. As far as she was concerned there wasn't any reason to wait. They were married. They knew each other better than most newlyweds. The certificate in Glenn's coat pocket granted them every right.

With her weight resting on the palm of one hand, she felt her heart throb painfully. "Glenn," she whispered brokenly, not knowing what to say, or how to say it.

The sound of her voice was drowned by the cork, exploding from the bottle. Fizzing champagne squirted across the dresser. Glenn deftly filled the two glasses and returned the dark bottle to its icy bed.

Handing her a goblet, Glenn joined her on the side of the mattress. "To my wife," he whispered tenderly and touched the edge of her glass to his.

"To my husband," she murmured in return. The bubbly liquid tickled her nose and she smiled shyly at Glenn as she took another sip. "I suppose this is when I'm supposed to suggest that I slip into something more comfortable."

"I'm for that." He quickly stood and strode across the room for the bottle, setting it on the floor next to the bed as he sat down again, avoiding her eyes the whole time.

"However, we both seemed to have forgotten something important." She bit her bottom lip in a gesture of uncertainty and laughter.

He glanced up expectantly. "What's that?"

"Clothes," she said and giggled. They had been so afraid to leave one another for fear something would happen to change their minds that they hadn't even stopped to pack an overnight bag.

"We're not going to need them." In that instant Glenn realized that they weren't going to wait. He wanted her. She wanted him; it was in her eyes and the provocative way she she regarded him. "We have two days," he murmured, "and I can't see any need we'll be having for clothes."

He was so utterly serious that laughter rumbled in her throat. Where there had once been anxiety there was expectancy. "Maybe we could get away with that sort of thing on the Riviera, but believe me, they arrest people for walking around nude in Reno."

Smiling, he tipped back his head and emptied his glass. "You know what I mean."

Maggie set their champagne glasses aside. "No," she said breathlessly as she lightly stroked the neatly trimmed hair at his temple. "I think you'll have to show me."

Gently, Glenn laid her back on the bed and joined

her so the upper portion of his body was positioned over the top of hers. His arms went around her, pressing her to his hard strength until her breasts strained against him. "I have every intention of doing exactly that."

His lips left hers to investigate her ear before tracing their way back across her cheek and reclaiming her mouth.

Maggie buried her face in the hollow of his throat, drawing in a deep shuddering breath as his busy hands fumbled with the effort to locate the tiny buttons at the back of her dress. Every place his fingers grazed her skin, a glowing warmth spread. Again Maggie opened her mouth to explore the strong cord of his neck, savoring his salty-tasting skin. She heard the harsh intake of his breath when she pulled his silk dress shirt free and stroked his muscular back.

"Oh, Glenn," she whispered when she didn't think she could stand it anymore. Her shoulders were heaving when he lifted his weight from her.

He rolled onto his back and she heard him release a harsh breath. "Maggie." His voice was thick and husky. "Listen, are you sure about this? We can wait."

"I'm sure," she whispered and switched positions so that now it was she who was sprawled half atop him. "Glenn, I'm so sure it hurts."

"Maggie, oh, Maggie." He repeated her name again and again in a broken whisper. "She'd spent a lifetime searching for him when all along he'd been so close and she hadn't known.

His arms crushed her then, and his mouth passionately sought hers with a greedy need that seemed to want to devour her. He took; she surrendered. He gave; she received. They were starved for each other and the physical love their bodies could share. With her arms wrapped securely around him, Maggie met his hunger with her own. When he half lifted her from the mattress she was trembling.

"Glenn," she whispered brokenly. "Oh, Glenn, don't ever let me go."

"Never," he promised, sitting on the edge of the bed with her cradled in his lap. "This is forever." His words were a vow. Carefully, in order not to tear her dress, his fingers released each tiny button at the back of her gown. As each one was freed he pressed his lips to the newly exposed skin.

"Forever," she repeated, and twisted so she could work loose the tuxedo tie and the buttons to the ruffled shirt. She pulled the shirt free of his shoulders and slid her hand down his chest to his tightening abdomen.

"Maggie," he warned hoarsely.

"Love me," she whispered. "Oh, Glenn, make me your wife."

Her fingers clutched frantically at his thick dark hair as he continued to stroke her breast.

All too soon she was on fire for him. Consumed with desire, lost in a primitive world, aware of nothing but the desperate need he awoke within her.

Moving quickly he laid her upon the mattress and eased his body over hers.

The loving was exquisite and when they'd finished a long moment passed before he gathered her in his arms. He rolled onto his side, taking her with him.

Lying cradled in his embrace, their legs entwined, Maggie closed her eyes and released a contented sigh.

"It was beautiful," she whispered, still overcome with emotion.

Glenn kissed the top of her head. "You're beautiful."

"So are you," she added quickly. "Oh, Glenn, we're going to have such a good life."

"Yes," he agreed and kissed her forehead.

Maggie snuggled closer against him and kissed the nape of his neck when he reached down to cover them with the sheet and blanket.

Glenn held her close, kissing the crown of her head until her eyes closed sleepily. Her last thought as she drifted into the welcoming comfort of slumber was of warmth and security.

Maggie woke a couple of times in the darkest part of the night, unaccustomed to sharing her bed. Each time she experienced the unexpected thrill of finding Glenn asleep at her side. No longer was she alone. Her joy was so great that she felt ten years old again, waking up on Christmas morning.

She cuddled him spoon fashion, pressing her softness to his backside. Her body fit perfectly to his. Edging her hand over his muscular ribs she felt his strength and knew that this man was as steady as the Rock of Gibraltar. She had chosen her life mate well. Content, she drifted back to sleep.

A low, grumbling sound woke her when morning light splashed into the room from the small crack between closed drapes. Sitting up, Maggie yawned and raised her arms high above her head. She was ravenous, and pressed a hand to her stomach to prevent her rumbling from waking Glenn. A menu for room service sat by the phone and Maggie reached for it, studying its contents with interest, wondering if it would wake him if she ordered anything.

Glenn stirred and rolled onto his back, still caught in the last dregs of sleep. Gloriously happy, Maggie watched as a lazy smile grew on his face. Pride swelled in her heart as she realized their lovemaking was responsible for his look of blessed contentment. Maybe she wasn't so hungry after all.

Her long, tangled hair fell forward as she leaned down to press her lips to his. As she drew near, he whispered something. At first Maggie couldn't understand his words, then she froze. Stunned, her hand flew to her breast at the unexpected pain that pierced her. The arctic chill extended all the way to her heart and she squeezed her eyes closed to fight back the burning tears. Choking on humiliation, she struggled to untangle herself from the sheet. Her frantic movements woke Glenn from the nether land of sleep to the world of consciousness.

He turned on his side and reached for her hand. "Good morning," he said cheerfully. At the sight of her stricken face, he paused and rose to a full sitting position. "What's wrong?"

"The name is Maggie," she whispered fiercely, shoving his hand away. "And in case you've forgotten, I'm your wife as well."

Four

Tugging the sheet loose from the mattress, Maggie climbed out of bed. Her hands were shaking so badly that she had trouble twisting the material around her. Glenn had mistaken her for another woman. A woman he had obviously once loved…and apparently still did. Holding it together with one hand she sorted through the tangled mess of clothes on the floor. The tightness in her chest was so painful she could barely breathe. The room swayed beneath her feet and she closed her eyes, struggling to maintain her balance and her aplomb. Everything had been so beautiful. So perfect. How readily she had fallen into the fantasy, believing in each minute with a childlike innocence and trust. She'd been living in a twenty-four-hour dream world. That fantasy had been shattered by the reality of morning and she was shamed to the very marrow of her bones.

Glenn wiped a hand over his face and struggled to a sitting position. He vaguely recalled the contented pleasure of sleeping with a warm body at his side. In his sleep he must have confused Maggie with Angie. He cursed Angie for haunting him in his marriage.

"Maggie, what did I say?"

Straightening, she turned to regard him coolly before speaking. "Enough." *More than enough,* her mind shouted. Clenching the sheet in one hand, her clothes in the other, she marched across the floor, her head tilted at a stately angle. She never felt more like crying in her life. Her pride and dignity remained intact but little else was as it should be.

Once inside the bathroom she leaned against the heavy door, her shoulders sagging. Covering her face with both hands in hurt and frustration, she let the sheet slip to the floor. Equal doses of anger and misery descended on her until she was convinced she'd slump under the force of their weight. She didn't know what do, but taking a bath seemed important.

"Maggie." Glenn stood on the other side of the door, his voice low and confused. "Tell me what I said. At least talk to me."

"No," she shouted, still reeling from the shock. "I don't want to talk. I've heard enough to last me a lifetime." Forcing herself into action, she turned on the faucet and filled the tub with steaming hot water. She had been a fool to believe in yesterday's illusions. The morning had shattered the dream—only she didn't want it to end. Glenn was someone she had thought she could trust. In her heart she knew that he wouldn't be like all the rest.

"Maggie, for the love of heaven give me a chance to explain."

Sliding into the steaming bath, Maggie bit into her

bottom lip and forced herself to think. She could demand that they divorce, but she didn't want that and Glenn didn't, either. For twelve hours she had been a happily married woman. Somehow Maggie had to find a way to stretch twelve hours into a lifetime.

In the other room Glenn dressed slowly, his thoughts oppressive. Things couldn't be worse. From the moment Maggie had met him at the airport he had seen how reserved and untrusting her inheritance had made her. Now he had hurt her, and he silently cursed himself for doing the very thing he vowed he never would. He could still see her stricken eyes glaring down at him when he woke. He'd wanted to take her in his arms and explain, but she'd jumped from the bed as if she couldn't get away fast enough. Not that he blamed her. The worst part was that he couldn't guarantee it wouldn't happen again. Angie had been an integral part of his life for nearly two years. He had cast her from his thoughts with an all-consuming effort, but he had no control over the ramblings of his mind while he slept. If only he knew what he'd said. He stroked his fingers through his hair and heaved a disgusted sigh. Whatever it was, he wouldn't allow it to ruin this marriage. Somehow he'd find a way to make it up to Maggie.

The bathroom door opened and Glenn turned anxiously. He studied Maggie's face for evidence of tears and found none. He had forgotten what a strong woman she was and admired her all the more. He vividly recalled the time she was fifteen and broke her arm skateboarding. She'd been in intense pain. Anyone else would have been screaming like a banshee, but not Maggie. She had gritted her teeth, but hadn't shed a tear. He also remembered how the only person she had trusted to help her had been him. The guilt washed over him in dousing waves.

"Can we talk now?" he asked her gently.

"I think we should," she said, pacing because standing in one spot seemed an impossible task. "We need to make some rules in this marriage, Glenn."

"Anything," he agreed.

"The first thing you have to do is stop loving that other woman right now. This minute." Her voice trembled and she battled for control.

Glenn felt physically ill. Maggie was unnaturally pale, her cheeks devoid of color. Her dark, soulful eyes contained a sorrow he longed to erase and yet he knew he couldn't. His thoughts were in turmoil. "You know I'd never lie to you."

"Yes." Glenn might be a lot of things, she knew, but a liar wasn't one of them.

"Maggie, I want this marriage to work, but what you're asking me to do is going to be hard."

A tingling sensation went through her that left her feeling numb and sick. She wouldn't share this man—not even with a memory.

"In that case," she murmured and swallowed, "I've got some thinking to do." She turned from him and started toward the door.

"Maggie." Glenn stopped her and she turned around. Their eyes met and held. "You don't want a divorce, do you?"

The word hit Maggie with all the impact of a freight

train. "No," she said, shaking her head. "I may be mad, Glenn Lambert, but I'm not stupid."

The door made an echoing sound that bounced off the walls as Maggie left the hotel room. Glenn felt his tense shoulder muscles relax. It had taken everything in him to ask her about a divorce. That was the last thing he wanted, but he felt he had to know where Maggie stood after what had happened that morning.

The curious stares that met Maggie as she stepped off the elevator convinced her that the first thing she had to do was buy something to wear that was less ostentatious. A wrinkled pink maid-of-honor gown would cause more than a few heads to turn, and the last thing Maggie wanted was attention. In addition, she couldn't demand that her husband give up his affection for another woman and love and care for her instead, when she looked like something the cat left on the porch.

The hotel had a gift shop where she found a summer dress of pale-blue polished cotton, which she changed into after purchasing it. A walk through the lobby revealed that Glenn was nowhere to be seen. With time weighing heavily on her hands, Maggie pulled a ten-dollar bill from her purse. Already the hotel casino was buzzing with patrons eager to spend their money. Standing in front of the quarter slot machine, Maggie inserted the first coin. Pressing the button, she watched the figures spin into a blur and slowly wind down to two oranges and a cherry. Maggie stared at the fifty cents she won in disbelief. She didn't expect to win. Actually, it was fitting that she was in Reno. She had just made the biggest gamble of her life. The scary part was that Maggie felt like a loser and had felt like one almost from the minute she inherited her Great-aunt Margaret's money. She felt the ridiculous urge to laugh, but recognized that if she gave in to the compulsion tears wouldn't be far behind.

Glenn found her ten minutes later, still playing the slot machine. For several moments he stood watching her, wondering how to approach this woman he had known most of his life. The woman who was now his wife. There were so many issues facing them that had to be settled before he left for Charleston. Maggie's inheritance was one thing he wouldn't allow to hang between them like a steel curtain. It was best to clear the air of that and everything else they could.

A discordant bell clanged loudly and a barrage of celebratory characters danced across the slot machine. She looked stunned and stepped back as the machine finished. Without emotion, she cashed out. As she turned, their eyes clashed. Her breath caught in her throat and she hesitated, waiting for him to speak first. Like her, he had purchased another set of clothes, and again Maggie wondered why she'd never noticed how extraordinarily good-looking Glenn was. He was a man any woman would be proud to call her husband. If he'd come to tell her he wanted out of the marriage, she didn't know what she would say. The time spent in front of the slot machine had given her the perspective to realize that Glenn was as shocked by what had happened as she was. She prayed that he hadn't come for the reason she suspected. Maggie wanted this marriage. She had been so lonely and miserable. The previous day with Glenn had been the most wonderful day of her life. Maybe she was still looking at the situation through rose-colored glasses, but the deed was done. They were married now. The other woman had no claim to him. He might murmur "her" name in his sleep, but he was married to Maggie.

"Our plane leaves in two hours," he said, stepping forward. "Let's get something to eat."

Nodding required a monumental effort. Her body went limp with relief.

The hostess at the restaurant led them to a booth and handed them menus. She gave Glenn a soft, slightly seductive smile, but Maggie was pleased to notice that he didn't pay the woman the least bit of attention. Glenn had never been a flirt. Beyond anything else, Maggie realized, Glenn was an intensely loyal man. For him to whisper another woman's name in his sleep had been all the more devastating for just that reason.

Almost immediately a waitress arrived, poured them each a cup of coffee and took their order.

"I want you to know that I'll do everything in my power to do what you asked," Glenn announced, his eyes holding hers. His hands cupped the coffee mug and there was a faint pleading note shining from his eyes. "About this morning; I suppose you want to know about her."

"Yes," Maggie whispered, hating the way his eyes softened when he mentioned his lost love.

A sadness seemed to settle over him. "Her name is Angie. We were…" He hesitated. "Engaged. She decided to marry her childhood sweetheart. It's as simple as that."

"You obviously cared about her a great deal," Maggie said softly, hoping to take some of the sting from her earlier comments. Talking about Angie, even now, was obviously painful for him.

He held her gaze without hesitation. "I did care for her, but that's over now. I didn't marry you longing for anyone else. You aren't a substitute. This marriage wasn't made on the rebound. We're both vulnerable for different reasons. I want you for my wife. Not anyone else, only you. We've known each other most of our lives. I like you a great deal and respect you even more. We're comfortable together."

"Yes, we are," she agreed. So Glenn regarded her as an old pair of worn shoes. He could relax with her and put aside any need for pretense…as she could. But then she hadn't exactly come into their marriage seeking white lace and promises. Or maybe she had, Maggie didn't know anymore; she was confused.

"We're going to work this out," he said confidently, smiling for the first time that day as he reached for her hand.

"We're going to try," she suggested cautiously. "I'm not so sure we've done the right thing running off like this. We were both half-crazy to think we could make a marriage work on a twenty-four-hour reacquaintance."

"I knew what we were doing every second," Glenn countered gruffly. "I wanted this, Maggie."

"I didn't know if it was right or wrong. I guess only time will tell if we did the right thing or not."

* * *

The flight back to San Francisco seemed to take a lifetime. Maggie sat by the window, staring at the miniature world far below. The landscape rolled and curved from jutting peaks to plunging valleys that reminded her of the first few hours of her marriage. Even now a brooding sense of unreality remained with her.

The days were shorter now that winter was approaching, and dusk had settled by the time the taxi pulled up in front of the beach house. While Glenn was paying the cabdriver, Maggie looked over the house where she'd voluntarily sequestered herself, wondering how Glenn would view the ostentatious showplace. Undoubtedly he would be impressed. Her friends had praised the beach house that seemed to lack for nothing. There was a work-out gym, a sauna, a Jacuzzi, a swimming pool and a tennis court in the side yard that Maggie never used. The house held enough attractions to keep even the most discriminating prisoner entertained.

On the way from the airport they had stopped off at Steve's empty apartment and picked up Glenn's luggage. Seeing it was a vivid reminder that he was scheduled to leave in the morning. "What time is your flight tomorrow?" she asked, wondering how long they'd be in Charleston. They had already decided to make their home in San Francisco, but arrangements would need to be made in Charleston.

His mouth hardened. "Are you so anxious to be rid of me?"

"No." She turned astonished eyes to him, stunned at his sharp tongue. He made it sound as though she wouldn't be going with him. She should. After all, she was his wife. She could make an issue of it now, or wait until she was certain she'd read him right. They had already experienced enough conflict for one day and Maggie opted to hold her tongue. Her fingers fumbled with the lock in an effort to get inside the house. "I have to phone my brother," she announced once the door was open.

"Denny?"

"Yes, Denny, or is that a problem, too?"

He ran his fingers through his hair and expelled an angry breath. "I didn't mean to snap at you."

Maggie lowered her gaze. "I know. We're both on edge. I didn't mean to bite your head off, either." They were nervous and unsure of each other for the first time in their lives. What had once been solid ground beneath their feet had become shifting sand. They didn't know where they stood…or if they'd continue to stand at all.

Glenn placed a hand at the base of her neck and gently squeezed it. "My flight's scheduled for three. We'll have some time together."

He didn't plan to have her travel with him! That was another shock. Fine, she thought angrily. If he didn't want her, then she wouldn't ask. "Good," she murmured sarcastically. Fine indeed!

The house foyer was paved with expensive tiles imported from Italy, and led to a plush sunken living room decorated with several pieces of furniture upholstered in white leather. A baby grand piano dominated one corner of the room. As she hung up Glenn's coat he wandered into the large living room, his hands in his pockets.

"Do you like it?"

"It's very nice" was all he said. He stood, legs slightly apart while his gaze rested on an oil painting hung prominently on the wall opposite the Steinway. It was one of Maggie's earlier works and her favorite, a beachscape that displayed several scenes, depicting a summer day's outing to the ocean. Her brush had captured the images of eager children building a sand castle. Another group of bikini-clad young girls were playing a game of volleyball with muscle-bound he-men. A family was enjoying a picnic, their blanket spread out on the sand, shaded by a multicolored umbrella. Cotton-candy clouds floated in a clear blue sky while the ocean waves crested and slashed against the shore. Maggie had spent hours agonizing over the minute details of the painting. Despite its candor and realism, Maggie's beachscape wasn't an imitation of a snapshot recording, but a mosaiclike design that gave a minute hint at the wonder of life.

"This is a marvelous painting. Where did you ever find it?" Glenn asked without turning around. "The detail is unbelievable."

"A poor imitation of a Brueghel." A smile danced at the corners of her mouth.

"Who?"

"Pieter Brueghel, a sixteenth-century Flemish painter."

"A sixteenth-century artist didn't paint this," Glenn challenged.

"No. I did."

He turned with a look of astonished disbelief. "You're not teasing, are you?" The question was rhetorical. His eyes narrowed fractionally as if reassessing her.

"It's one of my earliest efforts after art school. I've done better since, but this remains one of my favorite."

"Better than this?" His voice dipped faintly as though he doubted her words. "I remember you scribbling figures as a kid, but I never suspected you had this much talent."

A shiver of pleasure raced up her arm at the pride that gleamed from his eyes as he glanced from the painting back to her. "I had no idea you were this talented, Maggie."

The sincerity of the compliment couldn't be doubted. Others had praised her work, but Maggie had felt a niggling doubt as to the candidness of the comments. "Thank you," she returned, feeling uncharacteristically humble.

"I'd like to see your other projects."

"Don't worry, you'll get the chance. Right now, I've got to phone Denny. He'll wonder what happened to me."

"Sure. Go ahead. I'll wait in here if you like."

Maggie's office was off the living room. She hesitated a moment before deciding, then walked to the telephone on a table next to the couch. Her back was to Glenn as she picked up the receiver and punched out the number.

"Denny, it's Maggie."

"Maggie," he cried with obvious relief. "How was

the wedding? You must have been late. I tried to get hold of you all day."

It was on the tip of Maggie's tongue to tell him about her marriage, but she held back, preferring to waylay his questions and doubts. She would tell him soon enough.

Her brother's voice softened perceptibly. "I was worried."

"I'm sorry, I should have phoned." Maggie lifted a strand of hair around her ear.

"Did you get the money transferred?"

Maggie sighed inwardly, feeling guilty. Denny knew all the right buttons to push with her. "The money will be ready for you Monday morning."

"Thanks. You know Linda and I appreciate it." His voice took on a honey-coated appeal.

"I know."

"As soon as I talk to the attorney about my case I'll let you know where we stand."

"Yes, Denny, do that." A large portion of Denny's inheritance had been lost in a bad investment and Maggie was helping him meet expenses. She didn't begrudge him the money: how could she when she had so much? What she hated was what it was doing to him. Yet she couldn't refuse him. Denny was her brother, her only brother.

After saying her goodbye, she replaced the receiver and turned back to Glenn. "I gave the housekeeper the weekend off. But if you're hungry, I'm sure I'll be able to whip up something."

"How's Denny?" Glenn ignored her offer.

"Fine. Do you want something to eat or not?"

"Sure." His gaze rested on the phone and Maggie realized that he'd probably picked up the gist of her conversation with Denny. More than she had intended. As a stockbroker Glenn would know what a foolish mistake her brother had made and she wanted to save her brother the embarrassment if possible.

Determined to avoid the subject of her brother, Maggie strolled past Glenn, through the dining room and into the expansive kitchen that was equipped with every conceivable modern cooking device. The double-width refrigerator/freezer was well stocked with frozen meals so that all that was required of her was to insert one into the microwave, push a button and wait.

The swinging doors opened as Glenn followed her inside. He paused to look around the U-shaped room with its oak cabinets and marble countertops. His hands returned to his pockets as he cocked his thick brows. "A bit large, wouldn't you say? One woman couldn't possibly require this much space."

Of course the kitchen was huge, she thought, irritated. She hadn't paid an exorbitant price for this place for three drawers and a double sink. "Yes," she returned somewhat defensively. "I like it this way."

"Do you mind if I take a look outside?" he asked and opened the sliding glass doors that led to a balcony overlooking the ocean.

"Sure. Go ahead."

A breeze ruffled the drape as he opened and closed the glass French door. Maggie watched him move to the railing and look out over the beach below. If she paused and strained her ears, she could hear the the ocean as the wild waves crashed upon the sandy shore.

A crescent moon was barely visible behind a thick layer of clouds.

Leaning a hip against the counter, Maggie studied his profile. It seemed incomprehensible that the man who was standing only a few feet from her was her husband. She felt awkward and shy, even afraid. If he did head back to Charleston without her, their marriage would become increasingly unreal. Before Glenn turned to find her studying him, Maggie took out a head of lettuce from the refrigerator and dumped it into a strainer, and then placed it under the faucet.

Rubbing the chill from his arms, Glenn returned a few minutes later.

"Go ahead and pour yourself a drink," Maggie offered, tearing the lettuce leaves into a bowl. When he hesitated, she pointed to the liquor cabinet.

"I'm more interested in coffee if you have it."

"I'll make it."

"I'll do it."

Simultaneously they moved and somehow Maggie's face came sharply into contact with the solid mass of muscle and man. Amazingly, in the huge kitchen, they'd somehow managed to collide. Glenn's hand sneaked out to steady Maggie at the shoulders. "You okay?"

"I think so." She moved her nose back and forth a couple of times before looking up at him. "I should have known this kitchen wasn't big enough for the two of us."

Something warm and ardent shone from his eyes as his gaze dropped to her mouth. The air in the room crackled with electricity. The hands that were gripping her shoulders moved down her upper arms and tightened. Every ticking second seemed to stretch out of proportion. Then, very slowly, he half lifted her from the floor, his mouth descending to hers a fraction of an inch at a time. Maggie's heart skipped a beat, then began to hammer wildly. He deliberately, slowly, left his mouth a hair's space above hers so that their breaths mingled and merged. Holding her close, he seemed to want her to take the initiative. But the memory of that morning remained vivid in her mind. And now it seemed he intended to leave her behind in San Francisco as well. No, there were too many questions left unanswered for her to give in to the physical attraction between them. Still his mouth hovered over hers, his eyes holding her. At the sound of the timer dinging, Glenn released her. Disoriented, Maggie stood completely still until she realized Glenn had moved away. Embarrassed, she turned, making busywork at the microwave.

"That smells like lasagna," Glenn commented.

"It is." Maggie's gaze widened as she set out the dishes. What an idiot she'd been. The bell she heard hadn't been her heart's song from wanting Glenn's kisses. It had been the signal from her microwave that their dinner was ready. The time had come to remove the stars from her eyes regarding their marriage.

Maggie noted that Glenn's look was thoughtful when they ate, as if something was bothering him. For that matter, she was unusually quiet herself. After the meal, Glenn silently helped her stack the dinner plates into the dishwasher. "Would you like the grand tour?" Maggie inquired, more in an effort to ease the tension than from any desire to show off her home.

"You did promise to show me some more of your work."

"My art?" Maggie hedged, suddenly unsure. "I'm more into the abstract things now." She dried her hands on a terry-cloth towel and avoided looking at him. "A couple of years ago I discovered Helen Frankenthaler. Oh, I'd seen her work, but I hadn't appreciated her genius."

"Helen who?"

"Frankenthaler." Maggie enunciated the name slowly. "She's probably the most historically important artist of recent decades and people with a lot more talent than me have said so."

Glenn looped an arm around her shoulders and slowly shook his head. "Maggie, you're going to have to remember your husband knows absolutely nothing about art."

"But you know what you like," she teased, leading him by the hand to the fully glassed-in upstairs studio.

"That I do," he admitted in a husky whisper.

No one else had ever seen the studio, where she spent the vast majority of her time. It hadn't been a conscious oversight. There just had never been anyone she'd wanted to show it to. Not even Denny, who, she realized, only gave lip service to her work. She led Glenn proudly into her domain. She had talent and knew it. So much of her self-esteem was centered in her work. In recent years it had become the outpouring of her frustrations and loneliness. Her ego, her identity, her vanity were all tied up in her work.

Glenn noted that her studio was a huge room twice the size of the kitchen. Row upon row of canvases were propped against the walls. From the shine in her eyes, Glenn realized that Maggie took her painting seriously. She loved it. As far as he could see it was the only thing in this world that she had for herself.

He hadn't been pleased by what he'd overheard in her telephone conversation with Denny. He had wanted to ask Maggie about it over dinner, but hesitated. He felt that it was too soon to pry into her relationship with her brother. As he recalled, Denny was a decent guy, four or five years older than Maggie. From the sounds of it, though, Denny was sponging off his sister—which was unusual since he had heard that Denny was wealthy in his own right. It was none of his affair, Glenn decided, and it was best that he keep his nose out of it.

Proudly Maggie walked around the studio, which was used more than any other room in the house. Most of the canvases were fresh and white, waiting for the bold strokes of color that would bring them to life. Several of the others contained her early experiments in cubism and expressionism. She watched Glenn as he strolled about the room, studying several of her pictures. Pride shone in his eyes and Maggie basked in his approval. She wanted to hug him and thank him for simply appreciating what she did.

He paused to study a large ten-foot canvas propped at an angle against the floor. Large slashes of blue paint were smeared across the center and had been left to dry, creating their own geometric pattern. Maggie was especially pleased with this piece. It was the painting she had been working on the afternoon she was late meeting Glenn at the airport.

"What's this?" Glenn asked, his voice tight. He cocked his head sideways, his brow pleated in concentration.

"Glenn," she chided, "that's my painting."

He was utterly stupefied that Maggie would waste her obvious talent on an abstract mess. The canvas looked as though paint had been carelessly splattered across the top. Glenn could see no rhyme or pattern to the design. "Your painting," he mused aloud. "It's quite a deviation from your other work, isn't it?"

Maggie shrugged off his lack of appreciation and enthusiasm. "This isn't a portrait," she explained somewhat defensively. This particular painting was a departure from the norm, a bold experiment with a new balance of unexpected harmony of different hues of blues with tension between shapes and shades. Glenn had admitted he knew nothing about art, she thought. He wouldn't understand what she was trying to say with this piece, and she didn't try to explain.

Squatting, Glenn examined the large canvas, his fingertips testing the texture. "What is this material? It's not like a regular canvas, is it?"

"No, it's unprimed cotton duck—the same fabric that's used for making sails." This type of porous material allowed her to toss the paint across the canvas; then point by point, she poured, dripped and even used squeegees to spread the great veils of tone. She spent long, tedious hours contemplating each aspect of the work, striving for the effortless, spontaneous appeal she admired so much in Helen Frankenthaler's work.

"You're not into the abstract stuff, are you?" she asked with a faint smile. She tried to make it sound as if it didn't matter. The pride she'd seen in Glenn's eyes when he saw her beachscape and her other work had thrilled her. Now she could see him trying to disguise his puzzlement. "Don't feel bad, abstracts aren't for everyone."

A frown marred his smooth brow as he straightened and brushed the grit from his hands. "I'd like to see some more of the work like the painting downstairs."

"There are a couple of those over here." She pulled a painting out from behind a stack of her later efforts in cubism.

Glenn held out the painting and his frown disappeared. "Now this is good. The other looks like an accident."

An accident! Maggie nearly choked on her laughter. She'd like to see him try it. "I believe the time has come for me to propose another rule for this marriage."

Glenn's look was wary. "What?"

"From now on everything I paint is beautiful and wonderful and the work of an unrecognized genius. Understand?"

"Certainly," he murmured, "anything you say." He paused to examine the huge canvas a second time. "I don't know what you're saying with this, but this is obviously the work of an unrecognized and unappreciated genius."

Maggie smiled at him boldly. "You did that well."

Five

Glenn muttered under his breath as he followed Maggie out of her studio. Her dainty back was stiff as she walked down the stairs. She might have made light of his comments, but he wasn't fooled. Once again he had hurt her. Twice in one day. The problem was that he was trying too hard. They both were. "I apologize, Maggie. I didn't mean to offend you. You're right. I don't know a thing about art."

"I'm not offended," she lied. "I keep forgetting how opinionated you are." With deliberate calm she moved into the living room and sat at the baby grand piano, running her fingers over the ivory keys. She wanted to be angry with him, but couldn't, realizing that any irritation was a symptom of her own insecurity. She had exposed a deeply personal part of herself. It had been a measure of her trust and Glenn hadn't known or understood. She couldn't blame him for that.

"I don't remember that you played the piano." He stood beside her, resting his hand on her shoulder.

His touch was oddly soothing. "I started taking lessons a couple of years ago."

"You're good."

Maggie stopped playing; her fingers froze above the keys. Slowly, she placed her hands in her lap. "Glenn, listen, the new rule to our marriage only applies to my painting. You can be honest with my piano playing. I'm rotten. I have as much innate rhythm as lint."

Glenn recognized that in his effort to make up for one faux pas he had only dug himself in deeper. He didn't know anything about music. "I thought you played the clarinet."

"I wasn't much better on that, if you recall."

"I don't."

"Obviously," she muttered under her breath, rising to her feet. She rubbed her hands together in a nervous gesture. "It's been a long day."

Glenn's spirits sank. It had been quite a day and nothing like he'd expected. Yet he couldn't blame Maggie—he had brought everything on himself. His hand reached for hers. "Let's go to bed."

Involuntarily, Maggie tensed. Everything had been perfect for the wedding night, but now she felt unsure and equally uneasy. Glenn was her husband and she couldn't give him the guest bedroom. But things were different from what they had been. Her eyes were opened this time, and white lace and promises weren't filling her mind with fanciful illusions.

"Is something wrong?" Glenn's question was more of a challenge.

"No," she murmured, abruptly shaking her head. "Nothing's wrong." But then not everything was right, either. She led the way down the long hallway to the master bedroom, feeling shaky.

The room was huge, dominated by a brick fireplace, with two pale-blue chairs angled in front of it. The windows were adorned with shirred drapes of a delicate floral design that had been specially created to give a peaceful, easy-living appeal. The polished mahogany four-poster bed had a down comforter tossed over the top that was made from the same lavender floral material as the drapes. This room was Maggie's favorite. She could sit in it for hours and feel content.

If Glenn was impressed with the simple elegance or felt the warmth of her bedroom, he said nothing. Maggie would have been surprised if he had.

His suitcase rested on the thick carpet, and Glenn sighed, turning toward her. "We have a lot to do tomorrow." Frustrated anger filled Glenn at his own stupidity. Everything he had done that day had been wrong. From the moment he had opened his eyes to the time he'd mentioned going to bed. He couldn't have been more insensitive had he tried. He didn't want to argue with Maggie and yet, it seemed, he had gone out of his way to do exactly that. There would be a lot of adjustments to make with their marriage and he had gotten off on the wrong foot almost from the moment they'd started. Maggie was uncomfortable; Glenn could sense that. He could also feel her hesitancy. But he was her husband, and by heaven he'd sleep with her this and every night for the remainder of their lives.

The mention of the coming day served to remind Maggie that Glenn was planning on returning to Charleston alone. That rankled. Sometime during the evening, she had thought to casually bring up the return trip. But with what had happened in her studio and afterward, the timing hadn't been right. Crossing her arms over her breasts, she met his gaze.

"Oh. What are we doing tomorrow?" She couldn't think of anything they needed to do that couldn't be handled later.

"First we'll see a lawyer, then—"

"Why?" she asked, her voice unnaturally throaty. Alarm filled her. Glenn had changed his mind. He didn't want to stay married. And little wonder. She kept making up these rules and—

"I want to make sure none of your inheritance money is ever put in my name." With all the other problems they were facing, Glenn needed to assure Maggie that he hadn't married her for her wealth. If anything, he regretted the fact she had it. Her Great-aunt Margaret's money had been a curse as far as he was concerned. And judging by the insecure, frightened woman Maggie had become, she might even have realized that herself.

"I…I know you wouldn't cheat me." The odd huskiness of her voice was made more pronounced by a slight quiver. Of all the men she had known in her life, she trusted Glenn implicitly. He was a man of honor. He might have married her when he was in love with another woman, but he would never deliberately do anything to swindle her.

Their gazes melted into each other's. Maggie trusted him, Glenn realized. The heavy weight that had pressed against him from the moment she had turned her hurt, angry eyes on him that morning lessened. Surely there'd been a better way to handle that business with her paintings, he thought. She had talent, incredible talent, and it was a shame that she was wasting it by hiding it away.

"After the lawyer we'll go to a jeweler," he added.

"A jeweler?"

"I'd like you to wear a wedding ring, Maggie."

The pulse in her neck throbbed as she beat down a rush of pure pleasure. "Okay, and you too."

"Of course," he agreed easily. His gaze did a sweeping inspection of the room as if he'd noticed it for the first time. It reminded him of Maggie. Her presence was stamped in every piece of furniture, every corner. Suddenly, a tiredness stole into his bones. He was exhausted, mentally and physically. "Let's get ready for bed."

Maggie nodded, and some of her earlier apprehension faded. She wasn't completely comfortable sleeping with him after what had happened. Not when there was a chance he would take her in his arms, hold her close, kiss her, even make love to her, with another woman's name on his lips. "You go ahead, I've got a few odds and ends to take care of first."

Sitting at the oak desk in her office, Maggie lifted her long hair from her face and closed her eyes as weariness flooded her bones. She was tired—Glenn was tired. She was confused—Glenn was confused. They both wanted this marriage—they were both responsible for making it work. All right, there wasn't any reason to overreact. They'd share a bed and if he said "her" name in his sleep again, Maggie refused to be held responsible for her actions.

By the time Glenn returned from his shower, Maggie had gone back to the bedroom and changed into a sexless flannel pajama set that would have discouraged the most amorous male. She had slipped beneath the covers, and was sitting up reading, her back supported by thick feather pillows. Behind her book, she followed Glenn's movements when he reentered the bedroom.

He paused and allowed a tiny smile of satisfaction to touch his lips. He had half expected Maggie to linger in her office until he was asleep and was greatly pleased that she hadn't. Although she looked like a virgin intent on maintaining her chastity in that flannel outfit, he knew that this night wasn't the time to press for his husbandly rights. Things had gone badly. Tomorrow would be better, he promised himself.

Lifting back the thick quilt, Glenn slid his large frame into the king-size bed and turned off the light that rested on the mahogany nightstand on his side of the bed.

"Good night." His voice was husky and low with only a trace of amusement. He thought she would probably sit up reading until she fell asleep with the light on.

"Good night," she answered softly, pretending to read. A few minutes later, Maggie battled to keep her lashes from drooping. Valiantly she struggled as her mind conjured up ways of resisting Glenn. The problem was that she didn't want to resist him. He would probably wait until she was relaxed and close to falling asleep, she theorized. When she was at her weakest point, he would reach for her and kiss her. Glenn was a wonderful kisser and she went warm at the memory of what had happened their first night together. He had held her as if he were dying of thirst and she was a cool shimmering pool in an oasis.

Gathering her resolve, Maggie clenched her teeth. By heaven, the way her thoughts were going she'd lean over and kiss him any minute. Her hand rested on her abdomen and Maggie felt bare skin. Her pajamas might be sexless, but they also conveniently buttoned up the front so he had easy access to her if he wanted. Again she recalled how good their lovemaking had been and how she had thrilled to his hands and mouth on her. Her eyes drooped shut and with a start she forced them open. Lying completely still she listened, and after several long moments discovered that Glenn had turned away from her and was sound asleep.

An unexpected rush of disappointment filled her. He hadn't even tried to make love to her. Without a thought, he had turned onto his side and gone to sleep! Bunching up her pillow, Maggie rolled onto her stomach, feeling such frustration that she could have cried. He didn't want her, and as unreasonable as it sounded, Maggie felt discouraged and depressed. Her last thought as she turned out her light was that if Glenn reached for her in the night she would give him what he wanted...what she wanted.

Sometime in the middle of the night Maggie woke. She was sleeping on her side, but had moved to the middle of the bed. Her eyes fluttered open and she wondered what had caused her to wake when she felt so warm and comfortable. Glenn's even breathing sounded close to her ear and she realized that he was asleep, cuddling his body to hers. Contented and secure, she closed her eyes and a moment later a male hand slid over her ribs, just below her breasts. When he pulled her close, fitting his body to hers, Maggie's lashes fluttered open. Not for the first time, she was amazed at how perfectly their bodies fit together. Releasing a contented breath, Maggie shut her eyes and wandered back to sleep.

Glenn woke in the first light of dawn with a serenity that had escaped him for months. That morning he didn't mistake the warm body he was holding close. Maggie was responsible for his tranquility of spirit, Glenn realized. He needed Maggie. During the night, her pajama top had ridden up and the urge to move his hand and trace the soft, womanly curves was almost overpowering. Maggie was all the woman he would ever want. She was everything he had ever hoped to find in a wife—a passionate, irresistible mistress with an intriguing mind and delectable body, who surrendered herself willingly. Her passion had surprised and pleased him. She hadn't been shy, or embarrassed, abandoning herself to him with an eagerness that thrilled him every time he thought about it. She was more woman than he'd dared hope and he ached to take her again.

In her sleep, Maggie shifted and her breasts sprang free of the confining top. For an eternity he lay completely still until he couldn't resist touching her any longer. In his mind he pictured turning her onto her back and kissing her until her lips opened eagerly to his. With inhuman patience he would look into those dark beautiful eyes and wait until she told him how much she wanted him.

Groaning, he released her and rolled onto his back, taking deep breaths to control his frantic frustration. He had no idea how long it would be before he would have the opportunity to make love to his wife again. Two weeks at least, maybe longer. Almost as overwhelming as the urge to make love to her was the one to cherish and protect her. She needed reassurance and he knew she needed time. Throwing back the blankets he marched into the bathroom and turned on the cold water.

Maggie woke at the sound of the shower running. Stirring, she turned onto her back and stared at the ceiling as the last dregs of sleep drained from her mind. She had been having the most pleasant erotic dream. One that caused her to blush from the roots of her dark hair to the ends of her toenails. Indecent dreams maybe, but excruciatingly sensual. Perhaps it was best that Glenn was gone when she woke, she thought. If he had been beside her she didn't know what she would have done. She could well have embarrassed them both by reaching for him and asking him to make love to her before he returned to Charleston...alone.

Taking advantage of the privacy, she dressed and hurriedly made the bed. By the time she had straightened the comforter across the mattress, Glenn reappeared.

"Good morning," he said as he paused just inside the bedroom, standing both alert and still as he studied her. "Did you sleep well?"

"Yes," she responded hastily, feeling like a specimen about to be analyzed, but a highly prized specimen, one that was cherished and valued. "What about you?" she asked.

The hesitation was barely noticeable, but Maggie noticed. "Like a rock."

"Good. Are you hungry?" Her eyes refused to meet his, afraid of what hers would tell him.

"Starved."

"Breakfast should be ready by the time you've finished dressing," she said as she left the room. Glenn had showered last night, she remembered; she couldn't recall him being overly fastidious. Shrugging, she moved down the long hall to the kitchen.

The bacon was sizzling in the skillet when Glenn reappeared, dressed in dark slacks and a thick pullover sweater. Maggie was reminded once again that he was devastatingly handsome and experienced, and with a burst of pride, she remembered that he was married to her. At least legally, he was hers. However, another woman owned the most vital part of him—his heart. In time, Maggie trusted, she would claim that as well.

The morning swam past in a blur; such was their pace. They began by contacting Maggie's attorney and were given an immediate appointment. Together they sat in his office, although it was Glenn who did the majority of the talking. Maggie was uncomfortable with the rewording of her will, but Glenn was adamant. He desired none of her money and he wanted it stated legally. When and if they had children, her inheritance would be passed on to them.

From the attorney's they stopped off at a prominent San Francisco jeweler. Maggie had never been one for flashy jewels. All too often her hands were in paint solvent or mixing clay and she didn't want to have to worry about losing expensive rings or valuable jewels. Knowing herself and her often thoughtless ways, Maggie was apt to misplace a diamond and she couldn't bear the thought of losing any ring Glenn gave her.

"You decide," Glenn insisted, his hand at the back of her neck. "Whatever one you want is fine."

Sensing a sure sale, the young jeweler set out a tray of exquisite diamonds, far larger than any Maggie had dreamed Glenn would want to purchase. Her gaze fell on a lovely marquise and her teeth worried her bottom lip. "I...was thinking maybe something with a smaller stone would be fine," she murmured, realizing that she should have explained her problems about a diamond to Glenn earlier.

He pinched his mouth closed with displeasure, resenting her concern that he couldn't afford to buy her a diamond large enough to weight her hand.

"Try on that one," he insisted, pointing to the marquise solitaire with the wide polished band that she had admired earlier. The diamond was the largest and most expensive on the tray.

Maggie paled, not knowing how to explain herself. The salesman beamed, exchanging pleased glances with Glenn.

"An excellent choice," the jeweler said, lifting Maggie's limp hand. The ring fit as if it was made for her slender finger. But the diamond was so heavy it felt bulky and unnatural. In her mind Maggie could picture the panic of looking for it once it was mislaid... and it would be.

"We'll take it."

"Glenn." Maggie placed her hand on his forearm. "Can I talk to you a minute? Please."

"I'll write up the sales order," the jeweler said, removing the tray of diamonds. "I'll be with the cashier when you've finished."

Maggie waited until the salesman was out of earshot before turning troubled eyes to Glenn. Her heart was in her eyes as she recognized the pride and irritation that glared back at her.

"What's the matter, Maggie?" he growled under his breath. "Are you afraid I can't afford a wedding ring for my wife? I may not own a fancy beach house, but be assured, I can afford a diamond."

Glenn's words smarted and it was all Maggie could do to bite back a flippant reply. "It's not that," she whispered fiercely, keeping her voice low so the jeweler wouldn't hear them arguing. "If you'd given me half a chance, I'd have explained. I'm an artist, remember? If you buy me that flashy diamond, I'll be constantly removing it for one reason or another."

"So? What are you suggesting? No ring at all?"

"No…I'm sorry I said anything. The ring is fine." Maggie backed down, aware that anything said now would be misconstrued. Somehow she would learn to be careful with the diamond. Purchasing it had become a matter of male pride and Maggie didn't want to cause any more problems than the ones already facing them.

"Would a plain gold band solve that?" he asked unexpectedly.

"Yes," she murmured, surprised. "Yes, it would." To her delight, Glenn also asked the jeweler to size a band for her. Maggie felt wonderful when they stepped outside. The question of the ring might have been only a minor problem, but together they had settled it without wounding each other's sensitive pride. They were making progress and it felt good.

They ate lunch in Chinatown, feasting on hot, diced chicken stir-fried with fresh, crisp vegetables. All the time they were dining, Maggie was infinitely aware of two pressing items: the heavy feel of the ring on the third finger of her left hand, and the time. Within hours Glenn would be leaving for Charleston. A kaleidoscope of regrets and questions whirled through her mind. She wanted to go with him, but didn't feel she could make the suggestion. Glenn had to want her along, yet he hadn't said a word. Silence hung heavy and dark between them like a thick curtain of rain-filled clouds. He was going back to his lost love. Dread filled Maggie with each beat of her heart.

Glenn made several attempts at light conversation during their meal, but nothing seemed to ease the strained silence that had fallen over them. A glance at his watch reminded him that within a few hours he would be on a plane for Charleston. He didn't want to leave, but in some ways felt it was for the best. Maggie seemed to assume that she wouldn't be going with him and he was disappointed that she hadn't shown the willingness to travel with him. He might have made an issue of it if he hadn't thought a short separation would help them both become accustomed to their marriage without the issue of sleeping together. Those weeks would give Maggie the opportunity to settle things within her own mind. When he came back to her they would take up their lives as man and wife and perhaps she'd come to him willingly as she had that first night. That was what he wanted.

The drive back to the house and then on to the airport seemed to take a lifetime. With each mile, Maggie felt her heart grow heavier. She was apprehensive and didn't know how to deal with it. She and Glenn had been together such a short time that separating now seemed terribly wrong. Unreasonable jealousy ate at her and Maggie had to assure herself repeatedly that Glenn probably wouldn't even be seeing the other woman. She was, after all, married to another man or so Glenn had told her. But Maggie didn't gain a whit's comfort from knowing that. For the first time in memory, she found herself in a situation where money wasn't part of the solution.

As they left the airport parking garage, Glenn's hand took hers. "I won't be long," he promised. "I'll need to get everything settled at the office, list the condominium with a Realtor and settle loose business ties—that kind of thing. I can't see it taking more than two weeks, three at the most."

"The weeks will fly by," she said on a falsely cheerful note. "Just about the time I clean out enough closet space for you, you'll be back."

"I wouldn't leave if it wasn't necessary," Glenn assured her as they approached the ticketing desk to check in his luggage.

"I know that." Maggie hugged her waist, feeling a sudden and unexpected chill. "I'm not worried about… you know." *Liar,* her mind tossed back.

Their shoes made a clicking sound as they walked together toward security. Maggie had the horrible feeling she was about to cry, which, she knew, was utterly ridiculous. She rarely cried, yet her throat felt raw and scratchy and her chest had tightened with pent-up emotion. All the things she wanted to say stuck in her throat and she found that she couldn't say a thing.

"Take care of yourself," Glenn murmured, holding her by the shoulders.

"I will," she promised and buried her hands deep within the pockets of her raincoat. Even those few words could barely escape.

Glenn fastened the top button of her coat and when he spoke his voice was softly gruff. "It looks like rain. Drive carefully."

"I always do. You'll note that you're here on time." She made a feeble attempt at humor.

Tiny laugh lines fanned out from his eyes. "Barely. I don't suppose you've noticed that by now my flight's probably boarding. Married two days and I'm already picking up your bad habits."

His observation prompted a soft smile. "You'll phone?" She turned soft, round eyes to him.

"Yes," he promised in a husky murmur. "And if you need me, don't hesitate to call." He had written down both his work and home numbers in case she had to get in touch with him.

"You'll phone tonight." It became immensely important that he did. She pulled her hands from her pockets and smoothed away an imaginary piece of lint from his shoulder. Her hand lingered there. "I'll miss you." Even now if he hinted that he wanted her with him, she'd step on that plane. If necessary she'd buy the stupid plane.

"I'll phone, but it'll be late because of the time change," Glenn explained.

"I don't mind.... I probably won't sleep anyway." She hadn't meant to admit that much and felt a rush of color creep up her neck and into her cheeks.

"Me either," he murmured. His hands tightened on her upper arms and he gently brought her against his bulky sweater. With unhurried ease his mouth moved toward hers. The kiss flooded her with a swell of emotions she had tasted only briefly in his arms. She was hot, on fire and cold as ice. Hot from his touch, cold with fear. His kiss sent a jolt rocketing through her and she fiercely wrapped her arms around his neck. Her mind whirled and still she clung, afraid that if Glenn ever released her she'd never fully recover from the fall. Dragging in a deep breath, Maggie buried her face in his neck.

Glenn wrapped his arms around her waist and half lifted her from the floor. "I'll be back soon," he promised.

She nodded because speaking was impossible.

When he released her his gaze was as gentle as a caress and as tender as a child's touch. Maggie offered him a feeble smile. Glenn turned up the collar of her coat. "Stay warm."

Again she nodded. "Phone me."

Glenn claimed Maggie's lips again in a brief but surprisingly ardent kiss. "I'll call the minute I land."

With hands in her pockets for fear she'd do something silly like reach out and ask him not to go, or beg him to ask her to come. "Hurry now, or you'll miss the flight."

Glenn took two steps backward. "The time will go fast."

"Yes," she said, not exactly sure what she was agreeing to.

"You're my wife, Maggie. I'm not going to forget that."

"You're my husband," she whispered and choked back the tears that filled her eyes and blurred her vision.

Then tossing a glance over his shoulder, he hurriedly handed the TSA agent his boarding pass and identity.

Maggie pushed her. "Go on," she encouraged, not wanting him to see her cry. For all the emotion that was raging through her one would assume that Glenn was going off to war and was unlikely to return. Her stomach was in such tight knots that she couldn't move without pain. Rooted to the spot close to security, Maggie stood as she was until Glenn turned and ran toward his gate. When she could, she stepped to the window and whispered, "New rules for this marriage...don't ever leave me again."

The days passed in a blur. Not since art school had Maggie worked harder or longer. Denny phoned her twice. Once to thank her for the "loan" and later to talk to her about the top-notch lawyer he had on retainer. The attorney was exactly who he had hoped would pursue his case, and his spirits were high. Maggie was pleased for Denny and prayed that this would be the end of his problems.

Without Glenn, sound sleep was impossible. She'd

drift off easily enough and then jerk awake a couple of hours later, wondering why the bed seemed so intolerably large. Usually she slept in the middle of the mattress, but she soon discovered that she rested more comfortably on the side where Glenn had slept. She missed him. The worst part was the unreasonableness of the situation. Glenn had spent less than twenty-four hours in her home, yet without him the beach house felt like a silent tomb.

As he promised, Glenn had phoned the night he arrived back in Charleston and again three days later. Maggie couldn't recall any three days that seemed longer. A thousand times she was convinced her mind had conjured up both Glenn and their marriage. The marquise diamond on her ring finger was the only tangible evidence that the whole situation hadn't been a fantasy and that they really were married. Because she was working so hard and long she removed it for safekeeping, but each night she slipped it on her finger. Maggie didn't mention the wedding to her parents or any of her friends, and Denny didn't notice anything was different about her. She didn't feel comfortable telling everyone she was married, and wouldn't until Glenn had moved in with her and they were confident that their marriage was on firm ground.

Glenn phoned again on the fifth day. Their conversation was all too brief and somewhat stilted. Neither of them seemed to want it to end, but after twenty minutes, there didn't seem to be anything more to say.

Replacing the receiver, Maggie had the urge to cry. She didn't, of course, but it was several minutes before she had composed herself enough to go on with her day.

Nothing held her interest. Television, music, solitaire—everything bored her. Even the housekeeper lamented that Maggie had lost her appetite and complained about cooking meals that Maggie barely touched. Glenn filled every waking thought and invaded her dreams. Each time they spoke she had to bite her tongue to keep from suggesting she join him; her pride wouldn't allow that. The invitation must come from him, she believed. Surely he must realize that.

As for Angie, the woman in Glenn's past, the more Maggie thought about the situation, the more angry she became with herself. Glenn hadn't deceived her. They both were bearing scars from the past. If it wasn't love that cemented their marriage then it was something equally strong. Between them there was security and understanding.

The evening of the eighth day the phone rang just as Maggie was scrounging through the desk looking for an address. She stared at the telephone. Instantly she knew it was Glenn.

"Hello," she answered, happily leaning back in the swivel chair, anticipating a long conversation.

"Hi." His voice sounded vital and warm. "How's everything?"

"Fine. I'm a little bored." Maggie was astonished that she could sound so blasé about her traumatic week. "A little bored" soft-pedaled all her frustrations. "What about you?"

Glenn hesitated, then announced, "I've run into a small snag on my end of things." A small snag was the understatement of the century, he thought. Things had been in chaos from the minute he had returned. The company supervisor had paid a surprise visit to him Thursday afternoon and had suggested an audit because of some irregularity in the books. The audit had gone smoothly enough, but Glenn had worked long hours and had been forced to reschedule several appointments. In addition, the Realtor who listed the condominium offered little hope that it would sell quickly.

And worse, Glenn was miserable without Maggie. He wanted her with him. She was his wife, yet pride dictated that he couldn't ask her. The suggestion would have to come from her. Even a hint would be enough. He would pick up on a hint, but she had to be one to give it.

"A small snag?" Her heart was pounding so hard and strong that she felt breathless.

"I've got several accounts here that have deals pending. I can't leave my clients in the lurch. Things aren't going as smoothly as I'd like, Maggie," he admitted.

"I see." Maggie's vocabulary suddenly decreased to words of one syllable.

"I can't let them down." He sounded as frustrated as she felt. A deafening silence grated over the telephone line, and it was on the tip of Glenn's tongue to cast his stupid pride to the wind and ask her to join him.

"Don't worry, I understand," she said in an even tone, congratulating herself for maintaining firm control of her voice. On the inside she was crumbling to pieces. She wanted to be with him. He was her husband and her place was at his side. Closing her eyes she mentally pleaded with him to say the words—to ask her to come to Charleston. She wouldn't ask, couldn't ask. It had to come from Glenn.

"In addition there are several loose ends that are going to require more time than I originally planned." He sounded almost angry, an emotion that mirrored her own frustration.

"I think we were both naive to think you could make it back in such a short time."

"I suppose we were." *Come on, Maggie,* he pleaded silently. If you miss me, say something. At least meet me halfway in this.

The line went silent again, but Maggie didn't want to end the conversation. She waited endless hours for his calls. They would talk for ten minutes, hang up and immediately she'd start wondering how long it would be before he phoned again.

"The weather's been unseasonably cold. There's been some talk of freezing tempratures," Maggie said out of desperation to keep the conversation going.

"Don't catch cold." *Damn it, Maggie, I want you here, can't you hear it in my voice?*

"I won't," she promised. *Please,* she wanted to scream at him, *ask me to come to Charleston.* With her eyes shut, she mentally transmitted her need to have him ask her. "I've been too busy in the studio to venture outside."

"Brueghel or Frankenthaler?" Glenn questioned, his voice tinged with humor. "However, I'm sure that either one would be marvelous and wonderful." He smiled as he said it, wanting her with him all the more just to see what other crazy rules she'd come up with for their marriage.

"This one's a Margaret Kingsbury original," she said proudly. Maggie had worked hard on her latest project and felt confident that Glenn would approve.

"It can't be." Glenn stiffened and tried to disguise the irritation in his voice.

Maggie tensed, wondering what she had said wrong. He hadn't approved of her art, but surely he didn't begrudge her the time she spent on it when he was away.

"Your name's Lambert now," Glenn stated.

"I…forgot." *Remind me again,* she pleaded silently. *Ask me to come to Charleston.* "I haven't told anyone yet.… Have you?"

"No one," Glenn admitted.

"Not even your parents?" She hadn't told hers, either, but Glenn's family was in South Carolina. It only made sense that he'd say something to them before moving out west.

"That was something I thought we'd do together."

The sun burst through the heavy overcast and shed its golden rays on Maggie. He had offered her a way to Charleston and managed to salvage her pride. The tension flowed from her as her hand tightened around the receiver. "Glenn, don't you think they'll be offended if we wait much longer?"

"They might," he answered, unexpectedly agreeable. "I know it's an inconvenience, but maybe you should think about flying…."

"I'll be on the first flight out tomorrow morning."

Six

Glenn was in the terminal waiting when Maggie walked off the plane late the following afternoon. He was tall, rugged and so male that it was all Maggie could do not to throw her arms around him. He looked wonderful and she wanted to hate him for it. For nine days she had been the most miserable woman alive and Glenn looked as if he'd relished their separation, thrived on it. Renewed doubts buzzed about her like swarming bees.

Stepping forward, Glenn took the carry-on bag from her hand and slipped an arm around her waist. "Welcome to Charleston."

Shamelessly, Maggie wanted him to take her in his arms and kiss her. She managed to disguise the yearning by lowering her gaze. "I didn't know if you'd be here."

She tried to call to give him her flight number, but his phone had gone directly to voice mail. She'd left a message and then later sent him a text. If he hadn't gotten her message Maggie wouldn't have had a way of getting into Glenn's condominium.

"Of course I'm here. Where else would I be?"

"I'm so glad to see you." *Very glad,* her heart sang.

"How was the flight?"

"Just the way I like 'em," she said with a teasing smile. "Uneventful."

Glenn's features warmed and he grinned at her answer. Captivated by the tenderness in his eyes, Maggie felt her heart throb almost painfully. His eyes were dark, yet glowing with a warm light. Although he hadn't said a word, Glenn's gaze told her he was pleased she was with him.

"Your luggage is this way," he commented, pressing a hand to the middle of her back as he directed her toward baggage claim.

"I didn't bring much."

"Not much" constituted two enormous suitcases and one large carry-on. Maggie had spent half the night packing, discarding one outfit after another until her bedroom floor was littered with more clothes than a second-hand store. She wanted everything perfect for Glenn. She longed to be alluring and seductive, attractive without being blatant about it. She wanted his heart as well as his bed and only she realized how difficult that was going to be if Glenn was still in love with "her."

The more Maggie thought about the other woman who had claimed his heart the more she realized what an uphill struggle lay before her. Glenn wouldn't ever give his love lightly, and now that he had, it would take a struggle to replace her in his heart. Maggie yearned to know more of the details, but wouldn't pry. In the meantime, she planned to use every womanly wile she possessed and a few she planned to invent.

The leather strap of her purse slid off her shoulder and Maggie straightened it. As she did, Glenn stopped in midstride, nearly knocking her off balance.

"Where's your diamond?" he asked, taking her hand. Surprise mingled with disappointment and disbelief. "I thought you said the only time you wouldn't wear it was when you were working. You aren't painting now."

Maggie's mind whirled frantically. She had removed the diamond the morning before the phone call and placed it in safekeeping the way she always did. Then in her excitement about flying out to be with Glenn, she had forgotten to put it back on her finger.

"Maggie?"

Her fingers curled around the strap of her purse. "Oh, Glenn..."

He took her hand and examined the plain gold band that he had bought her with the marquise.

Maggie wanted to shout with frustration. From the moment they'd ended their phone conversation she had been carefully planning this reunion. Each detail had been shaped in her mind from the instant he picked her up until they dressed for bed.

"Maggie, where is the diamond?" he repeated.

"I forgot it, but don't worry... I have it with me." Her voice rose with her agitation. They hadn't so much as collected her luggage and already they were headed for a fight.

"You mean to tell me you packed a seven-thousand-dollar diamond with your underwear?" His voice was a mixture of incredulity and anger.

"I didn't do it on purpose, I...forgot I wasn't wearing it." Somehow that seemed even worse. "And furthermore it isn't in the suitcase, I have it in my carry-on."

Glenn's stride increased to a quick-paced clip that left Maggie half trotting in an effort to keep up. "Glenn," she protested, refusing to run through airports.

He threw an angry glare over his shoulder. "Forgive me for being overly concerned, but I work hard for my money."

The implication being, she thought, that she didn't work and the ring meant nothing to her. Little did he realize how much it did mean.

Maggie stopped cold as waves of anger hit her. Few words could have hurt her more. She was outraged he would say such a thing to her. For several minutes she found herself unable to speak. Nothing was going as she had planned. She'd had such wonderful images of Glenn sweeping her into his arms, holding her close and exclaiming that after the way he'd missed her, they'd never be separated again. He was supposed to tell her how miserable he'd been. Instead, he'd insulted her in a way that would hurt her the most.

Apparently he was angry because she had forgotten to slip on the diamond ring he'd gotten her, finding her casualness with the diamond a sign of irresponsibility. She had the ring; she knew where it was.

Glenn was standing outside the baggage-handling

system, waiting for it to unload the luggage from her flight, when she joined him.

"If you'd give me a second I'll..."

"Talk to me after you've gotten your ring, Maggie. At the moment I'm worried about losing an expensive diamond."

"And you work hard for your money. Right? At least that's what you claim. I don't doubt it. It's said that those who marry for it usually do."

Although he continued to look straight ahead, a nerve jumped convulsively in his clenched jaw, and Maggie was instantly aware of just how angry that remark had made him. Good, she meant it to do exactly that. If he wanted to hurl insults at her, then she could give as well as take.

"Can I have my carry-on?"

Without a word, he handed it to her. He studied the baggage conveyor belt as if it were the center of his world. Maggie wasn't fooled. Glenn was simply too outraged to look at her.

Maggie knelt down on the floor and flipped open the lid. Her small jewelry case was inside and the ring was tucked safely in that. With a brooding sense of unhappiness, Maggie located the marquise diamond and slipped it on her finger beside the plain gold band. Snapping the suitcase closed, she stood.

"I hope to hell you didn't mean that about me marrying you for your money."

Maggie regarded him coolly before answering. "I didn't," she admitted. "I was reacting to your implication that I diddn't have to work hard for my money."

He exhaled slowly. "I didn't mean it like that."

"I hope not."

They stood side by side, silent for several moments before his hand claimed hers. Right away he noticed the diamond was on her ring finger, he arched one brow expressively. "You had it with you all the time?"

"Yes."

He groaned inwardly. He had been wanting Maggie for days, longing for her. And now things were picking up right where they'd left off, with misunderstandings and sharp words. He had wanted everything perfect for her, and once again this bad start had been his own doing.

His fingers tightened over hers. "Can I make a new rule for this marriage?" he asked her with serious eyes.

"Of course."

"I want you to wear your wedding set all the time."

"But…"

"I know that may sound unreasonable," he interrupted, "and I'm not even entirely sure why my feelings are so strong. I guess it's important to me that your wedding bands mean as much to you as our marriage."

Slowly, thoughtfully, Maggie nodded. "I'll never remove them again."

Looking in her eyes, Glenn felt the overwhelming urge to take her in his arms and apologize for having started on the wrong foot once again. But the airport wasn't the place and now wasn't the time. From here on, he promised himself, he'd be more patient with her, court her the way he should have in the beginning.

They didn't say a word until the luggage was dispensed. Maggie pointed out her suitcases.

He mumbled something unintelligible under his breath and Maggie realized he was grumbling about the fact she claimed to have packed light for this trip. But he didn't complain strenuously.

The deafening quiet in the car was one neither seemed willing to wade into. Maggie wanted to initiate a brilliant conversation, but nothing came to mind and she almost cried with frustration. Their meeting wasn't supposed to happen this way. She sat uncomfortably next to a man she'd known most of her life and whom, she was discovering, she didn't know at all.

Glenn's condominium was situated just outside historic Charleston with a view of Colonial Lake. Maggie knew little about the area. Her head flooded with questions about the city that Glenn had made his home for a decade, but she asked none. While he took care of her luggage, she wandered into the living room to admire the view. The scenery below revealed magnificent eighteenth-century homes, large public buildings and meticulously kept gardens. The gentle toll of church bells sounded, and Maggie strained to hear more. Charleston was definitely a city of grace, beauty and charm. Yet Glenn was willing to sacrifice it all— his home, his family, his job, maybe even his career to move to San Francisco.

He must have suffered a great deal of mental anguish to be willing to leave all this, Maggie determined, experiencing an attack of doubt. Glenn had told her so little about this other woman, and Maggie had the feeling he wouldn't have told her anything if it hadn't been for the unfortunate scene the morning after their wedding. He was an intensely personal man.

The condominium was far more spacious than what Maggie had assumed. The living room led into a formal dining area and from there to a spacious kitchen with plenty of cupboards and a pantry. A library/den was separated from the living room by open double-width doors that revealed floor-to-ceiling bookcases and a large oak desk. She hadn't seen the bedrooms yet, but guessed that there were three, possibly four. The condo was much larger than what a single man would require. Her eyes rounded with an indescribable ache that came over her when she realized Glenn had purchased this home for Angie.

"Are you hungry?" he asked, halfway into the living room, standing several feet from her.

Maggie unbuttoned her coat and slipped the scarf from her neck. "No thanks, I ate on the plane, but you go ahead." The lie was a small, white one. The flight attendant had offered her a meal, but Maggie had declined. She'd been too anxious to eat when she was only a few hours from meeting Glenn.

He hesitated, turned, then whirled back around so that he was facing her again. "I regret this whole business with the ring, Maggie."

A shiver of gladness came over her at his offhand apology. "It's forgotten."

Something close to a smile quirked his mouth. "I'm glad you're here."

"I'm glad to be here."

He leaned around the kitchen door. "Are you sure you're not hungry?"

A small smile claimed her mouth. "On second thought, maybe I am at that."

A sense of relief flooded through Glenn's tense muscles. He hadn't meant to make such an issue of the diamond. For days he'd been longing for Maggie, decrying his earlier decision to leave her in San Francisco. They had so few days together that he'd thought the separation would give her the necessary time to adjust mentally to her new life. Unfortunately, it was he who had faced the adjustment...to his days... and nights without her. Now that she was here, all he wanted was to take her in his arms and make love to her. The level of physical desire she aroused in him was a definite shock. He hadn't expected to experience this intensity. All he had thought about since he'd known she was coming was getting her into his bed. He'd dreamed of kissing her, holding her and making love to his wife. She was the woman he'd married and he'd waited a long time for the privileges due a husband. He doubted that Maggie had any conception of.how deep his anger had cut when she had suggested that he'd married her for her money. That was a problem he had anticipated early on and it was the very reason he had insisted they see a lawyer as soon as possible.

Working together they cooked their dinner. Maggie made the salad while Glenn broiled thick steaks. Glenn didn't have a housekeeper to prepare his meals and for that matter, Maggie surmised, he might not even have someone in to do the housework. Now that she was here, she decided, she would take over those duties. Surprisingly, Maggie discovered she looked forward to being a wife. Glenn's wife.

Later, while he placed the few dirty plates in the

dishwasher, Maggie decided to unpack her bags. She located the master bedroom without a problem and gave a sigh of relief when she noticed that Glenn fully intended that she would sleep with him. It was what she wanted, what she had planned, but after their shaky beginning, Maggie hadn't known what to think. A soft smile worked its way across her face, brightening her dark eyes. Glenn longed for their marriage to work as much as she did, she thought. What they both needed to do was quit trying so hard.

When Maggie had finished unpacking, she joined Glenn in the living room. It amazed her how unsettled they were around each other still. Glenn suggested they turn on the last newscast of the evening. Readily, Maggie agreed. She supposed that this time could be thought of as their honeymoon. They were probably the only couple in America to watch television when they could be doing other...things.

After the news, Glenn yawned. Once again Maggie was reminded that his daily schedule was set with the routine of his job. Staying awake until two or three in the morning, watching a late late movie or reading would only cause problems the following morning. She would need to adjust her sleeping habits as well, although she had become a night person these past few years, often enjoying the peace and tranquility of the early-morning hours to paint. Glenn didn't live a life of leisure and she couldn't any longer, either.

Funny, Maggie thought, that the realization that she must now live according to a clock didn't depress her. She was willing to get up with him in the morning and cook his breakfast and even do the dishes.

She didn't know how long this "domesticated" eagerness would continue, and vowed to take advantage of it while it lasted. In the morning, she would stand at the front door, and send him off to the office with a juicy kiss. But from the frowning look he was giving the television, Maggie had the impression the goodbye kiss in the morning would be all the kissing she was going to get.

Glenn's thoughts were heavy. Maggie was sitting at his side and he hadn't so much as put his arm around her. He felt as though he were stretched out on a rack, every muscle strained to the limit of his endurance. It was pure torture to have her so close and not haul her into his arms and make love to her. If she could read only half of what was going through his mind, she would run back to California, he thought dryly. No, he wouldn't take her that night. He'd bide his time, show her how empty his life was without her, how much he needed a woman's tenderness. Then, in time, she would come to him willingly and desire him, maybe even as keenly as he did her.

"Don't you think we should go to bed? It's after eleven." Maggie broached the subject with all the subtlety of a locomotive. Sitting next to him was torture. They had hardly said two words all night. The thick, unnatural silence made the words all the more profound.

Smoothly rolling to his feet, Glenn nodded. He hadn't noticed that the news was over. For that matter, he couldn't recall the headlines or anything that had been reported. Not even the weather forecast, which he listened for each night. "I imagine you're tired," he finally answered.

"Dead on my feet," she confirmed, walking with him toward the hallway and the master bedroom. *You're wide awake,* her mind accused. She was on Pacific time and it was barely after eight in San Francisco.

Following a leisurely scented bath, Maggie joined him wearing a black nightshirt that buttoned up the front and hit her at midthigh with deep side slits that went halfway up to her hip. The satin top was the most feminine piece of sleepwear Maggie owned. The two top buttons were unfastened and she stretched her hands high above her head in a fake yawn, granting him a full glimpse of her upper thighs.

Glenn was in bed, propped against thick feather pillows, reading a spy thriller. One look at her in the black satin pajama top and the book nearly tumbled from his hands. Tension knotted his stomach and he all but groaned at the sight of his wife. Still wanting her was torture he endured willingly.

The mattress dipped slightly as she lifted back the blankets and slipped into the bed. Glenn set his novel aside and reached for the lamp switch. The room went dark with only the shimmering rays of the distant moon dancing across the far walls.

Neither moved. Only a few inches separated them, but for all the good it did to be sleeping with her husband, Maggie could well have been in San Francisco, she decided.

"Good night, Glenn," Maggie whispered after several stifled moments. If he didn't reach for her soon she'd clobber him over the head. Maybe she should say something to encourage him—let him know her feelings. But what? *Listen, Glenn, I've reconsidered and although I realize that you may still be in love with another woman I've decided it doesn't matter. We're married. I'm your wife....* Disheartened, Maggie realized she couldn't do it. Not so soon, and not in a condominium he probably bought with "her" in mind.

Glenn interrupted Maggie's dark thoughts with a deep, quiet voice. "Good night." With that he rolled onto his side away from her.

Gallantly, she resisted the urge to smash the pillow over the top of his head, pull a blanket from the mattress and storm into the living room to sleep. She didn't know how any man could be so unbelievably dense.

Maggie fell easily into a light, untroubled slumber. Although asleep, lying on her side, her back to him, she was ever conscious of the movements of the man who was sharing the bed. Apparently, Glenn was having more difficulty falling asleep, tossing to one side and then to another, seeking a comfortable position. Once his hand inadvertently fell onto her hip and for a moment he went completely still. Content now, Maggie smiled inwardly and welcomed the calm. Sleeping with him was like being in a rowboat wrestling with a storm at sea.

With unhurried ease the hand that rested against her bare hip climbed upward, stopping at her ribs. Shifting his position, Glenn scooted closer and gathered her into his embrace. As if he couldn't help himself, his hand sought and found a firm breast. His touch was doing insane things to her equilibrium and she was encompassed in a gentle, sweet warmth. Savoring the moment, Maggie bit into her bottom lip as he slowly, tantalizingly, caressed her breasts until she thought she'd moan audibly and give herself away.

Glenn was in agony. He had thought that he would wait and follow all the plans he'd made for courting his wife. But each minute grew more torturous than the one just past. He couldn't sleep; even breathing normally was impossible when she lay just within his grasp. He hadn't meant to touch her, but once his hand lightly grazed her hip he couldn't stop his mind from venturing to rounder, softer curves and the memory of the way her breast had fit perfectly into the palm of his hand. Before he could stop, his fingers sought to explore her ripe body. Maggie remained completely still, waiting patiently for him to roll her onto her back and make love to her. When he didn't move and she suspected that he might not ease the painful longing throbbing within her, she rolled onto her back and linked her arms around his neck.

"Kiss me," she pleaded.

"Maggie." He ground out her name like a man possessed, and hungrily devoured her lips with deep, slow, hot kisses that drove him to the brink of insanity. Groaning, he buried his face in her hair and he drew deep gulps of oxygen into his parched lungs. Again he kissed her, tasting her willingness, reveling in her eagerness. Her hands rumpled the dark thickness of his hair while she repeated his name again and again. Hungry for the taste of him, Maggie urged his mouth to hers, but his devouring kiss only increased her aching need.

"I want you," he groaned, breathing in sharply.

"Yes," she murmured, kissing the hollow of his throat and arching against him.

"Oh, Glenn," Maggie groaned in a harsh whisper. "What took you so long?" The sensation was so blissfully exultant that she felt she could have died from it.

"Took me so long?" he repeated and groaned harshly. "You wanted me to make love to you?"

Looping her arms around his neck, Maggie strained upward and planted a long, hot kiss on his parted mouth. "How can any man be so blind?"

"Next time, hit me over the head." He arched forward then, and buried himself deep within her.

Maggie moaned. "I will. Oh, Glenn, I will," she cried. He took her quickly, unable to bear slow torture. Their bodies fused in a glorious union of heart with soul, of man with woman, of Maggie with Glenn. They strained together, giving, receiving until their hearts beat in a paired tempo that left them breathless, giddy and spent.

Glenn gathered her in his arms and rolled onto his side, taking her with him. Her head rested in the crook of his shoulder, their legs entwined as if reluctant to release the moment.

Maggie felt the pressure of his mouth on her hair and snuggled closer into his embrace, relishing the feel of his strong arms wrapped securely around her.

Brushing a wayward curl from her cheek, Glenn's hand lingered to lightly stroke the side of her face. Maggie smiled gently up at him, the contented smile of a satisfied woman.

"Do you think you'll be able to sleep now?" she teased.

Glenn chuckled, his warm breath fanning her forehead. "Did my tossing and turning keep you awake?"

"Not really.... I was only half-asleep." Maggie lowered her chin and covered her mouth in an attempt to stifle a yawn. "Good night, Mr. Lambert," she whispered, dragging out the words as she swallowed back another yawn.

"Mrs. Lambert," he murmured huskily, kissing the crown of her head.

Maggie's last thought before slipping into an easy slumber was that she wasn't ever going to allow another woman's ghost to come between them again. This man was her husband and she loved him...yes, loved him with a ferocity she was only beginning to understand. Together they were going to make this marriage work. One hundred Angies weren't going to stand in the way of their happiness. Maggie wouldn't allow it.

Within minutes Maggie was asleep. Still awake, Glenn propped up his head with one hand and took delight in peacefully watching the woman who had become everything to him in such a shockingly short amount of time. She was his friend, his lover, his wife, and he had the feeling he had only skimmed the surface of who and what Maggie would be in his life. His finger lightly traced the line of her cheek and the hollow of her throat. As impulsive as their marriage had been, there wasn't a second when Glenn regretted having pledged his life to Maggie. She was fresh and warm, a loving, free spirit. And he adored her. She had come to him with an ardor he had only dreamed of finding in a woman. She was stubborn, impulsive, headstrong: a rare and exquisite jewel. His jewel. His woman. His wife.

The low, melodious sound of a ballad slowly woke Maggie.

"Good morning, Sleeping Beauty," Glenn said as he sat on the edge of the mattress and kissed her lightly. He finished buttoning his shirt and flipped up the collar as he straightened the silk tie around his neck.

"You're dressed," she said, struggling to a sitting position and wiping the sleep from her eyes. She had wanted to get up with him, but must have missed the alarm.

"Would you like to undress me?"

Leaning against the down pillow, Maggie crossed her arms and smiled beguilingly up at him. "What would you do if I said yes?"

Glenn's fingers quit working the silk tie. "Don't tempt me, Maggie, I'm running late already."

"I tempt you?" He'd never said anything more beautiful.

"If only you knew."

"I hope you'll show me." She wrapped her arms around her bent knees and leaned forward. "It...it was wonderful last night." She felt shy talking about their lovemaking, but it was imperative that he realize how much he pleased her.

"Yes it was," he whispered, taking her hand and kissing her knuckles. "I never expected anything so good between us."

"Me neither," she murmured and kissed his hand. "I wish you'd gotten me up earlier."

"Why?" He looked surprised.

Tossing back the covers, Maggie climbed out of bed and slipped into a matching black satin housecoat that she hadn't bothered to put on the night before— for obvious reasons. "I wanted to do the wifely thing and cook your breakfast."

"I haven't got time this morning." He paused, thinking he'd never seen any woman more beautiful. Her tousled hair fell to her shoulders, her face was free of any cosmetics, but no siren had ever been more alluring.

"Is there anything you'd like me to do while you're gone?" she offered. The day stretched before her and they hadn't made plans.

"Yes, in fact there are several things. I'll make a list." He reached for a pad and paper on his nightstand and spent the next few minutes giving her directions and instructions. "And don't plan dinner tonight," he added. "I phoned my parents yesterday and told them I had a surprise and to expect two for dinner."

Maggie sat on the bed beside him and unconsciously her shoulders slouched slightly. This was the very reason she'd come to Charleston, yet she was afraid. "Will they think we've gone crazy?"

"Probably," he returned with a short chuckle. "But they'll be delighted. Don't worry about it; they know you and have always liked you. Mom and Dad will be happy for us."

"I'm happy, Glenn." She wanted to reassure him that she had no regrets in this venture.

The smile faded from his dark eyes and his gaze held her immobile. "I am, too, for the first time since I can remember. We're going to make it, Maggie."

A grandfather clock in the den chimed the hour and reluctantly Glenn stood. "I've got to leave."

"Glenn." Maggie stopped him, then lowered her gaze, almost afraid of what she had to say. Waiting until the last minute to tell him wasn't the smartest thing to do.

"Yes?" he prompted.

"I'm… Listen, I think you should probably know that I'm not using any birth control."

His index finger lifted her chin so that her uncertain gaze met his. "That's fine. I want a family."

A sigh of relief washed through her and she beamed him a brilliant smile. "I probably should warn you, though, my mother claims the Kingsbury clan is a fertile one. We could be starting our family sooner than you expect."

"Don't worry about it; I'm not going to. When a baby comes, you can be assured of a warm welcome."

Maggie experienced an outpouring of love far too powerful to be voiced with simple words. Nodding demanded an incredible effort.

"I'll leave the car keys with you and I'll take public transportation. If you're in the neighborhood around noon stop into the office and I'll introduce you and take you to lunch."

"Maybe tomorrow," she said, stepping onto her tiptoes to kiss him goodbye. There was barely enough time to do everything she had to and be ready for dinner with his parents that evening.

A minute later Glenn was out the door. The condo seemed an empty shell without him. Maggie wandered into the kitchen with her list of errands, then poured a cup of coffee and carried it to the round table. She pulled out a chair and sat, drawing her legs under her. The first place she needed to stop was the bank to sign the forms that would add her name to the checking account. When she was there, Glenn had asked her to make a deposit for him.

She glanced at the front page of the paper he had left on the table and worked the crossword puzzle, then finished her coffee and dressed. The day held purpose. If she was going to see his parents it might not be a bad idea to find someplace where she could have her hair done.

With a jaunty step, Maggie found the deposit envelope Glenn had mentioned on the top of his desk. The room emanated his essence and she paused to drink it in. As she turned, Maggie caught a glimpse of a frame sticking above the rim of his wastepaper basket. What an unusual thing to do to a picture, she thought. As an artist, her sense of indignation rose until she lifted the frame from out of the basket and saw the multitude of small pictures with faces smiling back at her. Her breath came to an abrupt halt and the room crowded in on her, pressing at her with a strangling sensation. *So this was Angie.*

Seven

The first thought that came to Maggie was how beautiful Angie was. With thick, coffee-dark hair and intense brown eyes that seemed to mirror her soul, Angie had the ethereal look of a woman meant to be cherished, loved and protected. There was an inner glow, a delicate beauty to her that Maggie could never match. Angie was a woman meant to be loved and nurtured. It was little wonder that Glenn loved her. One glance at the woman who claimed his heart told Maggie that by comparison she was a poor second.

The frame contained a series of matted pictures that had obviously been taken over a period of several months. There was Angie on a sailboat, her windblown hair flying behind her as she smiled into the camera; Angie leaning over a barbecue, wearing an apron that said Kiss The Cook; Angie standing, surrounded by floral bouquets, in what looked like a flower shop, with her arms outstretched as though to signal this was hers. And more…so much more. Each picture revealed the rare beauty of the woman who claimed Glenn's heart.

A sickening knot tightened Maggie's stomach and she placed a hand on her abdomen and slowly released her breath. Although most of the photos were of Angie alone, two of them showed Glenn and Angie together. If recognizing the other woman's inner and outer beauty wasn't devastating enough, then the happiness radiating from Glenn was. Maggie had never seen him more animated. He seemed to glow with love. In all the years Maggie had known Glenn, she had never seen him look more content. He was at peace with his world, and so in love that it shone like a polished badge from every part of him. In comparison, the Glenn who had arrived in San Francisco was a sullen, doleful imitation.

Pushing the hair off her forehead, Maggie leaned against a filing cabinet and briefly closed her eyes. As early as the night before, she'd thought to banish Angie's ghost from their marriage. She had been a fool to believe it would be that easy. With a feeling of dread, she placed the frame back where she'd found it. Building a firm foundation for their marriage wasn't going to be easy, not nearly as easy as she'd thought. But then, nothing worthwhile ever was. Maggie loved her husband. Physically, he wanted her and for now that would suffice. Someday Glenn would look at her with the same glow of happiness that Angie evoked. Someday his love for her would be there for all the world to witness. Someday…

* * *

Glancing at her wristwatch, Maggie hurried from the bathroom into the bedroom. In a few hours she and Glenn were having dinner with his parents, Charlotte and Mel, people she'd known and liked all her life. Family friends, former neighbors, good people. Yet Maggie had never been less sure of herself. Already she had changed outfits twice. This one would have to do, she decided. There wasn't time to change her mind again. As she put the finishing touches on her makeup, Maggie muttered disparaging remarks over the sprinkling of freckles across the bridge of her nose; wanted to know why her lashes couldn't be longer and her mouth fuller. Mentally she had reviewed her body: her breasts looked like cantaloupes, her hips like a barge; her legs were too short, her arms too long. Maggie could see every imperfection. Finally she had been forced to admit that no amount of cosmetics was going to make her as lovely as Angie. She had to stop thinking of Charlotte and Mel as the mother- and father-in-law who would compare her to their son's first choice. She had to force herself to remember them instead as the friends she knew they were.

Perhaps if she'd had more time to prepare mentally for this dinner, she thought defensively. As it was, the list of errands had taken most of the day and Maggie had been grateful to have something to occupy her time and her mind. Instead of concentrating on being bright and witty for her meeting with Glenn's parents, her thoughts had returned again and again to the discarded series of photographs. If she had found those photos, she reasoned, then there were probably other pictures around. The realization that Angie could be a silent occupant of the condominium was an intolerable conjecture.

When Glenn had walked in the door that afternoon and kissed her, Maggie had toyed with the idea of confronting him with the pictures. Sanity had returned in the nick of time. He had obviously intended to throw them away, but surely must have realized that she would stumble upon them. Maybe it was cowardly of her, but Maggie had decided to ignore the fact that the pictures were in the other room, and pretended she hadn't seen them. For the first time since their marriage, things were going right and she didn't want to ruin that.

"Maggie, are you ready?" Glenn sauntered into the bedroom and hesitated when he saw her. "I thought you were wearing a blue dress."

"I…was," she answered slowly, turning and squaring her shoulders. "Do I look all right?"

"You're lovely." He placed a hand on each of her shoulders. "Maggie, I wish you'd stop worrying. Mom and Dad are going to be thrilled for us."

"I know." Absently she brushed her hand across the skirt of her black-and-red-print dress and slowly released her breath. "I've always been Muffie to them and I'm…I'm not sure they'll be able to accept me as your wife."

Glenn's chuckle echoed through the bedroom. "Maggie, how can they not accept you? You're my wife. Mother's been after me for years to marry and settle down. She'll be grateful I finally took the plunge."

"That's encouraging," she mumbled sarcastically. "So you were desperate to placate your mother and decided I'd do nicely as a wife. Is that supposed to reassure me?"

The muscles of his face tightened and a frown marred his wide brow as he dropped his hands to his side. "That's not true and you know it."

Ashamed, Maggie lowered her head and nodded. "I'm sorry, I didn't mean that. My stomach feels like a thousand bumblebees have set up camp. Even my hands are clammy." She held them out, palms up, for him to inspect. "Wait until we visit my parents, then you'll know how I feel."

Slipping an arm around her waist, Glenn led her into the living room. "If you're worried, stick to my side and I'll answer all the questions."

"I had no intention of leaving your side," she returned, slightly miffed.

A faint smile touched his mouth.

The ride to Glenn's parents' did little to settle her nerves. Maggie thought she would be glad when this evening was over. When Glenn turned off the main road and into a narrow street lined with family homes, Maggie tensed. Two blocks later he slowed and turned into a cement driveway.

Before Maggie was out of the car the front door opened and Mel and Charlotte Lambert were standing on the wide porch. Maggie was surprised by how little they'd changed. Glenn's father's hair was completely gray now and his hairline had receded, but he stood proud and broad shouldered just as Maggie remembered him. Glenn's mother was a little rounder, and wearing a dress. As a child, Maggie knew she was always welcome at the Lamberts' kitchen. Charlotte had claimed it was a pleasure having another woman around since she lived with a house full of men. Maggie had dropped over regularly when Dale, the youngest Lambert, was born. She had been at the age to appreciate babies and had loved to help feed and bathe him.

"Muffie!" Charlotte exclaimed, her bright eyes shining with genuine pleasure. "What a pleasant surprise. I had no idea you were in town."

Glenn joined Maggie and draped his arm around her shoulders as he boldly met his parents' gaze. To be honest, he had been dreading this confrontation himself. His parents would be pleased for him and Maggie, and do their best to hide their shock. But his father was bound to say something about Angie when they had a private moment. He might even suspect that Glenn had married on the rebound. He hadn't. Glenn tried not to think of Angie and ignored the nip of emotional pain associated with her name. His parents had loved her and encouraged him to marry her. Their disappointment had been keen when he told them she'd married Simon.

"Are you visiting from California?" Charlotte asked with a faint tinge of longing. "I do miss that old neighborhood. If we had a hundred years, we'd never find any better place to raise our family." Taking Maggie by the elbow, she led her into the house. "What's the matter with us, standing on the porch and talking when there's plenty of comfortable chairs inside."

Maggie tossed a pleading glance over her shoulder to Glenn, hoping he wouldn't leave the explaining to her.

The screen door closed with a bang as they entered the house. The small living room managed to hold a recliner, a sofa and an overstuffed chair and ottoman. In addition, a rocking chair sat in one corner. The fireplace mantel was lined with pictures of the three sons and the grandchildren.

"Mom, Dad," Glenn began, his expression sober as he met their curious faces. His arm slipped around Maggie as he stood stiffly at her side. He didn't know any better way to say it than right out. "Maggie is my wife. We've been married nearly two weeks."

"Married? Two weeks?" Charlotte echoed in a stunned whisper.

Mel Lambert recovered quickly and reached across the room to pump Glenn's hand. "Congratulations, son." Cupping Maggie's shoulders he gently kissed her cheek. "Welcome to the family, Muffie."

"Thank you." Her voice was both weak and weary. This was worse than she'd thought. Glenn's mother stood with a hand pressed over her heart and an absurd look of shock written across her face, which she was trying desperately to disguise.

"You two…are married," Charlotte whispered, apparently having recovered. "This is wonderful news. Mel, you open that bottle of wine we've been saving all these years and I'll get the goblets." Within seconds they had both disappeared.

Glenn took Maggie's hand and led her to the sofa where they both sat. "See, I told you it wouldn't be so bad." His hand squeezed hers and his eyes smiled confidently into hers. He smoothed a strand of hair from her temple with his forefinger in a light caress.

"How can you say that?" she hissed under her breath. "Your mother nearly fainted." To further her unease she could hear hushed whispers coming from the kitchen. The barely audible word "rebound" heightened the embarrassed flush in Maggie's red cheeks. She pretended not to hear, as did Glenn.

Glenn's handsome face broke into a scowl. It was a mistake not to have said something to his parents earlier. His better judgment had prompted him to tell them. But he had made such an issue of the necessity of Maggie and him confronting them together that he couldn't very well change plans. Informing his parents of their marriage had been what it took to get Maggie to join him in Charleston, and he would never regret that.

Mel and Charlotte reappeared simultaneously. Charlotte carried four shining crystal goblets on a silver tray and Mel had a wine bottle and corkscrew in one hand.

"Before leaving California," Mel explained as he pulled open the corkscrew, "Charlotte and I took a drive through the Napa Valley and bought some of the finest wines available. That was thirteen years ago now and we only open those bottles on the most special occasions."

"Let me see, the last time we opened our California wine was…" Charlotte paused and a network of fine lines knitted her face as she concentrated.

Glenn tensed and his hand squeezed Maggie's so tightly that she almost yelped at the unexpected pain.

Gradually he relaxed his punishing grip, and Maggie realized that the last special occasion in the Lambert family had been shared with Angie and Glenn.

"Wasn't it when Erica was born?" Mel inserted hastily.

"No, no," Charlotte dismissed the suggestion with an impatient wave of her hand. "It was more recent than that... I think it was..." Flustered, she swallowed and reached for a wineglass to hide her discomfort. "I do believe you're right, dear, it was when Erica was born. It just seems more recent is all."

The tension left Glenn, and even Maggie breathed easier. Mel finished opening the bottle and nimbly filled the four goblets. Handing Maggie and Glenn their wineglasses, he proposed a toast. "To many years of genuine wedded happiness."

"Many years," Charlotte echoed.

Later Maggie helped Charlotte set the table, carrying out the serving dishes while Glenn and his father chatted companionably in the living room. At dinner, the announcement that Glenn would be moving to San Francisco was met with a strained moment of disappointment.

"We'll miss you, son," was all that was said.

Unreasonably, Maggie experienced a flood of guilt. It hadn't been her idea to leave Charleston. She would make her home wherever Glenn wished, but apparently he wanted out of South Carolina.

"We'll visit often," Glenn assured his parents and catching Maggie's eye, he winked. "Especially after the children come."

Mel and Charlotte exchanged meaningful glances,

making Maggie want to jump up and assure them she wasn't pregnant...at least she didn't think so.

The meal was saved only because everyone felt the need to chat and cover the disconcerting silence. Maggie did her share, catching the Lamberts up on what had been happening with her parents and skimming over Denny's misfortunes, giving them only a brief outline of his life. In return, Charlotte proudly spoke of each of her three grandchildren, and while they cleared the table the older woman proudly brought out snapshots of the grandkids. Maggie examined each small smiling face, realizing for the first time that these little ones were now her nieces and nephew.

While Maggie wiped off the table, Charlotte ran sudsy water into the kitchen sink. "There was a time that I despaired of having a daughter," Charlotte began awkwardly.

"I remember," Maggie responded, recalling all the afternoons she had sat with Mrs. Lambert.

"And now I have three daughters. Each one of my sons have married well. I couldn't be more pleased with the daughters they've given me."

Maggie's hand pushed the rag with unnecessary vigor across the tabletop. "Thank you. I realize our marriage must come as a shock to you, but I want you to know, Mrs. Lambert, I love Glenn and I plan to be a good wife to him."

The dark eyes softened perceptively. "I can see that, Muffie. No woman can look at a man the way you look at Glenn and not love him." Hesitantly, she wiped her wet hands on her apron and turned toward Maggie. Her gaze drifted into the living room and she frowned slightly. "Are you free for lunch tomorrow? I think we should talk."

"Yes, I'd enjoy that."

Maggie didn't tell Glenn of her luncheon arrangement with his mother until the following morning. She woke with him and put on the coffee while he showered. When he joined her in the kitchen, Maggie had fried bacon and eggs, which was about the limit of her breakfast skills. Learning to cook was something she planned to do soon. Rosa, her housekeeper at the beach house, would gladly teach her. Thoughts of California brought back a mental image of her brother, and Maggie sighed expressively. "I'll need the car again today; do you mind?" Maggie asked Glenn, turning her thoughts from the unhappy subject of Denny.

Glenn glanced up from the morning paper. "Do you want to do some shopping?"

"No...I'm meeting your mother for lunch." With a forced air of calm she scooted out the chair across from him. Her hands cupped the coffee mug, absorbing its warmth. She was worried about letting Glenn know she was meeting his mother. "You don't mind, do you...I mean, about me using the car?"

"No." He pushed his half-eaten breakfast aside, darting a concerned look toward Maggie. "I don't mind." Great! he thought vehemently. He could only imagine what his mother was going to tell Maggie. If Maggie heard the details of his relationship with Angie, he'd prefer that they came from him, not his mother.

"Good." Despite his aloofness, Maggie had the impression that he wasn't altogether pleased. He didn't have to be—she was going and she sensed they both knew what would be the main subject of the luncheon conversation.

"Would you like to meet me at the health club afterward?" Glenn asked, but his attention didn't waver from the newspaper. "I try to work out two, sometimes three times a week."

It pleased Maggie that he was including her. "Sure, but let me warn you I'm terrible at handball, average at tennis and a killer on the basketball court."

"I'll reserve a tennis court," Glenn informed her, a smile curling up one side of his mouth. "And don't bother about dinner tonight. We'll eat at the club."

The morning passed quickly. Since she was meeting Glenn later, Maggie dressed casually in white linen slacks and a pink silk blouse, checking her appearance several times. All morning, Maggie avoided going near Glenn's den. She wouldn't torment herself by looking at the pictures again; stumbling upon them once had been more than enough. For all she knew, Glenn could have tossed them out with the garbage, but Maggie hadn't the courage to look, fearing that he hadn't.

Allowing herself extra time in case she got lost, Maggie left early for her luncheon date with Charlotte. She had some difficulty finding the elder Lamberts' home, and regretted not having paid closer attention to the route Glenn had taken the night before. As it turned out, when she pulled into the driveway it was precisely noon, their agreed time.

Charlotte met her at the door and briefly hugged her. "I got to thinking later that I should have met you someplace. You hardly know your way around yet."

"It wasn't any problem," Maggie fibbed, following the older woman into the kitchen. A quiche was cooling on the countertop, filling the room with the delicious smell of egg, cheese and spices.

"Sit down and I'll get you a cup of coffee."

Maggie did as requested, not knowing how to say that she didn't want to be thought of as company. Charlotte took the chair beside her. "The reason I asked you here today is to apologize for the way I behaved last night."

"No, please." Maggie's hand rested on her mother-in-law's forearm. "I understand. Our news must have come as a shock. Glenn and I were wrong not to have told you earlier."

"Yes, I'll admit that keeping it a secret for nearly two weeks was as much of a surprise as the deed." She lifted the delicate china cup to her mouth and took a sip. Glenn had always been close to his family; for him to have married without letting them know immediately was completely out of character. For that matter, their rushed marriage wasn't his style either. Maggie didn't need to be reminded that Glenn was a thorough person who weighed each decision, studied each circumstance. It was one reason he was such an excellent stockbroker.

"You have to understand," Maggie said, wanting to defend him. "We were as surprised as anyone. Glenn arrived for Steve and Janelle's wedding and everything seemed so right between us that we flew to Reno that night."

"The night of the wedding?" Charlotte did a poor

job of hiding her astonishment. "Why, he'd only arrived in San Francisco…"

"Less than twenty-four hours before the wedding." Maggie confirmed her mother-in-law's observation. "And we hadn't seen each other in twelve—thirteen years. It sounds impulsive and foolish, doesn't it?" Maggie wouldn't minimize the circumstances surrounding their marriage.

"Not that…Glenn's never done anything impulsive in his life. He knew exactly what he was doing when he married you, Maggie. Don't ever doubt that."

"I don't. But I know that Glenn was engaged to someone else recently and that he loved her a great deal."

Obviously flustered, Charlotte shook her head, her face reddening. "You don't need to worry any about her."

"I have, though," Maggie confirmed, being frank and honest. "Glenn hasn't told me much."

"He will in time," Charlotte said confidently. The older woman's brow was furrowed with unasked questions, and Maggie nearly laughed aloud at how crazy the situation must sound to someone else. Glenn and Maggie had grown up fighting like brother and sister, had moved apart for more than a decade and on the basis of a few hours' they'd decided to get married.

"I think I always knew there was something special between you and Glenn. He wasn't too concerned about girls during high school. Sports and his grades took up the majority of his energy. But he was at ease with you. If there was something troubling him, it wasn't me or his father he discussed it with; instead he talked it over with you. I suppose a few people will be surprised at this sudden marriage, but don't let that bother you. The two of you are perfect together."

"I won't." Maggie swallowed, the words nervously tripping over her tongue. "Neither of us came into this marriage the way normal couples do, but we're both determined to make it work. I'd been hurt, perhaps not as deeply as Glenn, but for the past few years I've been lonely and miserable. Glenn's still…hurting, but I've staked our future together on the conviction that time will heal those wounds."

"I'm pleased he told you about Angie." The look of relief relaxed Charlotte's strong face.

"Only a little. He loved her very much, didn't he?" Just saying the words hurt, but she successfully disguised a grimace.

"I won't deny it. Glenn did love her," Charlotte answered, then added to qualify her statement, "More than she deserved."

Maggie had guessed as much already. When Glenn committed himself to someone or something there would never be any doubts. He had loved her, but by his own words, he had no intention of pining away the rest of his life because she married another man. With their wedding vows, Glenn had pledged himself to Maggie. At moments like these and the one yesterday when she discovered the photos, this knowledge of his determination was the only thing that kept her from drowning in frustration.

"I think I always knew that Angie wasn't the right woman for Glenn. Something in my mother's heart told me things were wrong for them. However, it wasn't my place to intrude in his life. He seemed to love her so much."

This time Maggie was unable to hide the pain of Charlotte's words. She felt the blood drain from her face and lowered her eyes, not wanting her mother-in-law to know how tender her heart was.

"Oh dear, I've said the wrong thing again. Forgive me." Shaking her head as if silently scolding herself, Mrs. Lambert added, "That came out all wrong. He was happy, yes, but that happiness wouldn't have lasted and I suspect that even Glenn knew that." Charlotte stood and brought the quiche to the table along with two place settings.

"No, please continue," Maggie urged, needing to know everything about the situation she had married into.

Seeming to understand Maggie's curiosity, Charlotte rejoined her at the kitchen table. "Glenn cared enough for Angie to wait a year for her to decide she'd marry him. I've never seen Glenn so happy as the night she agreed to be his wife. We'd met Angie, of course, several times. She has the roundest, darkest eyes I've ever seen. She's an intense girl, quiet, a little withdrawn, exceptionally loyal, and although she's hurt Glenn terribly, I'm afraid I can't be angry with her. Ultimately she made the right decision. It would have been wrong for her to have married Glenn when she was in love with another man."

The irony of the situation was more than Maggie could stand. It was wrong for Angie to have married Glenn in those circumstances, yet he had done exactly that when he married her. Apparently, Charlotte didn't see it that way. For that matter, Maggie was convinced that had she known beforehand, she probably would have married him anyway.

"And she never did take the ring," Charlotte finished.

"The ring?"

"My mother's," the older woman explained. "She willed it to me as part of my inheritance, and when Glenn graduated from college I opted to make it his. It's a lovely thing, antique with several small diamonds, but of course, you've seen it."

Maggie thrust an expectant look at her mother-in-law. "No…I haven't. Glenn's never mentioned any ring."

Charlotte dismissed the information with a light shrug. "I wouldn't worry about it, you'll receive it soon enough. As I recall, Glenn had it sized and cleaned when he and Angie decided…" Realizing her mistake, Charlotte lowered her gaze and fidgeted with her coffee cup. "He's probably having it resized and is keeping it as a surprise for Christmas. As it is I've probably ruined that. I apologize, Maggie."

The racket slammed against the tennis ball with a vengeance and Maggie returned it to Glenn's side of the court with astonishing accuracy. So he had his grandmother's antique ring that was to go to his wife. She was his wife. Where exactly was the ring? *Slam.* She returned the tennis ball a second time, stretching as far as she could reach to make the volley. Not expecting her return, Glenn lost the point.

Maggie's serve. She aced the first shot, making his

return impossible. Fueled by her anger, she had never played a better match. The first two games were hers, and Glenn's jaw sagged open as he went into mild shock. He rallied in the third, and their fourth and fifth games were heated contests.

"I don't recall you ever being this good," he shouted from the other side of the court.

She tossed the ball into the air, and fully extending her body, wielded the racket forward, bending her upper torso in half.

"There are a lot of things you don't know about me, Lambert," she shouted back, dashing to the far end of the court to return the volley. She felt like a pogo stick hopping from one end of the clay surface to the other with a quickness she didn't know she possessed. At the end of the first set, Maggie was so exhausted that she was shaking. Good grief, she thought, she had a tennis court at the beach house that she never used. This match was a misrepresentation of her skill.

Wiping the perspiration from her face with a thick white towel, Maggie sagged onto the bench. Glenn joined her, taking a seat beside her. "You should have told me you were this good. I've never had to work this hard to win."

Her breath came in deep gasps. "That was quite a workout." She hoped he didn't suggest another one soon. A repeat performance of this magnitude was unlikely. The match had helped her vent her frustrations over the issue of his grandmother's ring—her normal game was far less aggressive.

Taking his mother's words at face value, Maggie decided the best thing she could do was patiently wait.

Glenn had originally intended the ring would go to Angie, but he'd married Maggie. When he felt comfortable with the idea he'd present her with the ring, not before. Christmas was less than seven weeks away, and Charlotte was probably right. He'd give it to her then.

Maybe.

Regaining his breath, Glenn leaned forward and placed his elbows on his knees. "What did you and my mother have to talk about?" The question wasn't an idle one. His brows were drawn into a single tense line. All afternoon he had worried about that luncheon date. Maggie had a right to know everything, but he didn't want the information coming from his mother. If anyone was going to tell her, it would come best from him. He had thought to call and talk to his mother, and discreetly explain as much, but the morning had been hectic and by the time he was out of the board meeting, it had been too late.

Wickedly, Maggie fluttered her thick, dark lashes. "I imagine you'd love to know what tales she carried, but I'm not breaking any confidences."

"Did she give you her recipe for my favorite dinner?"

"What makes you think we discussed you?" Maggie tilted her flushed face to one side and grinned up at him, her smile growing broader.

"It only seems natural that the two women in my life would talk of little else." He placed his arm around her shoulder and helped her stand, carrying her tennis racket for her.

Maggie placed her arm around his waist, pleased

with the way he linked her with his mother. "If your favorite meal is beef Stroganoff, then you're in luck."

"The luckiest day of my life was when you agreed to be my wife," Glenn murmured as he looked down on her with a haunting look so intense that Maggie's heart throbbed painfully. Her visit with his mother hadn't been easy for him, she realized. He had probably spent the entire day worrying about what she'd say afterwards.

Her voice grew husky with emotion. "What an amazing coincidence, that's my favorite day, too."

The longing in his eyes grew all the more poignant as Glenn weighed her words. If they'd been anyplace else, Maggie was convinced he would have tossed their tennis rackets aside and pulled her into his arms.

"Come on," she chided lovingly. "If you're going to beat me when I've played the best game of my life, then the least you can do is feed me."

Laughing, Glenn kissed the top of her head and led her toward the changing room and then to the restaurant.

His good mood continued when they reached the condominium. Maggie was bushed, and although she had taken a quick shower at Glenn's club, she couldn't resist a leisurely soak in a hot tub to soothe the aching cries of unused muscles. This day had been their best yet. The tension eased from her sore muscles and her heart. The matter with the ring no longer bothered her. When Glenn decided to give it to her, she'd know that it came from his heart and she need never doubt again.

With her hair pinned up, and a terry-cloth bathrobe

wrapped around her, Maggie walked into the living room, looking for her husband.

"Glenn."

"In here." His voice came from the den.

Remembering the photographs inside, Maggie paused in the doorway. Tension shot through her, although she struggled to appear outwardly composed. With monumental effort she kept her gaze from the large garbage can beside his desk.

"What are you doing?" She was exhausted and it was late. She'd have thought that after a workout on the courts he'd be ready for bed.

"I've got a few odds and ends to finish up here. I'll only be a few minutes," he answered without looking up, scribbling across the top of a computer sheet. When he did glance up he was surprised to find Maggie standing in the doorway as if she were afraid to come into the room. "I'd appreciate a cup of coffee."

Maggie shrugged. "Sure."

"Maggie." Glenn stopped her. "Is anything wrong?"

"Wrong?" she echoed. "What could possibly be wrong?" *Just that I'm such a coward I can't bear to look and see if those snapshots are still there,* she chastised herself, turning toward the kitchen.

"I don't know." Glenn's puzzled voice followed her.

The coffee only took a minute to make. Maggie stood in the kitchen, waiting for the liquid to drain into the cup and told herself she was behaving like an idiot.

She pasted a smile on her lips as she carried the mug into his den and set it on the edge of the desk. "Here you go."

"Thanks," Glenn murmured, busily working.

Maggie straightened and took a step backward. As she did, her gaze fell to the empty garbage can. Relief washed over her. He had gotten rid of them. She wanted to dance around the room and sing.

"Glenn." She moved behind his chair and slid her arms around his neck.

"Hmm…"

"How late did you say you'd be?" She dipped her head and nuzzled the side of his neck, darting her tongue in and out of his ear.

Glenn could feel the hot blood stirring within him. "Not long, why?"

"Why?" she shot back, giggling. "You need me to tell you why?"

Scooting the chair around, Glenn gripped her by the waist and pulled her into his lap. A brilliant smile came over her as she slid her arms around his neck.

Glenn's mouth twisted wryly as he studied her. He didn't know what had gotten into Maggie today. First she had surprised him on the tennis court. Then she had behaved like a shy virgin outside his door, looking in as if his office was a den of iniquity. And now she was a bewitching temptress who came to him with eyes that were filled with passion. Not that he was complaining, he'd never get enough of this woman.

Maggie's fingers fumbled with the buttons of his shirt so that she had the freedom to run her hands over his chest. She reveled in simply touching him, and pulled the shirt free of his shoulders. His muscles rippled as she slowly slid her hands upward to either side of his neck. Unhurried, she branded him with a kiss so hot it stole his breath.

"Maggie," he whispered hoarsely, intimately sliding his hands between her legs and stroking her bare thigh. "Maybe I haven't got so much paperwork to do after all."

Smiling dreamily, Maggie directed his mouth back to hers. "Good."

Eight

Two weeks passed and Maggie grew more at ease with her marriage. She realized that a silent observer to their world would have assumed that they had been married for several years. Externally, there was nothing to show that their marriage wasn't the product of a long, satisfying courtship. It didn't seem to matter that Glenn hadn't declared his love. He respected her, enjoyed her wit, encouraged her talent. They were happy…and it showed.

Maggie greeted each day with enthusiasm, eager to discover what lay in store for her. She purchased several cookbooks and experimented, putting her creativity to work in the kitchen. Glenn praised her efforts and accepted her failures, often helping her laugh when it would have been easy to lose patience. In the early afternoons, if there was time, Maggie explored Charleston with Glenn's mother and came to appreciate anew what a wonderful woman Charlotte Lambert was. They never spoke of Angie again.

South Carolina was everything Maggie had known

it would be, and more than she'd ever expected. She was thrilled by the eighteenth- and nineteenth-century paintings that displayed regional history in the Gibbes Art Gallery and explored the Calhoun Mansion and the Confederate Museum, examining for the first time the Civil War from the Confederate point of view. One hundred and fifty years after the last battles of the war had been waged, Maggie felt the anguish of the South and tasted its defeat.

Her fingers longed to hold a paintbrush, but she satisfied her urgings with a pen and pad, sketching the ideas that came to her. Charlotte was amazed at her daughter-in-law's talent, and Maggie often gave Glenn's mother her pencil sketches. At Sunday dinner with his family, Maggie was embarrassed to find those careless drawings framed and hanging on the living room wall. Proudly, Glenn's eyes had met hers. They didn't often speak of her art, and Maggie basked in the warm glow of his approval.

For his part, Glenn was happy, happier than he ever imagined he'd be. In the afternoons he rushed home from the office, knowing Maggie would be there waiting for him. Maybe he hadn't married her for the right reasons, maybe what they had done was half-crazy, but, he thought tenderly, he wouldn't have it any different now, and he thanked God every single day that he'd acted on the impulse. Maggie gave his life purpose. In the afternoons she would be there waiting. And the minute he walked in the door, she'd smile. Not an ordinary smile, but a soft feminine one that lit up her dark eyes and curved the edges of her mouth in a sultry way that sent hot need coursing through him. In his lifetime, Glenn never hoped to see another woman smile the way Maggie did. Often he barely made it inside the door before he knew he had to kiss her. He would have preferred to react casually to his desire for her, but discovered that was impossible. Some days he couldn't get home fast enough, using every ounce of self-control he possessed not to burst in the door, wrap his arms around her and carry her into their bedroom. He couldn't touch, or taste, or hold her enough. Glenn felt he'd choose death rather than a life without her. Angie might have possessed his heart, but Maggie had laid claim to his soul.

He wondered sometimes if she had even an inkling of what she did to him physically. He doubted it. If she wasn't pregnant soon, he mused, it would be a miracle. The thought of Maggie heavy with his child, her breasts swollen, her stomach protruding, produced such a shocking desire within him that it was almost painful. The feeling left him weak with wonder and pride. They'd have exceptionally beautiful children.

For the first time, Glenn understood his brothers' pride in and awe of their children. At thirty, Glenn hadn't given much thought to a family. Someday, he had always thought, he'd want children, but he hadn't put faces or names to those who would fill his life. With Maggie he envisioned a tall son and a beautiful daughter. Every man wanted an heir, and now he yearned for a son until some nights he couldn't sleep thinking about the children Maggie would give him. On those evenings, late, when his world was at peace, Glenn would press his hand over her satiny smooth stomach, praying her body was nurturing his seed. A child would cement Maggie and him so firmly together that only death would ever separate them.

Their evenings were filled with contentment. Only rarely did he bring work home, lingering instead in front of the television, using that as an excuse to have Maggie at his side, to watch her. If he did need to deal with some paperwork, she sat quietly in his den, curled up in a chair reading. It was as though they couldn't be separated any longer than necessary and every moment apart was painful.

Maggie enjoyed watching Glenn in his home office more than any other place. He sat with simple authority at his desk while she pretended absorption in a novel, when actually she was studying him. Now and then he would look up and they'd exchange warm, lingering glances that left her wondering how long it would be until they could go to bed.

When they did head toward the bedroom, it was ridiculously early. The instant the light went off Glenn reached for her with such passion that she wondered if he would ever get his fill of her—then promptly prayed he wouldn't. Their nights became a celebration for all the words stored in their hearts that had yet to be spoken. Never shy nor embarrassed, Maggie came to him without reserve, holding nothing back. She was his temptress and mistress. Bewitching and bewitched. Seduced and seducer.

Maggie had assumed that the fiery storm of physical satisfaction their bodies gave each other would fade with time, not increase. But as the days passed, she was pleased that Glenn's constant need equaled her desire for him. Each time they made love, Maggie would lie in his arms thinking that their appetite for each other would surely diminish, and knew immediately that it wouldn't.

In the mornings when she woke to the clock radio, Maggie was securely wrapped in Glenn's arms. He held her close and so tight she wondered how she had managed to sleep. Some mornings Maggie felt the tension leave Glenn as he emerged from the last dregs of slumber and realized she remained with him. It was as though he feared she would be gone. Once assured she was at his side, Glenn would relax. As far as Maggie could tell, this insecurity was the only part of his relationship with Angie that continued to haunt him. One hundred times each day, in everything she did, every place she went, Maggie set out to prove she would never willingly leave him.

Life fell into a comfortable pattern and the third full week after Maggie arrived in Charleston, the condominium sold. Maggie met Glenn at the door with the news.

"The Realtor was by with an offer," she said, draping her arms around his neck and pressing her body to his.

Glenn held her hips and placed his large hands on her hips, as he kissed her. "As far as I can see we should be able to make the move within a week, two at the most," he commented a few minutes later, as he curled an arm around her shoulder and deposited his briefcase in the den.

"A week?" Now that she was here, Maggie would have welcomed the opportunity to settle in South Carolina. California, Denny, the beach house seemed a million miles away, light-years from the life she shared with Glenn here.

"You sound like you don't want to move." He leaned against the edge of his desk, crossing his long legs at the ankles.

"South Carolina is lovely."

"So is California," Glenn countered. "You don't mind the change, do you?"

In some ways she did. Their time in Charleston was like a romantic interlude—the honeymoon they'd never gotten. They were protected from the outside world. No one knew who Maggie was, or cared. For the first time in several years she was a regular person and she loved it. In Charleston she had blossomed into a woman who boldly met a passerby's glance. She explored the art galleries without fear that someone would recognize her. No one came to her with "get rich quick" schemes, seeking naive investors. No one rushed to wait on her or gain her attention or her gratitude. However, Maggie was wise enough to know that those things would follow in time.

"No," she told Glenn soberly. "I don't mind the move."

He turned, sorting through the stack of mail she had set on the desktop, smiling wryly. Maggie wanted to stay in Charleston for the same reasons he wanted to move to San Francisco. They were each looking for an escape to problems they would need to face sooner or later. For his part, Glenn chose the West Coast more for nostalgia than any need to escape. San Francisco felt right and Charleston held too many painful memories.

"Will you want to live at the beach house?" Maggie's one concern was that Glenn might not like her home. Her own feelings toward the house were ambivalent. On some days, it was her sanctuary and on others, her prison. She liked the house; she was comfortable there, but she didn't know that Glenn would be.

"Sure. Is there any reason you'd want to move?"

"No, it's just that…" The telephone rang and Maggie paused as Glenn lifted the receiver.

After a moment he handed it to her. "It's for you."

"Me?" She felt her heart rate accelerate. She'd given specific instructions that she wasn't to be contacted except for her brother. And Denny would only call if he was in financial trouble.

"Hello." Her voice was wispy with apprehension.

"Who was that?"

"Denny, are you all right?"

"I asked you a question first. It's not often I call my sister and a man answers the phone. Something's going on. Who is it, Maggie?"

"I'm with Glenn Lambert."

A low chuckle followed, but Maggie couldn't tell if her brother was pleased or abashed. "So you and Glenn are together. Be careful, Maggie, I don't want to see you hurt again." He hesitated, as though he didn't want to continue. "Are you living with him?"

"Denny," Maggie had been foolish not to have told her family sooner, "Glenn and I are married."

"Married," he echoed in shock. "When did this happen?"

"Several weeks ago."

A short, stunned silence followed. "That's sudden,

isn't it? Linda and I would have liked to have attended the wedding."

"We eloped."

"That's not like you."

"It wasn't like either of us. I'm happy, Denny, really happy. You know what it's been like the past few years. Now don't worry about me. I'm a big girl. I know what I'm doing."

"I just don't want to see you get hurt."

"I won't," she assured him.

"Do Mom and Dad know?"

Denny had her there. "Not yet. We're planning to tell them once we're back in San Francisco."

"And when will that be?" His words were slow as if he were still thinking.

"A couple of weeks."

He didn't respond and the silence seemed to pound over the great echoing canyon of the telephone wire. Denny hadn't done a good job of disguising his reservations. Once he saw how good this marriage was for her, she was sure, he'd share her happiness. Her brother had been her anchor when she broke up with Dirk. He had seen firsthand the effects of one painful relationship and sought to protect her from another. Only Glenn wasn't Dirk, and when they arrived back in San Francisco Denny would see that.

"Is there a reason you phoned, Denny?"

"Oh, yeah." His voice softened. "Listen, I hate to trouble you but there's been some minor complications and the lawyer has to charge me extra fees. Also, Linda's been sick and the kids aren't feeling that well, either...."

"How much do you need?"

"I hate having to come to my sister like a pauper. But I swear as soon as everything's straightened out I'll repay every penny."

"Denny, don't worry about it. You're my brother, I'm happy to give you whatever you need. You know that." She couldn't refuse her own brother no matter what the reason.

"I know and appreciate it, Sis. I really do."

"You wouldn't ask if it wasn't necessary." She had hoped to make this difficult time in Denny's life smoother but sometimes wondered if she contributed more to the problem. Yet she couldn't say no. "I'll have Shirley write you a check."

Once he had gotten what he wanted the conversation ended quickly. Maggie replaced the receiver and forced a smile to her lips. "That was my brother," she announced, turning back to Glenn.

"Who's Shirley?" he asked starkly.

"My money manager." She lowered her gaze to the lush carpet, feeling her husband's censure. Glenn didn't understand the circumstances that had led to Denny's problems. They had both received a large inheritance. Maggie had received half of her great-aunt's fortune; her parents and Denny had split the other half. Everything had gone smoothly until Denny had invested in a business that had quickly gone defunct. Now his money—or what was left of it—was tied up in litigation.

"Does Denny need her name often?"

"Not really," she lied. "He's been having some cash flow problems lately." As in not having any, her mind added. "We were talking about the move to California when the phone buzzed, weren't we?"

"You don't want to discuss Denny, is that it?"

"That's it." Glenn couldn't tell her anything she didn't already know. She was in a no-win situation with her brother. She couldn't abandon him, nor could she continue to feed his dependence on her.

"Okay, if that's the way you want it." His eyes and voice silently accused her as he turned back and sorted through the mail.

"California will be good for us," Maggie said, hoping to lighten the atmosphere.

"Yes, it will," Glenn agreed almost absently, without looking up. "Before I forget, the office is having a farewell party for me Friday night. We don't have any plans, do we?"

Maggie had met Glenn's staff and seen for herself the respect his management had earned him. One afternoon when she had met him for lunch, Maggie had witnessed anew the quiet authority in his voice as he spoke to his associates. He was decisive and sure, calm and reassuring, and the office had thrived under his care. It went without saying that he was a popular manager and would be sorely missed.

Friday night Maggie dressed carefully, choosing a flattering cream-colored creation and pale blue designer nylons. She had never been one to enjoy parties, especially when they involved people she barely knew. This one shouldn't be so bad though, she reasoned. The focus would be on Glenn, not her.

"Am I underdressed?" she asked him, slowly rotating for his inspection. Not having attended this kind of function previously put her at a disadvantage. She didn't know how the other wives would dress and had chosen something conservative.

Glenn stood, straightening his dark blue silk tie. His warm chuckle filled their bedroom as he examined his wife. "As far as I'm concerned you're overdressed. But I'll take care of that later myself." His eyes met hers in the mirror and filled with sweet promise.

After inserting dangly gold earrings into her earlobes, Maggie joined Glenn in the living room. He was pouring them a drink and Maggie watched her husband with renewed respect. He was tall, athletic and unbearably handsome. Her heart swelled with the surge of love that raced through her. She hadn't been looking forward to the party; in fact, she had been dreading it from the moment Glenn had mentioned it. Early on, she had reconciled herself to being a good stockbroker's wife, and that meant that she'd be attending plenty of functions over the years. It would be to her advantage to adapt to them now. Although he hadn't said anything, Maggie was confident Glenn knew she was determined to make the best of this evening.

They arrived precisely at eight at the home of Glenn's regional manager, Gary Weir. Already the living room was filled with smoke, and from the look of things the drinks had been flowing freely. As Glenn and Maggie walked in the front door, spirited cheers of welcome greeted them. Maggie painted a bright smile on her lips as they moved around the room, mingling with the guests. Everyone, it seemed, was in a good mood. Everyone, that is, except Maggie.

She didn't know how to explain her uneasiness. There wasn't anything she could put a name to and she mentally chastised herself. Glenn's friends and associates appeared to be going out of their way to make her feel welcome. Her hostess, Pamela Weir, Gary's wife, was warm and gracious, if a bit reserved. Yet a cold persistence nagged at Maggie that something wasn't right. Glenn stayed at her side, smiling down on her now and then. Once her eyes fell upon two women whispering with their heads close together. They sat on the far side of the room and there wasn't any possibility that Maggie could hear their whispered conversation, but something inside told Maggie they were talking about her. A chill went up her spine and she gripped Glenn's elbow, feeling ridiculous and calling herself every kind of idiot. Lightly, she shook her head, hoping to toss aside those crazy insecurities.

A few minutes later Glenn was pulled into a conversation with some of the men and Maggie was left to her own devices. Seeing Maggie alone, Pamela Weir strolled over.

"It was such a pleasant surprise when Glenn announced he had married," Pamela said.

Maggie took a sip of her wine. Glenn was involved with his friends and moved to another section of the crowded room. "Yes, I imagine it was. But we've known each other nearly all our lives."

"That was what Glenn was saying." Pamela gave her a funny look and then smiled quickly. "For a long time Gary was worried that Glenn wanted the transfer because of a problem at the office."

Maggie forced a smile. "We decided when we married that we'd live in San Francisco," she explained to the tall, elegant woman at her side. "We were both raised there."

"Yes, Glenn explained that too."

Maggie's throat constricted and she made an effort to ease the strange tension she felt. "Although I've only been in Charleston a few weeks, I'm impressed with your city. It's lovely."

Pamela's eyes revealed her pride in Charleston. "We do love it."

"I know Glenn will miss it."

"We'll miss him."

Silence. Maggie could think of nothing more to comment upon. "You have a lovely home," she said and faltered slightly. "Glenn and I both appreciate the trouble you've gone to for this evening."

"It's no bother. Glenn has always been special to the firm. We're just sick to lose him." The delicate hands rotated the stem of the crystal wineglass. "I don't mind telling you that Glenn is the best manager Gary has. In fact—" she paused and gave Maggie a falsely cheerful smile "—Gary had been hoping to move Glenn higher into management. Of course that won't be possible now."

As with his parents, Maggie was again put on the defensive. Leaving Charleston hadn't been her idea and she didn't like being made the scapegoat. Swallowing back a retort, Maggie lowered her gaze and said, "I'm sure Glenn will do just as well in San Francisco."

"We all hope he does," Pamela said with a note of censure.

Glenn's gaze found Maggie several moments later.

She stood stiff and uneasy on the other side of the room, holding her drink and talking to Pamela Weir. Even from the other side of the room, he could see that Maggie was upset and he couldn't understand why. He had known from the beginning that she hadn't been looking forward to this party. He wasn't all that fond of this sort of affair himself. But since the party had been given in his honor, he couldn't refuse the invitation. Maggie's attitude troubled him. Earlier in the evening, he'd stayed at her side, but eventually he'd been drawn away for one reason or another. Good grief, he thought, he shouldn't have to babysit her. The longer he watched her actions with Pamela, the more concerned he became. He noticed Maggie wasn't making eye contact with Pamela and when his supervisor's wife moved away, Glenn crossed the room to Maggie's side.

She lifted her gaze to his and Glenn was shocked at the look of anger she sent him.

"What's wrong?" he asked.

She met his gaze with a determined lift to her chin. She was upset, more upset than she'd been since the first morning of their marriage. Glenn had let her walk into the party, knowing the resentment his co-workers felt toward her because he was leaving. "When we arrived tonight I kept feeling these weird vibes that people didn't like me. Now I know why...."

"You're being ridiculous," Glenn muttered, his hand tightening around his drink. "These are my friends and they accept you as my wife."

Glenn was on the defensive and didn't appear willing to listen to her. "You're wrong, Glenn," she murmured, "they don't like me and with good reason. We'll talk about it later."

Glenn said nothing. The sound of someone banging a teaspoon against the side of a glass interrupted their discussion.

"Attention everyone," Gary Weir called as he came to stand beside Glenn and Maggie. With dull blue eyes that revealed several drinks too many, Gary motioned with his arms that he wanted everyone to gather around.

Maggie felt like a statue with a frozen smile curving her mouth as she watched the party crowding around them. Glenn placed an arm at her neck, but his touch felt cold and impersonal.

Ceremoniously clearing his throat, Gary continued. "As you're all aware, tonight's party is being given in honor of Glenn and his—" he faltered momentarily, and seemed to have forgotten Maggie's name "—bride." A red blush attacked the cheeks of the supervisor and he reached for his drink and took a large swallow.

"As we know," he said, glancing over his shoulder to Glenn and Maggie, "Glenn has recently announced that he's transferring to California." Gary was interrupted with several low boos until he sliced the air, cutting off his associates. "Needless to say, everyone is going to miss him. Glenn has been a positive force within our company. We've all come to appreciate him and it goes without saying that he'll be missed. But being good sports, we want to wish him the best in San Francisco." A polite round of applause followed.

"In addition," Gary went on, his voice gaining volume with each word, "Glenn has taken a wife." He turned and beamed a proud smile at the two of them. "All of us felt that we couldn't send you away without a wedding gift. So we took up a collection and got you this." He turned around and lifted a gaily wrapped gift from behind a chair, holding it out to Glenn and Maggie.

Clearing his throat, Gary finished by saying, "This gift is a token of our appreciation and well wishes. We'd all like to wish Glenn and Angie many years of happiness."

Maggie's eyes widened and she swallowed hard at the unexpectedness of it. An embarrassed hush fell over the room and Maggie felt Glenn stiffen. Not realizing his mistake, Gary flashed a troubled look to his wife who was mouthing Maggie's name.

To cover the awkward moment, Maggie stepped forward and took the gift from Gary's hand. He gave her an apologetic look and fumbled, obviously flustered and embarrassed.

"Glenn and I would like to thank you, Larry."

"Gary," he corrected instantly, some color seeping back into his pale face.

A slow smile grew across Maggie's tight features. "We both seem to be having problems with names tonight, don't we?"

The party loved it, laughing spontaneously at the way she had aptly turned the tables on their superior. Laughing himself, Gary briefly hugged her and pumped Glenn's hand.

Not until they were on their way home did Glenn

comment on the mishap. "Thank you," he said as they headed toward the freeway.

"For what?"

"For the way you handled that." He didn't need to explain what "that" was. Maggie knew. Rarely in his life had Glenn felt such anger. He had wanted to throw Gary against the wall and demand that he apologize to Maggie for embarrassing her that way. Of course, the slip hadn't been intentional, but it hadn't seemed to matter.

Several times in the past few weeks, Glenn had questioned whether he was making the right decision leaving Charleston. Maggie had blossomed here and seemed to genuinely love the city. Now he knew beyond a shadow of a doubt that leaving was best. Angie would haunt their marriage in Charleston. He had been a fool not to realize why Maggie had been so miserable at the party. The thought that his co-workers would confuse her with Angie hadn't crossed his mind. It seemed impossible that only a few months back he had been planning to marry someone else. These days he had trouble picturing Angie and seldom tried. Angie would always hold a special place in his heart. He wished her a long and happy life with Simon. But he had Maggie now, and thanked God for the woman beside him. He might not have courted her the way he should have, the way she deserved, but he desperately needed her in his life.

He loved her. Simply. Profoundly. Utterly. He'd tell her soon. Not tonight though, he thought or she'd think the mistake at the party had prompted the admission. Glenn wanted to choose the time carefully. For several weeks now, he had realized she loved him. Yet she hadn't said anything. He couldn't blame her. Things would straighten themselves out once they were in San Francisco. The sooner they left Charleston the better. In California, Maggie need never worry that someone would bring up Angie's name again.

"Gary's mistake was an honest one. He didn't mean to embarrass anyone." Without a problem, Maggie excused Glenn's friend.

"I know," Glenn murmured, concentrating on his driving.

They didn't talk again until they were home and then only in polite phrases. They undressed in silence and when they lifted the covers and climbed into bed, Glenn gathered her close in his arms, kissing her softly. He was asleep long before she was and rolled away from her. Maggie lay staring at the ceiling, unable to shake what had happened earlier from her mind. The flickering moon shadows seemed to taunt her. All they had been doing for the past few weeks was pretending. The two of them had been so intent on making believe that there had never been another woman in Glenn's life that the incident tonight had nearly devastated them. That was the problem with fantasies—they were so easily shattered. Maggie didn't need to be told that Glenn had been equally disturbed. Angie was present in their lives; she loomed between them like an uninvited guest.

With a heavy heart, Maggie rolled over and tried to sleep, but she couldn't. Not until Glenn's arms found her and he pulled her into the circle of his embrace. But he had been asleep, and for all she knew, Maggie thought bitterly, he could have been dreaming it was "her" he was holding.

Monday morning after Glenn left for work, Maggie sat lingering over a cup of coffee, working the crossword puzzle. The first thing she should do was get dressed, but she had trouble shaking off a feeling of melancholy. No matter how hard she tried, she hadn't been able to forget what had happened Friday night. They hadn't spoken about it again, choosing to ignore it. For now the puzzle filled her time. Her pen ran out of ink and after giving it several hard shakes, she tossed it in the garbage. Glenn kept a dozen or more in his desk.

Standing, Maggie headed toward his office. One thing they had decided over the weekend was that Maggie would fly ahead of Glenn to California. Like a fool Maggie had suggested it on the pretense that she had several items that required her attention waiting for her. She had hoped that Glenn would tell her he wanted them to arrive together. But he had agreed all too readily and she'd been miserable for the remainder of the day.

Pulling open Glenn's drawer, she found what she needed and started to close the desk drawer. As she did it made a light, scraping sound. Her first inclination was to shove it closed. Instead, she carefully pulled the drawer free and discovered an envelope tucked away in the back that had been forced upward when she'd gotten the pen.

It wasn't the normal place for Glenn to keep his mail, and she examined the envelope curiously. The even, smooth flowing strokes of the handwriting attracted her artist's eye. This was a woman's handwriting—Angie's handwriting. Maggie felt the room sway as she sank onto the corner of the swivel chair, her knees giving out. The postmark revealed that the letter had been mailed a week before Steve and Janelle's wedding.

Perspiration broke out across Maggie's upper lip and she placed a hand over her mouth. Her heart hammered so loudly she was sure it rocked the room. The letter must have meant a great deal to Glenn for him to have saved it. Although she hadn't searched through the condominium, she had felt confident that he'd destroyed everything that would remind him of the other woman. Yet the letter remained.

Half of her wanted to stuff it back inside the drawer and pretend she'd never found it. The other half knew that if she didn't know the contents of the letter she would always wonder. Glenn had told her so little. She was his wife. She had a right to know. He should have explained the entire situation long ago and he hadn't, choosing instead to leave her curious and wondering. If she looked, it would be his own fault, she argued with herself. He had driven her to it.

It was wrong; Maggie knew it was wrong, but she couldn't help herself. Slowly, each inch pounding in nails of guilt, she withdrew the scented paper from the envelope.

Nine

Carefully Maggie unfolded the letter and was again struck by the smoothly flowing lines of the even handwriting. Angie's soulful dark eyes flashed in Maggie's memory from the time she'd seen the other woman's photograph. The handwriting matched the woman.

Dear Glenn,

I hope that I am doing the right thing by mailing you this letter. I've hurt you so terribly, and yet I owe you so much. I'm asking that you find it in your heart to forgive me, Glenn. I realize the pain I've caused you must run deep. Knowing that I've hurt you is my only regret.

Glenn, I don't believe that I'll ever be able to adequately thank you for your love. It changed my life and gave Simon back to me. Simon and I were destined to be man and wife. I can find no other way to explain it. I love him, Glenn, and

would have always loved him. You and I were
foolish to believe I could have forgotten Simon.

My hope is that someday you'll find a woman
who will love you as much as I love Simon. You
deserve happiness. Simon and I will never forget you. We both want to thank you for the sacrifice you made for us. Be happy, dear Glenn.
Be very happy.

With a heart full of gratitude,
Angie

With trembling hands, Maggie refolded the letter
and placed it back inside Glenn's drawer. If she had
hoped to satisfy her curiosity regarding Angie, the letter only raised more questions. Angie had mentioned a
sacrifice Glenn had made on her behalf. But what? He
was like that, noble and sensitive, even self-sacrificing.
Angie's marrying Simon clearly had devastated him.

All day the letter troubled Maggie, until she decided
that if she were to help Glenn bury the past, she had to
understand it. That night she would do the very thing
she had promised she wouldn't: she would ask Glenn
to tell her about Angie.

No day had ever seemed so long. She didn't leave
the house, didn't comb her hair until the afternoon, and
when she did, her mirrored reflection revealed troubled, weary eyes and tight, compressed lips. If Glenn
could talk this out with her, their chances of happiness
would be greatly increased. He had saved the letter,
risked her finding it. Although he might not be will-

ing to admit it, he was holding on to Angie, hugging the memory. The time had come to let go.

With her arms cradling her middle, Maggie paced the living room carpet, waiting for Glenn to come home from work. The questions were outlined in her mind. She had no desire to hurt or embarrass him. She wanted him to tell her honestly and freely what had happened with Angie and why he had stepped aside for Angie to marry Simon.

Yet for all her preparedness, when Glenn walked in the door Maggie turned abruptly toward him with wide, apprehensive eyes, her brain numb.

"Hello, Glenn." She managed to greet him calmly and walked across the room to give him a perfunctory kiss. She felt comfortable, but her cheeks and hands were cold. Earlier she had decided not to mention finding the letter, not wanting Glenn to know she had stooped so low as to read it. However, if he asked, she couldn't...wouldn't lie.

His hands found her waist and he paused to study her. "Maggie, what's wrong, you're as cold as an iceberg."

She felt ridiculously close to tears and nibbled at her lower lip before answering. This was far more difficult than she'd thought it would be. "Glenn, we need to talk."

"I can see that. Do you have another rule for our marriage?"

Absently, she rubbed the palms of her hands together. "No."

He followed her into the living room and took a seat while she poured him a glass of wine. "Do you think

I'm going to need that?" He didn't know what was troubling Maggie, but he had never seen her quite like this. She looked almost as if she were afraid, which was ludicrous. There was nothing she had to fear from him. He was her husband, and she should always feel comfortable coming to him.

Maybe she was pregnant. His pulse leaped eagerly at the thought. A baby would be wonderful, exciting news. A feeling of tenderness overcame him. Maggie was carrying his child.

"Maggie," he asked gently, "are you pregnant?"

She whirled around, sloshing some of the wine over the side of the glass, her eyes wide with astonishment. "No, what makes you ask?"

Disappointed, Glenn slowly shook his head. "No reason. Won't you tell me what's troubling you?"

She handed him the drink, but didn't take a seat, knowing she would never be able to sit comfortably in one position. She was too nervous. Hands poised, her body tense, she stood by the window and looked down at the street far below. "I've been waiting to talk to you all day."

He wished she'd get to the point instead of leaving him to speculate what troubled her. He had never seen her this edgy. She resembled a child who had come to her parent to admit a great fault. "If it was so important, why didn't you phone me at the office?"

"I...couldn't. This was something that had to be done in person, Glenn," she said, then swallowed, clenching and unclenching her fists as she ignored the impatience in his eyes. "This isn't easy." She resisted the urge to dry her clammy palms on the pockets of her navy-blue slacks.

"I can see that," he said gently. Whatever it was had clearly caused her a lot of anxiety. Rushing her would do no good, and so he forced himself to relax as much as possible. He crossed his legs and leaned back against the thick cushions of the chair.

"I thought for a long time I'd wait until you were comfortable about this…this subject. Now I feel like a fool, forcing it all out in the open. I wish I were a stronger person, but I'm not. I'm weak." Slowly she turned and hesitantly raised her eyes to his. "Glenn, I'm your wife. Getting married the way we did may have been unconventional, but I have no regrets. None. I'm happy being married to you. But as your wife, I'm asking you to tell me about Angie."

, Maggie watched as surprise mingled with frustration and grew across his face.

"Why now?" Angie was the last subject he had expected Maggie to force upon him. As far as he was concerned, his relationship with the other woman was over. He wouldn't deny that he had been hurt, but he had no wish to rip open the wounds of his pride. And that was what had suffered most. Even when he'd known he'd lost her, he had continued to make excuses to see and be with Angie. Something perverse within himself had forced him to go back again and again even when he had recognized that there wasn't any possibility of her marrying him. For weeks he had refused to let go of her even though he'd known he'd lost her and she would never be his.

Now was the opportunity to explain that she'd found

the letter, Maggie thought. But she couldn't admit that she'd stooped so low as to read the extremely personal letter. "I...wanted to know.... It's just that..."

"Is it because of what happened the other night?"

Glenn offered her an excuse that Maggie readily accepted. "Yes."

Glenn's mouth tightened, not with impatience, but confused frustration. Maggie should have put it out of her mind, long ago. No good would come from dredging up the past. "Whatever there was between us is over. Angie has nothing to do with you and me."

"But ultimately she does," Maggie countered. "You wouldn't have married me if your engagement hadn't been broken."

"Now you're being ridiculous. We wouldn't have married if I hadn't attended Steve and Janelle's wedding, either."

"You know what I mean."

"Maggie, trust me. There's nothing to discuss." The words were sharp.

Previously when Glenn was angry, Maggie had marveled at his control. He rarely raised his voice, and never at her. Until now. The only evidence she had ever had of his fury was a telltale leap of muscle in his jaw. He moved from his chair to the far side of the room.

"Glenn," she ventured. "I don't understand why you're so reluctant to discuss her. Is it because I've never told you about Dirk? I would have gladly, but you see, you've never asked. If there's anything you want to know, I'll be happy to explain."

"No, I don't care to hear the sorry details of your

relationship with another man, and in return I expect the same courtesy."

Her hand on the back of the sofa steadied her. All these weeks, she'd been kidding herself, living in a dreamer's world. As Glenn's wife, she would fill the void left when Angie married Simon, but now she knew she would never be anything more than a substitute. These glorious days in Charleston had been an illusion. She had thought they'd traveled so far and yet they'd only been walking in place, stirring up the roadway dust so that it clouded their vision and their perspective. Oh, she would cook his meals, keep his house and bear his children, and love him until her heart would break. But she would never be anything more than second best.

"All right, Glenn," she murmured, casting her eyes to the carpet. "I'll never mention her name again."

His eyes narrowed as if he didn't believe her. But he had asked her not to, and she wouldn't. She had swallowed her pride, and come to him when he must have known how difficult it had been for her. That meant nothing to him, she realized. It didn't matter what she said or did; Glenn wasn't going to tell her anything.

Purposefully, Maggie moved into the kitchen and started to prepare their evening meal. She was hurt and disillusioned. She realized that Glenn hadn't been angry, not really. The displeasure he had shown had been a reaction to the fact that he'd been unable to deal with his feelings for Angie. But he must, and she prayed he realized it soon. Only when he acknowledged his feelings and sorted it out in his troubled mind would he be truly free to love her.

It took Glenn several minutes to analyze his indignation. Of all the subjects in the world, the last thing he wanted to discuss was the past. He had handled it badly. Maggie was upset, and he regretted that, but it was necessary. The farewell party was responsible for this sudden curiosity; Maggie had said so herself. He should have realized earlier the repercussions. Glenn made his way to the kitchen and pretended to read the evening paper, all the while studying Maggie as she worked, tearing lettuce leaves for a salad. *Someday soon he'd make it up to her and she'd know how important she was in his life...how much he loved her and needed her.*

In bed that night, the entire Alaska tundra might as well have lain between them. Glenn was on his side of the bed, his eyes closed, trying to sleep. He had wanted to make love and reassure Maggie, but she had begged off. He did his best to disguise his disappointment. Other than polite conversation, Maggie hadn't said a word to him all evening. She cooked their dinner, but didn't bother to eat any of it. For his part, he could hardly stomach the fresh crab salad, although generally Maggie was a good cook and he enjoyed their meals together. Cleaning the kitchen afterward seemed to take her hours, and when she returned to the living room he had guiltily searched her face for evidence of what she was thinking. For a full ten minutes Glenn was tempted to wake Maggie and tell her he would answer any questions she had. Maggie was right. She did deserve to know and it was only his pride that prevented him from explaining everything. But she was asleep by then and he decided to see how things went in the morning. If Maggie was still troubled, then he'd do as she had asked. But deep down, Glenn hoped that Maggie would put the subject out of her mind so they could go on with their lives.

Maggie lay stiffly on her side of the bed, unable to sleep. That stupid comment about having a headache had been just that—stupid. Now she longed for the comfort of Glenn's body and the warmth of his embrace. He had hurt her, and refusing to make love had been her way of getting back. But she was the one who suffered with disappointment. She needed her husband's love more than ever. Her heart felt as if a block of concrete were weighing it down.

The more she thought about their conversation, the more angry she got. She was his wife and yet he withheld from her an important aspect of his life. Glenn was denying her his trust. Their marriage was only a thin shell of what it was meant to be. If Glenn wouldn't tell her about his relationship with Angie, then he left her no option. Maggie decided she would find Angie and ask her what had happened. From the pieces of information she'd gathered, locating the other woman wouldn't be difficult.

In the long, sleepless hours of the night, Maggie mentally debated the pros and cons of such an action. What she might discover could ruin her marriage. Yet what she didn't know was, in essence, doing the same thing. The thought of Glenn making love with the other woman caused such an intense physical pain that it felt as if something were cutting into her heart. Unable to bear it, she tried to blot the picture from her mind, but no matter how she tried, the fuzzy image stayed with her, taunting her.

By the early hours of the morning, Maggie had devised her plan. It worked with surprising ease.

Two days later Charlotte Lambert dropped Maggie off at the airport for a flight scheduled for San Francisco. As Glenn had agreed earlier, Maggie was going to fly ahead and take care of necessary business that awaited her. From the wistful look Glenn gave her that morning when she brought out her suitcases, she realized that he regretted having consented that she return before him. Some of the tension between them had lessened in the two days before the flight. With Maggie's plan had come a release. Glenn wouldn't tell her what she wanted to know, but she'd soon learn on her own.

The Delta 747 left Charleston for San Francisco on time, but Maggie wasn't on the flight. Instead, she boarded a small commuter plane that was scheduled to land in Groves Point. The same afternoon she would take another commuter plane and connect with a flight to Atlanta. If everything went according to schedule, Maggie would arrive in California only four hours later than her original flight.

Groves Point was a charming community. The man at the rental car agency gave her directions into town, and Maggie paused at the city park and looked at the statues of the Civil War heroes. She gazed at the drawn sword of the man standing beside the cannon and knew that if Glenn ever found out what she was doing then her fate would be as sure as the South's was to the North.

The man at the corner service station, wearing greasy coveralls and a friendly smile, gave her directions to Simon Canfield's home. Maggie drove onto the highway past the truck stop, as instructed. She would have missed the turnoff from the highway if she hadn't been watching for it. The tires kicked up gravel as the car wound its way along the curved driveway, and she slowed to a crawl, studying the long, rambling house. Somehow, having Angie live in an ordinary house was incongruous with the mental image Maggie had conjured up. Angie should live in a castle with knights fighting to protect and serve her.

A sleek black dog was alert and barking from the front step and Maggie hesitated before getting out of the car. She wasn't fond of angry dogs, but she'd come too far to be put off by a loud bark. Cautiously she opened the car door and stepped out, pressing her back against the side of the compact vehicle as she inched forward.

"Prince. Quiet." The dark-haired woman wearing a maternity top opened the back door and stepped onto the porch.

Instantly the dog went silent and Maggie's gaze riveted to the woman. Maggie stood, stunned. The photos hadn't done Angie's beauty justice. No woman had the right to look that radiant, lovely and serene. Angie was everything Glenn's silence had implied—and more. Her face glowed with her happiness, although she wasn't smiling now, but was regarding Maggie curiously. Maggie had been prepared to feel antagonistic toward her, and was shocked to realize that disliking the woman would be impossible.

"Can I help you?" Angie called from the top step, holding the dog by the collar.

All Maggie's energy went toward moving her head in a simple nod. Angie's voice was soft and lilting with an engaging Southern drawl.

"Bob phoned and said a woman had stopped in and asked directions to the house."

Apparently Bob was the man at the gas station. Putting on a plastic smile, Maggie took a step forward. "I'm Maggie Lambert."

"Are you related to Glenn?"

Again it was all Maggie could do to nod.

"I didn't know Glenn had any sisters."

Forcing herself to maintain an air of calm, Maggie met the gentle gaze of the woman whom Glenn had loved so fiercely. "He doesn't. I'm his wife."

If Angie was surprised she did an admirable job of not showing it. "Please, won't you come inside."

After traveling so far, devising the plan behind her husband's back and, worse, following through with it—Maggie stood cemented to the spot. After all that, without allowing anything to dissuade her from her idea, she was suddenly amazed at the audacity of her actions. Wild uncertainty, fear and unhappiness all collided into each other in her bemused mind until she was unable to move, struck by one thought: *it was wrong for her to have come here.*

"Maggie?" Angie moved down the steps with the dog loyally traipsing behind. "Are you all right?"

Maggie tasted regret at the gentleness in Angie's eyes. No wonder Glenn loved her so much, she thought. This wasn't a mere woman. Maggie hadn't known what to expect, but it hadn't been this. Angie was the type of woman a man yearned to love and protect. More disturbing to Maggie was the innate knowledge that Angie's inner beauty far surpassed any outer loveliness. And she was gorgeous. Not in the way the fashion models portrayed beauty, with sleek bodies and gaudy cosmetics. Angie was soft and gentle and sweet—a madonna. All of this flashed through Maggie's mind in the brief moment it took for Angie to reach her.

"Are you feeling ill?" Angie asked, placing a hand on Maggie's shoulder.

"I…I don't think so."

"Here," she said softly, leading her toward the house. "Come inside and I'll give you a glass of water. You look as if you're about to faint."

Maggie felt that a strong gust of wind would have blown her over. Mechanically, she allowed Angie to direct her through the back door and into the kitchen. Angie pulled out a chair at the table and Maggie sank into it, feeling more wretched than she had ever felt in her life. Tears were perilously close and she shut her eyes in an effort to forestall them. Maggie could hear Angie scurrying around for a glass of water.

She brought it to the table and sat across from Maggie. "Should I call the doctor? You're so pale."

"No, I…I'm fine. I apologize for putting you to all this trouble." Her wavering voice gained stability as she opened her dry eyes.

A few awkward seconds passed before Angie spoke. "I'm pleased that Glenn married. He's a good man."

Maggie nodded. Everything she had wanted to say

had been set in her mind, but all her well-thought-out questions had vanished.

"How long have you been married?" Angie broached the subject carefully.

"Five weeks." Holding the water glass gave Maggie something to do with her hands.

"Glenn must have told you about me?"

"No," Maggie took a sip of water. The cool liquid helped relieve the parched feeling in her throat. "He won't talk about you. He's married to me, but he's still in love with you."

A sad smile touched the expressive dark eyes as Angie straightened in the chair. "How well do you know Glenn?"

"We grew up together," Maggie said. "I…I thought I knew him, but I realize now that I don't."

"Do you love him?" Angie asked, then offered Maggie a faint smile of apology. "Forgive me for even asking. You must. Otherwise you wouldn't be here."

"Yes, I love him." Words felt inadequate to express t her feelings for her husband. "But that love is hurting me because I don't know how to help him forget you. He won't talk about what happened."

"Of course he wouldn't," Angie said with a sweet, melodic laugh. "His pride's at stake and as I recall, Glenn is a proud man."

"Very."

The dark eyes twinkled with encouragement. "First, let me assure you that Glenn isn't in love with me."

Maggie opened her mouth to contradict her, but Angie cut her off by shaking her head.

"He isn't, not really," Angie continued. "Oh, he may

think he is, but I sincerely doubt that. For one thing, Glenn would never marry a woman without loving her. He holds his vows too sacred. He could have married me a hundred times after I first saw Simon again, but he wouldn't. Glenn was wise enough to recognize that if we did marry I would always wonder about Simon. Glenn's a gambler, and he gambled on my love. At the time I don't think I realized what it must have cost him to give me the freedom to choose between the two of them."

"You mean you would have married Glenn?"

"At the drop of a hat," Angie assured her. "Glenn Lambert was the best thing to come into my life for twelve years and I knew it. I cared deeply for him, too, but that wasn't good enough for Glenn. He wanted me to settle my past, and heal all the old wounds before we made a life together. It was Glenn who led me by the hand back to the most difficult days of my life. Glenn's love gave me back Simon and I'll always be grateful to him for that. Both Simon and I will. We realize how dearly it cost Glenn to step aside so I could marry Simon."

Maggie grimaced at Angie's affirmation of love for Glenn and briefly closed her eyes to the pain. So this was the sacrifice Angie had mentioned in the letter.

"Knowing this, Maggie, you couldn't possibly believe that Glenn would take his vows lightly."

She made it all sound so reasonable and sure, Maggie thought uncertainly. "But...but if he was so strongly convinced that you should settle your past, then why is he leaving his own open like a festering wound?"

"Pride." There wasn't even a trace of hesitation in Angie's voice. "I doubt that Glenn continues to have any deep feelings for me. What happened between us is a painful time in his life he'd prefer to forget. Be patient with him."

Maggie realized that she had rammed heads with Glenn's pride when she'd asked him to tell her about Angie. His indomitable spirit had been challenged, and admitting any part of his pain to her went against the grain of his personality. Logically, knowing Glenn, it made sense.

"Glenn deserves a woman who will give him all the love he craves," Angie continued. "I could never have loved him like that. But he's found what he needs in you. Be good to him, Maggie, he needs you."

They talked nonstop for two hours, sometimes laughing, other times crying. Angie told Maggie of her own love story with Simon and their hopes and dreams for the child she carried. When it came time for Maggie to leave, Angie followed her to the airport and hugged her before she boarded her flight.

"You're a special lady, Maggie Lambert," Angie stated with conviction. "I'm confident Glenn realizes that. If he doesn't, then he's not the same man I remember."

Impulsively Maggie hugged Angie back. "I'll write once we've settled. Let me know when you have the baby."

"I will. Take care now, you hear?"

"Thank you, Angie, thank you so much. For everything."

Maggie's throat filled with emotion. There were so

many things she wanted to say. Glenn had given Angie her Simon, and in return Maggie now had Glenn. She could leave now and there would no longer be any doubts to plague her. Angie would always be someone special in Glenn's life, and Maggie wouldn't begrudge him that. She would leave him with his memories intact, and never mention her name. Angie was no longer a threat to their happiness. Maggie understood the past and was content to leave it undisturbed.

The flight from Groves Point to Atlanta and the connection from Atlanta to San Francisco went surprisingly well. Although before Maggie would have worried that each mile took her farther from Glenn, she didn't view the trip in those terms anymore. She was in love with her husband and the minute she touched down in San Francisco she planned to let him know her feelings.

A smile beamed from her contented face when she landed in the city of her birth. She took a taxi directly to the beach house, set her bags in the entryway and headed for the kitchen and the phone. She had to talk to Glenn; she burned with the need to tell him of her love. In some ways she was concerned. There was a better time and place, but she couldn't wait a second more.

His phone rang and she glanced at the clock. With the time difference between the East and the West Coast it was well after midnight in Charleston. Discouraged, she fingered the opening of her silk blouse, wondering if she should hang it up and wait until morning.

Glenn answered on the second ring. "Maggie?" The anger in his voice was like a bucket of cold water dumped over her head, sobering her instantly. Somehow, he had found out that she'd gone to Groves Point and talked to Angie.

"Yes," she returned meekly.

"Where the hell have you been? I've been half out of my mind worrying about you. Your flight landed four hours ago. Why did you have to wait so long to call me? You must have known I was waiting to hear from you." The anger in his voice had lessened, diluted with relief from his worries.

Maggie sagged with relief onto the bar stool positioned by the phone. He didn't know. "To be honest, I wasn't sure if you wanted me to phone or not."

"Not phone?" He sounded shocked. "All I can say is that it's a good thing you did." His voice grew loud and slightly husky. "It's like a tomb around here without you."

Maggie tried to suppress the happiness that made her want to laugh. *He missed her.* He was miserable without her and she hadn't even been away twenty-four hours.

"Whose idea was it for you to leave early anyway?"

"Mine," she admitted ruefully. "But who agreed, and said I should?"

"A fool, that's who. Believe me, it won't happen again. We belong together, Maggie." He made the concession willingly.

From the moment she had left that morning, he'd been filled with regrets. He should never have let her go, he had realized. He'd tried phoning an hour after her plane touched ground in California. At first it didn't bother him that she didn't answer her cell and when he tried the house, she didn't pick up ther either. He figured she'd probably gone to Denny's, Glenn assured himself earlier. Later, when he hadn't been able to get hold of her, Glenn assumed she had unplugged the phone and taken a nap. After a time his worry had grown to alarm, and from alarm to near panic. If she hadn't called him when she did—he hadn't been teasing—he would well have gone stir crazy. His feelings were unreasonable, Glenn knew that. His reaction was probably part of his lingering fear that he'd lose Maggie, he rationalized. But there was no denying it: the past few hours had been miserable.

Glenn said they belonged together with such meaning that it took a moment before Maggie could speak. "Glenn," she finally whispered, surprised at how low her voice dropped. "There's something you should know, something I should have told you long before now."

"Yes?" His voice didn't sound any more confident than her own.

"I love you, Glenn. I don't know when it happened, I can't put a time to it. But it's true. It probably embarrasses you to have me tell you like this, there are better times and places—"

"Maggie." He interrupted her with a gentle laugh. "You don't need to tell me that, I already know."

"You know?" All these weeks she'd kept her emotions bottled up inside, afraid to reveal how she felt—and he'd known!

"Maggie, it was all too obvious. You're an artist, remember? You don't do a good job of hiding your emotions."

"I see." She swallowed down the bitter disappointment. Although eager to tell him of her feelings, she had wondered how he'd react. In her mind she had pictured a wildly romantic scene in which he'd tenderly admit his own feelings. Instead, Glenn acted as if she were discussing the weather.

"Well, listen, it's late here, I think I'll go to bed." She tried to make her voice light and airy, but a soft sob escaped and she bit into her lower lip to hold back another.

"Maggie, what's wrong?"

"Nothing. I'll talk to you tomorrow. Maybe. There's lots to do and— "

"Maggie, stop. You're crying. You never cry. I want to know why. What did I say?"

The insensitive boor, she silently fumed, if he couldn't figure it out, she wasn't going to tell him. "Nothing," she choked out in reply. "It doesn't matter. Okay?"

"No, it's not all right. Tell me what's wrong."

Maggie pretended she didn't hear. "I'll phone tomorrow night."

"Maggie," he shouted. "Either you tell me what's wrong or I'm going to become violent."

"Nothing's wrong." Her heart was breaking. She'd just told her husband she loved him for the first time, and he'd practically yawned in her face.

"Listen, we're both tired. I'll talk to you tomorrow," she finished. Before he could argue, she gently replaced the receiver. The phone rang again almost immediately and Maggie simply unplugged it, refusing to talk to Glenn again that night. For a full five minutes she didn't move. She had left Atlanta with such high expectations, confident that she could create a wonderful life with Glenn. There was enough love in her heart to build any bridge necessary in their marriage. A half hour after landing in San Francisco, she was miserable and in tears. Maggie slept late, waking around eleven the next morning. She felt restless and desolate. Early that afternoon, she forced herself to dress and deal with her mail. By evening her desk was cleared and she phoned Denny. She was half-tempted to paint, but realized it would be useless with her mind in turmoil. Glenn would be furious with her for disconnecting the phone, and she had yet to deal with him. He might not have appreciated her actions, but it was better than saying things she was sure to regret later.

By early evening she had worked up her courage enough to dial his number. When he didn't answer she wasn't concerned. He was probably at the health club, she thought. An hour later she tried phoning again. By ten, Pacific Coast time, she was feeling discouraged. Where was he? She toyed with the idea of phoning his family and casually inquiring, but she didn't want to alarm them.

A noise in the front of the house alerted her to the fact that someone was at the door. She left her office and was halfway into the living room when she discovered Glenn standing in the entryway, setting his suitcases on the floor.

He straightened just in time to see her. Time went still as he covered the short space between them and reached for her, crushing her in his arms. "You crazy fool. If you'd given me half a chance I would have told you how much I love you."

"You love me?"

"Yes," he whispered into her hair.

With a smothered moan of delight, Maggie twined her arms around his neck and was lifted off the floor as his mouth came down hungrily on hers.

Ten

"Why didn't you say something earlier?" Maggie cried and covered Glenn's face with eager kisses, locking her arms around his neck.

"Why didn't you?" She was lifted half off the ground so that their gazes were level, his arms wrapped around her waist.

Maggie could hardly believe he was with her and stared at him in silent wonder, still afraid it could all be part of some fanciful dream. She couldn't very well admit that it had been her conversation with Angie that had convinced her that Glenn needed to know what was in her heart. The time had come to quit playing games with each other. The shock had come when he'd already known how she felt. Well, what did she expect? She'd never been good at disguising her feelings and something as important as love shouldn't be concealed.

"I take it you're pleased to see me?"

Happiness sparkled from her eyes as she raised her hands and lovingly traced the contours of his face. "Very."

His hold on her tightened. He hadn't slept in thirty hours. The first ten of those hours had been spent in complete frustration. He had tried countless times to get her to answer her cell until he realized she must have turned it off. The only thing that made sense was that she'd turned it off for the flight and then forgot to turn it back on, which was why he'd tried the house countless times. He needed to talk to her; to explain his reaction to her confession of loving him. It wasn't a surprise. He'd known almost from the first even if she hadn't verbalized her feelings. He'd been at a total loss to understand why she'd resorted to tears. He relived every word of their conversation and as far as he could see she was behaving like a lunatic. She announced she loved him and immediately shocked him by breaking into sobs. Maggie wasn't a crier. Several times in the first weeks of their marriage he would have expected a lot more than tears from her. He'd certainly given her enough reason. But Maggie had proudly held up her head unwilling to relinquish a whit of her pride. With startling clarity it had come to him in the early-morning hours. Maggie had expected him to declare his own love. What an idiot he'd been. Of course he loved her. He didn't know why she could ever question it. He had realized he felt something profound for Maggie the minute she had walked down the aisle at Steve and Janelle's wedding. She'd been vulnerable, proud and so lovely that Glenn went weak with the memory. He had originally assumed that his friends' wedding followed the lowest point of his life, but one look at Maggie and he'd nearly been blown over. She'd lived next door to him for most of his life and he'd blithely gone on his way not recognizing what was before his own eyes. Maggie shared his name and his devotion and, God willing, later she would bear his children. How could she possibly think he didn't love her? Just as amazing was the knowledge that he'd never told her. Glenn was astonished at his own stupidity. He would phone her as soon as she would talk to him, he had decided, and never again in her life would he give her reason to doubt.

In theory, Glenn felt , his plan sounded reasonable, but as the hours fled, and a rosy dawn dappled the horizon, he began to worry. In her frame of mind, Maggie might consider doing something stupid.

The first thing the following morning, Glenn decided not to jeopardize his marriage more than he had already. He would fly to Maggie on the first plane he could catch. When he tried phoning several times, and there wasn't any answer, he fretted all the more. For caring as much as he did he'd done a good job of messing things up.

Now that he was looking at her face flushed with a brilliant happiness, Glenn realized he'd done the right thing.

"Do you have to go back?"

"I probably should, but I won't." Her smile was solidly in place, he noticed. He adored that smile. "I don't deserve you, Maggie."

"I know."

Tipping back her head, she laughed and his heart was warmed by the sound. Maggie made his heart sing. Being around her was like lying on the sunny beach on a glorious day and soaking up energy. She was all warmth and vitality, both springtime and Christmas, and he couldn't imagine his life without her. Twisting her around in his embrace, he supported her with an arm under her legs and carried her down the long hall that led to the master bedroom.

"My dear Mr. Lambert, just where are you taking me?"

"Can't you guess?"

"Oh, yes," she said and her lips brushed his, enjoying the instant reaction she felt from him when her tongue made lazy, wet circles outlining his mouth.

"Maggie," he groaned. "You're going to pay for that."

"I'm looking forward to it. Very forward."

She couldn't undress fast enough. When Maggie's fingers fumbled with the buttons of her blouse in her eagerness, Glenn stopped her, placing her hand aside. Slowly, provocatively, he unfastened each one. As the new area of her skin was exposed, Glenn's finger lovingly trailed the perfection until he finally slipped the smooth material of her blouse from her shoulders and down her arms, letting it fall to the carpet. Maggie felt an exhilarating sense of power at the awe reflected in her husband's eyes. Impatience played no role in their lovemaking. Glenn had taught her the importance of self-control. The excruciating wait seemed only to enhance their pleasure; the disciplined pauses heightened their eagerness. Maggie was a willing pupil.

As if he couldn't deny himself a second longer, Glenn wrapped her in his arms and in one sweeping motion buried his mouth over hers.

What had begun with impatient eagerness slowed

to a breathless anticipation. When they moved, it was with one accord. They broke apart and finished undressing, then lay together on the thick, soft quilt.

"I love you," she whispered, raising her arms up to bring him to herself. "Please love me," she cried, surprised to hear her own voice.

"I do," Glenn breathed. "Always."

Afterwards, blissfully content, Maggie spread eager kisses over his face. Briefly she wondered if this exhilaration, this heartfelt elation would always stay with them. She wondered if twenty years from now she would still experience a thrill when Glenn made love to her. Somehow, Maggie doubted that this aspect of their marriage would ever change.

Glenn shifted positions so that Maggie was lovingly cradled in his arms and his fingers lightly stroked the length of her arm. Her fingers played at his chest, curling the fine dark hairs that were abundant there. A feeling of overpowering tenderness rocked him. He reveled in the emotion of loving and being loved, and knew what they shared would last forever. He was tired, more than tired—exhausted. He looked down and discovered Maggie asleep in his arms. Everything was going to work out, he thought sleepily. He wasn't going to lose her.... Slowly, his eyes drifted closed....

Maggie was his.

The following morning Maggie woke and studied her husband as he slept. A trace of a smile curved his mouth and her heart thrilled with the knowledge that she had placed it there. He must have been worried, terribly worried, she thought, to have dropped everything and flown to her. Surely, he couldn't believe that she'd ever leave him. A woman didn't love as strongly as she did and surrender without doing battle. Glenn's arrival had proved that Angie was right.... Glenn took his vows far too seriously to have married her or anyone when he was in love with another woman. Maggie didn't know what Glenn felt for the other woman anymore, but it wasn't love. Utterly content, she silently slipped from the bed and dressed, eager for the new day.

Glenn woke with a smile as Maggie's lips brushed his in a feather-light kiss. "Morning," he whispered, reaching up to wrap his arms around her waist.

"Morning," she returned brightly. "I wondered how long it'd take for you to join the living."

Glenn eased upright, using his elbow for support. "What time is it?"

"Noon."

"Noon!" he cried, rubbing the sleep from his face as he came fully upright. "Good grief, why didn't you wake me?"

Giggling, Maggie sat on the edge of the mattress and looped her arms around his strong neck. "I just did."

"You've been painting," he said, noticing that Maggie was in her smock.

"It felt good to get back to it. Charleston was wonderful, but it's great to be home and back into my regular schedule."

A light knock against the bedroom door attracted Maggie's attention. "Phone for you, Maggie," Rosa, the older Hispanic woman who was Maggie's housekeeper and cook, announced from the other side. "It's your brother."

"Tell him I'll be right there," Maggie said, and planted a tender kiss on Glenn's forehead. "Unfortunately, duty calls."

"Maggie." Glenn's hand reached for her wrist, stopping her. His eyes were questioning her as though he didn't like the idea of releasing her even to her own brother. "Never mind."

"I shouldn't be more than a few minutes. Do you want to wait for me here?"

He shook his head, already tossing aside the blankets as he climbed from the bed. "I'll be out of the shower by the time you've finished."

True to his word, Glenn leaned his hip against the kitchen counter, sipping coffee and chatting easily to Rosa when Maggie reappeared.

"I see that you two have introduced yourselves," Maggie said, sliding her arms around Glenn's waist.

"Si," Rosa said with a nod, her dark eyes gleaming. "You marry good man. You have lots of healthy *muchachos.*"

Maggie agreed with a broad grin, turning her eyes to her husband. "Rosa is going to teach me to cook, isn't that right?"

"Si. Every wife needs to know how to make her man happy," Rosa insisted as she went about cleaning the kitchen. "I teach Maggie everything about cooking."

"Not quite everything," Glenn whispered near Maggie's ear, mussing the tiny curls that grew at her temple. "In fact you wouldn't even need to go near a kitchen to keep me happy."

"Glenn," she whispered, hiding a giggle. "Quiet, or Rosa will wonder."

"Let her." His hold tightened as the housekeeper proceeded to chatter happily in a mixture of Spanish and English, scrubbing down already spotless counters as she spoke.

The lazy November day was marvelous. They took a dip in the heated pool and splashed and dunked each other like feisty teenagers at a beach party. Later, as they dried out in the sauna, Glenn carefully broached the subject of Maggie's brother.

"Was that Denny this morning?"

"Yes. He and Linda have invited us to Thanksgiving dinner. I didn't think you'd mind if I accepted."

"That'll be fine. How's Denny doing?"

Maggie wiped a thick layer of perspiration from her cheeks using both hands, biding time while she formed her thoughts. "Fine. What makes you ask?"

"He seems to call often enough. Didn't you get a couple of calls from him when we were in Charleston?"

"Yes. He's been through some rough times lately."

"How rough?"

Wrapping the towel around her neck, Maggie stood and paced the small enclosure while the heavy heat pounded in around her. "As you probably know, Denny and my parents inherited a portion of Greataunt Margaret's money. Denny made some bad investment choices."

"What happened?" As a stockbroker, Glenn felt his curiosity piqued.

"It's a long, involved story not worth repeating.

Simply put, Denny invested heavily in what he felt would be a good investment, trusting friends he shouldn't have trusted and lost everything. The case is being decided in the courts now, but it looks like he'll only get a dime back on every dollar invested."

"So you're bailing him out?" The statement was loaded with censure.

Maggie had to bite her tongue to keep from lashing out at Glenn for being so insensitive. He should know that litigation and lawyers were expensive. She was only doing what any sister would do in similar circumstances. "Listen, what's between my brother and me is private. You don't want to talk about certain things in your life, and I don't, either. We're both entitled to that."

"Don't you think you're being overly defensive?"

Maggie looked at him sharply. "So what? Denny's my brother. I'll give him money any time I please."

Glenn was taken back by her bluntness. "Fine." He wouldn't bring up the subject again…at least not for a while.

Thanksgiving arrived and Maggie's parents flew out from Florida. The elder Kingsburys had reacted with the same pleased surprise as Glenn's family had when Maggie phoned to announce that she and Glenn had married. The gathering at Denny and Linda's was a spirited but happy one. Neither of Maggie's parents mentioned how brief her and Glenn's courtship had been, nor that they were shocked at the suddenness of the ceremony. The questions were in their eyes, but Maggie was so radiantly happy that no one voiced any doubts.

The traditional turkey was placed in the oven to be ready to serve at the end of the San Francisco 49ers football game. They ate until they were stuffed, played cards, ate again and watched an old movie on television until Maggie yawned and Glenn suggested they head home. The day had been wonderful and Maggie looked forward to Christmas for the first time since moving to the beach house.

Glenn's days were filled. He started work at Lindsey & McNaught Brokerage the Monday after his arrival in San Francisco, and continued to work long hours to build up his clientele. More often than not, it was well past seven before he arrived home. Maggie didn't mind the hours Glenn put in away from home. She understood his need to secure his position with the company branch. The competition was stiff and as a new boy on the block, the odds were against him.

"How are things going at the office?" she asked him one evening the first week of December.

"Fine," he responded absently as he sorted through the mail. "How about a game of tennis? I need to work out some of my frustrations."

"Everything's fine at the office, but you want to use me as a whipping boy?" she joked lovingly.

Glenn raised his gaze to hers and met the teasing glimmer mingled with truth in her eyes.

"Are you sorry we're here?" she asked on a tentative note. In Charleston, Glenn had held more than a hundred million dollars in assets for his firm, a figure that was impressive enough for him to have quickly worked his way into a managerial position. In San Francisco, he was struggling to get his name out and establish himself with new clients. Some of his previous ones had opted to stay with him but others had decided to remain with the same brokerage. From the hours he was putting in during the day and several long evenings, the task must be a formidable one.

"I'm not the least bit sorry we're living in San Francisco," he said. "Where you and I are concerned, I have no regrets. Now," he added, releasing a slow breath, "are we going to play tennis or stand here and chat?"

Just as he finished speaking the telephone rang. "Saved by the bell," Maggie mumbled as she moved across the room to answer it. "Hello."

"Hi, Maggie," Denny said in the low, almost whiny voice she had come to know well.

"Hi. What's up?" She didn't want to encourage Denny to drag out the conversation when Glenn was in the room. Denny was a subject they avoided. She knew her husband disapproved of her handing over large sums of money to her brother, but she didn't know what else she could do—Denny needed her. The money wasn't doing her any good, and if she could help her only brother, then why not?

The argument was one Maggie had waged with herself countless times. As long as she was available to lean upon, the opposing argument went, then Denny would be content to do exactly that. He hadn't accomplished anything worthwhile in months. From conversations with her sister-in-law, Linda, Maggie had learned that Denny did little except decry his misfortune and plot ways of regaining his losses. Maggie could understand his circumstances well enough to realize he was in an impossible position. He didn't like it, she didn't like it, but there was nothing that either of them could do until the court case was settled.

"I just wanted you to know that I'll be meeting with the lawyers tomorrow afternoon."

"Good luck," she murmured.

A silence followed. "What's the matter? Can't you talk now?"

"That about sizes up the situation." Glenn was studying her and Maggie realized her stalling tactics weren't fooling him. He knew exactly whom she was talking to and did nothing to make the conversation any easier by leaving the room.

"Maybe I should phone you tomorrow," Denny suggested.

"That would be better." Maggie forced a carefree note into her tone. "I'll talk to you tomorrow then."

"Okay." Denny sounded disappointed, but there wasn't anything Maggie could do. She wanted to avoid another confrontation with Glenn regarding her brother.

Replacing the receiver, she met her husband's gaze. "You said something about tennis?" Her voice was remarkably steady for all the turmoil going on inside her.

"You're not helping him, you know," Glenn said calmly. "All you've done to this point is teach him to come to you to solve his financial problems."

It was on the tip of her tongue to tell him that she was aware of that. She had seen it all herself, but she was caught in a vicious trap where her brother was concerned. "He needs me," she countered.

"He needs a job and some self-worth."

"I thought you were a stockbroker, not a psychologist."

Maggie could tell by the tightness in his jaw that she had angered Glenn. "Look, I'm sorry, I didn't mean to snap at you. Denny's in trouble. I can't let him down when he needs me the most. If you recall, I did ask you to stay out of it."

"Have it your way," he mumbled and handed her a tennis racket.

Their game wasn't much of a contest. Glenn overpowered her easily in straight sets, making her work harder than ever. Maggie didn't know if he was venting his frustrations from the office or if he was angry because of Denny. It didn't matter; she was exhausted. By the time he'd finished showering, she was in bed half-asleep. Glenn's pulling the covers over her shoulders and gently kissing the top of her head were the last things Maggie remembered.

With the approach of the Christmas holidays, Maggie felt a renewed sense of rightness. She was in love with her husband, they were together and her world seemed in perfect balance. Glenn worked hard and so did she, spending hours in her studio doing what she enjoyed most—painting. With her marriage, Maggie had discovered that there was a new depth to her art. She had once told Glenn that color was mood and brushwork emotion. Now with Glenn's love, her brush painted bold strokes that revealed a maturity in her scenes that had been missing before their wedding.

She was happy, truly happy, and it showed in ways she'd never expected.

Maggie didn't mention Glenn's grandmother's antique ring, confident that he'd gift her with it on Christmas morning. And she would react with the proper amount of surprised pleasure.

She wore her wedding ring continually now, even when she worked. Glenn glanced at her hand occasionally to be sure it was there. It was an odd quirk of his, but she didn't really mind. The ring meant as much to her as their marriage vows and that was all he wanted. They had come a long way from the night she'd arrived in Charleston.

For their first Christmas, Maggie wanted to buy Glenn a special gift, something that would show the depth of her love and appreciation for the good life they shared. But what? For days she mulled over the problem. She could give him one of her paintings for his office, but he had already asked her for one. She couldn't refuse him by telling him that that was what she planned to give him for Christmas. He took one of her seascapes and she was left without an idea. And she so wanted their first Christmas together to be special.

For the first time in years Maggie went Christmas shopping in stores. Usually she ordered through the mail or over the Internet, but she feared missing the perfect gift that would please Glenn most. Janelle joined her one day, surprised at the changes in Maggie.

"What changes?"

"You're so happy," Janelle claimed.

"I really am, you know."

"I can tell. You positively glow with it."

The remark pleased Maggie so much she repeated it for Glenn later that evening.

"So you were out Christmas shopping. Did you buy me anything?"

How she wished. Nothing seemed special enough. She had viewed a hundred jewelry display cases, visited the most elite men's stores and even gone to obscure bookstores, seeking rare volumes of Glenn's favorite novels. A sense of panic was beginning to fill her.

"You'll have to wait until Christmas morning to find out," she told him, coyly batting her long lashes.

With so many relatives on their list, Glenn and Maggie were in and out of more department stores the following Saturday than Maggie cared to count. Soft music filled the stores and bells chimed on the street corners, reminding them to be generous to those less fortunate. The crowds were heavy, but everyone seemed to expect that and took the long waits at the cash registers in stride.

While Maggie stood in line buying a toy farm set for Glenn's nephew, Glenn wandered over to the furniture department. Lovingly, Maggie's gaze followed him as he looked over cherry wood bookcases in a rich, deep-red color. Bookcases? Glenn wanted something as simple as bookcases? Maggie couldn't believe it. After days of looking at the latest gadgets and solid-gold toys, she stared in disbelief that he could be interested in something as simple as this. When the salesman approached, Glenn asked several questions and ran his hand over the polished surface.

"Did you see something?" she asked conversationally when he returned to her side. He wanted those bookcases, but she doubted that he'd mention it to her.

"Not really," he replied, but Maggie noted the way his gaze returned and lingered over the cases.

Maggie's heartbeat raced with excitement. At the first opportunity she'd return and buy Glenn those bookcases.

"You're looking pleased about something," Glenn commented over dinner Wednesday evening.

His comment caught her off guard and she lightly shook her head. "Sorry, I was deep in thought. What did you say?"

"I could tell," he chided, chuckling. Standing, he carried his clean plate to the sink. "Do you want to talk about it, or is this some deep dark secret you're hiding from your husband?"

"Some deep dark secret."

"What did you do today?" he asked, appreciating anew how beautiful his wife had become. She was a different woman from the one who'd met him at the airport months ago. He liked to think the changes in her were due to their marriage. He was different too and credited Maggie with his renewed sense of happiness.

"What did I do today?" Maggie repeated, her dark eyes rounding with shock. Swallowing back her unease, she cast her gaze to her plate. "Christmas cards." The truth nearly stuck in her throat. She had written Christmas cards, but in addition she had penned a long letter to Angie, thanking her for everything the other woman had shared the day of their brief visit. In the letter, Maggie told Angie how improved her marriage was now that she'd told Glenn how much she loved him, and was confident that he loved her in return.

As impractical as it sounded, Maggie would have liked to continue the friendship with Angie. Rarely had Maggie experienced such an immediate kinship with another woman. Impractical and illogical. Of all the people in the world, Maggie would have thought she'd despise Angie Canfield. But she didn't. Now, weeks later, Maggie felt the need to write the other woman and extend her appreciation for their afternoon together and to wish her and Simon the warmest of holiday greetings. The letter had been interrupted by Glenn's homecoming and she had safely tucked it away from the other cards she kept on top of her desk.

"I still have several things that need to be done before Christmas," she said in order to hide her discomfort.

Glenn was silent for a moment. "You look guilty about something. I bet you went out shopping today and couldn't resist buying yourself something."

"I didn't!" she declared with a cheery laugh.

Later, in the den, when Glenn was looking over some figures, Maggie joined him. She sat in the chair opposite his desk. When Maggie glanced up she found her husband regarding her lazily with a masked expression, and she wondered at his thoughts.

On the other side of the desk, Glenn studied his wife, thinking that she was more beautiful that night than he ever remembered. Her eyes shone with a translucent happiness and a familiar sensation tugged at his heart. Something was troubling her tonight…no, troubling was too strong a word. She was hiding something from him. Which was natural, he supposed. It was Christmastime and she had probably cooked up some scheme for his gift, yet Glenn had the feeling this had nothing to do with Christmas.

Convinced he shouldn't go looking for trouble, he shook his mind free of the brooding sensation. Whatever it was probably involved Denny, and it was just as well that he didn't know. It would only anger him.

Glenn pushed back his chair and stood. "I'll be right back. I'm going to need a cup of coffee to keep these figures straight. Do you want one?"

Maggie glanced up from the book she was reading and shook her head. The caffeine would keep her awake. "No, thanks," she said as he left the room.

The phone rang and Glenn called out that he'd answer it. The information didn't faze Maggie until she realized that he had probably gone into her office since the phone was closer there.

He returned a minute later, strolling into the room with deceptive casualness. "It's your leeching brother," he told her.

Eleven

"Glenn, what a nasty thing to say." Maggie couldn't help knowing that Glenn disapproved of the way she gave Denny money, but she hadn't expected him to be so blunt or openly rude. "I hope Denny didn't hear you," she murmured, coming to her feet. "He feels terrible about the way things have turned out."

"If he honestly felt that, he wouldn't continue to come running to you at every opportunity."

Straightening her shoulders to a military stiffness, Maggie marched from the room and picked up the telephone. "Hello, Denny."

A short silence followed. "Hi. I take it I should call back another time."

"No," she contradicted firmly. She wasn't going to let Glenn intimidate her out of speaking to her own brother. "I can talk now."

"I just wanted to tell you that my lawyer didn't have anything new to tell me regarding our case. It looks like this thing could be tied up in the courts for years.

I'm telling you, Maggie, this whole mess is really getting me down."

"But you don't need to worry, I'm here to help you." she offered sympathetically.

"But Glenn…"

"What I do with my money is none of his concern." In her heart Maggie knew that Glenn was right, but Glenn was a naturally strong person, and her brother wasn't to be blamed if he was weak. They had to make allowances for Denny, help him.

"You honestly mean that about helping, don't you?" Denny murmured, relief and appreciation brightening his voice.

"You know I do."

Ten minutes later Maggie rejoined her husband. All kinds of different emotions were coming at her. She was angry with Glenn for being so unsympathetic to her brother's troubles, infuriated with Denny because he pushed all the right buttons with her, and filled with self-derision because she gave in to Denny without so much as a thoughtful pause. Denny had only to give his now familiar whine and she handed him a signed check.

"Well?" Glenn glanced up at her.

"Well what?"

"He asked for money, didn't he?"

"Yes," she snapped.

"And you're giving it to him?"

"I don't have much choice. Denny is my brother."

"But you're not helping him, Maggie, don't you see that?"

"No," she cried, and to her horror tears welled in

her eyes. It was so unlike her to cry over something so trivial that Maggie had trouble finding her breath, which caused her to weep all the louder.

Glenn stood and gently pulled her into his arms. "Maggie, what is it?"

"You…Denny…me," she sobbed and dramatically shook her hands. "This court case might take years to decide. He needs money. You don't want me to lend him any, and I'm caught right in the middle."

"Honey, listen." Glenn stood and gently placed his arms around her. "Will you do something for me?"

"Of course," she responded on a hiccupping sob. "What?"

"Call Denny back and tell him he can't have the money…."

"I can't do that," she objected, shaking his arms free. She hugged her waist and moved into the living room where a small blaze burned in the fireplace. The warmth of the fire chased the chill from her arms.

"Hear me out," Glenn said, following her. "Have Denny give me a call at the office in the morning. If he needs money, I'll loan it to him."

Maggie was skeptical. "But why…?"

"I don't want him troubling you anymore. I don't like what he's doing to you, and worse, what he's doing to himself." He paused, letting her take in his offer. "Agreed?"

She offered him a watery smile and nodded.

With Glenn standing at her side, Maggie phoned Denny back and gave the phone over to her husband a few minutes later. Naturally, Denny didn't seem overly pleased with the prospect of having to go through

Glenn, but he had no choice. Maggie should have been relieved that Glenn was handling the difficult situation, but she wasn't.

In the morning, Maggie woke feeling slightly sick to her stomach. She lay in bed long after Glenn had left for the office, wondering if she could be pregnant. The tears the evening before had been uncharacteristic and she'd had a terrible craving for Chinese food lately that was driving her crazy. For three days in a row she had eaten lunch in Chinatown. None of the symptoms on their own was enough for her to make the connection until this morning.

A smile formed as Maggie placed a hand on her flat stomach and slowly closed her eyes. A baby. Glenn would be so pleased. He'd be a wonderful father. She'd watched him with Denny's girls on Thanksgiving and had been astonished at his patience and gentleness. The ironic part was all these weeks she'd been frantically searching for just the right Christmas gift for Glenn, and all along she'd been nurturing his child in her womb. They both wanted children. Oh, she'd get him the bookcases he had admired, but she'd keep the gift he'd prize most a secret until Christmas morning.

Not wanting to be overconfident without a doctor's confirmation, Maggie made an appointment for that afternoon, and her condition was confirmed in a matter of minutes. Afterward she was bursting with excitement. Her greatest problem would be keeping it from Glenn when she wanted to sing and dance with the knowledge.

When Maggie returned to the beach house Rosa

had left a message that Denny had phoned. Maggie returned his call immediately.

"How did everything go with Glenn?" she asked him brightly. Nothing would dim the brilliance of her good news, not even Denny's sullen voice.

"Fine, I guess."

"There isn't any problem with the money, is there?" Glenn wouldn't be so cruel to refuse to make the loan when he'd assured her he'd help her brother. Maggie was confident he wouldn't do anything like that. Glenn understood the situation.

"Yes and no."

Her hand tightened around the receiver. "How do you mean? He's giving you the money, isn't he?"

"He's lending me the money, but he's got a bunch of papers he wants me to sign and in addition he's set up a job interview for me. He actually wants me to go to work."

By the time Denny finished with his sorry tale, Maggie was so furious she could barely speak. Lending him the money—making him sign for it—a job interview. Glenn had told her he was going to help her brother. Instead he was stripping Denny of what little pride he had left.

By the time Glenn arrived home that evening, he found Maggie pacing the floor. Sparks of anger flashed from her dark eyes as she spun around to face him.

"What's wrong? You're looking at me like I was Jack the Ripper."

"Did you honestly tell Denny that he couldn't borrow the money unless he got a job?" she said in accusation. Her hands were placed defiantly on her hips, challenging Glenn to contradict her.

Unhurriedly, Glenn removed his raincoat one arm at a time and hung it in the hall closet. "Is there something wrong with an honest day's toil?"

"It's humiliating to Denny. He's…accustomed to a certain lifestyle now…. He can't lower himself to take a job like everyone else and…"

Maggie could tell by the way Glenn's eyes narrowed that he was struggling to maintain his own irritation. "I live in a fancy beach house with you and somehow manage to suffer the humiliation."

"Glenn," she cried. "It's different with Denny."

"How's that?"

Unable to remain still, Maggie continued to stalk the tiled entryway like a circus lion confined to a cage. "Don't you understand how degrading that would be to him?"

"No," Glenn returned starkly. "I can't. Denny made a mistake. Any fool knows better than to place the majority of his funds in one investment no matter how secure it appears. The time has come for your brother to own up to the fact he made a serious mistake, and pay the consequences of his actions. I can't and won't allow him to sponge off you any longer, Maggie."

The tears sprang readily to the surface. Oh how she hated to cry. Hopefully she wouldn't be like this the entire pregnancy. "But don't you understand?" she blubbered, her words barely intelligible. "I inherited twice the money Denny did."

"And he's made you feel guilty about that."

"No," she shouted. "He's never said a word."

"He hasn't had to. You feel guilty enough about it, but my love, trust me. Denny will feel better about you, about himself, about life in general. You can't give him the self-worth he needs by handing him a check every time he asks for it."

"You don't understand my brother," Maggie cried. "I can't let you do this to him. I...I told you once that I wanted you to stay out of this."

"Maggie—"

"No, you listen to me. I'm giving Denny the money he wants. I told him that he didn't need to sign anything, and he doesn't need to get a job. He's my brother and I'm not going to turn my back on him. Understand?"

Silence crackled in the room like the deadly calm before an electrical storm. A muscle leaped in Glenn's jaw, twisting convulsively.

"If that's the way you want it." His voice was both tight and angry.

"It is," she whispered.

What Maggie didn't want was the silent treatment that followed. Glenn barely spoke to her the remainder of the evening, and when he did his tone was barely civil. It was clear that Glenn considered her actions a personal affront. Maybe it looked that way to him, she reasoned, but she'd explained long ago that she preferred to handle her brother herself. Glenn had interfered and now they were both miserable.

When morning arrived to lighten the dismal winter sky, Maggie rolled onto her back and stared at the ceiling, realizing she was alone. The oppressive gray light of those early hours invaded the bedroom and a heaviness settled onto Maggie's heart. She climbed from the bed and felt sick and dizzy once again, but her symptoms were more pronounced this morning. Her mouth felt like dry, scratchy cotton.

Glenn had already left for the office and the only evidence of his presence was an empty coffee cup in the kitchen sink. Even Rosa looked at Maggie accusingly and for one crazy instant Maggie wondered how the housekeeper knew that she and Glenn had argued. That was the crazy part—they hadn't really fought. Maybe if they had, the air would have been cleared.

The crossword puzzle didn't help occupy her mind and Maggie sat at the kitchen table for an hour, drinking cup after cup of watered-down apple juice while sorting through her thoughts. With a hand rubbing her throbbing temple, Maggie tried to recall how Glenn had been as a youth when he was angry with someone. She couldn't remember that he had ever held a grudge or been furious with anyone for long. That was a good sign.

Tonight she'd talk to him, she decided, try to make him understand why she had to do this for Denny. If the situation was reversed and it was either of his brothers, Glenn would do exactly the same thing. Maggie was sure of it.

Because of the Christmas holidays, the stock market was traditionally slow, and Glenn had been home before six every night for the past week. He wasn't that night. Nor was he home at seven, or eight. He must be unbelievably angry, she thought, and a part of Maggie wondered if he'd ever be able to completely understand her actions. Apparently, he found it easier to blame her than to realize that he'd forced her into the situation. Maggie spent a miserable hour watching a television program she normally disliked.

The front door clicked open and Maggie pivoted sharply in her chair, hoping Glenn's gaze would tell her that they'd talk and clear up the air between them.

Glenn shrugged off his coat and hung it in the hall closet. Without a word he moved into his den and closed the door, leaving Maggie standing alone and miserable.

Desolate, she sat in the darkened living room and waited. She hadn't eaten, couldn't sleep. Leaving the house was impossible, looking and feeling the way she did. Her only companion was constant anxiety and doubt. There wasn't anything she could do until Glenn was ready to talk.

When he reappeared, Maggie slowly came to her feet. Her throat felt thick and uncooperative. Her hands were clenched so tightly together that the blood flow to her fingers was restricted. "Would you like some dinner?" The question was inane when she wanted to tell him they were both being silly. Arguing over Denny was the last thing she wanted to do.

"I'm not hungry," he answered starkly without looking at her. His features tightened.

Undaunted, Maggie asked again. "Can we at least talk about this? I don't want to fight."

He ignored her and turned toward the hallway. "You said everything I needed to hear last night."

"Come on, Glenn, be reasonable," she shouted after him. "What do you want from me? Are you so insensitive that you can't see what an intolerable situation you placed me in?"

"I asked you to trust me with Denny."

"You were stripping him of his pride."

"I was trying to give it back to him," he flared back. "And speaking of intolerable positions, do you realize that's exactly what you've done to me?"

"You... How...?"

"You've asked me to sit by and turn a blind eye while your brother bleeds you half to death. I'm your husband. It's my duty to protect you, but I can't do that when you won't let me, when you resent, contradict and question my intention."

"Glenn, please," she pleaded softly. "I love you. I don't want to fight. Not over Denny—not over anything. It's Christmas, a time of peace and goodwill. Can't we please put this behind us?"

Glenn looked as weary as she felt. "It's a matter of trust too, Maggie."

"I trust you completely."

"You don't," Glenn announced and turned away from her, which only served to fuel Maggie's anger.

Maggie slept in the guest bedroom that night, praying Glenn would insist she share his bed. She didn't know what she had thought sleeping apart would accomplish. It took everything within Maggie not to swallow her considerable pride and return to the master bedroom. A part of her was dying a slow and painful death.

Maggie couldn't understand why Glenn was behaving like he was. Only once had he even raised his voice to her in all the weeks they'd been married. But now the tension stretched between the two bedrooms was so thick Maggie could have sliced it with a dull knife. Glenn was so disillusioned with her that even talking to her was more than he could tolerate. He wasn't punishing her with the silent treatment, Maggie realized. He was protecting her. If he spoke it would be to vent his frustration and say things he'd later regret.

Instead of dwelling on the negative, Maggie recalled the wonderful love-filled nights when they had lain side by side and been unable to stay out of each other's arms. The instant the light was out, Glenn would reach for her with the urgency of a condemned man offered a last chance at life. And when he'd kissed her and loved her, Maggie felt as though she was the most precious being in the world. Glenn's world. He was a magnificent lover. She closed her eyes to the compelling images that crowded her mind, feeling sick at heart and thoroughly miserable.

In the other room Glenn lay on his back staring at the ceiling. The dark void of night surrounded him. The sharp edges of his anger had dulled, but the bitterness that had consumed him earlier had yet to fade. In all his life he had never been more disappointed and more hurt—yes, hurt, that his wife couldn't trust him to handle a delicate situation and protect her. He wasn't out to get Denny; he sincerely wanted to help the man.

Morning arrived and Maggie couldn't remember sleeping although she must have closed her eyes sometime during the long, tedious night. The alarm rang and she heard Glenn stirring in the other room.

While he dressed, Maggie moved into the kitchen and put on coffee. Ten minutes later, he joined her in the spacious room and hesitated, his gaze falling to her wide, sad eyes. Purposely he looked away. There was no getting around it. He had missed sleeping with his wife. A hundred times he had had to stop himself from going into the bedroom and bringing her back to his bed where she belonged. Now she stood not three feet from him in a sexy gown and his senses were filled with her. He should be aware of the freshly brewed coffee, but he discovered the elusive perfumed scent of Maggie instead. Silently he poured himself a cup of coffee and pulled out a kitchen chair. He tried to concentrate on something other than his wife. He reached for the newspaper and focused his attention on that. But mentally his thoughts were involved in this no-win situation between him and her blood sucking brother. When he'd learned exactly how much money Denny had borrowed he'd been insensed. This madness had to stop and soon or he'd bleed Maggie dry.

Sensing Glenn's thoughts, Maggie moved closer, wanting to resolve this issue, yet unsure how best to approach a subject that felt like a ticking time bomb.

Propping up the newspaper against the napkin holder, Glenn hid behind the front page, not wanting to look at Maggie yet he struggled to keep his eyes trained on the front page headlines. "Will you be home for dinner?" Maggie forced the question out. Leaning against the kitchen counter, her fingers bit into the tiled surface as she waited for his answer.

"I've been home for dinner every night since we've been married. Why should tonight be different?"

Maggie had only been trying to make idle conversation and break down the ice shield that positioned between them. "No reason," she murmured and turned back to the stove.

A few minutes later Glenn left for the office with little more than a casual farewell.

By noon Maggie was convinced she couldn't spend another day locked inside the confines of the beach house. Even the studio that had been her pride now became her torture chamber. One more hour dealing with this madness and she'd go stir-crazy.

Aimlessly, she wandered from room to room, seeking confirmation that she had done the right thing by Denny and finding none. She took a long, uninterrupted walk along the beach where gusts of ocean air carelessly whipped her hair across her face and lightened her mood perceptibly. Christmas was only a week away, and there were a hundred things she should be doing. But Maggie hadn't the heart for even one.

Recently she had been filled with such high expectations for this marriage. Now she realized how naive she'd been. She had always thought that love conquered all. What a farce that was. She had been unhappy before marrying Glenn; now she was in love, pregnant, and utterly miserable. And why? Because she'd stood by her brother when he needed her. It hardly seemed fair.

A light drizzle began to fall and she walked until her face felt numb with cold. She trekked up to the house, fixed herself something hot to drink and decided to go for a drive.

The ride into the city was sluggish due to heavy traffic. She parked on the outskirts of Fisherman's Wharf and took a stroll. A multitude of shops and touristy places had sprung up since her last visit—but that had been years ago, she realized. She dropped into a few places and shopped around, finding nothing to buy. An art gallery caught her eye and she paused to look in the window at the painting on display. A card tucked in the ornate frame revealed the name of the painting was *The Small Woman.* The artist had used a black line to outline the painting, like lead surrounding the panes in a stained-glass window. The colors were bold, the setting elaborate. The simple woman, however, was strangely frail and pathetic, detached from the setting as though she were a sacrifice to be offered to the gods in some primitive culture. Examining the painting, Maggie saw herself in the tired woman and didn't like the reflection.

A blast of chilling wind whipped her coat around her legs, and to escape the unexpected cold, Maggie opened the glass door and entered the gallery. The room was deceptively large, with a wide variety of oil paintings, some watercolors, small sculptures and other artworks in opulent display.

"Can I help you?"

Maggie turned toward the voice to find a tall, slender woman dressed in a plaid wool skirt and creamy white silk blouse. She appeared to be studying Maggie closely, causing Maggie to wonder at her appearance. The wind had played havoc with her hair and...

"Maggie?"

Maggie blinked twice. She didn't recognize the woman. "Pardon?"

"Are you Maggie Kingsbury?"

"Yes…my married name is Lambert. Do I know you?"

The woman's laugh was light and sweetly musical. "I'm Jan Baker Hammersmith. Don't you remember we attended…"

The name clicked instantly. "Jan Baker." The two had been casual friends when Maggie was attending art school. "I haven't seen you in years. The last I heard, you were married."

"I'm divorced now."

Maggie dropped her gaze, desperately afraid that she would be adding that identical phrase someday when meeting old friends. "I'm sorry to hear that."

"I am, too," Jan said with a heavy sadness. "But it was for the best. Tell me, are you still painting?" Maggie noted how Jan quickly diverted the subject away from herself.

"Occasionally. Not as much since I married."

Jan strolled around the gallery with proud comfort. "I can still remember one of your paintings—a beach scene. The detail you'd put into it was marvelous. Whatever happened to that?"

"It's hanging in our living room."

"I can understand why you'd never want to sell that." Jan's eyes were sincere. "Rarely have I seen a painting with such vivid clarity and color."

"It would sell?" Maggie was surprised. Ridiculous as it seemed, she'd never tried to sell any of her paintings. There hadn't been any reason to try. She gave them away as gifts and to charities for auctions but she didn't have any reason to sell them. She didn't need the money and inwardly she feared they might not sell. Her artwork was for her own pleasure. The scenes painted by her brush had been the panacea for an empty life within the gilded cage.

"It'd sell in a minute," Jan stated confidently. "Do you think you'd consider letting the gallery represent you?"

Maggie hedged, uncertain. "Let me think about it."

"Do, Maggie, and get back to me. I have a customer I know who'd be interested in a painting similar to the beachscape, if you have one. Take my card." They spoke for several minutes more and Maggie described some of her other works. Again Jan encouraged her to bring in a few of her canvases. Maggie noted that Jan didn't make any promises, which was reasonable.

Sometime later, Maggie returned to her car. Meeting Jan had been just the uplift she'd needed. Already her mind was buzzing with possibilities. There wasn't any reason she shouldn't sell her work. Glenn's car was in the driveway when she returned and she pulled to a stop in front of the house and parked there. A glance at her watch told her that it was later than she suspected. Her spirits were lighter than at any time during the past two days, but she didn't hurry toward the house.

"Where have you been?" Glenn asked the minute she walked in the door. Not granting her the opportunity to respond, he continued. "You made an issue of asking me if I was going to be home for dinner and then you're gone."

Carelessly, Maggie tossed her coat over an armchair. "I lost track of the time," she explained on her way into the kitchen. Glenn was only a step behind. From the grim set of his mouth, Maggie recognized that once again she'd displeased him. Everything she'd done the past few days seemed to fuel his indignation.

He didn't say another word as she worked, dishing up the meal of baked pork chops and scalloped potatoes Rosa had prepared for them. Maggie could feel his gaze on her defeated shoulders, studying her. He looked for a moment as if he wanted to say something, but apparently changed his mind.

"I was in an art gallery today," she told him conversationally.

"Oh."

"I'm thinking of taking in some of my work."

"You should, Maggie."

Silence followed. This was the first time they'd had a decent conversation since she'd sided with her brother against him.

Their dinner was awkward, each trying to find a way to put their marriage back on track. Glenn sat across from her, cheerless and somber. Neither ate much.

"Did the mail come?" Maggie asked, setting the dinner dishes aside.

"It's in your office," Glenn answered without looking up. "Would you like me to bring it in to you?"

"Please. I'll finish up here in a minute." Well, at least they were speaking to each other, she thought. It was a start. Together they'd work things out. The situation with Denny was probably the first of many disagreements and misunderstandings they would face through the years. It might take time, she told herself, but they'd work it out. They loved each other too much to allow anything to wedge a space between them for long. They had both behaved badly over this issue with Denny, but if she'd bend a little, Glenn would, too.

When Glenn returned to the living room, he said her name with such fervor that her head came up. Unconsciously Maggie pressed farther back into the thick cushions of her chair, utterly stunned by the look that flashed from her husband's eyes. She could think of nothing that would cause him such anger.

"Explain this," he said and thrust her letter to Angie in front of Maggie's shocked face.

Twelve

Maggie's mind was in complete turmoil. She'd known it was a risk to write Angie, and later had regretted it. She hadn't mailed the card. Yet she'd left the letter on top of her desk for Glenn to find. Perhaps subconsciously she had wanted him to discover what she'd done.

Tension shot along her nerves as she struggled to appear outwardly calm. Lifting the chatty letter Glenn handed her, she examined it as if seeing it for the first time, amazed at her detachment. Whatever she wished, consciously or subconsciously, Glenn had found it and the timing couldn't be worse. They were just coming to terms with one major disagreement and were about to come to loggerheads over another. Only this issue was potentially far more dangerous to the security of their marriage. Going behind Glenn's back had never felt right. Maggie had regretted her deception a hundred times since. And yet it had been necessary. Long ago Maggie had admitted that Glenn had forced her into the decisive action. She had asked him about Angie and he'd refused to discuss the other woman. Maggie was his wife and she loved him; she had a right to know. But all the rationalization in the world wasn't going to help now.

"How do you explain this?" His voice went deep and low, as though he couldn't believe what he'd found. Maggie hadn't trusted him to help her brother, he thought, somewhat dazed, and now he'd learned that she had betrayed his trust in another situation as well.

Glenn knew he should be furious. Outraged. But he wasn't. His emotions were confused—he felt shocked, hurt and discouraged. Guilt was penned all over Maggie's pale face as she sat looking up at him, trying to explain. There couldn't possibly be a plausible one. Not one. Feeling sick with defeat, he turned away from her.

Maggie's heartbeat quickened at the pained look in Glenn's dark eyes. "I met Angie."

"When?" he asked, still hardly able to comprehend what she was saying. He paced the area in front of her in clipped military-like steps as if standing in one place were intolerable.

Maggie had never seen any man's features more troubled. "The...the day I flew to San Francisco...I took a flight to Groves Point first and then flew from there to Atlanta before heading home."

If possible Glenn went even more pale.

"I asked you to tell me about the two of you but—" Maggie attempted to explain and was quickly cut off.

"How did you know where she lived?"

Admitting everything she had done made it sound all the more sordid and deceitful. She hesitated.

"How did you know where she lived?" he repeated, his rising voice cold and deliberate. Maggie was pressed as far back against the chair cushion as possible as dread settled firmly over her.

"I found her letter to you…and read it." She wouldn't minimize her wrongdoing. The letter had been addressed to him and she had purposely taken it from the envelope and read each word. It was wrong. She knew it was wrong, but given the opportunity, she would do exactly the same thing again.

Shocked, all Glenn seemed capable of doing was to stare back at her. She yearned to explain that she hadn't purposely searched through his drawers or snooped into his private matters. But she could see that expounding on what had happened wouldn't do any good. Reasoning with Glenn just then would be impossible. She felt wretched and sick to her stomach. The ache in her throat was complicated by the tears stinging her eyes. With everything in her, she struggled not to cry.

"What else did you try to find?" he asked. "How many drawers did you have to search through before you found the letter? Did you take delight in reading another woman's words to me? Is there anything you don't know?"

"It wasn't like that," she whispered, her gaze frozen in misery.

"I'll bet!" He moved to the other side of the living room. His anger died as quickly as it came, replaced by a resentment so keen he could barely stand to look at Maggie. She couldn't seem to let up on the subject of Angie. For months he had loved Maggie so completely that he was amazed that she could believe that he could possibly care for another woman. Worse, she had hounded the subject of Angie to death. It was a matter of trust, and she'd violated that and wounded his pride again and again.

"Are you satisfied now? Did you learn everything you were so keen to find out?" His voice was heavy with defeat. "You don't trust me or my love, do you, Maggie? You couldn't, to have done something this underhanded."

"That's not true," she cried. Glenn wanted to wound her; she understood that. She had hurt him when all she'd ever wanted to do was give him her love, bear his children and build a good life with him. But their marriage had been clouded with the presence of another woman who stood between them as prominently as the Cascade mountain range. Or so it appeared at the time.

With a clarity of thought Glenn didn't realize he possessed, he knew he had to get out of the room... out of the house. He needed to sit down and do some serious thinking. Something was basically wrong in a relationship where one partner didn't trust the other. He loved Maggie and had spent the past few months trying to prove how much. Obviously he'd failed. He acrossed the living room and jerked his raincoat off the hanger.

"Where are you going?" Maggie asked in a pathetically weak voice.

He didn't even look at her. "Out."

Trapped in a nightmare, her actions made in slow motion, Maggie came to her feet. The Christmas card and letter were clenched in her hand. Glenn turned to look back at her and his gaze fell to the brightly colored card. His mouth twisted into a scowl as he opened the door and left Maggie standing alone and heartbroken.

Maggie didn't allow the tears to escape until she was inside their bedroom with the door securely closed. Only then did she vent her misery. She wept bitter tears until she didn't think she could stop. Her throat ached and her sobs were dry; her eyes burned and there were no more tears left to shed. She had hoped to build a firm foundation for this marriage and had ruined any chance. Glenn had every reason to be angry. She had deceived him, hurt him, invaded his privacy. The room was dark and the night half-spent when Glenn came to bed. His movements sounded heavy and vaguely out of order. The dresser drawer was jerked open, then almost immediately slammed shut. He stumbled over something and cursed impatiently under his breath as he staggered to the far side of the bedroom.

Remaining motionless, Maggie listened to his movements and was shocked to realize that he was drunk. Glenn had always been so sensible about alcohol. He rarely had more than one drink. Maggie bit into her lower lip as he jerked back the covers and fell onto the mattress. She braced herself, wondering what she'd do if he tried to make love to her. But either he was too drunk or he couldn't tolerate the thought of touching her.

She woke in the morning to the sounds of Glenn moving around the room. Her first thought was that she should pretend to be asleep until he'd left, but she couldn't bear to leave things unsettled any longer.

"Glenn," she spoke softly, rolling onto her back. At the sight of his suitcase she bolted upright. "Glenn," she said again, her voice shaking and urgent. "What are you doing?"

"Packing." His face devoid of expression, told her nothing.

He didn't look at her. With an economy of movement he emptied one drawer into a suitcase and returned to the dresser for another armload.

Maggie was shocked into speechlessness.

"You're leaving me?" she finally choked out. He wouldn't…couldn't. Hadn't they agreed about the sanctity of marriage? Hadn't Glenn told her that he felt divorce was wrong and people should work things out no matter what their problems?

Glenn didn't answer; apparently his actions were enough for her to realize exactly what he was doing.

"Glenn," she pleaded, her eyes pleading with him. "Please don't do this."

He paused mid-stride between the suitcase and the dresser. "Trust is vital in a relationship," he said and laid a fresh layer of clothes on top of the open suitcase.

Maggie threw back the covers and crawled to the end of the mattress. "Will you stop talking in riddles for heaven's sake. Of course trust is vital. This whole thing started because you didn't trust me enough to tell me about Angie."

"You knew everything you needed to know."

"I didn't," she cried. "I asked you to tell me about her and you refused."

"She had nothing to do with you and me."

"Oh, sure," Maggie shouted, her voice gaining volume with every word. "I wake up the morning after our wedding and you call me by her name. It isn't bad enough that you can't keep the two of us straight. Even…even your friends confuse our names. Then… then you leave her picture lying around for me to find. But that was nothing. The icing on the cake comes when I inadvertently find a letter tucked safely away in a drawer to cherish and keep forever. Never mind that you've got a wife. Oh, no. She's a simpleminded fool who's willing to overlook a few improprieties in married life."

Rising to her knees, Maggie waved her arms and continued. "And please note that word 'inadvertently,' because I assure you I did not go searching through your things. I found her letter by accident."

Glenn was confused. His head was pounding, his mouth felt like sandpaper and Maggie was shouting at him, waving her arms like a madwoman.

"I need to think," he murmured.

Maggie hopped off the bed and reached for her bathrobe. "Well, think then, but don't do something totally stupid like…like leave me. I love you, Glenn. For two days we've behaved like fools. I'm sick of it. I trusted you enough to marry you and obviously you felt the same way about me. The real question here is if we trust our love enough to see things through. If you want to run at the first hint of trouble then you're not the Glenn Lambert I know." She tied the sash to her robe and continued, keeping her voice level. "I'm going to make coffee. You have ten minutes alone to 'think.'"

By the time she entered the kitchen, Maggie's knees

were shaking. If she told Glenn about the baby he wouldn't leave, but she refused to resort to that. If he wanted to stay, it would be because he loved her enough to work out their differences.

The kitchen phone rang and Maggie stared at it accusingly. The only person who would call her this time of the morning was Denny. If he asked her for another penny, she'd scream. It used to be that he'd call once or twice a month. Now it was every other day.

On the second ring, Maggie nearly ripped the phone off the hook. "Yes," she barked.

"Maggie, is that you?" Denny asked brightly. "Listen, I'm sorry to call so early, but I wanted to tell you something."

"What?" Her indignation cooled somewhat.

"I'm going to work Monday morning. Now don't argue, I know that you're against this. I'll admit that I was, too, when I first heard it. But I got to thinking about what Glenn said. And, Maggie, he's right. My attitude toward life, toward everything, has been rotten lately. The best thing in the world for me right now is to get back into the mainstream of life and do something worthwhile."

"But I thought…" Maggie couldn't believe what she was hearing.

"I know. I thought all the same things you did. But Linda and I had a long talk a few days ago and she helped me see that Glenn is right. I went to an interview, got the job and I feel terrific. Better than I have in years."

Maggie was dumbfounded. She lowered her lashes and squeezed her eyes at her own stupidity. Glenn had been right all along about Denny. Her brother had been trapped in the same mire as she had been. Maggie should have recognized it before, but she'd been so defensive, wanting to shield her brother from any unpleasantness that she had refused to acknowledge what was right in front of her eyes. Denny needed the same purpose that Glenn's love had given her life.

The urge to go back to their bedroom and ask Glenn to forgive her was strong, but she resisted. Denny was only one problem they needed to make right.

Glenn arrived in the kitchen dressed for the office. Silently he poured himself a cup of coffee. Maggie wondered if she should remind Glenn that it was Saturday and he didn't need to go to work. No, she'd let him talk first, she decided.

He took a sip of the hot, black coffee and grimaced. His head was killing him. It felt as if someone was hammering at his temple every time his heart beat. Furthermore he had to collect his car. He'd taken a taxi cab back to the house, far too drunk to get behind a wheel.

"Who was on the phone?" he asked. The question was not one of his most brilliant ones. Obviously it had been Denny, but he hoped to get some conversation going. Anything.

"Denny."

Glenn cocked a brow, swallowing back the argument that sprang readily to his lips. If she was going to write WELCOME across her back and lie down for Denny to walk all over her there wasn't anything he could do. Heaven knew he'd tried.

"He…he called because…"

"I know why he phoned," Glenn tossed out sarcastically.

"You do?"

"Of course. Denny only phones for one reason."

"Not this time." Her pride was much easier to swallow after hearing the excitement and enthusiasm in her brother's voice. "He's got a job."

Glenn choked on a swallow of coffee. "Denny? What happened?"

"Apparently you and Linda got through that thick skull of his and he decided to give it a try. He feels wonderful."

"It might not last."

"I know," Maggie agreed. "But it's a start and one he should have made a long time ago."

Her announcement was met with silence. "Are you telling me I was right?"

"Yes." It wasn't so difficult to admit, after all. Her hands hugged the milk-laced herbal tea and lent her the courage to continue. "It was wrong to take matters into my own hands and visit Angie. I can even understand why you loved her. She's a wonderful person."

"But she isn't you. She doesn't have your beauty, your artistic talent or your special smile. Angie never made up crazy rules or beat me in a game of tennis. You're two entirely different people."

"I'll never be like her," Maggie murmured, staring into the creamy liquid she was holding.

"That's a good thing, because I'm in love with you. I married you, Maggie, I don't want anyone else but you."

Maggie's head jerked upright. "Are you saying…?

Do you mean that you're willing to forgive me for taking matters into my own hands? I know what I did wasn't right."

"I'm not condoning it, but I understand why you felt you had to meet her."

If he didn't take her in his arms soon, Maggie thought, she'd start crying again and then Glenn would know her Christmas secret for sure.

He set the coffee cup aside and Maggie glanced up hopefully. But instead of reaching for her, he walked out of the kitchen and picked up the two suitcases that rested on the other side of the arched doorway.

Panic enveloped her. "Glenn," she whispered. "Are you leaving me?"

"No. I'm putting these back where they belong." He didn't know what he'd been thinking this morning. He could no more leave Maggie than he could stop breathing. After disappearing for a moment, he returned to the kitchen and stood not more than three feet from her.

Maggie's heart returned to normal again. "Are we through fighting now? I want to get to the making up part."

"We're just about there." The familiar lopsided grin slanted his mouth.

"Maybe you need a little incentive."

"You standing there in that see-through outfit of yours is giving me all the incentive I need." He wrapped his arms around her then and held her so close that Maggie could actually feel the sigh that shuddered through him.

She met his warm lips eagerly, twining her arms

around his neck and tangling her fingers in the thick softness of his hair. Maggie luxuriated in the secure feel of his arms holding her tight. She smiled up at him dreamily. "There's an early Christmas gift I'd like to give you."

Unable to resist, Glenn brushed his lips over the top of her nose. "Don't you think I should wait?"

"Not for this gift. It's special."

"Are you going to expect to open one of yours in return?"

"No, but then, I already have a good idea of what you're getting me."

"You do?"

Maggie laughed outright at the way his eyes narrowed suspiciously. "It wasn't really fair because your mother let the cat out of the bag."

"My mother!"

"Yes, she told me about your grandmother's ring."

His forehead wrinkled into three lines. "Maggie, I'm not giving you a ring."

He couldn't have shocked her more if he'd dumped a bucket of ice water over her head. He wasn't giving her the ring! "Oh." She disentangled herself from his arms. "I...guess it was presumptuous of me to think that you would." Her eyes fell to his shirt buttons as she took a step backward.

"Just so there aren't any more misunderstandings, maybe I should explain myself."

"Maybe you should," she agreed, feeling the cold seep into her bones. It never failed. Just when she was beginning to feel loved and secure with their marriage, someone would throw a curve ball at her.

"After the hassle we went through with the wedding rings—"

"I love my rings," she interrupted indignantly. "I never take them off anymore. You asked me not to and I haven't." She knew she was babbling like an idiot, but she wanted to cover how miserable and hurt she was. All those months she had put so much stock in his grandmother's ring and he wasn't even planning on giving it to her.

"Maggie, I had the ring reset into a necklace for you."

"A necklace?"

"This way you won't need to worry about putting it on or taking it off, or losing it, for that matter."

The idea was marvelous and Maggie was so thrilled that her eyes misted with happiness. "It sounds wonderful," she murmured on a lengthy sniffle and rubbed the tears from her face.

"What is the matter with you lately?" Glenn asked, his head cocked to one side. "I haven't seen you cry this much since you were six years old and Petie Phillips teased you and pulled your braids."

Maggie smiled blindly at him. "You mean you haven't figured it out?"

"Figured what out?"

Glenn's dark brown eyes widened as he searched her expression as if expecting to find the answer hidden on her face. His eyebrows snapped together. "Maggie," he whispered with such reverence one would assume he was in a church, "are you pregnant?"

A smile lit up her face, and blossomed from ear to ear. "Yes. Our baby is due the first part of August."

"Oh, Maggie." Glenn was so excited that he longed to haul her into his arms and twirl her around the room until they were both dizzy and giddy. Instead, he pulled out a chair and sat her down. "Are you ill?"

"Only a little in the mornings," she informed him with a small laugh. "The worst thing is that I seem to cry over the tiniest incident."

"You mean like me packing my bags and leaving you."

"Yes." She giggled. "Just the minor things."

"A baby." Glenn paced the area in front of her, repeatedly brushing the hair off his forehead. "We're going to have a baby."

"Glenn, honestly, it shouldn't be such a shock. I told you in the beginning I wasn't using any birth control."

"I'm not shocked...exactly."

"Happy?"

"Very!" He knelt in front of her and gently leaned forward to kiss her tummy.

Maggie wrapped her arms around his head and held him to her. "Merry Christmas, my love."

Glenn heard the steady beat of Maggie's heart and closed his eyes to the wealth of emotions that flooded his being. She was a warm, vital woman who had made him complete. Wife, friend, lover...the list seemed endless and he had only touched the surface.

"Merry Christmas," he whispered in return and pulled her mouth to his.

* * * * *

FRIENDS—AND THEN SOME

One

The thick canvas sail flapped in the breeze before Jake Carson aligned the boat to catch the wind. The *Lucky Lady* responded by slicing through the choppy waters of San Francisco Bay. Satisfied, Jake leaned back and closed his eyes, content with his life and with the world.

"Do you think I'm being terribly mercenary?" Lily Morrissey asked as she stretched her legs out and crossed them at the ankles. "It sounds so coldhearted to decide to marry a man simply because he's wealthy. He doesn't have to be *that* rich." She paused to sigh expressively. Lately she'd given the matter consideration. For almost a year now she'd been playing the piano at the Wheaton. Only wealthy businessmen could afford to stay at a hotel as expensive as the Wheaton. And Lily was determined to find herself such a man. Unfortunately, no one had leaped forward, and she'd grown discouraged. Each day she told herself that she would meet someone soon. That hope was what kept Lily going back night after night.

"I'd only want someone rich enough to appreciate opera," she added thoughtfully. "Naturally it'd be nice if he drove a fancy car, but that isn't essential. All I really care about is his bank account. It's got to be large enough to take care of Gram and me. That doesn't sound so bad, does it?"

A faint smile tugged at the corners of Jake's mouth.

"Jake?" she repeated, slightly irritated.

"Hmm?"

"You haven't heard a word I said."

"Sure I have. You were talking about finding yourself a wealthy man."

"Yes, but that's what I always talk about. You could have guessed." Maybe she was foolish to dream of the day when a generous man would adorn her with diamonds.

"I wasn't guessing. I heard every word."

Lily studied him through narrowed eyes. "Sure you did," she mumbled under her breath.

Jake's slow, lazy smile came into play again.

Lily studied the profile of her best friend. Jake drove a taxi and they'd met the first week she worked at the Wheaton. She owed him a lot. Not only did he give her free rides back and forth to work when he was available, which was just about every day, but he'd rescued Gram and Lily from the Wheaton's manager.

Lily's starting salary had been less than what Gram had paid for an hour of piano lessons. Gram had raised Lily from the time her mother had died and her father had sought his fortune as a merchant marine. Gram had been outraged by the manager's unintended slight. And Gram, being Gram, couldn't do anything without a production. She'd shown up at the hotel in authentic witch doctor's costume and proceeded to chant a voodoo rite of retribution over the manager's head.

Luckily, Lily had gotten her grandmother out of the lobby before the police arrived. Jake had been standing next to his taxi and had witnessed the entire scene. Before everything exploded in Lily's face, Jake held open the cab door and whisked Gram and Lily away from any unpleasantness. Over the months that followed, the three had become good friends.

Jake was actually a struggling writer. He lived on his boat and worked hard enough to meet expenses by driving the taxi. He didn't seem to take anything too seriously. Not even his writing. Lily sometimes wondered how many other people he gave free rides to. Money didn't matter to Jake. But it did to Lily.

"I *am* going to meet someone," Lily continued on a serious note.

"I don't doubt it," Jake said and yawned, raising his hand to cover his mouth.

"I mean it, Jake. Tonight. I bet I meet someone tonight."

"For your sake, I hope you're right," Jake mumbled in reply.

Her words echoed in her ears several hours later when Lily pulled out the bench of the huge grand piano that dominated the central courtyard of the Wheaton. Dressed in her full-length sleeveless dress and dainty slippers, she was barely recognizable as the woman who'd spent the afternoon aboard Jake's boat.

Deftly her fingers moved over the smooth ivory

keys as her upper body swayed with the melody of a Carpenters' hit.

Some days Lily felt that her smile was as artificial as her thick, curling eyelashes. After twenty-seven hundred times of hearing "Moon River," "Misty" and "Sentimental Journey," Lily was ready to take a journey herself. Maybe that was why she had talked to Jake. If she was going to meet someone, surely it would have happened by now. Sighing inwardly, she continued playing, hardly conscious of her fingers.

Five minutes later when Lily glanced up, she was surprised to find a ruddy faced cowboy standing next to the piano, watching her.

She smiled up at him and asked, "Is there something you'd like to hear?" He had to be close to forty-five, with the beginnings of a double chin. A huge turquoise buckle dominated the slight thickening at his waist. He was a good-looking man who was already going to seed.

"Do you know 'Santa Fe Gal of Mine'?" The slight Southern drawl wasn't a surprise. His head was topped with a Stetson although he was dressed in a linen sport coat that hadn't cost a penny under five hundred dollars. A Texan, she mused; a rich Texan, probably into oil.

"'Santa Fe Gal of Mine,'" she repeated aloud. "I'm not sure that I do," she answered with a warm smile. "Hum a few bars for me." She didn't usually get requests. People were more interested in checking into the hotel or meeting their friends for a drink in the sunken cocktail lounge to care about what she was playing.

The man placed a steadying hand against the side of the piano and momentarily closed his eyes. "I can't remember the melody," he admitted sheepishly. "Sorry, I'm not much good with that sort of thing. I'm an oil-man not a singer."

So he was into oil just as she suspected. Lily got a glance at his feet and recognized the shoes from an advertisement she'd seen in *Gentlemen's Quarterly*. Cowboy boots, naturally, but ones made of imported leather and inlaid with silver. Leather, Lily felt, made the difference between being dressed and well dressed. This gentleman was definitely well dressed.

"Do you know who sang the popular version?" she questioned brightly, her heart pounding so hard it felt as though it would slam right out of her chest. She'd told Jake she was going to meet someone. And that someone had appeared at last! And he wasn't wearing a wedding band either.

"Nope, I can't say that I do."

"Maybe there's another song you'd like to hear?" Without conscious thought her hands continued to play as she glanced up at the cowboy with two chins and reminded herself that looks weren't everything. But, then again, maybe he had been married and had a son her age—an heir.

"One day I'm going to find some sweet gal who knows that blasted song," he muttered. "It always was my favorite."

Already Lily's mind had shifted into overdrive. Somehow she'd locate his long-lost song and gain his everlasting gratitude. "Will you be around tomorrow?"

"I should be."

"Come back and I'll see what I can do."

He straightened and gave her a brief salute. "I'll do that, little filly."

Lily's heart was pounding so hard that by the time she finished an hour later, she felt as if she'd been doing calisthenics. Maybe he'd be so grateful he'd insist on taking her to dinner. This could be the break Lily had waited months for. It hadn't happened exactly as she'd expected, but it was just the chance she'd been wanting. Already she could picture herself sitting in an elegant restaurant, ordering almond-saffron soup and lobster in wine sauce. For dessert she'd have Italian ice cream with walnuts and caramel oozing from the sides. Her mouth watered just thinking about all the wonderful foods she'd read about but never tasted. Her Texan would probably order barbecued chicken, but she wouldn't care. He could well be her ticket to riches and a genteel life…if she played her cards right. And for the first time in a long while, Lily felt she'd been dealt a hand of aces.

Jake was in his cab, parked in front of the hotel when she stepped into the balmy summer night. Eagerly she waved and hurried across the wide circular driveway to the bright-yellow taxi.

"Jake!" she cried. "Didn't I tell you today was the day? Didn't I? The most fantastically wonderful thing has happened! I can't believe I'm so lucky." She felt like holding out her arms and twirling around and bursting into song.

With one elbow leaning against the open window, Jake studied her with serious dark eyes and a slow, measured smile that lifted one corner of his full mouth. "Obviously Daddy Warbucks introduced himself."

"Yes," she giggled. "*My* Daddy Warbucks."

Leaning across the front seat, Jake swung open the passenger door. "Climb in and you can tell me all about it on the way to your house."

Rushing around the front of the car, Lily scooted inside the cab and closed the door. Jake started the engine and pulled onto the busy street, skillfully merging with the flowing traffic. "I was so surprised, I nearly missed my chance," Lily started up again. "Suddenly, after all these months, he was there in a five-hundred-dollar sport coat, requesting a song. He called me 'little filly,' and, Jake, he's rich. Really, really rich. I can just see that Texas oil oozing from every pore." She paused long enough to inhale before continuing. "He's older, maybe forty-five or fifty, but that's not so bad. And he's nice. I can tell that about a man. Remember how I met you and instantly knew what a great person you were? That's just the kind of feeling I had tonight." She continued chattering for another full minute until she realized how quiet Jake had become. "Oh, Jake, I'm sorry, I've been talking up a storm without giving you a chance to think."

"You're talking with a drawl."

"Oh, yeah, I'm practicing. I was born in Texas, you know."

"You were?"

"No, of course not, but I thought it'd impress him."

The slow, lazy smile came into play again.

Lily studied the intense profile of her friend as he steered. Jake wasn't handsome—not in the way the models for *Gentlemen's Quarterly* were. He was tall with broad shoulders and a muscular build. But with those sea-green eyes and that dark hair, he could be attractive if he tried. Only Jake couldn't care less. Half the time he dressed in faded jeans and outdated sweaters. Lily doubted that he even owned a suit. Formal wear wasn't part of Jake's image.

As she studied Jake, Lily realized that she really didn't know much about him. Jake kept the past to himself. She knew he'd been a medic in the Army, and had an engineering degree from a prestigious college back east someplace. From tidbits of conversation here and there, she'd learned that he'd worked at every type of job imaginable. There didn't seem to be anything he hadn't tried once and—if he liked it—done again and again. In some ways Jake reminded Lily of her father who had been in the merchant marine and brought her a storehouse of treasures from around the world. Jake was the kind of man who could do anything he put his mind to. He was creative and intelligent, proud and resourceful. Lily supposed she loved him but only as a friend. He was her confidant and in many ways, her partner. Her feelings were more like those of a young girl for an endearing older brother or an adventurous sidekick. Love, real love between a man and a woman was an emotion Lily held in reserve for her husband. But first she had to convince a rich man that she would be an excellent wife.

Studying Jake now, Lily noted that something had displeased him. She could tell by the way he tucked back his chin, giving an imitation of a cobra prepared to strike. He exuded impatience and restrained anger.

From past experience, Lily knew that whatever was bothering him would be divulged in his own time and in his own way.

"Well?" he snapped.

"Well, what?"

"Are you going to tell me your plan to snag this rich guy or not?"

"Are you sure you want to hear? You sound like you want to snap my head off."

"Darn it, Lily, one of these days..." He paused to inhale sharply as if the night were responsible for his wrath. Several moments passed before he spoke, and when he did his voice was as smooth as velvet, almost caressing.

Lily wasn't fooled. Jake was furious. "All right, tell me what's wrong. Did you get stiffed again? I thought you had a foolproof system for avoiding that."

"No one stiffed me."

"Then what?"

He ignored her, seeming to concentrate on the traffic. "Listen, kid, you've got to be careful."

Lily hated it when Jake called her "kid" and he knew it. "Be careful? What are you talking about? You're acting like I'm planning to handle toxic waste. Good grief, I don't even know his name."

"You could be playing with fire."

"I'm not playing anything yet. Which reminds me, have you ever heard the song 'Santa Fe Gal of Mine'?"

"'Santa Fe Gal of Mine'?" The harsh disgruntled look left his expression as a smile split his mouth. "No, I can't say that I have."

"Gram will know it," Lily said with complete confidence. Her grandmother might be a bit eccentric, but the woman was a virtual warehouse of useless information. If that wealthy Texan's favorite song was ever on the charts, Gram would know it.

Jake eased to a stop in front of the large two-story house with the wide front porch.

"Can you come in now or will you be by later?"

"Later," he answered with apparent indifference.

Lily walked toward the house and paused on the front steps, confused again. A disturbing shiver trembled through her at the cool, appraising way Jake had behaved this evening. His smooth, impenetrable green eyes resembled the dark jade Buddha her father had brought her from Hong Kong. Nothing about Jake had been the same tonight. Lily attributed it to his having had a bad day. But it shouldn't have been. They'd spent the majority of it sailing and they both loved that. But then everyone had a bad day now and again. Jake was entitled to his.

Shaking off the feelings of unease, Lily stepped inside the fifty-year-old house, pausing to pat Herbie. Herbie was her grandmother's favorite conversation piece—a shrunken head from South America. A zebra-skin rug from Africa rested in front of the fireplace.

The television blared from Gram's bedroom, but the older woman was snoring just as loudly, drowning out the sounds of the cops-and-robbers movie. With an affectionate smile, Lily turned off the set and quietly tiptoed from the darkened room. She'd talk to Gram in the morning.

After changing out of the red gown, Lily inspected

her limited wardrobe, wondering what she'd wear first if the Texan asked her to dinner. Possibly the dress with the plunging neckline. No, she mentally argued with herself. That dress could give him the wrong impression. The lavender chiffon one she'd picked up at Repeaters, a secondhand store, looked good with her dark eyes and had a high neckline. Lily felt it would be best to start this relationship off right. She was sitting beside the old upright piano, sorting through Gram's sheet music that was stored in the bench when Jake returned. He let himself in, hung his jacket on the elephant tusks and picked up a discarded Glenn Miller piece from the top of the pile.

"Hi."

"Hi." At least he sounded in a better mood than earlier. "It'd be just like Gram to have that song and not even know it."

"You're determined to find it, aren't you?" Jake asked with a faint smile.

"I've got to find it," Lily shot back. "Everything will be ruined if I don't." Her sharp words bounced back without penetrating his aloof composure. "He won't be grateful if I can't find that song."

Jake sat on the arm of the sofa and idly flipped through the stack she'd already sorted. He didn't like the sounds of this Texan. He wasn't sure what he was feeling. Lily was determined to find herself a rich man and, knowing her persistence, Jake thought she probably would. When Lily wanted something, she went after it with unwavering resolve. In his life, there wasn't anything he cared that much about. Sure, there were things he wanted, but nothing that was worth abandoning the easygoing existence he had now. Lily's dark-brown eyes had sparkled with eager excitement when she'd told him about the Texan. He'd never seen anyone's eyes light up that way.

"Did you get a chance to do any writing today?"

Jake straightened the tall stack of sheet music and sat upright. "I finished that short story I was telling you about and e-mailed it off."

Lily smiled up at him, her attention diverted for the moment. Jake had talent, but he wasted it on short stories that didn't sell when he should be concentrating on a novel. That's where the real money was. "Are you going to let me read this one?" He usually gave her his work to look over, mainly for grammar and spelling errors—Jake was a "creative" speller.

"Later," he hedged, not knowing why. He preferred it when Lily had a chance to correct his blatant errors, but there was something of himself in this story that he'd held in reserve, not wishing her to see. The interesting part of being a writer was that Jake didn't always like the people inside him who appeared on paper. Some were light and witty while others were dark and dangerous. None were like him and yet each one was a part of himself.

"I know Gram's got tons more sheet music than this," Lily mumbled, thoughtfully chewing on her bottom lip. "Do you want to go to the attic with me?"

"Sure."

He followed her up the creaky stairs to the second floor, then moved in front and opened the door that led to another staircase, this one narrower and steeper.

Lily tucked her index finger in Jake's belt loop as the light from the hallway dimmed. They were surrounded by the pitch-black dark, two steps into the attic.

"Where's the light?"

An eerie sensation slowly crept up Lily's arm and settled in her stomach. The air was still with a stagnant heaviness. "In the center someplace. Jake, I'll do this tomorrow. It's creepy up here."

"We're here now," he argued and half turned, bringing her to his side and loosely taking her by the hand. "Don't worry, I'll protect you."

"Yeah, that's what I'm afraid of." She tried to make light of her apprehensions, and managed to squelch the urge to turn back toward the dim hallway light. Involuntarily she shivered. "Gram's got some weird stuff up here."

"It can't be any worse than what's downstairs," he murmured, and chuckled softly as he edged their way into the black void, taking short steps as he swung his hand out in front of him to prevent a collision with some inanimate object.

Gradually, Lily's eyes adjusted to the lack of light. "I think I see the string—to your left there." She pointed for his benefit and squeezed her eyes half-closed for a better view. It didn't look exactly right, but it could be the light.

"That's a hangman's noose."

"Good grief, what's Gram doing with that?" In some ways, she'd rather not know what treasures Gram had stored up here. The attic was Gram's territory and Lily hadn't paid it a visit in years. In truth, Lily didn't really want to know what her sweet grandmother was doing with a hangman's noose.

"She told me once that her great-grandfather is said to have ridden with Jesse James. The noose might have something to do with that." As he spoke, Jake's foot collided with a box and he stumbled forward a few steps until he regained his balance.

Lily let out a sharp gasp, then held her breath. "Are you all right?"

"I'm fine."

"What was that?"

"How would I know?"

"Jake, let's go back down. Please." Her greatest fear was walking into a bat's nest or something worse.

"We already went over that. The light's got to be around here someplace."

"Sure, and in the meantime we don't know…"

"Damn."

Lily's hand tightened around his, her fingers clammy. "Now what's wrong?"

"My knee bumped into something."

"That does it. We're going back." Jake could stay up here if he wanted, but she was leaving. From the minute they'd stepped inside this tomb, Lily had felt uneasy.

"Lily," he argued.

Jerking her hand free, she turned toward the stairs and the faint beam of light. It looked as though the attic door had eased shut, cutting off what little illumination there had been from the hall. Everything was terribly dark and spooky. "I'm getting out of here," she declared, unable to keep the catch out of her voice.

"This place is giving me the heebie-jeebies." More interested in making her escape than being cautious, Lily turned away and walked straight into a spider's web. A disgusted sound slid from her throat as her hands flew up to free her face from the fine, sticky threads. A prickling fear shot up her spine as she felt something scamper across her foot.

Her heart rammed against her breast like a jackhammer as the terror gripped her and she let out a bloodcurdling cry. "Jake...Jake."

He was with her in seconds, roughly pulling her into his arms. She clung to him, frantically wrapping her arms around his neck. Her face was buried in his shoulder as she trembled. His arms around her waist half lifted her from the floor. "Lily, you're all right," he whispered frantically. His hold, secure and warm, drove out the terror. "I've got you." It took all the strength she could muster just to nod.

Jake's hand brushed the wispy curls from her temple. "Lily," he repeated soothingly. "I told you I'd protect you." His warm breath fanned her face, creating an entirely new set of sensations. His scent, a combination of sweat and man, was unbelievably intoxicating. For the first time Lily became aware of how tightly pressed her body was to the rock hardness of his. Her grip slackened and she slid intimately down the length of him until her feet touched the floor. The hem of her blouse rode up, exposing her midriff so that her bare skin rubbed against the muscular wall of his chest. His hands found their place in the small of her back and seemed to hold her there, pressing her all the closer.

Her breasts were flattened to his upper torso and her nerves fired to life at the merest brush of his body.

As if hypnotized, their eyes met and held in the faint light. It was as though they were seeing each other for the first time. Her pulse fluttered wildly at his look of curious surprise as his gaze lowered to her mouth.

"Jake?" Her voice was the faintest whisper, wavering and unsure.

His eyes darkened and a thick frown formed on his face. Slowly, almost as if drawn by something other than his will, Jake lowered his mouth to hers. Warm lips met warm lips in an exploratory kiss that was as gentle as it was unhurried. "Lily." His mouth left hers and sounded oddly raspy and unsure. Her eyes remained tightly closed.

Somehow she found her voice. "That shouldn't have happened."

"Do you want an apology?"

Her arms slid from around his neck and fell to her side as he released her. "No…" she whispered. "I should be the one to apologize…I don't know what came over me."

"You're right about this place," he admitted on a harsh note. "There is something spooky about it. Let's get out of here."

By the time they'd returned to the living room, Lily had regained her equilibrium and could smile over the peculiar events in the attic.

"What's so amusing?" He didn't sound the least bit pleased by their adventure, and stalked ahead of her, sitting in the fan-back bamboo chair usually reserved for Gram.

"Honestly, Jake, can you imagine *us kissing*?"

"We just did," he reminded her soberly, his voice firm as his watchful eyes studied her. "And if we're both smart, we'll forget it ever happened."

Lily sat on the sofa, tucking her legs under her. "I suppose you're right. It's just that after being such good friends for the past year, it was a shock. Elaine would never forgive me."

"Would you lay off Elaine? I've told you a thousand times that it's been over for months." Jake grimaced at the sound of the other woman's name. His relationship with Elaine Wittenberg had developed nicely in the beginning. She was impressed with his writing, encouraging even. Then bit by bit, with intrusive politeness, Elaine had started to reorganize his life. First came the suggestion that he change jobs. Driving a cab didn't pay that well, and with his talents he could do anything. She started introducing him to her friends, making contacts for him. The problem was that Jake liked his life exactly the way it was. Elaine had been a close call—too close. Jake had come within inches of waking up one morning living in a three-bedroom house with a white picket fence and a new car parked in the garage—a house and a car with big monthly payments. True, Lily was just as eager for the same material possessions, but at least she was honest about it.

"Well, you needn't worry," Lily told him, taking a deep breath and releasing it slowly. "Just because we kissed, it doesn't mean anything."

Her logic irritated him. "Let's not talk about it, all right? It was a mistake and it's over."

Lily arched a delicate brow and shrugged one shoulder. "Fine." His attitude didn't please her in the least. As far as she knew, Jake wasn't one to sweep things under the carpet and forget they existed. If anything, he faced life head-on.

Abruptly getting to his feet, Jake stalked to the other side of the living room. Confused, Lily watched the impatient, angry way he moved. "I'll see you tomorrow," he said on his way to the front door.

"Okay."

The door closed and Lily didn't move. What an incredibly strange night it had been. First, the golden opportunity of finding that crazy song for the Texan. Then, wilder still was Jake's kissing her in the attic. Even now she could feel the pressure of his mouth on hers, and the salty-sweet taste of him lingered on her lips. He'd held her close, his scent heightened by the stuffy air of the attic.

But, Lily realized with a start, the kiss had been a moment out of time and was never meant to be. Jake was right. They should simply put it out of their minds and forget it had happened. A single kiss should be no threat to a year of solid friendship. They knew each other too well to get caught up in a romantic relationship. Lily had seen the type of woman Jake usually went for, and she wasn't even close to it. Jake's ideal woman was Mother Theresa, Angelina Jolie and Betty Crocker all rolled into one perfect female specimen. Conversely, her ideal man was Daddy Warbucks, Bruce Willis and Mr. Goodwrench. No…Jake and she would always be friends; they'd make terrible lovers….

* * *

The next morning when Lily found her way into the kitchen, Gram was already up and about. Her bright-red hair was tightly curled into a hundred ringlets and held in place with bobby pins.

"Morning," Lily mumbled and pulled out a kitchen chair, eager to speak to her grandmother.

Gram didn't acknowledge the greeting. Instead, the older woman concentrated on opening a variety of bottles, extracting her daily quota of pills.

Lily waited until her grandmother had finished swallowing thirteen garlic tablets and a number of vitamins, and had chewed six blanched almonds. This daily ritual was Gram's protection from cancer. The world could scoff, but at seventy-four Gram was as fit as someone twenty years her junior.

"I didn't hear you come in last night."

A smile played at the edges of Lily's mouth. "I know. Gram, have you ever heard of the song 'Santa Fe Gal of Mine'?"

The older woman's look was thoughtful and Lily nibbled nervously on her bottom lip. "It's been a lotta years since I heard that ol' song."

"You remember it?" Relief washed through Lily until she sagged against the back of the chair. Lily marveled again at her grandmother's memory.

"Play a few bars for me, girl."

Lily tensed and the silence stretched until her nerve endings screamed with it. "I don't know the song, Gram. I thought *you* did."

"I do," she insisted, shaking her bright red head. "I don't remember it offhand, is all."

Is all, Lily repeated mentally in a panic. "When do you think you'll remember it?"

"I can't rightly say. Give me a day or two."

A day or two! "Gram, I haven't got that long. Our future could depend on 'Santa Fe Gal of Mine.' Think."

Stirring the peanut butter with a knife, Gram picked up a soda cracker and dabbed a layer of chunky-style spread across the top before popping it into her mouth.

Lily wanted to scream that this wasn't a time for food, but she pressed her lips tightly shut, forcing down the panic. Gram didn't do well under pressure.

"What do you want to know for?" Gram asked after a good five minutes had lapsed. Meanwhile, she'd eaten six soda crackers, each loaded with a thick layer of peanut butter.

"A rich man requested that song last night. A very rich man who had a generous look about him," Lily explained, doing her best to keep the excitement out of her voice. "If I can come up with that song, he'd probably be willing to show his appreciation."

"We could use a little appreciation, couldn't we, girl?"

"Oh, Gram, you know we could."

"If I can't think of it, Gene Autry would know." Gram often spoke as if famous personalities were her lifelong friends and all she had to do was pick up the phone and give a jingle.

"Did Gene Autry sing the original version?"

"Now that you mention it, he might have been the one," she said, scratching the side of her head.

Lily perked up. Gram had a recording of every song Gene Autry had ever sung. "Then you have it."

"I must," she agreed. "Someplace."

"Someplace" turned out to be in the furnace room in the basement five hours later. The next few hours were spent transposing the scratchy old record into notes Lily could play on the piano.

When she sat at the grand piano at five that evening in the Wheaton lobby, 'Santa Fe Gal of Mine' was forever embedded in her brain. Each note had been agonized over. There couldn't be a worse way to memorize a song. Lily had never been able to play very well by ear.

As it worked out, the timing had been tight and consequently Lily had been unable to pay the amount of attention she would have liked to her dress and makeup.

The lobby was busy with people strolling in and out, registering for a wholesale managers' conference. At the moment the only thing Lily was interested in was one Texan with a love for an ol' Gene Autry number.

During the evening, Lily twice played the song she had come to hate more than any of the others. Her only reward was a few disgruntled stares. The lively Western piece wasn't the "elevator" style she'd been hired to play. The second go-around with 'Santa Fe Gal' and Lily caught the manager's disapproving stare. Instantly, Lily switched over to something he'd consider more appropriate: 'Moon River.'

As the evening progressed, Lily's plastic smile became more and more forced. She'd gone to all this trouble for nothing. Her stomach felt as if it were weighted with a lead balloon. All the hassle she'd gone through, all the work, had been for nothing. Gram would be so disappointed. Heavens, Gram nothing. Lily felt like crying.

As usual, Jake was waiting for her outside the hotel.

"How'd it go?" he asked as she approached the cab. One look at her sorrowful dark eyes and Jake climbed out of the cab. "What happened?"

"Nothing."

"Mr. Moneybags wasn't the appreciative type?"

She shook her head, half expecting Jake to scold her for being so incredibly naive. "No."

"What, then?"

"He didn't show."

Jake held open the taxi door for her. "Oh, Lily, I'm sorry."

"It's not your fault," she returned loyally. "I was the stupid one. I can't believe that I could have gotten so excited over an overweight Texan who wanted to hear a crummy song that's older than I am."

"But he was a rich Texan."

"Into oil and maybe even gold."

"Maybe," Jake repeated.

He'd walked around the front of the taxi when the captain of the bellboys came hurrying out of the hotel. "Miss Lily!" he called, flagging her down. "Someone left a message for you."

Two

"A message?" Lily's gaze clashed with Jake's as excitement welled up inside her, lifting the dark shroud of depression that had settled over her earlier.

"Thanks, Henry." Lily gave the hotel's senior bellhop a brilliant smile. Two minutes before, Lily would never have believed that something as simple as an envelope could chase the clouds of doubt from her heart.

"Well, what does it say?" Jake questioned, leaning through the open car window. He appeared as anxious as Lily.

"Give me a minute to open it, for heaven's sake." She ripped apart the beige envelope bearing the Wheaton's logo. Her gaze flew over the bold pen-strokes, reading as fast as she could. "It's him."

"Daddy Warbucks?"

"Yes," she repeated, her voice quavering with anticipation. "Only his real name is Rex Flanders. He says he got hung up in a meeting and couldn't make it downstairs, but he wanted me to know he heard the song and it was just as good as he remembered. He wants to thank me." Searching for something more, Lily turned over the single sheet, thinking she must have missed or dropped it in her hastiness. Surely he meant that he wanted to thank her with more than a simple message. The least she'd expected was a dinner invitation. With hurried, anxious movements she checked her lap, scrambling to locate the envelope she'd so carelessly discarded only a moment before.

"What are you looking for?" Jake asked, perplexed.

"Nothing." Defeat caused her voice to drop half an octave. Lily couldn't take her eyes from the few scribbled lines on the single sheet of hotel stationery. Shaking her head, she hoped to clear her muddled thoughts. She'd been stupid to expect anything more than a simple thank-you. Rich men always had women chasing after them. There wasn't one thing that would make her stand out in a crowd. She wasn't strikingly beautiful, or talented, or even sophisticated. Little about her would make her attractive to a wealthy man.

"Lily?" Gently, Jake placed a hand on her forearm. His tender touch warmed her cool skin and brought feeling back to her numb fingers. "What's wrong?"

A tremulous smile briefly touched her lips. "Me. I'm wrong. Oh, Jake, I'm never going to find a rich man who'll want to marry me. And even if I caught someone's eye, they'd take one look at Gram and Herbie and start running in the opposite direction."

"I don't see why," he contradicted sharply. "I didn't."

"Yeah, but you're just as weird as we are."

"Thanks." Sarcasm coated his tongue. So Lily thought he was as eccentric as her grandmother. All

right, he'd agree that he didn't show the corporate ambitions that drove so many of his college friends. He
liked his life. He was perfectly content to live on a sailboat for the remainder of his days, without a care or
responsibility. There wasn't anything in this world that
he couldn't walk away from, and that was exactly the
way he wanted it. No complications. No one to answer
to. Except Gram and Lily. But even now his platonic
relationship with Lily was beginning to cause problems. He admired Lily. What he liked best about her
was that she had no designs on his heart and no desire
to change him. She was an honest, forthright woman.
She knew what she wanted and made no bones about
it. Their kiss from the day before had been a fluke
that wouldn't happen again. He'd make sure of that.

"I didn't mean that the way it sounded," Lily mumbled her apology. "You're the best friend I've got. I'm
feeling a bit defeated at the moment. Tomorrow I'll be
back to my normal self again."

Silently walking around the front of the taxi, Jake
climbed into the driver's seat and started the engine
with a flick of his wrist. "I can't say I blame you."
And he didn't. After everything she'd gone through to
find that song, she had every right to be disappointed.

"It's me I'm angry with," Lily said, breaking the
silence. "I shouldn't have put such stock in a simple
request."

Jake blamed himself. He should have cautioned her,
but at the time he'd been so surprised that he hadn't
known what he was feeling—maybe even a bit of jealousy, which had shocked the hell out of him. Later he'd
discarded that notion. He wanted Lily to be as happy

as she deserved, but there was something about this Texan that had troubled him from the beginning.

The moment Lily had mentioned she'd met someone, warning lights had gone off inside his head. His protective instinct, for some reason he couldn't put into words, had been aroused. That alien impulse had been the cause of the incident in the attic. He didn't regret kissing Lily, but it was just that type of thing that could ruin a good friendship. The Texan meant trouble for Lily. It'd taken him half the night to realize that was what bothered him, but he was certain. Now, after Lily's revelation, Jake could afford to be generous.

"How about if we go fishing tomorrow?"

Lily straightened, her dark eyes glowing with pleasure at the invitation. Over the past year, Jake had only taken her out on the sloop for short, limited periods of time. Lily loved sailing and was convinced that the man she married would have to own a sailboat.

"With Gram," he added, smiling. "We'll make a day of it, pack a bottle of good wine, some cheese and a loaf of freshly baked French bread, and beer for me."

"Jake, that sounds wonderful." Already her heart was lifting with anticipation. Only Jake would know that an entire day on his sailboat would cheer her up like this.

"We deserve a one-day vacation from life. I'll park the cab, shut down the laptop and take you to places you have never been."

Lily expelled a deep sigh of contentment. "It sounds great, but Thursday's Gram's bingo day. Nothing will convince her to give that up."

A smile sparked from Jake's cool jade eyes. Lily's grandmother had her own get-rich schemes going. "Then it'll have to be the two of us. Are you still game?"

"You bet." Lily pictured the brisk wind whipping her hair freely about her face as the boat sliced through the deep-green waters of San Francisco Bay.

Within ten hours, the daydream had become reality. The wind carried Lily's low laugh as she tossed back her head and the warm breeze ruffled her thick, unbound hair. The boat keeled sharply and cut a deep path through the choppy water. Lily had climbed to the front of the boat to raise the sails and was now sitting on the bow, luxuriating in the overwhelming sense of freedom she was experiencing. She wanted to capture this utopian state of being and hug it to her breast forever. She didn't dare turn back and let Jake see her. He'd laugh at her childish spirit and tease her unmercifully. Lily wanted nothing to ruin the magnificent day.

For the first hour of their trip, Lily remained forward while Jake manned the helm. Keeping his mind to the task was difficult. He couldn't ever remember seeing Lily so carefree and happy. She was a natural sailor. He'd taken other women aboard *Lucky Lady* and always regretted it. Elaine, for one. In the beginning, she'd pretended to love his boat as much as he, but Jake hadn't been fooled. Elaine's big mistake had come when she suggested that he move off the boat and into an apartment. Pitted against his only true love, Jake decided to keep *Lady* and dump Elaine. And not a moment since had he regretted the decision.

Watching Lily produced a curious sense of pride in
Jake. Laughing, she turned back and shouted something to him. The wind whirled her voice away and he
hadn't a clue as to what she'd said, but the exhilaration in her flushed face wasn't something that could be
manufactured. It surprised Jake how much he enjoyed
watching her. She reminded him of the sea nymphs
sailors of old claimed inhabited the waters.

As he watched her, Jake realized that Lily was his
friend and they were fortunate to share a special kind
of relationship. But it wasn't until that moment that
Jake noticed just how beautiful she was. In the year
he'd known her, Lily's youthful features had filled
out with vivid promise. Her long hair was a rich, dark
shade of mahogany and he'd rarely seen it unbound.
That day, instead of piling it on top of her head the
way she normally did, Lily had left it free so that it
fell in gentle waves around her shoulders. Her natural
gracefulness was what struck Jake most. Her walk was
decidedly provocative. Jake smiled to himself with an
inner pride at the interest Lily's gently rounded hips
generated from the opposite sex. If that Texan had
seen her walk he would have given her more than a
simple thank you. But what Jake loved mainly about
Lily was her eyes. Never in his life had he met anyone with eyes so dark and expressive. Some days they
were like cellophane and he could read her moods as
clearly as the words in a book. He could imagine what
it would be like making love to her. He wouldn't need
to see anything but her eyes to…

He shook his head and dispelled the disconcerting
thoughts. His fingers tightened around the helm and

he looked sharply out to sea. What was the matter with him? He was thinking of Lily as a prospective lover.

"How about a cup of coffee?" Lily called, standing beside the mast. The wind whipped her hair behind her like a magnificent flag and Jake sucked in his breath at the sight of her.

"I'll get it," he shouted. "Take over here for me, will you?"

A quick, tantalizing smile spread across her features as she nodded and hurried down to join him at the helm. She laughed as he gave her careful instructions. She didn't need them. She felt giddy and reckless and wonderful.

Turning away, it was all Jake could do not to kiss her again. Mumbling under his breath, he descended to the galley and sleeping area of the boat.

Lily didn't know what was troubling Jake. She'd witnessed the dark scowl on his face and been surprised. He returned a few minutes later with two steaming mugs, handing her one.

"Is something wrong?" she ventured.

"Nothing," he said, keeping his gaze from lingering on her soft, inviting mouth.

"You look like you want to bite off my head again."

"Again?" Jake was stalling for time. This foul mood was Lily's fault. She didn't know what she was doing to him, and that was his problem.

"Yes, again," she repeated. "Like you did the other night when I told you about Rex."

"I've been doing some thinking about that ungrateful Texan," he said, narrowing his eyes. "There's something about him I don't trust."

"But you've never seen him," Lily countered, confused.

"I didn't have to. Just hearing about him was enough. I don't want you to see him again."

"Jake!"

"I mean it, Lily."

Astonished, Lily sat with her jaw sagging and turned away from him, cupping the steaming mug with both hands. Jake had never asked her to do anything. It wasn't like him to suddenly order her about and make demands. She swallowed her indignation. "Will you give me a reason?"

Drawing in a deep, irritated breath, Jake looked out over the green water and wondered at his own highhandedness. The Texan had been bothering him for two days. He hadn't wanted to say anything and even now, he wasn't entirely convinced he was doing the right thing. "It's a gut feeling I have. My instincts got me out of the war alive. I can't explain it, Lily, but I'm asking you to trust me in this."

"All right," she agreed, somewhat deflated. At the rate things were progressing with Rex What's-his-name, she wouldn't have the opportunity to see him again anyway. In reality, Jake wasn't asking much. He was her friend and she trusted his judgment, albeit at the moment reluctantly.

"Someone else will come along," Jake assured her, and a lazy grin crept across his face. "If not, you'll trap one as effectively as the fish we're about to lure to our dinner plates."

"You make it sound too easy." He wasn't the one

who sat at that piano night after night playing those same songs again and again and again.

"It is." He handed her a fishing pole and carefully revealed to her the finer points of casting. Luckily, Lily was a fast learner and he took pains not to touch her. Shaking off his mood, he gave her a friendly smile. "Before you know it, our meal will mosey along," he said with a distinct Southern drawl. "And who knows? It could be an oil-rich Texan bass."

Lily laughed, enjoying their light banter.

"Every woman scheming to marry money has to keep her eye out for a tightfisted shark, but then again " he paused for emphasis "—you might stumble upon a flounder in commodities."

"A generous flounder," Lily added.

"Naturally." Cupping his hand behind his head, Jake leaned back, crossed his long legs at the ankle and closed his eyes. He felt better. He hadn't a clue why he felt so strongly about that rich Texan. He just sensed trouble.

"There's another message for you, Miss Lily," Henry informed her when she arrived at the hotel the following evening.

Lily stared at the envelope as if it were a snake about to lash out at her. "A message?" she repeated, her voice sounding like an echo.

"From the same man as before," Henry explained with ageless, questioning eyes.

Undoubtedly the elderly bellboy couldn't understand her reluctance now when only the day before she behaved as if she'd won the lottery.

"Thank you." Lily took the folded note and made her way into the grand lobby. The manager acknowledged her with a faint nod, but Lily's answering smile was forced. The message lay on the keyboard of the piano for several moments before she had the courage to open it.

Hello, Lily—the bellhop told me your name. He also told me what time you'd be in today. I've thought about you and your music. I'm hoping that a sweet filly like you won't think it too forward of me to suggest we meet later for a drink.

Rex Flanders

A drink…surely that would be harmless, especially if they stayed right here in the hotel. Jake wouldn't mind that. Her hands moved to the ivory keys and automatically began the repertoire of songs that was only a step above the canned music that played in elevators.

Although her fingers moved with practiced ease, Lily's thoughts were in turmoil. She'd promised Jake she wouldn't get involved with Rex. At the time it had seemed like a little thing. It hadn't seemed likely she'd have the chance to see him again. Now she regretted having consented to Jake's request so readily. Her big break had arrived and she was going to have to refuse probably the richest man she'd ever met. And all because Jake had some stupid *feeling*. It wasn't fair. How could anyone have a feeling about someone they hadn't even met?

Later, when she had a moment, Lily penned a note

to Rex, declining his invitation. She didn't offer an excuse. It'd sound ludicrous to explain that a friend had warned her against him. *You see, my friend, Jake, who has never even met you, has decided you're bad news. He felt so strongly about it that he made me promise I wouldn't see you again.* Rex would laugh himself all the way home to Texas. No one in their right mind would blame him.

Jake was out front, standing beside his taxi when she appeared. She suddenly felt like taking the bus, but one look at the darkening sky convinced her otherwise. The night was overcast, with thick gray clouds rolling in over the bay. Lily didn't need the weather to dampen her already foul mood.

"I hope you're happy," she announced as she opened the car door.

"Relatively. What's your problem?"

"At the moment, you."

Their gazes met, a clash of befuddled emerald and blazing jet. Lily had been waiting months for this opportunity—months of built up fanciful dreams—months when she'd schemed and planned for exactly this moment. And now, because of Jake, she was walking away from the opportunity of a lifetime.

"Me!" Jake cocked his head to one side, studying her as his gaze narrowed thoughtfully. "What do you mean?" His tone told her clearly that he didn't appreciate being put on the defensive.

"Rex asked me out."

"And you refused?" Instinctively he felt the hard muscles of his shoulders tense. So Daddy Warbucks was back. Somehow Jake had known the man would return.

"I'm here, aren't I? But I'll have you know that I regret that promise and would take it back in a minute if you'd let me." She eyed him hopefully, but at the sight of the deep grooves that were forming at the sides of his mouth, Lily could tell he wouldn't relent.

Jake was conscious of an odd sensation surging through his blood. He'd experienced it only a few times in his life and always when something monumental was about to happen. The first time had been as an eight-year-old kid. He'd been lost in the downtown area at Christmastime and frightened half out of his wits. The huge skyscrapers had seemed to close in around him until he could taste panic. Then, the feeling had come and he'd stopped, got his bearings and found his way home on his own, astonishing his mother. Later, in high school, that same feeling had struck right before he played in a football game during which he scored three touchdowns and went on to be the MVP for the season. He'd felt it again in the desert in Iraq and that time, it had saved his life. Jake had never told anyone about the feeling. It was too complex to define.

"No," he said with cold deliberation. "I'm not changing my mind."

"Jake," she moaned, feeling wretched.

"I'm asking you to trust me." He said it without looking at her, not wanting her to see the intensity of his determination. His fists were clenched so tightly at his sides that his fingers ached. Lily could bat her long eyelashes at him all she wanted and it wouldn't change how he felt. Truth be known, he wished she'd find her Daddy Warbucks and get married if that was what she wanted so badly. But this Texan wasn't the right man for Lily.

Without further discussion, Lily slid inside the cab. Disappointment caused her shoulders to droop and her head to hang so low that her chin rested against the bright-red collar of her gown. She was more tired than she could remember having been in a long time. Of all the men in the world, she trusted Jake the most. More than her father. But then it was difficult to have too much confidence in a vague childhood memory. Lily's father had died when she was twelve, but she had trouble picturing him in her mind. As far as Lily could recall, she'd only seen her father a handful of times. In some ways Lily wished she didn't trust Jake so much; it would make things a whole lot easier.

Jake closed her door, his hands gripping the open window as he watched her through weary eyes. For half a second, he toyed with the idea of releasing her from the promise. But he entertained the idea only fleetingly. He knew better.

"Can you take me home now?"

"Sure." He hurried around the cab and climbed into the front seat beside her. A flick of the key and the engine purred. "You won't regret this," Jake said, flashing her one of his most brilliant smiles.

"I regret it already," she said and stared out the side window.

Those thoughtless words hounded Lily for the remainder of the evening. Jake was her friend—her best friend—and she was treating him like the tax man. Usually, at the end of the evening Jake would stop by the house on his way back to the dock where his sail-boat was moored. But he didn't show up, although Lily waited half the night. She didn't blame him. They'd hardly said a word on the way home and when he pulled to the curb in front of Gram's rickety old house, Lily had practically jumped out of the taxi. She hadn't even bothered to say good-night.

The following morning Lily was wakened by Gram singing an African chant. Tossing aside the covers, Lily leaped from the bed and rushed into the kitchen. Gram only sang in Swahili when things were look-ing up.

"Gram, what happened?" she asked excitedly, rub-bing the sleep from her eyes. Two steps into the large central kitchen and Lily discovered Gram clothed in full African dress. Yard upon yard of bold chartreuse printed fabric was draped around her waist with deep folds falling halfway to the floor. The shirt was made of matching material and hung from her shoulders, falling in large bell sleeves. Wisps of bright-red hair escaped the turban that was wrapped around her head. Ten thin gold bracelets dangled like charms from each wrist.

"Gram." Lily stopped cold, not knowing what to think.

The older woman made a dignified bow and hugged Lily fiercely. *"Nzuri sana,"* she greeted her, ceremoni-ously kissing her granddaughter on the cheek.

Lily was too bemused to react. *"Nzuri sana,"* she returned, slowly sinking into a kitchen chair. Her grandmother might behave a bit oddly on occasion, but nothing like this.

Continuing to chant in low tones, Gram turned and pulled a hundred-dollar bill from the folds of her outfit and waved it under Lily's nose.

"Gram, where did you get that?" All kinds of anxious thoughts were going through her mind. Maybe Gram was so worried over their finances that she'd done something illegal.

Hips swaying, Gram crossed the room and chuckled. The unmusical sound echoed against the walls. "Bingo," she cried, and removed four more hundred-dollar bills.

"You won at bingo!" Lily cried, jumping up from the chair and dancing around the room. Their arms circled each other's waists and they skipped around the kitchen like schoolgirls until Lily was breathless and dizzy.

"You buy yourself something special," Gram insisted when they'd settled down. "Something alluring so those rich men at the Wheaton won't be able to take their eyes off you."

Lily did her utmost to comply. She left the house and spent the rest of the morning shopping. Half the day was gone by the time she'd located the perfect outfit. It was a silky black dress with a fitted bodice that dipped provocatively in the front, granting a glimpse of cleavage and hinting at the fullness of her breasts. Studying herself in the mirror, Lily turned sideways, one hand on her hips, and rested her chin on her shoulder as she pouted her lips. It was perfect. After paying for the dress, Lily hurried home. She rushed up to her bedroom and donned her new purchase, eying her reflection in the mirror. Jake would tell her if the dress had the desired effect. Besides, she owed him an apology.

His boat was in the slip at the marina when she arrived at the marina a short time later. Lily had never visited him without an invitation and felt uneasy about doing so now.

"Jake," she called from the dock. "Are you there?" The boards rolled slightly under her heels and Lily had to brace herself. "Jake," she repeated louder, hugging the full-length coat close to her.

"Coming." His tone sounded irritated and he was frowning as he stuck his head out from below deck. He stopped when he saw it was Lily and smoothed a hand through his thick hair. "Hi." Slowly he came topside. "What are you doing here? And why in heaven's name are you wearing that ridiculous coat?"

Lily glanced down over the long wool garment that had once belonged to Gram and felt all the more silly. "Gram won five hundred dollars at bingo last night. I bought a new dress and want your opinion on it. Can I come aboard?"

"Sure." Jake didn't sound nearly as eager as she'd hoped he would.

She lifted the gray wool coat from her shoulders and let it slip down her arms. "What do you think?" she asked. "Be honest, now."

One glance at Lily in that beautiful dress, and Jake could barely take his eyes off her. She looked sensational—a knockout.

"I...I didn't know if you'd want to see me," she continued.

"Why wouldn't I?" His answer was guarded, his words quiet. Still he couldn't take his eyes from her.

"I feel terrible about yesterday."

"It's no problem." He reached out his hand in silent invitation for her to join him and Lily deftly crossed the rough wooden dock to his polished deck.

"Gram insisted I buy something new. How do you like it?"

"I like it fine," he murmured, doing his best to avoid eye contact. "You look great, actually." That had to be the understatement of the century.

"Do you honestly think so?" she asked excitedly.

Jake smiled. "You look really nice."

"That's sweet," she said softly. "Thank you."

"Think nothing of it." With a sweep of his arm, he invited her below. "Do you want a cup of coffee?"

"Sure." She paused to remove her shoes and handed them to Jake. "Would you put these someplace where I won't forget them?"

"No problem." He went down before her and waited at the base of the steps in case she needed help. One bare foot appeared on the top rung of the ladder and the side split in the skirt revealed the ivory skin of her thigh as the next foot descended. Jake felt his heart constrict. He sighed with relief as she reached the bottom rung and turned around to face him, eyes sparkling. "I'll get you a cup," he announced, disliking the close confines of his cabin for the first time. Lily seemed to fill up every inch of available space, looming over him with that alluring scent of hers.

"How's the writing going?"

"Good." It wasn't. Actually he'd faced writer's block all day, and determined that it was Lily's fault. He didn't like what was happening between them and yet seemed powerless to stop it.

"Heard any more from Rex?"

"No." Lily slid into the tight booth that served as a seat around the kitchen table. "I won't see him again," she told him. "I promised you I wouldn't."

"Someone else will come along." And soon, he hoped. The quicker Lily found herself a sugar daddy, the better it would be for him.

"I know." She smiled up at him briefly as he set the mug on the table.

He didn't join her, fearing that if he slid into the seat beside her, they might accidentally brush against one another. And touching Lily while she looked so tempting in that dress shook Jake. It would be the attic all over again and he knew he wouldn't be able to stop himself. As it was now, he could barely tear his eyes from her. She lifted her mug and blew against the edge before taking a sip. Her dewy lips drew his gaze like a magnet. Jake turned around and added some sugar to his coffee.

"I didn't know you used sugar."

"I don't," he said, turning back to her.

"You just dumped three tablespoons into your cup." She sounded as perplexed as he felt.

Jake lifted one shoulder in a halfhearted shrug. "It must be something in the air."

"Must be," Lily agreed, not knowing what he was talking about. She dropped her gaze to the dark, steaming liquid. "I've been thinking that I need lessons on how to flirt."

Jake nearly choked on his coffee and did an admirable job of containing himself. Lily was so unconsciously alluring, that he couldn't believe that any man could ignore her.

"Will you teach me, Jake?" There wasn't anyone she trusted more. Jake had been all over the world and done everything she hadn't. Lily didn't think there was a thing he didn't know. With that, he did choke on a mouthful of coffee. "Me?"

"Yes, you."

"Lily, come on. I don't know anything about feminine stuff like that."

"Sure you do," she contradicted, warming to her subject. "Every time I bat my eyelashes at a man, I'm convinced he thinks I've got a nerve disease."

"Ask Gram."

"I can't do that." She waved her hand dismissively. "Just tell me what Elaine did that made you go all weak inside."

" I don't remember."

"Something like this?" She dropped her eyes and parted her lips, giving him her most sultry look.

Jake experienced a tenderness unlike anything he'd ever known. He couldn't teach her to flirt. She was a natural. "Yeah," he murmured at last.

Discouraged, Lily straightened. Elaine had known exactly what to do to make a man notice her. For months, Jake had been so crazy over the other woman that he'd hardly ever come by for a visit. It had shocked Lily when they'd split. Maybe Jake wasn't the best person to teach her what she needed to know. But she knew he wasn't immune to a woman's wiles. The problem was he thought of her as a sister. She could probably turn up on his dock naked and he'd barely notice.

"Forget it," she mumbled. "I'll ask Gram."

Three

Jake paced the small confines of his galley like a man trapped in an obligatory telephone conversation. He had to do something, and fast. Roughly he combed his fingers through his hair and caught his breath. Lily was beginning to look good to him. Real good. And that was trouble with a capital *T*. Either he found himself a woman, and quick, or…or he'd take it upon himself to find Lily a wealthy man. Both appeared formidable tasks.

If he involved himself in another relationship, it would surely end in disaster. No woman would be satisfied with his carefree lifestyle. Every woman he'd known, with the exception of Lily, had taken it upon herself to try to "save" him. The problem was, Jake didn't want to be redeemed by a woman's ambitions.

But locating a rich man for Lily wouldn't be easy either. It wasn't as if he traveled in elite circles. He had a few contacts—buddies from school—but he didn't know anyone who perfectly fit the wealthy profile Lily was after.

The only potential option was Rick, his friend from college days. From everything Jake had heard, Rick had done well for himself and was living in San Francisco. It wouldn't hurt to look him up and see if he was still single. Jake didn't like the idea, but it couldn't be helped.

Humming softly, Lily smiled at the doorman at the Wheaton and sauntered into the posh hotel as if she owned it. She was practicing for the time when she could enter a public place and cause faces to turn and whispers to fill the air. Lily felt good. The meeting with Jake hadn't turned out to be the confrontation she'd expected. Jake had every reason to be angry with her, and wasn't. If anything he'd behaved a bit weirdly. He'd seemed to go out of his way to be distant. When she was on one side of the boat, he'd stand on the other. He'd avoided eye contact as though he were guilty of something. The large bouquet of red roses on the piano was a nice surprise. A small white envelope propped against the ivory keys caused her eyes to widen, and her heart to do a tiny flip-flop. Lily knew without looking that Rex had sent the flowers. Her hands trembled noticeably as she removed the card and read the bold handwriting:

Sorry you couldn't make it, little filly. I'll see you next month on the 25th at nine.

Lily swallowed a nervous lump that clogged her throat. Next month or next year; it wouldn't make any difference. She'd given Jake her word and she wouldn't go back on it no matter how tempting. And tempting it was. Rex was interested. He must be, to send her the flowers and ask her out again.

With a heavy heart, Lily pulled out the piano bench and sat, her hands poised over the pearly keys before starting in on the same old songs.

As usual, Jake was waiting for her at the end of her shift. His gaze focused on the roses and narrowed fractionally.

"Daddy Warbucks?"

"Yeah." Lily didn't know why she felt so guilty, but she did. This was the first time in her life that anyone had sent her roses and she wasn't about to leave them at the Wheaton. "He's gone."

Jake felt a surge of relief wash over him. He wished that he felt differently about that Texan. It would have been the end of his troubles. Lily could have her rich man and he could go about his life without complications.

"He left a note with the roses, asking me out next month. Apparently he'll be back in town then."

"Are you going?"

The muscles at the side of her mouth ached as Lily compressed her lips into a tight line. "No."

"Good."

Maybe it was good for Jake, but Lily was miserable.

"Will I see you later?" she asked when he dropped her off in front of Gram's house.

"I'll be by."

Even with all his hang-ups about personal freedom and restricting schedules, Lily knew that if Jake said he'd be someplace, he'd be there eventually. Purposely waiting up for him, she sat watching the late-

late show dressed in a worn terry-cloth housecoat that was tightly cinched at the waist. In an effort to stay awake, she sipped Marmite, a yeast extract, which had been stirred into hot water. Years ago while traveling in New Zealand, Gram had had her first taste of the thick, chocolate-like substance and she had grown to love it. She received the product on a regular basis from family friends now and spread it lightly over her morning toast. Lily preferred the dark extract diluted.

The movie was an old Gary Cooper one that had been filmed in the late nineteen fifties. Soon Lily was immersed in the characters and the plot and loudly blew her nose to hold back tears at a tender scene. A light knock against the front door announced Jake's arrival. She opened the door, waved him inside and sniffled as he took the seat opposite her.

Jake eyed her curiously. "You sick?"

Lily sucked in a wobbly breath and pointed to the television screen with her index finger. "No…Gary Cooper's going to be killed in a couple of minutes and I hate to see him die."

Jake scooted forward in the thickly cushioned chair and linked his hands. "I talked to an old friend today."

Lily's eyes didn't leave the black-and-white picture tube. "That's nice."

"Rick's a downtown attorney and has made quite a name for himself in the past few years."

Lily didn't know why Jake found it so important to tell her about his friend in the middle of the best scene of the movie.

Jake hated it when Lily ignored him. He couldn't imagine how she could be so engrossed in a film that made her weep like a two-year-old. "Lily," he demanded, "would you listen to me?"

"In a minute," she sobbed, wrapping a handkerchief around her nose and blowing. Tears streamed down her cheeks and she wiped them aside with the back of her hand.

Knowing that there wasn't anything he could do but wait, Jake settled back in the upholstered chair that had once belonged to a Zulu king and impatiently crossed his arms over his chest. He had terrific news to share—and she found it more important to cry over Gary Cooper than to listen to him. Ten minutes later, Lily grabbed the remote and turned off the TV. "That's a great movie."

"You cried through the whole thing," Jake admonished.

"I always cry during a Gary Cooper movie," she shot back. "You should know that by now."

Rather than argue, Jake resumed his earlier position and leaned forward in the chair toward her. "As I was saying…"

"Do you want a cup of Marmite?" Remembering her manners, Lily felt guilty about being such a poor hostess. Gram had taught her better than this.

"What I want," Jake said with forced patience, "is for you to sit down and listen to me."

Meekly lowering herself to the sofa, Lily politely folded her hands in her lap and looked at Jake expectantly. "I'm ready."

"It's about time," he muttered.

"Well. I'm waiting." Sometimes it took Jake hours to get to the point. Not that he did a lot of talking. He'd say a few words here and there and she was expected to get the gist. The problem was, Lily rarely did and he'd end up staring at her as if her head were full of holes.

"I saw Rick—my lawyer friend—this afternoon."

"The one from school?"

"Right. Anyway, Rick has become a regular socialite in the past few years and he's invited me to a cocktail party he's having Saturday night."

Lily blinked twice. She wouldn't have thought Jake would be so enthusiastic about a bunch of people standing around holding drinks and exchanging polite inanities. "That's interesting." She tried to hide a yawn and didn't succeed. Belatedly she cupped her mouth and expelled a long whiney breath.

Jake's face fell into an impatient frown. He didn't usually look that way until he was five minutes into his monologue.

"I thought you'd be thrilled," he murmured. It hadn't been easy to reach out to Rick—Mr. Success—and strike up a conversation after so many years.

"To be perfectly honest, I wouldn't have believed you'd enjoy a cocktail party."

"I won't. I'm doing it for you."

"For me?"

"There are bound to be a lot of rich men there, Lily. Undoubtedly some of them will be single and on the lookout for an attractive woman."

"What do you plan to do? Hand them my name and phone number?" she asked.

"You're going with me," he barked.

"Well, for heaven's sake, why didn't you say so?"

"Anyone with half a brain would have figured that

out. You should know that I wouldn't be willing do something like this without an ulterior reason."

They stood facing each other, not more than two feet apart. The air between them was so heavy that Lily expected to see arcs of electricity spark and flash. Jake's breathing was oddly raspy. But then hers wasn't any better. They shouldn't be arguing—they were friends. Neither of them moved. Lily couldn't stop looking at him. They were so close that she could see every line in his face, every groove, every pore. Even the hairs of his brows seemed overwhelmingly interesting. Her gaze located a faint scar on his jawline that she'd never noticed before and she wondered if this was a souvenir from Iraq. He'd told her little of his experiences there.

His eyes were greener tonight than she'd remembered. Green as jade, dark as night, alive and glittering with an emotion Lily couldn't read. His mouth was relaxed and slightly parted as if beckoning her, telling her that she must make the first move. Surely she'd misinterpreted him. Jake wouldn't want to kiss her. They were friends—nothing more. What had happened in the attic had been a moment out of time and place. Still not believing what she saw, Lily raised her gaze to his and their eyes met and clashed. Jake did want to kiss her. And even more astonishing was that she wanted it, too. "Lily." He breathed heavily and turned away from her, stalking to the opposite side of the room. "I think I will have something to drink after all."

"Marmite?"

"Sure—anything."

Lily was grateful that she had something to occupy her hands and her mind. Jake didn't follow her into the kitchen, and she needed to have time to compose her thoughts. Good grief, what was happening to them? After all these months there wasn't any logical explanation why they should suddenly be physically attracted to each other. Something must be in the air—but spring was nine months away. A laugh hovered on her lips as she pictured tiny neon lights that flashed on and off across her forehead, telling Jake: *Kiss Lily.* But Lily knew it wasn't right. Jake was wonderful, but he wasn't the man for her. Thank heaven he'd had enough sense to turn away when he did.

Lily carried a steaming cup into the living room and carefully handed it to him. She wasn't so much afraid of being burned by the near-boiling water as she was fearful of her reaction if she touched him.

"I want you to attend that party with me." Jake picked up the conversation easily, pretending nothing had happened. Even though it was obvious they'd been a hair's breadth from hungrily falling into each other's arms.

"Saturday?" Her mind filled with niggling thoughts. She was scheduled to work, but she would be free at nine; she could wear her new dress. No, that was a bit too daring for a first meeting.

"Do you or don't you want to go?" Jake still hadn't taken a sip of his Marmite.

"Sure. I'll be happy to attend. Thanks for thinking of me." That sounded so stilted, Lily instantly wanted to grab back the words and tell him how pleased she was that he'd thought of her and was willing to help her out.

"I'll see you Saturday, then."

"Saturday," she echoed, and watched as Jake set aside his untouched drink and walked out of the house.

Lily didn't see Jake for two days. That wasn't as unusual as it was unsettling. It was almost as if they were afraid to see each other again.

During that time, Lily thought about Jake. She didn't know what was happening, but it had to stop. Jake was the antithesis of everything she wanted in a man. He had no real ambitions and was perfectly content to live out his days aboard his sailboat, doing nothing more than write short stories that didn't pay. Usually he received three free copies of the publication in compensation for his hundred hours of sweat and toil. Sometimes Lily wondered why Jake wrote when each word seemed so painful for him. Jake was a paradoxical sort of person. He hid behind his computer screen and revealed his soul in heart-wrenching stories no one would ever read.

While Jake was perfectly content with his life, Lily desperately wanted to improve hers. She longed to explore the world, to travel overseas and dine in the shadow of the Eiffel Tower. She yearned to see China and lazily soak up the sun on a South Pacific island. And she didn't want to ever agonize over a price tag again. Bargain basements and secondhand stores would be forever behind her. But most of all, Lily never wanted to hear "Moon River" again.

* * *

On Saturday evening Lily dressed carefully. Her dark curls were swirled high on her head and held in place with combs her father had brought her from India when she was twelve. He'd died shortly afterward and Lily had treasured this last gift, wearing them only on the most special occasions. At the end of her shift, with the thirty-ninth rendition of "Moon River" ringing in her ears, Lily stepped out of the hotel, expecting Jake to meet her. She didn't see him, and for half a second, panic filled her.

"Lily," Jake said, stepping forward.

Lily blinked and placed her hand over her heart at the sight of the tall, handsome man who stood directly in front of her. She squinted, sure she was seeing things. "Jake, is that you?"

"Who else were you expecting? Prince Charming?"

"You're wearing a suit!" A gray one that could have been lifted directly from the pages of *Gentlemen's Quarterly*, Lily realized in bemusement. The simple, understated color was perfect for Jake, emphasizing his broad shoulders and muscular build. "You look… wonderful!"

Jake ran his finger along the inside of his collar as if he needed the extra room to breathe properly. "I don't feel that way."

"But why?" She'd never seen Jake in anything dressier than slacks and a fisherman's bulky-knit sweater.

" I don't know. But knowing Rick, this party is bound to be an elaborate affair and it's best to dress the part."

Lily could hardly take her eyes from him. He looked dashing. Her gaze dropped to her own much-worn dress. "Am I overdressed? Underdressed? I don't want to give the wrong impression." Her insecurities dulled the deep brilliance of her eyes.

Jake glanced at her and shrugged. "You look all right."

All right? She'd spent half the day getting ready, fussing over each minute detail. "I hope you know you're about as charming as the underside of a toad."

"Hey, if you want romance, try Hugh Jackman. I ain't your man."

"You're telling me!" she huffed.

"Are we going to this thing or not?" He held the taxi's passenger door open for her, but didn't wait until she was inside before walking around the front of the car.

The first ten minutes of the ride down Golden Gate Avenue past the Civic Center was spent in silence.

Lily felt obligated to ease the tension. Both were on edge. "I didn't know you owned a suit."

Jake's response was little short of a grunt. The expensive suit had been Elaine's idea. She was the one who'd insisted he needed some decent clothes. She had dragged him around town to several exclusive men's stores and fussed over him like a drone over a queen bee. He'd detested every second of it, but he'd been so crazy about her that he'd stood there like a stooge and done exactly as she dictated. His weak-mindedness shocked him now. In thinking over his short but fiery relationship with Elaine, Jake was dismayed by some of the things he'd allowed her to do to him. The last party he'd attended had been with Elaine. He'd sat back and listened as she introduced him to her phony friends, telling them that Jake owned his own company and lived on a yacht. To hear her tell it, Jake was a business tycoon. In reality, he owned one taxicab that he drove himself, and his "yacht" was a ten-year-old, twenty-seven-foot, single-mast, fore- and aft-rigged sailboat that most of Elaine's colleagues could have bought with their pocket change.

"Are you going to sit there and sulk all night?" Lily questioned, growing impatient.

"Men never sulk," Jake declared, feeling smug just as Rick's house came into view. Jake parked several yards away in the closest available space. His five-year-old Chevy looked incongruous on the same street with all the fancy foreign cars, so he patted his steering wheel affectionately as if to assure his taxi that it was as good as the rest of them.

Rick's house was an ostentatious colonial-style, with thick white pillars and a well-lit front entrance. Jake swallowed nervously. Old Rick had done well for himself, even better than Jake had assumed.

"It's lovely," Lily murmured, and sighed with humble appreciation. This was exactly the kind of home she longed to own someday—one with crystal chandeliers, Persian carpets and gold fixtures.

"Lovely if you like that sort of thing," Jake grumbled under his breath.

Lily liked it just fine. "Oh, but I do. Thank you, Jake."

The genuine emotion in her voice was a surprise

and he tore his gaze away from the house long enough to glance her way.

"I should have been more appreciative. I'd never thought I'd be able to attend something as wonderful as this. Oh, Jake, just think of all the wealthy men who'll be here."

"I'm thinking," he mumbled, pleased for the first time that he'd accepted Rick's invitation.

If Lily was impressed with the outside of the house, she was doubly so with the interior. She resisted the urge to run her hand over the polished mahogany woodwork and refused to marvel at the decor for too long. A maid perfunctorily accepted their coats at the front door and directed them toward a central room where drinks were being served.

"Jake, old buddy."

Lily felt Jake stiffen, but was proud of the way he disguised his uneasiness and shook hands with the short man with a receding hairline. Lily could easily picture the man as a successful attorney. She could see him pacing in front of the jury box and glancing acrimoniously toward the defendant.

"Rick," Jake said with a rare smile. "It's good to see you. Thanks for the invitation."

"Any time." Although he spoke to Jake, Rick's gaze rested on Lily. "Jake, introduce me to this sweet cream puff."

"Rick, Lily. Lily, Rick."

"I'm most pleased to make your acquaintance," Lily murmured demurely. "Jake has told me so much about you."

Briefly, Rick's enthralled gaze left Lily to glance at Jake. "Where did you find this jewel?"

Lily's gaze pleaded with Jake to not tell Rick the real story of Gram confronting the Wheaton manager in full witch doctor's costume, outraged over Lily's starting wages. "We met at the Wheaton," Jake explained and Lily reached for his hand, squeezing it as a means of thanking him.

"Are you visiting our fair city?" Rick directed the question to her.

"No, I play the piano there."

"A musician!" Rick exclaimed. "I imagine you're a woman of many talents."

Jake didn't know what Rick was implying, but he didn't like the sound of it. He bunched up his fist until he realized that Lily's fingers were linked with his and he forced his hand to relax.

"Only a few talents, I fear," Lily answered with such self-possession that Jake wanted to kiss her. "But enough to impress my friends."

"Then I'd consider it an honor to be your friend."

Lily batted her lashes. "Perhaps."

From the way Rick's eyes widened, Jake knew that Lily had impressed his old friend. A surge of pride filled Jake and he struggled not to put his arm around Lily's shoulders.

Rick reached out to take Lily's hand. "Do you mind if I steal your girl away for a few minutes?"

Jake did mind, but this was exactly why he'd brought Lily to the party. She would make more contacts here than she would during a year of playing piano at the Wheaton. "Feel free," he murmured, lifting a glass of champagne from the tray of the passing server. He didn't watch as Lily and Rick crossed the room, Lily's arm tucked securely in the crook of Rick's elbow.

The bubbling liquid in the narrow crystal glass seemed to be laughing at him and, almost angrily, Jake set it aside. He hated champagne and always had. He much preferred a hearty burgundy with some soul to it. He found an obscure corner and sat down, giving anyone who approached him a look that would discourage even the most outgoing party guest. He could hear Lily's laugh drift from another section of the house and was pleased she was enjoying herself. At least one of them was having a decent time.

Another waiter came past and Jake ordered Ouzo, a Greek drink. Gram had given him his first taste of the anise-flavored liqueur she drank regularly. Lily claimed it had made her teeth go soft, and to be honest, the licorice-tasting alcohol had curled a few of Jake's chest hairs. But he was in the mood for it tonight—something potent to remind himself that he was doing the noble thing. Now he knew how Joan of Arc must have felt as she was tied to the stake and the torches were aimed at the dry straw. No, he was being melodramatic again. What did it matter? He'd known all along that he was going to lose *his* Lily. But Lily wasn't his; had never been his. He drank down the liqueur with one swallow and felt it sear a path to his stomach. Lily was his good friend. He'd do anything for her and Gram—well, almost anything.

Jake asked for another Ouzo and drank it down with the same eagerness as the first. Another followed shortly after that. His eyes found a woman sitting on the sofa on the other side of the room, and she smiled. Hey, Jake mused, maybe this party wasn't such a loss after all. Maybe Lily wasn't the only one destined to have a good time.

He stood, surprised that a house as expensive as Rick's had a floor that swayed like a ship at sea. Suavely, he tucked one hand in his pants pocket and paused to smooth the hair along the side of his head. There wasn't any need to look like a slob.

Just when he was prepared to introduce himself to Goldilocks across the way, he heard the piano and stopped cold. "Moon River." Oh no. Rick had convinced Lily to entertain him. Jake knew how she felt about that song. Rick couldn't do that to Lily. Jake wouldn't let him. Rushing forward, he raised his hand and started to say something when the floor suddenly, unexpectedly, came rushing up to meet him.

Four

Holding a small bouquet of flowers, Lily traipsed through the hospital lobby to the open elevator, stepped inside and pushed the button for the appropriate floor. She'd worried about Jake all night. He'd looked so pale against the starched white hospital sheets. Pale and confused. Lily should never have left his side, but Rick had convinced her that there wasn't any more either of them could do. Jake had been given a shot and would soon be asleep. Nonetheless, Lily had lingered outside the hall until the shot took effect, then reluctantly left.

When the heavy metal doors of the elevator parted, Lily stepped out eagerly. She had so much to tell Jake. He'd been such a dear to have taken her to the party. Everything had turned out beautifully—except for his fall, of course. Lily had met several men, all of whom had an aura of wealth. She prided herself on her ability to recognize money when she saw it. Rick had insisted on buying her a new dress since the one she'd worn to the party had gotten stained. But Lily had adamantly refused. The dress wasn't ruined. Gram had used vinegar and a few other inventively chosen ingredients to remove Jake's blood.

Lily stepped past the nurse's station and headed down the wide hall to Jake's room. The faint smell of antiseptic caused her to wrinkle her nose. Jake would be glad to get out of there.

The door to his room was open and Lily paused in the doorframe, looking at the nurse's aide who was stripping the bed of the sheets and blankets. Troubled, Lily's gaze slid to the number printed on the door for a second time to be sure she had the right room.

"Good morning," Lily murmured.

"Morning," the other woman answered flatly. "Is there something I can do for you?"

"Do you know where Jake Carson is?"

"Mr. Carson signed himself out early this morning."

Lily swallowed to relieve her voice of its shock and surprise. "Signed himself out? But why?"

"I believe Mr. Carson had several reasons, all of which were described in colorful detail."

"Oh, dear." Lily was shocked to realize she'd spoken out loud.

"I'm afraid so. He also insisted on paying his own tab and wanted the bill brought to him immediately." Impatiently, the woman jerked the bottom sheet from the raised hospital bed. "I've seen a few stubborn men in my day, but that one takes the cake."

It didn't take much imagination for Lily to picture the scene. Jake could be a terror when he wanted to be, and from the frustrated look on the nurse's flushed face, Jake had outdone himself this time. Lily was all the more convinced that she shouldn't have left him.

She shouldn't have listened to Rick. Next time, she'd follow her instincts.

"Did he say where he was going?" Lily pressed.

The woman hugged the sheet to her abdomen and slowly shook her head. "No, but I'm sure the staff could give you a few suggestions about where we'd like to see him."

"I am sorry." Lily felt obliged to apologize for Jake, although she was convinced he wouldn't appreciate it. "I'm sure he didn't mean…whatever it was he said."

"He meant it," the woman growled, placing the sheet with unnecessary force inside a laundry cart at her side.

"Well, thank you, anyway," Lily stammered. "And here…" She shoved the small bouquet of daisies into the woman's hands. "Please take these." With that, Lily turned and hurried from the room.

By the time she arrived back at Gram's, Lily was more worried than before. "Gram, Jake's left the hospital."

Gram stood at the ironing board, pressing dried flowers between sheets of waxed paper. "I know."

"You know!"

"Why yes. He called earlier."

"Where is he?" Lily demanded, the wobble in her voice betraying her concern. "He shouldn't be alone… not with a head injury."

"He sounded perfectly fine," Gram contradicted, moving from the iron to the stove where she stirred the contents of a large stockpot.

"Is he at the marina? I should probably go there, don't you think? Something could happen." Not waiting for a response, Lily made a sharp about-face and headed out of the kitchen. For a panicked second, she imagined a dizzy, disoriented Jake stumbling about the sailboat. He could slip and fall overboard and no one would know.

"It'd be a waste of time."

"A waste of time? Why?" Lily paused and turned around to face Gram, her thoughts scrambled.

Humming an old Beatles tune, Gram continued stirring. "Jake's on his way over here."

"Now?"

"That's what he said."

"Why didn't you tell me that earlier?" Lily cried.

Gram turned away from the stove and studied Lily with narrowed, knowing eyes. "You seem worried, girl. Jake can take care of himself."

"I know…but he's lost a lot of blood. He had ten stitches and…"

"He's not going to appreciate it if you make a fuss over him."

Lily forced the tense muscles in her back and shoulders to relax. Gram was right. Jake would hate how concerned she was.

"What else did he say?" Trying to disguise how disquieting Lily found this entire matter, she pushed the kitchen chair under the table.

"Do you want some split-pea soup?" Gram asked as though she hadn't heard Lily's question.

"No, thanks." An involuntary grimace crossed her face. Gram loved split-pea soup, but Lily didn't know why she would be eating it in the middle of the morning.

A loud knock against the front door announced

Jake's arrival. Lily battled the urge to run across the room to meet him.

Jake let himself inside. "Morning."

"Hello, Jake." Lily laced her fingers in front of her. "How are you feeling?"

"Great," he answered, breezing right past her and into the kitchen.

"Soup's ready," Lily heard her grandmother tell him.

"I appreciate it, Gram."

"When it comes to restoring a person's health, it's better than chicken noodle."

"Anything you cook is better than my futile attempts."

Shocked and a little hurt at Jake's abrupt greeting, Lily stood stiffly, halfway between the kitchen and the front door. Jake may have said only one word to her, but his eyes spoke volumes. Over the past year they'd often informed her of what he was thinking and feeling before he could say a word. They were a stormy shade of jade when he was angry, and that seemed to be happening on a regular basis lately. At other times they were a murky green, but that was generally when he was troubled about something. Then there were rare times when they sparked with what seemed a thousand tiny lights. They'd glittered like that when he'd first seen her in the dress she'd bought with Gram's bingo winnings and again later, when they'd met before Rick's party. But then they'd quickly changed to that murky shade of green. Lily didn't know what to make of that. Jake had been so easy to read in the past, but either he was changing or she was losing her ability to understand the one man she thought she knew so well.

"How are you feeling?" Lily asked for the second time, coming into the kitchen.

Jake pulled out a chair at the table, and sat drinking Gram's soup from a ceramic mug.

"Fine," he answered curtly.

"You look better." Some color had returned to his face. Yet he remained so pale that the tiny creases around his eyes were more noticeable than ever.

Gram joined Jake at the table, pouring two additional servings of soup.

"Here." She gave one to Lily who wrinkled her nose at it.

"No thanks, I prefer chicken noodle."

Jake's snort was almost imperceptible. "I'll be ready in a minute here," he added.

Lily glanced at Gram, who appeared oblivious to the comment. "Ready for what?" Lily inquired.

"Shopping."

"You're going shopping?" Good grief, he'd just been released from the hospital. "Whatever for?" If he needed anything, she'd be happy to make the trip for him.

"We're going out."

"Us?"

Jake caught Gram's eye. "You didn't tell her?"

"I didn't get a chance."

"Tell me!" Lily demanded, not liking the way Jake was ignoring her.

"Jake's taking you out to buy you a new dress," Gram informed her.

"The dress is fine," Lily protested loudly. "Didn't you tell him that?"

"I did," Gram huffed. "But he insists."

Jake's gaze bounced from Gram to Lily and back again. "Did you tell Lily that it won't do any good to argue with me on this one? I saw what I did to her dress. I'm buying her another one and that's all there is to it."

Lily sank into the chair across from Jake and boldly met his gaze. "In case you hadn't noticed, I'm standing right here. There's no need to ask Gram to tell me anything when you and I are separated by less than two feet." The words came out sharp and argumentative despite her effort to sound casual.

"If you insist." Gram chuckled. "You two remind me of Paddy and me."

Paddy was Lily's grandfather. He'd died several years before Lily was born, but the tales Gram told about him were very telling of the deep love and commitment her grandparents had shared. Lily hoped to find the same deep and lasting love with her own husband.

"You ready?" Jake asked, standing.

Lily looked at Gram for support, then back to Jake. "I hate to have you spend money on me. It isn't necessary."

"Would you like it better if Rick bought you a dress? Is that it?"

"Of course not." She hardly knew Rick and didn't want him buying her clothes.

"Then let's get this over and done with." He was halfway across the living room before Lily moved.

"Gram, what's wrong with Jake? He's not himself."

Gram shook her pin-curled head and laughed. "I can't say I rightly know, but I have my suspicions."

With Jake marching ahead, Lily had little choice but to follow him. He was sitting in the driver's seat of his taxi and glaring impatiently toward Lily as she came down the front steps.

"How'd you get your cab back?" she asked, opening the car door. They'd left it parked in front of Rick's house and Lily had wondered if Jake wanted her and Gram to pick it up for him. That was one of the things she'd planned to ask him that morning at the hospital.

"I have my ways," he grumbled, checking the sideview mirror before pulling onto the street. A heavy pause followed. "Did you have a good time last night?"

The question repeated in Lily's mind. Had she? Yes and no. The evening had been one she'd dreamed about for years. She'd met several interesting men who might be worth her time. Rick had been a gentleman, kind and considerate and genuinely concerned when Jake had fallen. He'd taken charge immediately and knew exactly what to do. Lily had been surprised at her own response to Jake's injury. She'd fallen to pieces, and Rick had been there to lend his support. "Hello? Earth to Lily," Jake said. "Did you or did you not have a good time?"

"The evening was grand. Thank you, Jake, for inviting me."

"Did you meet someone?" Anticipating her answer, his grip tightened around the steering wheel. He wanted Lily to assure him that she had found the rich man of her dreams. But in the same breath, he wanted her to tell him she'd found no one.

"Not really."

"What about Rick?"

"He was very nice."

The corner of Jake's mouth curved up sarcastically. Her word choice was comforting. "Anyone else?"

"Not really. A couple of others said they planned to visit the Wheaton to hear me play, but I don't think they'll show."

"Who?" Jake demanded.

Lily lifted one shoulder in a delicate shrug, surprised that Jake would sound angry when meeting eligible wealthy men was the reason he'd taken her to the party. "I don't remember their names."

"If they do come, I want to know about it so I can have them checked out." He was eager to know for other reasons as well—ones that weren't clearly defined in his mind. He wanted Lily married and happy and he wished to heaven that he could forget the taste of her. Every time he looked at her, he had trouble not kissing her again. He'd received a head injury, Jake told himself. One that was apparently affecting his reasoning ability. He shouldn't be thinking of Lily in that way. His only option was to set her up with Rick or one of the others—and quickly.

"Jake," Lily said softly.

"Yes?" He swallowed hard.

"Why are you insisting on buying me a dress?"

"What's the matter? Do you think Rick could afford a better one?"

"Oh, Jake, of course not."

From the soft catch in her voice, Jake knew he'd hurt her to even imply such a thing. "It's a matter of pride," he explained. "You told me Rick wanted to replace the one I ruined. My blood stained it, so I should be the one to buy you another dress."

"But Gram got the stain out."

"It doesn't matter."

"But…"

"I'm buying you the dress. Understand?"

She didn't answer.

"Understand?" he repeated forcefully.

"Repeaters is off Thirty-second."

"What?"

"The secondhand store where I usually buy my dresses." It took all of her willpower to give in to his pride. Jake had always been so reasonable, but his harsh tone told Lily she'd best concede gracefully. Either Jake would go with her or he'd buy something for her on his own.

"I'm not getting you anything secondhand."

"All right," she agreed reluctantly. "Either Sears or Penney's is fine."

"We're going to Neiman-Marcus."

"Neiman-Marcus, Jake!" Lily's jaw fell open. Jake couldn't afford to shop there.

The announcement was as much of a shock to Jake as it was to Lily. He'd driven toward downtown, thinking they'd figure out where to shop once he'd found parking. But now that he'd spoken the words, he wouldn't back down. If he was going to buy Lily a dress, it would be one she'd remember all her life.

"I saw a dress I liked on display in Penney's." Her

hands felt clammy just at the thought of spending all Jake's money on some silly dress. He worked too hard and saved so little.

"And I saw one at Neiman-Marcus," Jake countered. "You're always talking about how you want to shop there someday. I'm giving you the chance."

A hundred arguments crossed her mind as they parked and Jake escorted her through the elite department store.

"Jake," Lily pleaded.

"And nothing on sale." Jake paused in front of a mannequin. "Nice," he said to no one in particular.

"It should be," Lily informed him stiffly, reading the price tag. "This little piece of chiffon is fifteen hundred dollars."

It demanded all of his discipline for Jake to bite his tongue. Fifteen hundred dollars for a dress? He had no idea. He hesitated a second longer. "So?"

"Jake, honestly, fifteen hundred dollars would wipe you out." Lily was growing more uneasy by the minute. This whole idea was ridiculous. Pride or not, Jake had no business buying her clothes. Not here.

"May I help you?" An attentive salesclerk approached them.

"Yes," Jake insisted.

"No," Lily countered.

"Perhaps if I came back in a few minutes." The salesclerk took a step in retreat.

"My friend here would like to try on this dress," Jake said, lifting the hem of the pricey dress on the mannequin.

"Jake," Lily hissed under her breath.

"And a few more just like this," Jake continued.

The clerk gave a polite nod. "If you'll come this way."

Jake's hand on the small of Lily's back urged her forward.

"Do you have any color in mind?"

"Midnight blue, red, and maybe something white." The choices came off the top of his head. Once, a long time back, it had occurred to him that with Lily's dark hair she'd look like an angel in white.

"I have just the thing." The clerk motioned toward the dressing rooms on the other side of the spacious floor.

Like a small duckling marching after its mother, Lily walked behind the salesclerk through rows and rows of expensive dresses.

Sitting in a deep, cushioned chair outside the dressing room, Jake leaned against the padded back and crossed his legs, playing the part of a generous benefactor. This was just the type of thing Rick would relish. Jake had recognized the look in Rick's eyes the minute he laid eyes on Lily. He'd wanted her. Jake knew the feeling. He'd wanted Elaine from the first minute he'd seen her; had lusted after her and been so thoroughly infatuated with her that he couldn't think straight. But Lily was different. She wasn't Elaine—knowledgeable in the ways of the world and practiced in controlling men. No, Lily was an innocent.

Changing positions, Jake uncrossed his legs and folded his arms over his chest. He didn't know what could be taking so long—or how he was going to pay for whichever dress Lily chose. But it would be worth it to salvage his pride.

"Jake," Lily whispered, coming out of the dressing room. She wore a deep-blue dress with a scalloped collar and short sleeves. "How do you like it?"

Jake watched her walk self-consciously in front of him. It was a dress, nothing special. "What do you think?" he asked.

"The saleslady called it Spun Sapphires."

"It has a name?"

"Yes." She inserted her hand inside the thin belt. "It's a little big around the waist."

"Then try on another."

Relieved, Lily returned to the dressing room. The dress was nice, but she hated the thought of Jake spending nine hundred dollars on it. As tactfully as possible, she asked the clerk to bring dresses that were in a lower price range. Eager to please, the woman returned with a variety in the colors Jake had requested. A white crepe frock with feminine tucks and simulated pearl embellishments caught her eye.

Jake felt a little too conspicuous as he sat and waited. Since Iraq he liked to think of himself as an island, an entity unto himself. His life was comfortable. He needed no one. There were no ties to the mainland, no bridges, no sandbars. Nothing. Elaine had been the first to tug him closer to the shore. And now Lily... Just when he wanted to cast thoughts of her from his mind, he glanced up to discover her standing in front of him. She was breathtakingly beautiful in a simple, white dress. He felt the air constrict in his lungs. Without realizing what he was doing, he slowly rose to his feet. Their eyes met for an instant before Lily turned away. Jake could hardly breathe, let alone speak. He'd never seen anyone more lovely.

"What's this one called?" He swallowed and held his breath, trying to slow his racing heart. The task was impossible. Lily was a vision; she was everything that Jake had ever wanted in a woman. His fingers ached with the need to trace her cheekbones and touch the fullness of her lips.

"It's called Angel's Breath," she said.

"We'll take it," Jake informed the salesclerk, without glancing her way. Tearing his eyes away from Lily was unthinkable. He wanted to hold the memory of her in his mind and carry it with him for the remainder of his days.

"But you don't even know how much it is," Lily objected.

"The price doesn't matter." Her nose was perfect, Jake decided, with a soft sprinkling of freckles across the narrow bridge. He adored every single one.

Jake paid the salesclerk while Lily changed back into her clothes. The woman smiled warmly at him as he signed the credit card receipt for three hundred and sixty-five dollars. On Lily it would have been a bargain at twice the price.

"That dress is gorgeous on your wife," the sales-clerk told him with a sincerity Jake couldn't doubt. It wasn't until they were at the car that Jake realized he hadn't corrected her. Not only was she not his wife, but he was doing everything he could to marry her off to a wealthy man so she could have everything she desired. When the time came, he'd let her go without regret. When the time came…but not today.

"Thank you, Jake," Lily told him once they were outside the store.

He looked down at her, captivated by the warmth of her smile. "Any time." He reached for her hand, linking their fingers. "Are you hungry?"

"Starved. But it's my turn to treat you. What would you like?"

"Food."

"That's what I love most about you," Lily teased. "You're so articulate." The word *love* echoed in the corners of her mind, sending a shaft of sensation racing through her to land in the pit of her stomach. They took the cable car down to Fisherman's Wharf and stood in line with hordes of tourists. Lily's favorite part of San Francisco was the waterfront. The air smelled of saltwater and deep-fried fish. The breeze off the bay was cool and refreshing. They ate their lunch on the sandy beach behind the Maritime Museum. Lily took off her sandals and stepped to the water's edge, teasing the tide and then retreating to Jake's side when the chilly water touched her toes. For his part, Jake leaned back against the sand and closed his eyes. Lily's musical laugh lulled him into a light slumber. He was content with his world, content to have Lily nearby. He thought about the characters in the short story he'd recently submitted to the *New Yorker*. Lily had claimed it was his best story yet and had encouraged him to dream big. Personally, Jake thought it was a waste of time but to appease her, he'd sent it to the prestigious publisher.

"Jake?"

"Hmm?"

Lily sat at his side, drawing up her legs so that her arms crossed her knees. "It's almost four."

"Already?" He sat up. The day had slipped past too quickly.

"You're not working tonight, are you?"

Lily hesitated. "No." Jake knew her schedule as well as she did.

"Good." He settled back on the sand, folding his arms behind his head. "I'm too relaxed to move."

"Me too," Lily said with a sigh and joined him, lying back in the sand. They were in such close proximity and Jake squeezed his eyes shut at the surge of emotion that burned through him at the merest brush of her leg against his. Slow, silent seconds ticked past, but Lily didn't move and Jake hadn't the will. The summer air felt heavy with unspoken thoughts and labored heartbeats. It demanded everything within Jake not to reach for Lily's hand. He felt so close to her. His heart groaned. Lily wasn't Lily to him anymore, but a beautiful, enticing woman. "Jake?"

He rolled his head to the side and their eyes met,. Her warm breath tickled his face. "Yes?"

"I've enjoyed today."

"Me, too."

"Can we do it again?"

Jake turned his head and stared into the clear blue sky. For a long minute he didn't say anything. He couldn't do this again and remain sane; having Lily this close and not touching her was the purest form of torture. But he could never be the man she wanted.

"I don't know." He would be doing them both a favor if he got out of her life and moved further down the coast. That was the nice thing about owning a sailboat and driving a taxi; he didn't have a string of responsibilities tying him down.

"You're right," Lily concurred. "It's probably not a good idea."

"Why?" Something perverse within him insisted that he ask.

"Well..." Lily hedged. "Just because."

"Right," he agreed. "Just because." Standing up, Jake wiped the granules of sand from his clothes. "I think I should take you home."

"You probably should." But Lily's tone lacked enthusiasm. The day had been charmed, a gift she had never expected to receive. "Gram will wonder about us."

"We might cool her wrath if we bring a peace offering," Jake suggested.

"What do you have in mind?"

"Chinese food."

"But, Jake..."

"Gram loves it."

"I know, but—"

"No buts."

They took the cable car back to where Jake had parked his taxi. Lily tried to talk to him twice on the way through Chinatown. Jake knew his way around, popping in and out of shops, greeting friends and exchanging pleasantries along the way, and all the while ignoring Lily.

"I didn't know you spoke Chinese," Lily commented, hurrying after him.

"Only a little." He didn't mention that half of everything he'd said had been an explanation about Lily.

"Not from what I heard."

"I'm a man of many talents," he joked, loading her arms with the brown paper sacks that contained their meal.

Again on the way home, Lily tried to talk to Jake, but he sang at the top of his lungs, infecting her with his good mood. Soon Lily's sweet voice joined his. At a stoplight, their smiling eyes met briefly and the song died on his lips. Without thinking, Jake leaned over and touched his lips to hers. His hand brushed the hair from her temple and lingered in the thick dark strands.

A blaring horn behind him rudely alerted Jake of the fact that the light had changed. Forcing himself to sing again, Jake stepped on the accelerator and sped ahead.

Lily had a more difficult time recovering from the casual kiss. Had that really just happened? It somehow felt so right to have Jake claim her lips as if he'd been doing it for a lifetime. His light touch left her longing for more.

When Jake glanced at her curiously out of the corner of his eye, she forced her voice to join his, but it wasn't the same and both of them knew it.

Jake eased to a stop in front of the house. Gram was standing on the front porch, her hands riding her round hips as she paced the small area. "It's about time you got home, girl. Rick called. He's on his way over."

Five

The sensation of dread went all the way through Jake. He'd known from the minute they entered Chinatown that Lily had been trying to talk to him. But in his stupidity, Jake feared that she was going to mention things he didn't want to discuss—mainly that something rare and special was happening between them. Such talk was best delayed and, if possible, ignored entirely.

"Rick's coming?" he questioned, turning to Lily and trying to disguise the raging battle that was going on inside him. Rick was better for Lily than he'd ever be. Rick could give her the world. But Jake didn't like it. Not one bit. There was something very wrong about spending the day with Lily and then watching her march off with Rick that evening. His gut instinct told him Rick was wrong for Lily, but he couldn't say anything without making a fool of himself. He'd been doing enough of that lately as it was.

"I tried to tell you earlier," she mumbled, feeling guilty. "I…we…Rick and I, that is, we're going to dinner…"

"No problem," Jake said, feigning a shrug of indifference. "Gram and I will have a good time without you." He walked ahead of Lily and took the older woman by the hand. "I guess you're stuck with me tonight."

"I'd consider it a privilege," Gram said with a smile.

Jake responded with one of his own. He led the way into the house, carrying the sacks of spicy Chinese food to the kitchen. If Lily wore the white dress he bought her, he didn't know what he'd do. She couldn't. Not after all they'd shared that day. Deep down, Jake knew she wouldn't do that to him.

Lily walked to her room with all the enthusiasm of someone going to the dentist for a root canal. She felt terrible. Everything had been so perfect today with Jake. When they'd stopped at the red light and Jake had kissed her, Lily had died a little. The kiss had felt so right—as though they were meant to be together forever. Only they weren't.

Taking her new dress from its box, Lily hung it in her closet. She wouldn't wear it for anyone but Jake. It was the most beautiful article of clothing she'd ever owned and she'd treasure it for the rest of her life.

After checking the contents of her meager closet, Lily chose a midi-length straight black skirt and matching top. She dressed hurriedly, then took a moment to freshen her makeup and run a brush through her tangled hair. She'd just finished when the doorbell chimed. A glance at her watch confirmed that he was right on time.

Gram was introducing herself to Rick when Lily appeared.

"Lily." Rick looked at her appreciatively and stepped toward her. Claiming both hands, he kissed her lightly on the cheek.

Lily had to resist wiping his touch from her face. She hadn't found it offensive, only wrong. It wasn't Jake who was kissing her and it felt unnatural. "Hello, Rick." Automatically, her gaze shifted to Jake, who had just emeged from the kitchen.

Rick's eyes followed hers. "Glad to hear you're okay after that fall, Carson."

"Yeah, thanks." Jake's reply was as abrupt as a shot.

"I'll be home early," Lily told Gram, hoping to avoid a confrontation between the two men.

Rick's hand curved around the back of Lily's neck. "But not too early."

At the front door, she turned to Jake. "Thank you for today."

He pretended not to hear her and strode back into the kitchen. He didn't like her going out with Rick, but he hadn't said a word.

"Jake doesn't mind you dating me, does he?" Rick asked when they reached his car. He drove a Mercedes convertible. Lily had often dreamed of riding in one with the top down and the wind whipping through her thick hair. Now that she was standing in front of one, she couldn't seem to muster the appropriate level of enthusiasm.

"No, he doesn't mind," she told Rick.

"I don't want to horn in on you two if you've got something going. But from what Jake said…"

"There's nothing between us," Lily said, fighting the heavy sadness that permeated her voice. "We're only friends." *And then some*, she added silently. But the *some* hadn't been defined.

"Did I tell you where we were going?" Rick asked next, politely opening the car door for her.

"No."

"The Canlis."

Her returning smile was weak. "Thanks. Sounds fantastic."

They arrived at the popular restaurant a half-hour later. From everything she'd read, Lily knew the Canlis was highly rated and extremely expensive. For the first time she'd have the opportunity to order almond-saffron soup. Funny, now that the time had arrived, she'd have given almost anything to sit at the kitchen table across from Gram and Jake and struggle with the chopsticks Jake insisted they use to eat pork-fried rice.

"You have heard much about this place?" Rick asked.

"Oh, yes. From what I understand, the food's wonderful."

"Only the best for you, Lily. Only the best."

Rick took Lily out for two evenings straight. On Sunday night, following their dinner at the Canlis, he took her to the Cliff House and ordered champagne at three hundred dollars a bottle. After years of scrimping by with Gram for the bare necessities, Lily discovered her sense of priorities was offended by seeing good money wasted on something as frivolous as overpriced champagne.

When she mentioned it to Gram later, her grandmother simply shook her head. "Did it taste better than the cheap stuff?"

"That's the problem," Lily admitted, and sighed dejectedly. "I don't know. I've had champagne that was plenty good at a fraction of the cost."

"Rick must want to impress you."

Lily's gaze fell to her lap. "I think he does." Rick wined and dined her and claimed he found her utterly refreshing. He called her his "sunbeam" and was kind and patient. Lily should have been in ecstasy to have someone like Rick interested in her. She liked him, enjoyed his company and looked forward to seeing him again; but something basic was missing in their relationship—something that Lily couldn't quite put her finger on.

On Monday evening Jake was waiting outside the Wheaton for her as usual. A warm smile lit up Lily's dark eyes as she spotted him from the lobby, standing outside his taxi.

"Hello, Jake," she said, walking toward him, her heart pounding.

"Lily." He uncrossed his long legs and slowly straightened. "How'd it go tonight?"

"Good." About as good as it ever goes, playing the same songs night after night.

"Meet any more rich Texans?" He forced the joke when the last thing he felt was cheerful.

"Not tonight."

"How did everything go with Rick?" Jake had thought of little else over the past two days. It felt good to be responsible for giving Lily what she wanted most.

And wretched because it went against his instincts. But Rick was a decent sort. He'd be good to Lily.

"Rick's very nice."

"I knew you'd like him."

"I do." But not nearly as much as I like you, she added silently.

"Where'd he take you?"

"The Canlis."

"Rick always did have excellent taste." Most especially in women, Jake thought to himself. His friend wasn't going to let Lily slip away. She was a priceless gem, rare and exquisite, and it hadn't taken Rick long to covet her. Jake couldn't regret having introduced them; he'd planned it. But he hadn't expected that letting Lily go would be so difficult.

"How'd the writing go today?"

"Pretty good. I've got a story for you to read when you have the time." He reached inside the cab for a manila envelope and handed it to her.

Pleased, Lily hugged it to her breast. "Is there anything special you want me to look for?"

"The usual."

"Have you heard anything back on that one you sent to the *New Yorker*?"

Jake snickered and shook his head. "Lily, I only sent it there to please you. Trust me, the *New Yorker* isn't going to be interested in a story from me."

"Don't be such a defeatist. Who can say? That story was your best. I liked it."

The corner of his mouth edged up in a self-mocking grimace. "You like all my stories."

"You're good, Jake. I just wish…"

"What?" He opened the passenger side for her and walked around the front of the vehicle.

"I think you ought to think about novels," Lily told him, once he was seated beside her.

"Maybe someday," he grumbled.

The evening traffic was lighter than usual as Jake drove the normal route to Gram's in the Sunset district. They didn't talk much after Lily suggested Jake consider writing novels. Ideas buzzed through his mind. Maybe he ought to think about it. Almost always the characters in his stories were strong enough to carry a book-length story. Naturally it would call for more plot development, and that could be a problem, but one he could work at learning. To his surprise, he found the idea appealing.

Lily studied the man sitting on the seat beside her. His gaze was centered on the street, his dark-green eyes narrowed in concentration. Sensing Lily's gaze, Jake turned toward her.

"Are you coming in tonight?"

Mentally Jake weighed the pros and cons. He liked talking over his day with Lily and Gram. They offered him an outlet to the everyday frustrations of life. Yet, coming around every night the way he used to could mean problems. The day they'd gone shopping proved that. But did he really need to worry with Gram around? "If you don't mind?"

Lily laughed, surprised that he'd even suggest such a thing. "Of course I don't mind. You're always welcome. You know that."

He smiled then until the emerald light sparkled in

his eyes and Lily discovered she couldn't look away. "Yes, I suppose I do," he said finally.

By the time Jake returned it was after eleven. Lily sat in the living room with Gram. She'd read over Jake's short story and made several markings on the manuscript. Every time she read something of Jake's she was stirred by the powerful emotion in his stories. This one was particularly heart wrenching. The story involved a grumpy old man who lived alone. He had no women or children in his life, but he had a soft spot in his heart for animals. Late one night, the crotchety old man found a lost dog that had been frightened and had nearly drowned in a bad storm. He brought the dog, a miniature French poodle, into his home and fed it some leftovers. As he worked at drying off the dog, he complained gruffly that Miss Fifi, as he'd named her, deserved to be left out in the storm. The little dog ignored the surly voice and looked up at him adoringly with dark eyes. She was so grateful to have been rescued that she followed the old man around the house. Soon she was sleeping on the end of his bed and working her way into his crusty heart. People who saw the man with the fancy poodle were amused by the sight of them. The old man felt torn. Miss Fifi was a damn nuisance and he definitely didn't like drawing attention to himself. Yet every day, he grew more attached to the dog. At the end of the story he found her a good home and, without a second thought, went about his life as before.

Lily was sitting on the sofa with her feet tucked up under her when Jake knocked once before letting himself inside.

His gaze fell to the manila envelope. "Did you read it?"

"Yes."

Gram was swaying in her rocker, watching the news. She acknowledged Jake and returned her attention to the television set.

"Well?" He shouldn't have let her read it. Lily was frowning. The story wasn't one of his best. He should have ditched it. He sat on the end of the coffee table and leaned forward, resting his elbows on his knees.

"You're getting better and better," she hedged. "The best thing about your writing, Jake, is that you're a natural storyteller."

"But?" He could tell she was leading up to something unpleasant by the way her eyes avoided his. "But...the ending's wrong."

"What do you mean?"

"The little dog loved that lonely old man."

"He wasn't lonely."

"But he was!" Lily protested. "That's the reason the old man came to love the dog so much. He longed for companionship."

"You're thinking like a woman again. The old man liked his life. He was content. He didn't need anyone or anything."

"But he loved that fancy dog."

"And people laughed at him." His gaze centered on her breasts and he cursed himself for being so weak.

"Why should he care what people think? He didn't like them anyway. You've set him up to be so antisocial. The only friend he's got is that dog."

Smiling sadly, Jake shook his head. "That crusty

old man knows that dog isn't right for him. He's doing the only thing he can by giving her to someone who will appreciate and love her."

"*He* appreciates and loves her," Lily countered hotly.

"But he isn't right for her. He loves her, but he knows he has to let her go. You missed the point of the story."

"I didn't miss it," Lily told him shortly. "It's right here, hitting me between the eyes. That old man, who you want the reader to see as strong and fiercely proud, is actually shallow and foolish."

"Shallow and foolish?" Jake spat the words back at her. "He's noble and unselfish." It astonished him that Lily, who was generally so intuitive, could be so off base in her assessment.

"Let's agree to disagree," he proposed.

"It won't sell, Jake."

"So? I've got tons of stories that'll never see a printed page."

"But this one could, if you'd change the plot around."

"I'm not changing a thing."

"That's your choice." She folded her arms over her chest and stared past him to the picture on the wall. Any other time Jake would have taken her feedback to heart. Usually he appreciated her insight and made the changes she suggested, but she was wrong about this one.

"Yes, it is my choice," he said through gritted teeth.

A heavy silence settled over them.

"Would you like a glass of Marmite?" Lily asked

five minutes later, seeking some way to smooth matters over. She was uncomfortable when things weren't right between her and Jake.

"Sure." Jake followed her into the kitchen. "You disappoint me, Lily."

"I do?" She hesitated before returning the teakettle to the stove. "How?"

"With the story. You're thinking like a woman and forgetting that this is a man's story."

"Women buy the majority of magazines."

"Maybe."

"Maybe nothing—that's a fact. And what's so wrong with thinking like a woman? In case you hadn't noticed, I *am* one."

Oh, he'd noticed all right. Every time she moved in that T-shirt she was wearing, he noticed. From the instant he'd walked in the door, her breasts had enthralled him, pressed against the thin material of her shirt, round and full. Stalking to the other side of the room, Jake swallowed tightly and forced his gaze in the opposite direction.

"The fact is," Lily continued, "I don't much like the hero in your story."

"I thought we were through discussing the story."

"You were the one who brought it up."

"My mistake." Jake ground his teeth in an effort to hold her eye and not allow his gaze to drop.

"What are you two shouting about?" Gram asked, joining them.

"Jake's story."

"Nothing," Jake countered, and at her fiery gaze, he added, "I thought we agreed not to discuss it."

"Fine." Lily's arms hugged her waist.

"You two sound like snapping turtles."

"We aren't going to argue anymore, Gram," Lily promised.

"The way you two have been carrying on lately, one would think you were married. Me and Paddy sounded just like the two of you. We'd fight, but then we'd make up, too. Those were the best times," she chuckled. "Oh, yes, making up was the best part."

"We aren't fighting," Lily insisted.

"And there isn't a snowball's chance in hell that we'd ever marry," Jake barked angrily.

Involuntarily, Lily winced. She was surprised by how much his words hurt her. "You aren't exactly my idea of good husband material, either."

"Of course I'm not," Jake growled. "You're like every other woman—you want someone who can run a four-minute mile after a fast buck."

"And what's wrong with that? A girl can dream, can't she? At least I'm honest about it." Lily battled to hold on to her temper, pausing to take several deep breaths. "Maybe it would be best if I didn't read your stories anymore, Jake."

"You're right about that," he declared, marching into the living room. He jerked the manila envelope off the coffee table with such force he nearly knocked the table over. "Damn right," he said again on his way out the front door.

The screen door slammed and Lily cringed, closing her eyes.

"More and more, the two of you sound like Paddy and me," Gram announced a second time.

Lily's answering smile was nearly nonexistent. She and Jake weren't anything like Gram and Paddy. Her grandparents shared a mutual trust and a love so true that it had spanned even death.

Unshed tears brightened Lily's eyes as she turned off the lights one by one and went to bed.

The next evening Jake wasn't outside the Wheaton when Lily was finished for the night. Standing in the lobby she looked out at the long circular driveway and she'd hoped they would have a chance to talk. But Jake was angry, probably angrier than he'd ever been with her. Lily couldn't stand it. Their friendship was too important to let something as petty as a short story stand between them.

Feeling dejected, Lily secured her purse strap over her shoulder and walked into the cool evening air. She was at the end of the long driveway when she recognized Jake's cab barreling down the street. He eased to a stop along the curb beside her.

Her heart leaped at the sight of him. Jake leaned across the front seat and opened the door. "Are you talking to me?"

"Of course."

"Climb in and I'll give you a ride home."

Lily didn't hesitate. "Jake…"

"No, let me go first. I apologize. You were right about the story. I don't know what was wrong with me."

"No," she said in a hurried breath. "I was the one who was wrong. I've felt wretched all day. We shouldn't fight."

"No, we shouldn't." He grinned at her then—that

crooked, sexy grin of his that melted her insides—
and reached for her hand. "Let's put it behind us,"
Jake suggested.

Lily smiled and felt the tension of the last twenty
hours drain from her. "What did you do with the
story?"

"I trashed it."

"But Jake, it was a good story. With a few changes,
I know it would sell."

"Maybe. But I wasn't willing to change the ending.
The best place for it was the recycling bin."

"I wish you hadn't."

"Friends?" he questioned.

"Friends." Jake may have given up on the story,
but they'd learned something about each other in the
process. Their friendship was important. Whatever
else happened, they couldn't discard what they shared.

Her regret over the discarded story persisted as Jake
drove her home, but she bid him goodnight and raced
up the walk toward the house.

"Rick called," Gram told Lily when she walked in
the front door.

"Okay." Lily stood at the window, watching Jake
drive away. "Jake and I are friends again."

"Were you enemies before?"

"No, but we had a fight and now that's over."

"And you fretted about it most of the day."

"I was worried," Lily corrected, releasing the drape
so that it fell against the window. "I don't like there to
be tension between Jake and me."

"I know what you mean. I felt the same way when
Paddy and I fought."

Lily remained at the window long after Jake had driven out of sight. Rick was waiting for her to phone back and Gram was walking around comparing Lily and Jake to her and Paddy. They weren't anything alike. Jake and Lily were friends…and then some, her mind echoed…and then some.

"Gram, how do I look?" Lily had swirled her hair high atop her head and put on a striking red dress.

"As pretty as a picture," Gram confirmed without looking up from the crossword puzzle she was working on.

"Gram, you didn't even look."

"But you're always pretty. You don't need me to tell you that." She yawned loudly, covering her red lips with a veined hand. "You seeing Rick or Jake tonight?"

"Rick." She hoped the lack of enthusiasm wasn't evident in her voice.

"You don't sound pleased about it."

It did show. "We're going to the opera."

"You'll love that."

Rick had managed to obtain tickets to Mozart's *Così Fan Tutte*, which was being performed by the Metropolitan Opera Company from New York. From what little Lily knew, the performance had been sold out for months. She didn't know how Rick had managed it. He'd mentioned it once in passing, much to her delight, and the next thing she knew, he had tickets.

"It's something I've always wanted to do," Lily agreed. She was fascinated by the costumes and extravagance. Rick would be the type of husband who'd take pleasure in taking his wife out and buying her huge diamonds and an expensive wardrobe. Lily forced a smile. Those things had been important to her for so long, she hated the thought of doing without them. But Rick deserved someone who would love him for who he is and not what he could provide.

The sound of footsteps pounding up the cement walkway snapped Lily out of her daydream.

"Lily!" Jake burst in the front door and grabbed her by the waist. His handsome face was flushed and his emerald eyes sparked with excitement.

"I just heard back from the *New Yorker*. They want my story!"

"Oh, Jake!" She threw her arms around his neck and gleefully tossed back her head, squealing with delight.

Jake lifted her from the carpet and whirled her around until they were both dizzy.

"Plus they're actually paying me," he added. He set her back on the carpet but kept his arms around her. Nor did her hands leave his shoulders as she smiled up at him, her eyes filled with warmth and happiness.

"I knew it would sell," she told him. "I knew it."

Jake felt he had to either let go of Lily or pull her to him and kiss her senseless. Reluctantly, he chose the former and turned to Gram who was sitting in her old rocker, swaying.

"Nzuri sana," Gram cried, resorting to the happy Swahili word to express her congratulations.

Jake bent down and kissed the older woman soundly on the cheek. "We're celebrating. All three of us. A night on the town, dinner, dancing. No more beer and television for us."

Lily's heart sank all the way to her knees. "When?"

"Right now." Jake paused, seeming to notice her dress for the first time, and sobered. "You're going somewhere." There was no question in his voice. He knew. The joy bubbling inside him quickly went flat.

"To the opera with…"

"…Rick," he finished for her. He rammed both hands into his pants pockets and gestured outwardly with his elbows. "Listen, that's not a problem. We'll do it another time."

"I don't want to do it another time."

"It works out this way sometimes," Jake announced. "Don't worry about it." He headed out the door.

"Gram?" Lily turned frustrated, unhappy eyes to her grandmother and cried. "What should I do?"

"That's up to you, girl," Gram answered obliquely.

"Jake—" Lily rushed out the door after Jake. "Wait up." The screen slammed and Lily hurried down the stairs of the porch.

Jake paused in front of his cab, keys in hand. "What?"

"Don't go," she pleaded.

"From the look of you, Rick will be here any minute."

"Yes, but I want to go with you."

"For as long as I've known you, you've talked of wanting to attend an opera. You're going. We'll celebrate another time."

"But I want to be with you."

"No."

Lily battled with herself. She couldn't wait. Jake deserved this celebration. This sale was a victory, a triumph. Ever so briefly, Jake had held her with an exhilaration that would fade in time. She wanted to be with him tonight more than anything—more than seeing an opera or sharing almond-saffron soup with Rick.

"Please, please come back in three hours," she pleaded, holding his hand. "I'll be waiting for you." Because she couldn't stop herself, Lily stood on her tiptoes and planted a warm, heartfelt kiss on the side of his mouth.

Six

"Are you sure you're going to be all right?" Rick asked with such tender concern Lily thought she might cry.

In response, she pressed her palms against her stomach and leaned her head against the headrest in the luxury car. "I'm sure it's nothing serious."

"I should have known you weren't feeling well." Rick's gentle voice was tinged with self-derisive anger. "You haven't been yourself all evening."

Because Lily had felt guilty all evening!

"You've been so quiet."

It wasn't like her to deceive anyone!

"I only wish you'd said something earlier."

She couldn't. When she had asked Rick to take her home because she wasn't well, Lily had felt as if there were a neon light identifying her as a scheming liar flashing across her forehead.

When Rick parked the Mercedes in front of Gram's, Lily automatically looked around for Jake's cab. She saw no sign of it and didn't know whether to be grateful or concerned.

Rick climbed out of the car and crossed over to her side, opening her door. He gave her his hand and studied her with worried eyes. "You're so pale. Are you sure you don't want me to stay with you?"

"No," she cried quickly, perhaps too quickly. "But thank you, Rick, for being so good to me." Her lashes fluttered against her cheek as she dismally cast her gaze to the sidewalk.

"I hope to be good to you for a very long time," Rick announced softly, slipping an arm around her waist and guiding her toward the house. "I never imagined I'd find someone like you, Lily."

The stomach ailment Lily had invented became increasingly more real. Her insides knotted. They paused on the porch and Rick tucked a finger under her chin, raising her eyes to his. Ever so gently, he brushed his mouth over her cheek. "Can I see you next week?"

Lily would have agreed to anything if it would help lessen her intense feeling of guilt. "If you'd like."

"Oh, I'd like, my sunbeam, I'd like it very much." With that he tenderly lifted the hair from her forehead and kissed her again.

Lily had the physical response of a rag doll. She didn't lift her hands to his shoulders or encourage him, but Rick didn't appear to care or notice.

"I'll call you in the morning," he promised. Within a minute, he was gone.

Like a soldier returning to camp after a long day in the field, Lily marched into the house. Gram was asleep and snoring in her rocking chair. The crossword puzzle had slipped unnoticed to the floor. Gently, Lily shook her grandmother.

"Come on, Gram, let me help you into bed."

Gram jerked awake with a start. "Oh, it's you."

"Who were you expecting?"

"Jake. You did say he was coming back, didn't you?"

"Yes…but he isn't here."

"He will be," Gram stated confidently, sitting upright. She rubbed a hand over her eyes and looked around her as though half expecting Jake to be there without either of them noticing. "Trust me, girl, he'll be here."

Lily wasn't as certain. He hadn't actually agreed to come back, but he hadn't told her he wouldn't either. Lily had been the one to convince Jake to submit it to the *New Yorker*. They should be celebrating together.

Lily changed out of her evening gown and into the white dress that Jake had bought her. A night as significant as this one demanded a dress that was just as special.

Pausing at her bedroom window, Lily parted the drapes and stared into the starlit sky. The street was empty and her heart throbbed with anticipation. If Jake didn't come, she didn't know what she'd do. Perhaps go to his boat. Tonight he wouldn't escape her.

A half-hour later, Lily sat in the still living room, staring silently at the elephant tusks that adorned the wall. The moving shadows cast by the trees outside, dancing in the moonlight, seemed to taunt her for being so foolish.

Gram's last words before heading to bed were that Jake would come. The sound of Jake's cab registered in her mind and she bolted to her feet, sucked in a calming breath and rushed to the door. He was really there. She was standing on the porch by the time he'd parked. He didn't look eager to see her and stopped the instant he realized she was wearing the dress. When he started toward her again, he trod heavily—like someone being led to a labor camp.

"Gram said you'd come." She rubbed her hands together to dispel her nervous energy.

Jake spread his fingers wide in a gesture that told her he hadn't wanted to return. But something stronger than his will had led him back to her.

"What did you tell Rick?" Jake stood on the sidewalk as if he wasn't quite sure he wanted inside.

"That I wasn't feeling well."

"And he bought that?"

"By the time we left the opera, it was true."

"And how are you feeling now?"

"Terrible." She hung her head so that her hair fell forward.

"I shouldn't be here."

Why did Lily have to look so beautiful standing there in the moonlight? She was miserable and confused and it took everything in him not to reach for her and haul her into his arms and comfort her. Rick had probably wanted to do that. Involuntarily, Jake's fist clenched. The thought of Rick holding Lily produced such a rage within him that he felt like smashing his hand through a wall. "I'm glad you came back," Lily said softly.

Her intense gaze commanded his attention, and Jake knew he could refuse her nothing.

"I'm glad I did too," he admitted with reluctance, walking toward her.

"It's a little late for going out to eat. I thought…that is, if you don't mind…that we could order a pizza."

"With anchovies?"

Her eyes lit up with a smile. "Only on your half."

"Agreed." He took the stairs two at a time and paused at the darkened living room. "Where's Gram?"

"She fell asleep. I'll wake her."

"No." A hand on Lily's forearm stopped her. No, tonight was for them. "Let her rest."

"All right."

She smiled at him and Jake felt his stomach twist. If he had any sense left, he'd get out of there right away. But the ability to reason had left him the first time he'd kissed Lily that night in the attic. From that minute on he'd behaved like a fool. He'd like to blame Lily for what he was feeling, but he couldn't. With her, everything had been of his own making.

"I brought some wine." Actually he'd left it in the front seat of the cab. He hadn't been sure he'd be staying. "I'll be right back."

Lily had the wineglasses out by the time he returned. She turned to him when he walked into the kitchen and Jake found he couldn't look away from her no matter how hard he tried. "Do you want a corkscrew?"

Lily's words shook him from his trance. "Yeah, sure." He paused to clear his throat. "You look nice in that dress." That had to be the understatement of the year. She was the personification of the very name of the gown: Angel's Breath—so soft and delicate. It was the purest form of torture to be near her and not touch her.

Lily handed him the corkscrew and while he fiddled to open the wine bottle, she casually browsed a pizza flyer she grabbed from the side of the fridge. "Should we pick the pizza up ourselves or have it delivered?"

"That's up to you."

"Have it delivered." Lily didn't want to go out again or do anything that would disrupt the evening. "What toppings do you want?"

"Anchovies, pepperoni, olives, green pepper—" he paused "—and sausage. What about you?"

"Cheese," she told him, and laughed at the doubtful look on his face. "I'm just teasing. I'll have the same except for those disgusting little fish."

The cork came out of the wine bottle with a popping sound and Jake filled both glasses. "Here."

Lily accepted the wine and took a small sip. It was excellent. "This is good."

"I wanted something special."

She touched the edge of her wineglass to his. "To Jake: a master of words, a skilled storyteller, a man of obvious talent and virtue."

"And to Lily, who lent me her support."

"Moral and immoral," she added with a small laugh.

"Mostly moral."

Together they tasted the wine and then moved into the living room to sit on the zebra skin beside the wide ottoman. Lily had a fleeting thought to suggest they light a fire in the fireplace, but the evening was warm. "Thank you, Lily, for all your encouragement."

"Thank you, Jake, for being such a talented storyteller."

"To friendship." His eyes didn't leave hers.

"To friendship," she repeated in a hushed whisper.

They each drank their first glass and Jake replenished their supply.

"Jake."

"Hmm?"

"What really happened between you and Elaine?"

The question was so unexpected that his mouth parted, searching for words. "What do you want to know for?"

She lifted one shoulder and lowered her gaze to the red liquid. "You were so close to her."

"Yeah. So?"

"And then everything blew up."

"She wanted me to be something I couldn't."

"But that's part of what's great about you, Jake. You're so versatile. You can do anything."

"But only if I want to." Jake had no qualms about his talents. He'd tried enough things in life to know what Lily said was true. He wasn't being egotistical in admitting as much, only honest.

With a lazy finger, Lily drew imaginary circles over the top of her wineglass. "Were you lovers?"

"What?" Jake sat up so quickly that the wine nearly sloshed over the sides of his glass. "What kind of question is that?"

"I just want to know." Morbid curiosity had driven her to ask.

"That's none of your business." He downed the remainder of his glass in one giant swallow. "Do you mind if we don't talk about Elaine?"

"All right." Already Lily regretted having brought up the other woman. It was a sore subject. But Lily couldn't regret that Jake had broken things off with Elaine. She wasn't nearly good enough for him.

"What about you and Rick?"

She straightened. "What about us?"

"Has he kissed you?"

Lily clamped her upper teeth over her bottom lip and hunched her shoulders. "Sort of."

"How does a man 'sort of' kiss you?"

Lily rose to her knees, planted her hands on his shoulders and slanted her mouth over Jake's. "Like this," she whispered, gently grazing his mouth with hers. Their mouths barely touched in a soft caress.

Jake nearly choked on his own breath as a shaft of desire shot through him. He broke contact and leaned back, lowering his gaze. Lily was achingly close; she smelled like summer and sunshine and everything good. He had to look away, fearing he'd feel compelled to toss aside the wineglass and pull her into his arms. "Yes, well, I see what you mean."

"You knew Rick was married before, didn't you?"

"I seem to remember something about that."

"He's been divorced less than a year."

"What happened?" Jake didn't care two cents about the breakup of Rick's marriage, but he needed the distraction. Anything to take his mind off how badly he wanted Lily. "I'm not exactly sure, but apparently she left him for another man."

"That must've hurt." The remark was inane, but every second was torture having Lily so close.

"He's insecure and lonely."

"So are a lot of people."

Lily rotated the stem of the wineglass between her thumb and fingers. "I know."

"You like Rick, don't you?" Jake pressed. His gut feeling that Rick wasn't right for Lily persisted, but he wouldn't say anything. Not after what happened with that oil-rich Texan. Jake was beginning to doubt that anyone would ever be good enough for Lily.

"He's a nice man."

"Rich."

Softly, Lily cleared her throat. "Yes, he seems to be."

"That's what you wanted."

Lately, Lily wasn't so sure. She set the wineglass aside, got up, and moved to the window to stare into the night. The city lights obliterated the brilliance of the stars, but Lily was only pretending to look into the sky.

Jake joined her, coming to stand behind her. He raised his hands to cup the gentle curve of her shoulders and rested his cheek against the side of her head. "It's a beautiful night, isn't it?" He shouldn't be touching her like this, even in the most innocent way. Her nearness was a stimulant he didn't need. She smelled much too good for his sanity. Rick could give her all the things he'd never be able to afford. A knot of misery tightened in his chest.

"Yes, it's lovely," she mumbled. Without meaning to, she leaned back against Jake. He accepted her weight and slid his hands down the length of her arms. Desperately he wanted to hold her—to touch her without giving in to the temptation to kiss her. Lily was meant to be cherished and treasured, and he couldn't do her justice. Lily didn't move, barely breathed. The light touch of Jake's hands stirred her blood. She yearned to turn and have his arms surround her. The taste of his mouth lingered on hers unbearably.Without thinking, Jake turned his face into her hair and breathed in the fragrance of her shampoo. He lowered his face and nuzzled her ear. Lily tilted her head, luxuriating in the warm sensation that flooded through her.

"Lily," Jake breathed desperately. "I shouldn't be holding you like this."

"I like it."

"I do too. Too much."

"But I want you to hold me."

"Lily, please."

"Don't hold me then," she murmured. "Let me hold you." Without warning, she turned and slipped her arms around his waist and pressed her ear against his heart.

"Lily."

"It feels good in your arms," she purred, tightening her grip so that he couldn't break the contact. "How can it be wrong when it feels this good?"

"I don't know. Oh, Lily…" He whispered her name as he lowered his head, searching out her mouth. He touched his lips against hers, savoring her. She tasted like melting sugar, unbearably sweet and highly addictive.

Restlessly she moved against him, caught up in the moment as her passion for him took over.

"Lily," he pleaded against her mouth. "Hold still. We shouldn't let things get out of hand."

"I can't help it." She combed her fingers through his hair and looked up at him with wide, adoring eyes. "This feels so right."

"Lily…"

"Shh," she whispered and planted her mouth over his. She wound her arms around his neck and caressed his mouth with hers. "Your kiss is irresistible."

"So is yours." He paused to study the desire in her eyes. They were playing a dangerous game, which they both stood to lose. Yet he was unable to resist and he lowered his mouth to capture hers again.

Lily moaned softly, her lips moving against his. A low groan slipped from Jake's throat and he forced deeper contact, gripping the sides of her face and fusing their mouths together.

He came away from her weak, his resolve diminishing by the second. He hugged her hard, struggling deep within himself to find the willpower to release her. With a superhuman effort, he broke contact, stepping back and holding her at arm's length. "The wine went to our heads."

Her small smile contradicted his words. "We didn't have that much."

"Obviously more than we should have."

"I like what you do to me."

"Well, I don't like it," he hissed. "Tonight was a fluke and best forgotten."

"I'm not going to forget it."

"Well, I am. This isn't going to happen again. Do you understand? It's not right."

"But Jake…"

"I'm leaving. Right now,. If you have half the intelligence I credit you with, you'll forget this ever happened." He dropped his arms, and rubbed a hand over his face. "Goodnight, Lily."

She could hardly see him. Salty tears clouded her vision. "Goodnight, Jake." He was gone before she could utter another word.

"Morning." Gram greeted Lily cheerfully the following day. "I see Jake came. I told you he would."

Lily pulled out a kitchen chair and sat. After a restless, unhappy night she wasn't feeling very motivated.

"Yes, he was here."

"You coming down with a cold, girl? Your eyes are all red like you were awake half the night."

Lily blinked and offered her grandmother a feeble smile. "I think I might be."

Gram pushed a handful of vitamins and herbal supplements in Lily's direction. "You better start taking these."

"All right."

Gram gave her an odd look as Lily downed each capsule without argument. "I see you two celebrated with some wine."

Her explanation was mumbled. "Jake brought it."

"Where'd he take you for dinner?"

They had never gotten around to ordering the pizza. "We…we just had the wine."

"Ah," Gram muttered knowingly. "So you sat around and talked."

Lily pulled out the chair and stood in front of the old porcelain sink, her back to her grandmother. "Yes, we talked." Her fingers tightened around her mug. They'd talked, and a lot more. It was the "lot more" that would be difficult to explain.

"What did Jake have to say?"

"This and that." Nervously, Lily set the mug on the long counter. "I think I'll go get dressed."

"You do that," Gram said with a knowing chuckle. "Me and Paddy used to talk about 'this and that' ourselves. Some of our best conversations were spent discussing those very things."

On Monday evening Jake wasn't parked in his usual spot outside the Wheaton when Lily finished her shift. She lingered around the lobby for an additional fifteen minutes, hoping he'd arrive and they'd have a chance to talk. He didn't. And he wasn't there the next evening, either. Lily didn't require a typed message to know that Jake was avoiding her. Maybe he felt they needed a break from each other to give ample thought to what had happened. But Lily would have felt better if Jake hadn't been playing a silly game of hide-and-seek with her.

Early Wednesday evening, Rick appeared in the lobby of the Wheaton and sat listening to Lily play. He clapped politely at the end of a series of numbers. No one applauded her playing; she was there for mood and atmosphere, not as entertainment.

When she had finished, Lily slid off the polished piano bench and Rick rose to join her.

"You're very gifted," he said, kissing her on the cheek.

"Thank you."

"Would you like a cocktail?"

Lily hesitated. She wanted to check if Jake was out front. If he was, Lily had everything she wanted to tell him worked out in her mind. She had no intention of mentioning what had happened over the wine. She'd decided that she'd play Jake's game and pretend the alcohol had dictated their uncharacteristic behavior. She planned to be witty and clever and show him that she hadn't been nearly as affected by his kiss as he seemed to believe. Playing this role was a matter of pride now. "Let me tell Jake first," Lily told Rick.

"Sure." A guiding hand at her elbow led her through the hotel and into the foyer. "Why do you need to talk to Jake?"

"He usually gives me a ride home."

"Every night?" Rick uttered a faint sound of disapproval. "I wasn't aware that you saw Jake that often."

"That's how we got to be such good friends." Lily stood between the two sets of thick glass doors, scanning the long circular driveway. Jake wasn't there. Her heart sank.

"Apparently he can't tonight."

"Apparently not."

"I'll take you home. For that matter, there isn't any reason why I can't see you home every night. I hate the thought of you having to rely on Jake's schedule for a ride home."

"I'm not relying on Jake's schedule. He's here when he can be, and not here when it's inconvenient or he's got a fare. The agreement works well for us both." Perhaps she did depend more on Jake than she should. But Jake would be as offended as she to have Rick suggest as much. "And as for you seeing me home every night, that's ridiculous."

"But I want to take care of you," Rick protested, his arm closing around her waist. "Let's go have that drink and we'll talk it over."

"There's nothing to discuss." Now Rick was irritating her. She didn't want to have a drink with him; she wanted to talk to Jake. Only Jake wasn't around and hadn't been for three days. Lily missed him. She hadn't realized how much she shared with Jake—nonsensical things about her day that only he would understand.

By Saturday afternoon, Lily was irritable and snapping at Gram. Rick had declared that he was coming to listen to her again and Jake continued to avoid her. Lily couldn't recall a time in all her years when she felt more frustrated.

"I haven't seen Jake around lately," Gram complained as Lily pulled weeds from the front flower beds. Alongside her, Gram groomed her African violets, smiling under a huge straw hat with a brightly colored bandanna wrapped around the brim.

"He's been busy." With unnecessary force, Lily jerked a weed free of the soft soil. "I haven't seen him for an entire week."

"Not since you two discussed 'this and that'?" Gram asked with a knowing glance.

"Nope." The cool earth felt good against Lily's

hands. For once she didn't care if there was grit and grime under her manicured nails. Everything felt different after what has happened with Jake. "Gram, what would you say about me changing jobs?"

"Changing jobs? But I thought you liked it at the Wheaton. Or is it Jake that's worrying you?"

"Jake hasn't got anything to do with it."

"This decision seems sudden."

"Forget it, then. I'll stay at the Wheaton and play 'Moon River' for the rest of my life. I don't care if I ever see Jake again." The minute the words escaped her lips, Lily realized what she'd said, and snapped her mouth closed.

"Seems to me that you're more worried about seeing Jake than you are about playing that song."

Lily kept her mouth shut. She had already said more than she'd intended.

"Why don't you just pay him a visit?," Gram asked, undaunted.

"Should I?" Lily's first inclination was to hurry to the marina, but she had her pride to consider. Already it had taken a beating, and Lily doubted it could go another round.

"I can't see what harm it'd do."

To Lily's burdened mind it could solve several problems. To hell with her pride! "Maybe I will drop by and see how he is. Perhaps he's been ill or something."

"He could even be waiting for you to come."

Lily sat back on her haunches and brushed a stray curl from her face. A thin layer of mud smeared her cheek. "All right, I'll do it."

By the time Lily had showered and changed clothes,

she had grown nervous and fidgety. Maybe going to Jake's wasn't the best idea, but Lily couldn't stand the terrible silence any longer.

On her way to the marina, she made a stop to order the pizza they hadn't gotten around to eating that other night. Carrying the thin cardboard box in both hands, Lily walked down the long, rolling dock to where his sailboat was moored.

"Jake!" Her voice trembled as she called out his name.

Below deck, Jake heard Lily calling for him and quickly closed the story he was writing on his laptop.

Seven

Jake's heart sped up at the sound of Lily's voice. He got up slowly, unsure of what he should do. He'd avoided her all week and with good cause. After what had happened at their "victory celebration," they needed to stay away from each other.

Besides, he reasoned, Lily didn't need him anymore; she had Rick. Jake had seen Rick's car at the Wheaton nearly every evening. He still couldn't reconcile himself to Lily's dating the guy. But he had no one else to blame. He'd introduced them. He couldn't protest at this point. He was snared in a trap of his own making. The best thing for him to do was make himself scarce.

"Jake, I know you're in there," Lily called again.

Jake's fist clenched at his side and an irritated noise slipped from deep inside his throat. If he didn't react it would be just like that stubborn woman to hop on board the *Lucky Lady* and search him out. Then he'd look like even more of a fool than he did already. Reluctantly, he climbed on deck.

"Hello, Jake," Lily began.

He tucked in his shirttails, giving the impression that he'd been preoccupied. "Lily."

"Did I catch you at a bad time? You weren't asleep, were you? Gram thought you might be sick."

His gaze just managed to avoid hers. "This is a bit of a bad moment. I'm busy."

"Oh." She dropped her gaze. "I brought a pizza. We…the other night we forgot about it."

"We didn't exactly forget it," he corrected her. "We just didn't get around to ordering it." His eyes delved into hers. Already it was happening. He couldn't help noticing how beautiful she was standing there with those huge brown eyes, looking betrayed and hurt.

"Anyway, I thought I could bring a pizza now."

Jake shifted his gaze to the flat box in her arms.

"But if you're busy, I'll understand." She didn't, not really. He must realize that coming here had cost her a lot of pride. The least he could do was make it easier on her.

Something in her voice reminded Jake that this wasn't any less difficult for Lily. It ws wrong of him to protect his ego at her expense. "It was thoughtful of you to come."

The tension eased from Lily's shoulders as Jake stretched out his hand to help her aboard. The boat rocked gently as she shifted her weight from the narrow dock to the *Lucky Lady.*

"There are anchovies on your half." She smiled up at him and Jake knew instantly that he was in trouble.

Lily drew in a long breath as though she didn't know what to say now that she was aboard the boat.

"It looks like rain, doesn't it?" she suggested, casting a discerning eye toward the thick gray clouds. "Maybe we should take this below."

Jake's chest tightened. Being alone with Lily was bad enough, but the thought of being next to her in the close confines of the cabin was almost more than he could bear.

"Jake?"

"Yeah, sure." He led the way and Lily handed the pizza down to him before expertly maneuvering the few steps that led below deck.

"Have you been working on another story?" Lily asked as she spied his laptop. Crumpled yellow sticky notes littered the tabletop and filled what limited space there was in the dining area. "It looks like you're having a few problems. Do you want to tell me your plot? That helps, sometimes."

Setting the pizza beside the tiny sink, Jake cleared away his mess. "No," he answered starkly.

Lily was taken aback by his answer. For a minute neither spoke.

"Why not?" Lily asked, trying to sound curious instead of hurt. Jake often talked out his plot ideas with her and listened to her reactions. Invariably, he argued his point and then, more often than not, accepted her suggestions.

"Every writer comes to the time when he has to break away…"

Lily sighed and shook her head regretfully. "Why are you so angry with me?"

"I'm not." The words came quickly.

"I thought we were friends, and all of a sudden you're treating me like I'm your worst enemy."

"I'm not mad."

"I haven't seen you in a week. Friends don't avoid each other like that'."

"I've been busy." Even to his own ears, the excuse sounded lame.

"Friends are honest with each other," Lily continued.

"I haven't lied."

"Friends tell each other what's on their minds."

"Nothing's bothering me. Why can't you accept that?"

Lily made a tsking noise that sounded remarkably like Gram when she was displeased about something.

"All right," Jake countered. "You want to talk about being friends? Fine. Then maybe you should think about what's been going on between us. You may be innocent, Lily Morrissey," Jake retorted, "but you're not naive enough to believe that friends kiss the way we do." Hoping to give the appearance of nonchalance, Jake leaned against the counter and crossed his arms. "I don't like what's happening."

"Nothing's happening," Lily said, struggling to keep her voice from rising. "We aren't any different than we were six months ago."

"Oh, I beg to differ!"

"All right, I concede that our relationship has gone to a deeper level, but we're still good friends. At least that's what I'd like to think."

Jake snorted. "We're in serious trouble."

"You're being overdramatic. I...I like kissing you.

You make me feel warm and tingly inside. I just don't think that's wrong."

"Not wrong; bad."

"You're only saying that because you think kissing me will lead to something more."

Jake looked nonplussed. "And it doesn't?"

"Not if we don't want it to."

"Lily." Her name came out in a rush of breath as if he were reasoning with a young child. "Kissing is only the first step. The next thing you know, we'll be in bed together and wondering how we let things go so far."

"You seem to be equating a simple friendly kiss with love and marriage. Good grief, Jake. We're friends and we just happen to like to kiss each other. It doesn't have to lead to anything."

"If we don't stop thinking like this, the next thing I know I'll be shopping for diapers."

Lily laughed. "Honestly, Jake, you make it sound far more dreadful than it is. Here, let me show you." She moved across the narrow confines of the cabin and placed her hands on his shoulders.

Jake stiffened and jerked away as if her touch burned him. "No."

"It's only a kiss, not a hand grenade."

"I don't think we should be kissing."

"But I want to prove something." Her voice was small and she couldn't keep the disappointment out of it. Before Jake had the opportunity to react, she moved her mouth against his in a soft caress.

Jake felt liquid fire seep through him. "See?" Lily announced proudly. "And I'm not humming the 'Wedding March' or anything. From everything Gram's told me, there isn't the slightest possibility of my getting pregnant from a kiss."

The thoughts Jake was having didn't have anything to do with marriage and a family. His gaze fell past her to the small area where he slept. He thought about sleeping with Lily at his side and seeing her hair spread out on his pillow. The vision of her lying there without clothes and reaching her arms out to him nearly ate a hole right through him.

"Right," he grumbled.

"To further prove the point, I think we should do it again."

"I don't know." He closed his eyes, knowing that one pleading glance from Lily and he'd give her anything she wanted. He hated his lack of self-control. It had never been like this with other women. He had always been the one calling the shots. Jake opened his eyes to discover Lily standing so close that all he had to do was lean forward and their bodies would touch. He could feel the heat radiating from her. So little would be required of him to press his thigh to hers, to feel her breasts against his chest. His senses were suddenly awake to her every curve and it was slowly driving him insane.

Unable to keep his hands away, Jake tenderly cupped her cheek. Her thick lashes fluttered closed as she turned her face into his palm. Ever so gently, she kissed the inside of his hand. The inch or so between them was eliminated before another second could pass. They stood thigh to thigh, breasts to chest, and feasted on the feel of each other. With a reverence that shocked him, Jake lowered his head and claimed Lily's mouth.

Their lips met in the sweetest, most profound kiss Lily had ever experienced. Passion smoldered just beneath the surface, but this was a different kind of kiss—one that Lily didn't know how to define. Her hand crept up his chest and closed around the folds of his shirt collar as she clung to him.

When Jake lifted his mouth from hers, Lily smiled up at him and tears clouded her eyes. "That was beautiful," she whispered.

"You're beautiful." He tucked a strand of hair around her ear and traced her temple with his fingertips.

She had that dreamy look of a person in love.

Lightly, he kissed her again. "Lily, believe me when I tell you that this has to stop right now."

"Okay," she murmured. She looped her arms around his neck and buried her face in his throat. He smelled of the sea and the sun. Vital and alive. Her tongue discovered his pulse.

"Lily," he groaned, moving his hands to set her away.

"You taste good."

Already, he was wavering. He hadn't wanted her on his boat and here she was a few feet from his bed. They were in each other's arms, and from the way things were progressing, only heaven knew where they'd end up.

"I said, no more." Forcefully Jake moved away from her. Lily's expression fell into a mixture of bewilderment and hurt.

"I told you before, I want to put an end to this nonsense. You women are all alike."

"Jake—"

"It was the same thing with Elaine." It hadn't been, but Lily didn't know that and Jake was desperate to extract himself before things went any further. He had to act fast.

"I'm not anything like Elaine."

"The two of you could be sisters. You think a woman has the right to drive a ring through a man's nose and lead him around."

"That's not true." Lily struggled to swallow back her indignation.

"You women are never satisfied. There's always something that needs to be changed."

"What have I ever asked you to change?"

"My writing. At first you were content to read the short stories, but oh no, those didn't make enough money, so you started pressing me to write novels."

"But I thought…"

"The crazy part of all this is that for a time I even considered it."

Lily took a step back, staring up at Jake. She slowly shook her head, still having trouble believing that this was Jake speaking to her—the man who only minutes ago had kissed her and held her so lovingly in his arms.

"Elaine almost ruined my life and I almost let her. Thank God I saw the light in time."

"Jake…" Recklessly, Lily tried one last time to reason with him.

"You aren't any better than Elaine, worming your way into my life, using me, and then taking it upon yourself to mold me into whatever you want."

"I've never tried to change you."

"Oh that's right. You want to *save* me. Well, listen and listen good. I like my life. I don't want to be saved. Got it?"

"Would you stop shouting long enough for me to say something?" Lily demanded.

"No. Enough's been said."

"It hasn't!" she shouted. "I like you the way you are and I have no intention of saving you."

Jake snorted. "That was what Elaine said."

"I'm not Elaine!" She stabbed a finger in his direction.

"Right," he snickered.

"There's no reasoning with you when you're like this."

"Then it would be best if you left, wouldn't it?"

She didn't say anything for several seconds. "Are you kicking me off your boat?"

"I'm saying—"

"Don't say anything…it's not necessary. I get the picture. I won't bother you again…and I'll never, ever come on board the *Lucky Lady* again. You've made your point perfectly clear." She turned quickly and moved up the steps in a huff.

Jake didn't move. Above him, he heard Lily's footsteps as she hurried across the deck. Her steps were heavy and their echo cut straight into his heart. The frustrations of a lifetime of bitterness suddenly surfaced and he struggled against the urge to ram his fist through the side of the boat. He paced the tiny, enclosed area in an effort to compose himself. It was what he wanted. Lily was gone. He didn't doubt her word; she wouldn't be back. He'd driven her away for good. But Jake couldn't imagine what his life would be like without her. There were better ways of handling this situation. He could apologize, but his pride sneered at the thought. No, he'd bide his time and try to forget how deeply he cared for her. That was the only solution to avoid ruining both their lives.

By the time Lily slid into her seat at the grand piano at the Wheaton that evening, she was outwardly composed. But the inner battle continued to rage. She didn't know which had hurt the most—Jake comparing her to that horrible Elaine, or when he'd told her to get off his boat. Both had devastated her to the point that she hadn't been able to talk to Gram. Lily placed her hands over the ivory keys and her fingers moved automatically, playing from memory. Lily had learned not to involve her mind in the music. If she did, she'd have been half-crazy by now. Her smile was pasted on her mouth, curving her full lips slightly upward.

The manager strolled past her once and Lily dropped her gaze to her hands. Usually his presence meant she had done something that annoyed him. Lily no longer cared. If he fired her, she'd find another job. The monotony of playing the same songs night after night had robbed her musical gift of the natural spark she'd once possessed. She hardly ever sat at the piano to goof around anymore. And all this for what? The only wealthy man she'd met in a year's time at the hotel was Rex Flanders and that had turned out to be a bust. Even now, Jake's negative reaction to the Texan confused her. He hadn't so much as seen Rex and he'd forced Lily into promising that she wouldn't go out with the middle-aged man.

When Lily had finished the first half of the evening's set of music, she took a break. Henry, the senior bellhop, stopped her halfway across the lobby.

"Miss Lily, there's a message for you." He strolled across the carpet to hand her a beige envelope.

Lily accepted the letter and her heart flip-flopped in her chest. For one insane moment, Lily thought it might be from Jake. After a glance at the slanted strokes of the cursive script, she recognized the handwriting as Rex Flanders's.

The first genuine smile of the evening came.

Hello Lily,

I've been thinking about you lately, and about that old song you hunted down for me. As I promised, I'm back in San Francisco and I'm hoping that you'll allow me to show you my appreciation. I meant what I said about taking you to dinner. I insist. It's the least I can do to thank you. I'll meet you in the lobby at nine-thirty. Don't disappoint me this time.

Rex

Folding the single sheet over, Lily tucked it inside the envelope. She would join Rex for dinner. Her promise to Jake had been made under duress. Besides, she owed him nothing now. He'd made that clear. He had no reason to care if she saw Rex or any other man, for that matter.

* * *

Parked outside the Wheaton, Jake leaned against the side of his cab and crossed his arms, watching the entrance. Lily was due out in another hour. He needed to talk to her so he could explain that he hadn't meant what he'd said. The anger had been a ploy to keep her out of his arms, but he hadn't meant to insult her. The apology burned in his chest. The minute she came through those doors he'd go to her and admit he was wrong. That was the very least he could do. She deserved that and a lot more.

Once he'd made his peace with Lily, Jake decided, they had to have a serious discussion about what was going on between them. They had to stop pretending their kisses didn't mean something, that they were simply friends. For his part, Jake was convinced that a serious relationship between them wouldn't work. Their life goals couldn't be more different. He wasn't going to change. And if Lily wanted a wealthy man, then she ought to look elsewhere. She was putting her schemes in jeopardy by flirting with him.

They were reasonable adults. After they'd talked this craziness out of their systems, they could go back to the way things used to be, and continue as friends. They had to acknowledge those feelings for what they were—infatuation. He was flattered that Lily found him attractive. But they could only be one or the other. They could be great friends or good lovers. Of the two, Jake sought her friendship.

Satisfied with his reasoning, Jake checked his watch

again. It wouldn't be long. A crooked grin spread across his face. He felt much better now than he had that afternoon.

Lily nervously smoothed a wrinkle from the skirt of her blue dress. She glanced up to find Rex strolling toward her, his eyes alight with appreciation.

"Lily," he whispered, and collected her hands. "You're as lovely as I remember."

Rex looked even bigger and taller than she had recalled. "Thank you."

"Have you been waiting long?"

"No. Only a minute." Actually, she'd changed her mind twice. Not until she neared the huge glass doors at the Wheaton's entrance had she decided to go back and meet Rex.

"Good." His gaze claimed hers. "It doesn't seem a whole month since I first laid eyes on you."

"Time has a way of slipping past, doesn't it?" Once she'd worried about appearing witty and attractive. Now she didn't care; she could only be herself.

"It sure does." He offered her his elbow in gentlemanly fashion. "I know a quiet little French restaurant where the food is excellent."

"That sounds lovely."

"You do like French food?"

"Oh, yes."

Smiling at her, Rex directed Lily toward the front entrance. Once outside, he stepped forward and raised his hand, calling for a taxi.

Jake was parked in the driveway, chewing on the end of a toothpick, wondering what was taking Lily so long. He had almost made up his mind to go inside and find out. As he straightened, the toothpick slipped from his mouth and fell to the ground. Lily was with that Texan. Jake was incredulous. She'd only mentioned the man a couple of times, but Jake knew instantly that the man she'd told him about was the one escorting her now. She'd promised to stay away from that pot-bellied fool. Promised. He'd been right all along. She wasn't any different from Elaine.

Stupefied, Jake watched as one of his colleagues pulled toward the front. The doorman opened the cab door and Lily climbed in the back with the Texan. Jake was so furious that he slammed his fist against the side of his taxi, momentarily paralyzing his fingers.

Well, fine, Lily could date whomever she liked. She was nothing to him. Nothing.

Inside the cab, Lily tossed a glance over her shoulder, wondering if Jake had been out front. Silently she lambasted herself for even looking. He wouldn't be there, of course, especially after a whole week of avoiding her. After what had happened that afternoon, the Wheaton would be the last place Jake would show.

Feeling agitated, Lily fiddled with her fingers. She regretted having agreed to go with Rex. She'd accepted the date for all the wrong reasons.

Rex must have sensed her uneasiness since he chatted the whole way, his deep voice filling the taxi. When she responded with only a polite word or two, he struck up a conversation with the cabdriver.

Lily wondered if the driver, who was a friend of Jake's, would mention it to him. Fervently she prayed he wouldn't, then doubted that Jake would care either way.

The restaurant, Chez Philippe, was one of the most expensive and highly rated in all of San Francisco. Famous people from all over the world were reputed to have dined there. Lily had often dreamed of sampling the excellent cuisine and catching a glimpse of a celebrity.

After arriving at the restaurant, they were seated by the maître d' and handed huge, odd-shaped menus. Lily noted that the prices weren't listed, so she was left to guess at what this dinner would cost Rex. However, she learned long ago that anyone who needed to ask about the price probably couldn't afford it.

"Do you see anything that looks good to you, little filly?"

Their eyes met over the top of the menu. "What would you suggest?" Rex listed a couple of items and Lily smiled absently. The waiter returned and filled their water glasses with expensive bottled water.

With each passing minute, Jake's anger grew until he could almost taste his fury with every breath. Slamming the door of his cab, he cursed his lack of decisive action when he'd seen Lily with the rich Texan. She'd promised him she wouldn't go out with Daddy Warbucks and with God as his witness, Jake was going to hold her to her word. As hard as it was on his patience, he waited until the cabbie who drove Lily and the Texan returned to the Wheaton.

"Where'd you take them?" Jake demanded in a tone that caused the other driver to cringe.

"Who?"

"You know who. Lily."

"Oh, yeah. That was her, wasn't it?"

"Where did you take them?" Jake demanded a second time.

The driver cleared his throat. "That fancy French place on Thirty-third."

"Chez Philippe's?"

"That's the one."

Jake breathed a quick word of thanks then rushed back to his cab, revving the engine with such force that a billow of black smoke shot from the tailpipe.

Jake's cab roared through the streets toward Chez Philippe's. He ran two red lights and prayed a cop wouldn't pull him over for speeding.

Once he was within a block of the restaurant, Jake pulled to a dead stop. What was he going to do once he arrived? To rush in and demand that Lily leave with him simply wouldn't work. He'd only end up looking like a jealous idiot. He could picture her now, looking up at him with disdain and quietly asking him to leave. He needed a plan. He parked on the street, not wanting the valet to take his cab. The fact was, Jake wasn't sure the valet *would* take it.

Hands buried deep inside his pants pockets, Jake strolled into the classy place as if he'd been dining there for years. The maître d' stepped forward expectantly.

"May I help you, *monsieur*?"

"A table for one," Jake said confidently.

"*Monsieur*, I regret that we only seat gentlemen wearing a suit and tie."

"You mean I have to have a suit and tie even before I can spend my money?"

"That is correct. I sincerely regret the inconvenience."

Jake scowled. "Do you mind if I sit and wait?" He motioned toward an empty chair.

"Sir, we aren't going to change our dress code this evening."

"That's fine, I'd just like to wait."

The stoic expression altered for the first time as the maître d' arched a skeptical brow. "As you wish."

The rush of whispers from the front of the restaurant caused Lily to glance up from her plate. As she did, her breath caught in her lungs. Jake was standing there, and from the look he tossed at her, he was furious.

Eight

Lily felt the blood drain from her face. Jake was looking at her as though it required every ounce of restraint he'd ever possessed not to march across the room and confront her.

"Doesn't that sound like fun?" Rex was saying.

Lily stared at him blankly. "Yes, it does." She hoped her response was appropriate.

"Good. Good," Rex continued, obviously pleased. "I thought a young filly like you would enjoy an evening on the town."

The first time she'd met Rex, Lily had torn Gram's house apart looking for that crazy song on the chance he'd suggest spending an evening with her. A lavish date with a rich man had been Lily's dream for many years. She was a fool if she was going to allow Jake's foul temper to ruin tonight. She forced her chin up a notch. Jake had made his views of her plain, and she wasn't going to let him wreck her evening.

"Where would you like to start?" She planted her

elbows on the white linen tablecloth and rested her chin atop her folded hands, staring at him expectantly.

"There's a small dance floor at the St. Francis."

"That sounds grand," Lily simpered.

"We could have our after-dinner drink there as well, if you like."

"That would be wonderful."

From the corner of her eye, Lily noted that Jake was pacing the small area in front of the maître d's desk. A smile tugged at the edges of her mouth. She certainly hoped he got an eyeful. The memory of the insults he'd hurled at her earlier was enough to encourage Lily. She wasn't much of a flirt but with Rex sitting across from her and Jake just waiting for the opportunity to pounce on her, Lily gave it all she had.

Jake had claimed she was a schemer; she was only proving him right. Once he saw the way she behaved with Rex, he would get the message and leave.

The waiter approached their table with the bill. While Rex dealt with it, Lily took the opportunity to glance in Jake's direction. The shock of seeing him had faded and was being replaced by indignation. Jake had a lot of nerve.

"Are you ready?" Rex asked.

"Yes." Lily's heart constricted as Rex pulled out her chair and she stood.

Her wealthy escort placed a hand on the small of her back, urging her forward. Lily looked up at him with adoring eyes, ignoring Jake. She held her breath as they approached the front desk, wondering if Jake would cause a scene. Indecision showed in his eyes and she quickly glanced away.

For his part, Jake battled with uncertainty. He'd been a fool to have followed her there. He felt he ought to punch the lights out of that oil-rich Texan and grab Lily while he had the chance. But he couldn't do that. Lily would never forgive him and he already owed her one apology.

The hem of her skirt brushed his leg as she scooted past him and Jake jumped back as though he'd been burned. His eyes demanded that she look at him, but Lily refused. She tucked her hand in the crook of the Texan's elbow and glanced up at him adoringly.

Unsure of what he should do, Jake stood where he was for an entire minute, silently cursing. If he had any sense left, which he was sincerely beginning to doubt, he'd go back to the marina and forget that Lily had broken her promise.

Once outside, Jake's feet felt as though they were weighted with concrete blocks. He gave a companionable salute to the valet as he passed.

Lily and the Texan were in the backseat of another cab, pulling out of the circular driveway and Jake stepped back as they sped away.

As he returned to his taxi he increased his pace. He couldn't ignore the gut feeling that something was wrong with Lily and Rex. The *feeling* had always perplexed him. He hadn't *felt* right about Lily and Rick either, but this time the sensation was far stronger. If anything happened to Lily, he'd never be able to forgive himself. Foolish pride no longer dictated his actions; he was driven by something far stronger: fear.

His hand slapped the side of the taxi and he jumped inside and revved the engine. It only took a minute to locate the other cab driving Lily and Rex. Jake stayed a fair distance behind them, fearing that the other driver would suspect that he was following him.

When they entered the downtown core, Jake relaxed. The other cab was in his territory now and Jake wove in and out of traffic without a problem. The driver dropped Lily and the Texan off at the St. Francis Hotel. Jake couldn't fault the man's taste. He rounded the corner and was lucky enough to locate a parking space.

The doorman opened the tall glass door as Jake approached the hotel entrance. Music from the piano bar filtered into the lobby from the cocktail lounge and he headed toward it. Although his gait was casual, his eyes carefully scanned the darkened area for Lily. When he spotted her sitting at a tiny table in the middle of the room, he heaved a sigh of relief.

As inconspicuously as possible, he took a seat at the far corner of the bar so he could keep an eye on her without being seen.

"Can I help you?" The bartender spoke and Jake swiveled in his seat to face him.

"A beer," he replied. "Any kind. It doesn't matter."

"Right away."

Sitting sideways, Jake propped an elbow against the edge of the bar and centered his attention on Lily. She really was lovely. Jake couldn't blame Rex for being interested. Jake recalled the day he'd taken her out on the *Lucky Lady* and the way she'd sat perched on the bow, laughing. The wind had tossed her hair in every direction, making her resemble a sea nymph, soaking in the early summer sun. Something had happened to him that day—something so significant that he had yet to determine its meaning. From that moment on, Jake concluded, his life had been in a tailspin.

The bartender delivered his beer and Jake absently placed a bill on the counter. Holding the thick glass with one hand, he took a long sip. It felt cool and soothing against his parched throat. He set the glass back on the bar.

Glancing in Lily's direction again, Jake noted that Rex had reached for her hand and held it in his own as he leaned across the small table, talking intimately with her. From this distance Jake couldn't read Lily's reaction.

Without thinking, Jake slid off the bar stool and stood. His fist knotted, but he managed to control his immediate outrage. Another man was touching Lily and although it appeared innocent enough, Jake didn't like it. He didn't like it one bit. Furthermore, he trusted that overweight Texan about as much as he did a rattlesnake.

Several couples were gliding around on a small dance floor on the other side of the lounge and Jake watched as Rex stood and helped Lily to her feet. Jake downed the remainder of his beer when the Texan escorted Lily to join the dancing couples, bringing her into his arms. Holding hands was one thing, but dancing was another. There was nothing more Jake could do, but act. He ate up the distance to the dance floor in three huge strides.

Lily wished she hadn't agreed to come to the bar with Rex. She felt like a fraud. She had no desire to share a drink and conversation and had even less enthusiasm for dancing. Rex's hands felt warm and clammy against her back and she resisted the subtle pressure of his arms to bring her closer.

They'd already circled around the small dance area once when Lily glanced up and noticed Jake coming toward her with abrupt, angry strides. She knew she should be furious, but her heart responded with a wild leap of pleasure. After her behavior in the restaurant, Lily had been disappointed in herself. Rex was a nice man. He didn't deserve to be used. Jake tapped Rex's shoulder. "I'm cutting in." He didn't ask, but simply announced it.

Rex looked stunned. "Lily?"

"That's fine," she murmured, dropping her gaze. "I…I know him. This is Jake Carson."

Jake took Lily by the waist, pressing her to him as he whirled her away.

"Jake—"

"No, you listen to me. What kind of game are you playing?" He pushed the words through clenched teeth. He was being unreasonable but he didn't care. He wanted answers.

"I'm not playing…"

"You assured me that you wouldn't be seeing Daddy Warbucks."

"That was before."

"Before what?"

"Before you *assured me* that I was a nuisance and asked me to leave your precious boat."

"Consequently your promise doesn't mean anything?"

"No," she cried, then changed her mind. "Yes."

"Dinner was bad enough, but did you have to come here as well? What's the matter? Didn't that fancy restaurant give you ample opportunity to flaunt yourself?"

Lily was too outraged to answer. "Let me go."

"No. I'm taking you home."

"Rex will take me home."

"No way. You promised me you wouldn't be seeing that rich bullfrog, and I'm holding you to your word."

"You can't make me do anything." Lily didn't understand why she was fighting Jake when the very sight of him made her heart race. If only he'd stop behaving like an arrogant fool, she'd tell him that she longed for him to take her home.

"I don't have much taste for making a scene, but I won't back away from one if that's what you want."

"You're acting crazy."

"Perhaps."

"There's no question about it. You're bossy, stubborn and unreasonable."

"Great. Now that you've named my personality traits, we can leave."

"Not without saying something to Rex."

Jake relaxed his hold. "I'll do the talking."

"That's hardly necessary."

He didn't answer as he gripped her hand in his and led the way off the dance floor. The other couples cleared a path for them and Lily wondered how much of their heated conversation had been overheard. Embarrassment brought a flush of color to her cheeks.

Rex stood as they approached the small table.

"I'm taking Lily home," Jake informed the older man.

"Lily, is that what you want?" Rex eyed her seriously. His brows formed into a sharp frown as he waited for her to respond.

"Jake's an old friend," she said, trying to explain.

"I see," Rex said slowly.

"I hope you do," Jake added. His hand continued to grip hers as he headed out of the cocktail lounge, half pulling Lily as he went.

In her heels she had difficulty keeping up with his wide strides and paused momentarily to toss an apologetic look over her shoulder, wanting Rex to know she was sorry for everything.

"Are you happy?" she asked, once they hit the sidewalk.

"Very." He thrust his face toward her. "Don't ever pull that trick on me again."

Recalling all lessons on ladylike behavior Gram had drilled into her over the years, Lily battled to keep her temper. She only partially succeeded. "And don't you *ever* do that to me again."

"Keep your promises and I won't," Jake barked.

They didn't say another word until they were inside the cab, headed home.

The anger was slowly dissolving inside Lily. Everything had changed in the past few weeks and she didn't know if it was for the better. A year ago, she'd started playing piano at the Wheaton with so many expectations. In that time she'd dated two wealthy men and met Jake. Rick and Rex weren't anything like she'd dreamed. Jake was Jake: proud, stubborn, and so very good to her and Gram. She'd ached over the loss of something precious and wonderful—her relationship with Jake—and prayed it wasn't too late to salvage it.

"I thought you didn't care anymore what I did," she murmured, longing to explain why she'd accepted Rex's invitation.

"Believe me, it wasn't by choice." His hands tightened on the steering wheel.

"Then why did you…"

"I couldn't care less who you date," he lied smoothly. "But you'd given your word about that Texan and I was determined to see that you kept it."

"That's why you followed me tonight?" Her voice was little more than a whisper.

"Right."

"I see." She clasped her hands together tightly in her lap. She'd hoped that he'd admit that he cared for her and had been concerned about her welfare. But that was clearly too much to expect in his present frame of mind.

Jake dropped her off in front of Gram's and drove away as soon as she closed the car door. Once inside the house she struggled to maintain her composure. Gram was asleep and Lily was grateful for that. She would have had trouble recounting the events of this evening. Nothing had gone right, starting with accepting Rex's invitation to dinner.

Knowing that any effort to sleep would be useless, Lily wandered into the kitchen and set the kettle on the burner to boil. When it whistled, she poured the boiling water into a mug before adding a tea bag. A loud knock at the front door surprised her and her heart rocketed to her throat. She didn't have time to react when Jake burst in.

"We need to talk," he announced, coming toward her.

Lily couldn't have moved if her life depended on it.

"Well?" he demanded.

"Would you like a cup of tea?" Lily noticed that his defenses relaxed at the offer.

"Yes."

She busied herself bringing down another cup from the cupboard and adding a tea bag to the steaming water. The action gave her a moment to compose her thoughts. Her head buzzed with all the things she longed to say. As much as she tried, she couldn't keep her gaze off the man who filled the doorway, staring at her.

She gestured toward a chair, indicating that Jake should take a seat. She found it bewildering that only minutes before they had been shouting at each other and now they were behaving like polite strangers.

She set the second steaming mug on the tabletop across from her own and sat facing Jake. She gripped her mug and stared down into the black liquid.

The silence grew heavy and Lily was unsure if she should be the first one to wade into it.

But then they spoke simultaneously.

"Lily—"

"Jake—"

"You first," Jake said and motioned toward her with his hand.

"No…you go first."

"All right." Another lengthy pause followed. "I'm here to apologize."

"For what?"

"Come on, Lily, don't play dumb," He accused.

"I'm not." Her own temper flared. "Are you apologizing for this afternoon or for what happened this evening?"

Jake raked his fingers through his hair. The kitchen suddenly felt small and Jake seemed so large, filling every corner. Despite everything she longed to feel his arms around her again, comforting and gentle.

"I see," Jake said finally. "I guess I do owe you an apology for both." His finger fiddled with the handle of the mug. As yet he hadn't tasted the tea, but then neither had Lily.

"I owe you one myself. I don't know what possessed me to go out with Rex. I shouldn't have. I don't know why I did." Her voice was husky. "That's not exactly true. I went with him because I wanted to get back at you for this afternoon."

"I didn't mean what I said." A telltale muscle twitched along his jaw.

Lily raised her eyes to meet Jake's, unsure that she had understood him correctly.

"Those things I said on the boat were spoken in desperation."

"But why?"

"Come on, Lily, surely you've figured it out by now." He pushed back the chair and stood, taking his tea with him. He marched to the sink and then turned back to her, leaning against the counter as he finally took a sip from his mug.

"You mean because we were kissing again?"

"Bingo."

"But I like kissing you."

"That's the problem, kid."

Lily winced at the use of the childish term. "All right, well, we don't ever have to touch each other again."

It wasn't what Jake wanted, but for his peace of mind and for the sake of a treasured relationship, he had little choice but to agree. "That would be best."

"The kissing was just the result of my own curiosity."

"So you said."

Lily's heart was hammering in her throat. She was forced to admit how much she'd come to enjoy Jake's touch and the thought of them never kissing again filled her with regret. She took a sip of her tea, which had grown lukewarm.

Jake followed suit. There didn't seem to be anything more to say but he wasn't ready to leave, so he searched for an excuse to linger. "You were right about me being unreasonable this evening."

She released a short, audible breath that told of her own remorse. "Going out with Rex and flaunting it in your face like that was childish of me."

"So you knew I was waiting tonight."

"No." Her stare found his. She'd hoped, of course, but she hadn't guessed that he'd be there after their confrontation on the sailboat. "My feelings were hurt and I didn't think you'd care one way or the other if I saw Rex—especially after today—so I agreed to dinner. I regretted it from the minute we left the hotel."

"You seemed to be enjoying your meal." His jaw clenched at the memory of Lily in that fancy French restaurant.

Lily swallowed at the lump of pride that constricted her throat. She'd come this far. "That was an act for your benefit. It's stupid, I know, but at the time it made sense."

A crooked grin lifted one corner of his mouth. "You're lucky that me making a scene in that restaurant *didn't* make sense."

"I guess I am." She returned his smile, wondering if there would ever be a time when his expressive eyes wouldn't affect her.

Jake glanced at his watch. "I suppose I should think about heading home." A few more nights like this one and he'd have trouble paying his bills.

"It is late." Lily couldn't disagree with that, but she didn't want him to leave. She never did.

He took one last swallow of the tea and placed the mug in the sink. "I'm glad we were able to resolve our differences."

"We were both wrong."

"Are you working tomorrow?" He already knew she wasn't, but asking delayed his departure.

"No."

"How about an afternoon on the boat?" It was the least he could do.

Instantly, her dark eyes brightened. Lily loved the *Lucky Lady*, and the thought of spending a carefree afternoon with Jake was an opportunity she couldn't refuse. "You're sure?"

No, he wasn't. Spending the day beside her without

being able to touch her would be pure torture for him. But he knew it would make her happy.

"Jake?"

"I invited you, didn't I?"

"Then I'd love to."

"It's a date then. Meet me around noon?"

"I'll be there." She followed him through the living room to the front door. "Jake."

He turned, his brow knit with doubts over the sailing invitation. "Yeah?"

"Thank you for coming back. I wouldn't have been able to sleep if you hadn't."

His body relaxed. "Me neither." With that he was gone.

The following morning Lily was humming as she worked around the kitchen. She had a lemon meringue pie baking in the oven and was assembling some pastrami sandwiches when Gram returned from the garden nursery. The older woman carted in a full tray of potted plants.

At Lily's dubious look, Gram explained, "They were on sale."

Continuing to pack the sandwiches, Lily commented, "But aren't you the one who insists that we don't save money by spending money?"

"Good grief, no."

"Are you sure?" Lily tried unsuccessfully to hide a smile.

"Of course I'm sure. I may be seventy-four, but my mind is still good. I'm the one who says that when the going gets tough, the tough go shopping."

Lily burst out laughing. "I love you, Gram. I don't think I let you know that nearly often enough."

"Sure you do, girl."

Lily hugged her grandmother. Gram might be a bit eccentric, but she had given Lily a good life, taking her in and raising her in a home full of love. "I've got some news for you."

"What?" Gram leafed through the mail, tossing the junk mail without a second glance. The rest she stuffed into an overflowing basket on the kitchen counter.

"I'm giving the Wheaton my two-week notice."

Gram looked doubtful. "Now why would you do that?"

"I don't like it there. This morning I saw a job posting for a music director at a daycare center. I already called and booked an interview."

"And you'd enjoy that?" Gram regarded her skeptically.

"I'm sure I would. You know how much I like children."

"That you do. You're as natural with them as you are with us old folks."

Opening the refrigerator, Lily scouted its contents, taking out two red apples.

"You going somewhere?"

"Jake and I are taking out the *Lucky Lady*."

Gram sank into a kitchen chair and propped her feet up on the one across from it. "Rick phoned last night. I forgot to tell you."

"What did he want?"

"Just to remind you that he was taking you to dinner tonight."

Lily bit into her bottom lip. "Darn." She'd forgotten about that. "Did he say what time he'd be by?"

"Seven. He didn't seem too happy when I told him you were going out with that fellow from Texas."

Hands on her hips, Lily swiveled around. She'd phoned Gram during her break to explain why she'd be late. "You told him?"

"Had to, girl. He'd mentioned swinging by the hotel to see you."

"Great," Lily grumbled. On second thought it was probably just as well. Rick seemed to want to get too serious too quickly, but Rick was nice and deserved someone who would appreciate him.

"How much do you like this Rick fellow?" Gram wanted to know.

"He's all right."

"Seems to be well off."

"He's got money, if that's what you mean."

"That's what you've been wanting."

The words had a brittle edge to them. Lily opened her mouth to argue that Gram made her sound calculating and shallow, but she found she had no ground. That was exactly the way she'd been in the past. Her ambition to marry rich had made her so narrow-minded that it was little wonder she'd been disappointed with both Rick and Rex.

"I'm not so sure anymore," Lily murmured, tucking the lunch supplies into the bottom of a wicker basket. "I've been doing some thinking lately and I feel that there are certain things in life more valuable than a fat bank account."

"Oh?" Gram gave her a look of mock surprise.

"Money's nice, but it isn't everything."

"The next time house taxes are due I'll tell that to the county clerk."

"We've always managed in the past; we'll do so again."

Gram mumbled something under her breath, but she was smiling and Lily wondered what her game was.

"So you're going to spend the day with Jake? I take it you two have resolved your differences?"

"We're working on it," Lily hedged. They'd taken one step forward, but at the moment it seemed a small one. There was so much she wanted to share with Jake and feared she couldn't. Her job at the Wheaton was coming to an end, but she wouldn't tell Jake until she had another one to replace it. Otherwise he might worry. He cared for Gram and her. Lily only wished he cared a little bit more.

Nine

Jake placed the jib sail on the bow of the *Lucky Lady*. He was nervous about this excursion with Lily and regretted having suggested it. However, he realized that Lily loved being on the water and that the invitation to sail would go a long way toward repairing their friendship.

Strolling down the long dock that led to Jake's boat, Lily saw him working on the bow. She paused to admire him. Her heart fluttered at the sight of his lean, brawny figure. He was all man, rugged and so completely different from Rick that it was difficult to picture them as friends. Jake possessed an indomitable spirit and a fierce pride. Of the two men, Rick was the more urbane and sophisticated, but there was a purity of character in Jake. He was true to himself and his beliefs. Rick was too easily influenced by those around him. He considered it important to flow with the tide. Jake was the type of man who *moved* the tide.

"Morning," she called, standing on the pier and waving at him.

"Good morning." Jake straightened and Lily noted he wasn't smiling. Wasn't he pleased to be sailing today? Was he only doing this for her? Hoping to turn things around, she held up the picnic basket enthusiastically. "I packed us a lunch."

"Good thinking." He climbed down from the bow. "Are you ready to cast off?"

"Aye, aye, captain." She saluted and handed him the basket before climbing aboard. While he fiddled with the ropes, Lily took off her light summer jacket. She'd worn jeans and a sleeveless top, hoping to catch a bit of a tan on her arms. She didn't hold out much hope for this day, but desperately yearned to smooth over the rough edges of their relationship. Jake had been such a good friend. There were things in her life that only Jake knew. She could tell him anything without fear of being criticized or harshly judged. Anyone else would have called her hard-hearted and callous to set her sights on a wealthy man. Not Jake. He'd even gone so far as to introduce her to Rick and try to help her fulfill her ambitions. And she had helped him. Jake longed to be a successful author. He could do it, too. The *New Yorker* wouldn't buy a short story from someone without talent.

"We're going to have nice weather," Jake said, looking to the blue sky.

"Yes, we are." They were tiptoeing around each other, Lily realized, each afraid of the other's response. "Can I raise the sails again?"

"If you want." He kept his sights straight ahead, manning the helm.

Feeling self-conscious and a little unsteady on her feet, Lily climbed to the bow and prepared to raise the sails. She waited until they were clear of the waterway that led from the marina to the deep, greenish waters of San Francisco Bay before hoisting the sails and tying them off. The boat instantly keeled and sliced through the rolling waves.

Holding on to the mast, Lily threw back her head and raised her closed eyes to the warm rays of the summer sun. A sense of exhilaration filled her. Her unbound hair blew behind her head like a flag waving in the breeze. She loved this. Her skin tingled with the force of the wind and the spray of saltwater. "This is great," she called down to Jake a moment later. Finding a comfortable spot, she sat and wrapped her arms around her bent knees. She felt marvelous—better than she had in weeks; giddy with happiness. She looked at Jake and their eyes met. Lily's cheeks grew warm as he studied her. His eyes became serious and seemed to linger on her mouth. She smiled at him. He responded with a short, almost involuntary, grin.

Jake found himself incapable of looking away. Lily was so lovely that the picture of her at this moment, her dark hair wind-tossed and free, would be forever seared in his mind. He yearned to go to her, kneel at her feet, and promise her the world.

He felt as though he'd been punched in the gut. The emotion he felt for her went far beyond friendship. He was in love. All this time he'd *been* in love with her and hadn't been able to admit it—not even to himself.

A frown drove deep grooves in his brow. What was he supposed to do now? He'd always cared for her. Recognizing his feelings couldn't make a difference. There were things that Lily wanted that he could never give her. Fancy parties, diamonds and expensive clothes. From the pittance he earned driving a taxi and writing stories, it was unlikely that he could ever afford those things. He might love her, but he wouldn't let that love destroy her dreams.

Lily studied Jake and noted that he was brooding. She couldn't recall a time when he'd been more withdrawn.

Concerned, she cupped her hands around her mouth and called out: "Are you hungry?"

Jake stared out across the water before answering. "I could eat something." Actually, he was ravenous but he wasn't sure he was ready for Lily to join him on deck. Now that he'd acknowledged his feelings, it would be ten times more difficult to keep her out of his arms.

Lily hadn't eaten since early morning. "I'm starving." Watching her step, she worked her way toward the opposite end of the sailboat to join him.

Jake watched her as she approached. The sun glittered through her hair, giving it an almost heavenly shine. Her lips were pink and so inviting that the muscles in his abdomen tightened. Each step she took emphasized the lovely lines of her neck and shoulders and the curve of her breasts…Jake's thoughts came to an abrupt halt.

This type of thinking wouldn't do either of them any good. He could fantasize until doomsday about making love to Lily and it wouldn't change anything. She was going to marry some rich man and Jake was going to let her.

Lily glanced up from the picnic basket to find Jake watching her, clearly amused. "Is something funny?"

"No." His gaze shot past her to the water, but when he turned back to her, he smiled, his face relaxing and his eyes growing gentle and warm.

Lily experienced the effects of being near Jake almost immediately. She was so tempted to just reach out and touch him. She sat as far away as she dared without being obvious. Yet she was drawn to him like a homing pigeon to its place of rest.

"What did you pack?" Jake asked.

"Pastrami sandwiches and homemade lemon meringue pie." She removed the cellophane and handed him a sandwich.

"Mustard?" He cocked one dark brow with the question.

"Your wish is my command."

"Your memory impresses me."

I'm glad something does, she mumbled to herself, suddenly feeling gloomy. She didn't dare get close to Jake, even in the most innocent way. Lily was tired, having slept only a few hours the previous night. She yearned to curl up in his arms and nestle her head against his chest. She looked away, fearing he would take one look at her and know what she was thinking.

"Aren't you going to eat something?" Jake asked. "I thought you said you were hungry."

"I am," she answered, somewhat defensively. Reaching inside the basket, she withdrew another sandwich, unwrapped it and took a bite. "There's cold beer if you want one," she told him.

"Sure." Lily grabbed one for him and another for herself.

"I didn't know you liked beer. I thought you preferred wine."

"I do sometimes. Beer's good too. It's an acquired taste. Gram says it's good for what ails you."

Jake downed a large swallow and wiped his mouth off with the back of his hand. "Gram's right."

Lily took a more delicate swig. The liquid felt cold all the way to her stomach. She took another bite of the sandwich. "My dad was a big beer drinker."

"You've never spoken much of your father."

"He died when I was young." Lily looked at the sails as they billowed in the wind, avoiding eye contact with Jake.

"What about your mother?"

"I don't remember her," she said, her voice growing soft. "The pictures Gram gave me of her make me wish I had. She was really beautiful. But she died of complications following surgery."

"You must have been very young."

"Three. Gram took me in then because Dad traveled so much. I don't think Dad ever recovered from losing my mother. Gram says they loved each other like no two people she'd ever known, except her and Paddy. Yet my parents were nothing alike. Mom was delicate. From her pictures, she looks like a fragile princess. And Dad was this big hulk of guy—a lumberjack sort of fellow. I have wonderful memories of him. Whenever he'd come home it was like Christmas;

he brought Gram and me the most marvelous gifts. I saved every one. Mom and Dad's picture sits on my dresser. I'll show it to you sometime if you'd like."

The smile in Jake's eyes widened and spread to his mouth. "You must resemble her."

"Me?" Lily laughed. "No, I'm more like my dad. I've got this big nose and fat cheeks and ears that tend to stick out."

"You're lovely."

"Why, Jake, what a nice thing to say." She laughed and took another swallow of the beer. "When was the last time you had your eyes examined?" It felt good to tease him again. "What about your parents?"

"There's not much to tell. They're both still alive. I don't see them often. I'm kind of the black sheep of the family. My two brothers are successful. One's a bank executive and the other's a physician."

"And you're the almost famous writer." Lily was obliged to defend him. This past month when Lily had been seeing Rick and Rex had taught her how unfair it was to judge people by their bank balance.

"No, I'm a cabdriver and a failure. After all, they paid for four years of college for me that have completely gone to waste."

"It hasn't been wasted."

"In their eyes it has."

"You're a strong and solid man and if your parents don't see that, then I pity them." Jake was earthy and intelligent. A man of character and grit. He may have chosen a different path than his brothers, but that didn't make him any less a success.

"My mother would like you." His voice was oddly

gruff. "She'd see you as just the type who could reform me."

"But you don't want to be saved. Remember?"

"You're right about that." But if anyone could ever do it, it would be Lily. A house, family and responsibilities wouldn't be half bad if he shared his life with her. The change wouldn't come easy, but he would be more prone to consider it with her.

They finished their beer and sandwiches and Jake ate a thick slice of pie, praising her efforts.

The sun shone brightly against the horizon and the boat plowed smoothly ahead through the choppy waters. Gradually, Lily's head began to droop. The beer had added to her sleepiness, and now she fought to keep her eyes open.

Intent on his duties, Jake didn't seem to notice until Lily started to slouch against his side. Instinctively he reached for her, looping an arm around her shoulders and pressing her weight to his side. The sheer pleasure of holding her was overwhelming. And yet it felt so natural. Pressing his face into her hair, he breathed in the fresh scent of her. She reminded him of summer wine.

Closing his eyes, Jake took in another deep breath and held it. He'd never told another living soul about his parents' disappointment in him. His love for Lily surged at the way she'd wanted to defend him. Her eyes had sparked with fiery indignation. A lazy smile spread over his features. The wind changed directions and he expertly manipulated the canvas sails around to catch the power of the moving air.

Relaxed now, he stretched out his legs and crossed

them at the ankles. A man could get accustomed to this. The woman he loved was in his arms and the sea was at his command.

Lily stirred, feeling secure and warm. Slowly she opened her eyes and realized the cause of this incredible relaxed sensation. Suspecting that any sudden movement would destroy the moment, Lily gradually raised her face to Jake. His serious eyes met hers.

The sails flapped in the breeze and still Jake didn't move. Lily remained motionless and the moment stretched out until she lost all concept of time. It could have been seconds or even minutes, she didn't know. Jake's face was so close to hers that she could see every line etched in his face. Jake smiled. Then, a fraction of an inch at a time, his mouth edged toward hers.

Lily closed her eyes, surrendering to him. Ever so gradually, his mouth eased onto hers. Lily felt her heart melt, but resisted the urge to lock her arms around his neck. Although she yearned for more, she was unwilling to invite it. Only the day before, Jake had ardently claimed he hadn't wanted this. Yet here he was, holding her, kissing her and looking as though it would take all the forces of heaven and hell to drive them apart.

The kiss lindered for what seemed like a lifetime. When he finally dragged his mouth from hers, Lily didn't protest. Her response had to be careful. It would be tragic to destroy this moment. She kept her eyes closed and savored the feel of his breath as it continued to fan her lips. She could tell that Jake was as affected by the kiss as she.

"Oh, Lily," he whispered. Jake bent his index finger and gently pressed it to her lips. "Did you enjoy your nap?"

Her response was a faint nod.

"Good."

Unhurriedly, as if moving in slow motion, Jake lifted his arm from her shoulders. Lily shifted her weight and stretched. Sitting up straight, she smoothed her hands over her jean-clad thighs, searching for something to say.

"We're doing it again and we said we wouldn't," Jake said.

Lily cast her gaze to the deck. "You're right."

"We should think about heading back. It's been a full afternoon."

Lily felt hurt and cheated. Why did Jake find it so objectionable to kiss her? Every time he did, it was wonderful. "Okay," she mumbled. "If that's what you want."

"Don't you?"

"No. Yes. I don't know anymore. What's wrong with kissing me?" she asked him bluntly.

"Plenty. I'm not right for you." His brow narrowed into a heavy frown. "I'd never make you happy."

"I'm happy with you now," she cried, her voice breaking.

"Sure you are, but it won't last, Lily. I'm saving us both a lot of heartache, understand?"

"No, I don't."

His mouth hardened and he stared straight ahead, effectively closing her out. Lily had seen that look often enough to realize that she might as well argue with a brick wall, for all the good it would do her.

A sudden chill went all the way to her bones. She reached for her jacket. Jake was freezing her out again; but somehow it hurt more this time.

As they neared the marina, Jake momentarily gave her the helm and moved forward to lower the sails. The lump in the back of her throat had grown so large she could barely swallow. Even breathing was difficult. Today should have been special. And now it was ruined.

"Lily, listen. I'm doing this for your own good."

"Stop it, Jake," she all but shouted. "Why can't you be honest, for once? I don't know what you're trying to prove. I couldn't even begin to guess. I'm tired of playing your games."

The *Lucky Lady* glided smoothly into her berth. Lily waited just long enough for the boat to steady before leaping onto the dock.

"Lily, wait." Jake jumped after her, pausing to secure the vessel. "Don't leave like this. We need to talk this out." He didn't know what he could say, but seeing Lily this upset was more than he could bear. He had to find some way to reason with her.

She turned to face him squarely. "Sorry, no time. I've got a date with Rick."

The words hit Jake with all the force of a freight train. She had a date? Jake held her gaze and a muscle flexed convulsively in his jaw. Apparently it didn't bother her to go from one man's arms to another's. "Then what's keeping you?"

"You certainly wouldn't be interested in keeping me, would you?" Maybe it was cruel of her but she wanted him to experience just a little of what she was feeling. "Rick likes me. He isn't hot and cold."

Sadly she shook her head. "Goodbye, Jake." She turned and walked up the narrow dock. Every step took her farther from Jake and somehow Lily felt she'd never be coming back.

Jake watched her go, his fist knotted at his side. Half of him demanded that he race after her, but the other commanded that he stay exactly where he was. Against all good sense, he'd done it again. He'd kissed her and regretted it, punishing Lily for his own weakness. It wasn't Lily's fault he couldn't control himself around her. Nor was it her problem that he'd fallen in love with her. But something had to be done. And quickly.

In the past, he'd toyed with the idea of packing up and moving down the coast. They couldn't continue on this way. They were confusing one another, fighting their feelings, denying what they yearned for most. He had to get out of her life completely. There was no help for it. He had to leave.

Jumping back on the deck of his boat, Jake moved with determined strides. Now that he'd made up his mind, he felt better.

Belowdecks, he reached for the sea maps, charting his course down the California coast. He was a free man, no ties, no bonds. He could go without a backward glance. Except...

Jake paused. *Except.*

He slumped against the counter. He couldn't leave Lily. It would be like leaving a part of himself behind. Who was he trying to fool? He loved her. Loved her enough to give up the precious freedom he'd struggled to maintain all these years.

He'd sell the boat before he'd lose Lily. The thought nearly paralyzed him. He'd meant it. Lily was worth ten thousand *Lucky Lady*'s.

When a man felt that strongly for a woman there was only one option: marriage. He waited for the natural aversion to overtake him. It didn't. The startling fact was that it actually sounded quite appealing.

His mind conjured up a house with a white picket fence around it. He could see Lily in the front yard planting flowers, pregnant.

That, too, had a nice feel to it. Jake hadn't thought of it much, but he'd like to have a son. And a daughter would be a joy if she looked anything like Lily.

Marriage, a family, responsibilities, a regular job—those were all the things he'd despised over the years. Jake had claimed they weren't for him. But they would be if he had Lily at his side. All this time he'd had the gut feeling that Rex and Rick were wrong for her. Of course they were. *He* was the one meant for Lily. In time, Jake would give her the fancy things she wanted. He even looked forward to doing it.

Shuffling through his closet, Jake took out his best clothes. He'd shower and shave first so he'd look halfway decent. A man didn't ask a woman to be his wife every day of the week.

"Hi, Gram." Lily walked in the front door and tried to put on a happy face.

Rocking in her chair, Gram glanced away from the TV show she was watching. "You've been crying."

"It…just looks that way. I've got something in my eye."

"Like tears," Gram scoffed, slowly getting to her feet. "What happened?"

"Nothing." Lily's could feel her control slipping. "Jake kissed…me," she finally said.

"Why, that's no reason to cry, child." Gram gave her a perplexed look as if she couldn't comprehend why Lily would find Jake's kiss so repulsive.

"I—I…know…but…he…doesn't…want…me."

"He'd hardly be kissing you if it wasn't what he wanted."

"You don't understand." She wiped the tears from her face. "I'm so in love with him, Gram. But you know Jake. He doesn't want a woman in his life. Loving him has ruined everything. We've lost him."

Gram's look was thoughtful as she slipped her arm around Lily's waist and hugged her close. "Dry those tears. You and I have weathered worse over the years. And as for losing Jake, we can't lose something we never had. Let Jake sort this out for himself. He's a smart man."

"I don't ever want to see him again."

The older woman smiled. "You don't mean that. But I know how you feel. Paddy and me had some pretty good fights in our time."

"We didn't fight," Lily insisted. In some ways she wished they had. An argument would have cleared the air. It might even have brought out the truth and helped them find a solution—if there was one.

Slowly Gram walked into the kitchen and put on the kettle. "I'll make you a cup of Marmite."

"Thanks, Gram," she said solemnly. She'd spent so much time trying to find herself a wealthy man that she'd allowed herself to be blind to the treasures she already possessed.

The last thing Lily felt like doing was getting ready for her date with Rick. She had to end things. She'd been using him and that couldn't continue.

The doorbell chimed just when Lily was touching up her makeup. The telltale redness around her eyes had faded and she looked reasonably attractive.

Lily stuck her head around the corner to be sure that Gram had answered the door. With the television blaring, Gram often didn't hear the bell. It had gotten so bad that Jake had become accustomed to knocking once and letting himself in. At the thought of Jake, a tiny shudder went all the way through her.

Rick stood awkwardly in the living room and Lily offered him her brightest smile. She wasn't looking forward to this evening. "I'll be with you in a minute."

"Take your time," he said, smiling back at her.

Tonight wouldn't be easy, but she wasn't going to be maudlin.

After grabbing her purse and a light wrap, she rejoined Gram and Rick in the living room, forcing herself to smile.

Knowing Lily would be out with Rick, Jake waited for what he considered a reasonable amount of time before heading over to Gram's. Content now that he'd made his decision, he climbed inside his faithful taxi and absently ran his hand along the empty seat. He'd sell the cab. That would be the first thing to go. While waiting, he'd scanned the newspaper. Finding a decent job shouldn't be too difficult. Engineers seemed to be in demand, and although his degree had several years' dust on it, he'd been a good student. An employer would recognize that soon enough.

On impulse, Jake stopped at a corner market and picked up a small bouquet of flowers. He didn't know what kind they were; flowers were Lily and Gram's department. Humming, he eased to a stop in front of Gram's house, climbed out of the car and slapped his hand across the hood as he ventured past. He felt good. Once everything was straightened out with Lily, he'd be on cloud nine.

Gram answered his knock and he proudly shoved the flowers in her direction. "Is Lily home yet?"

"Are these for me or her?"

"Both."

"I'd say you're a bit late."

It wasn't like Gram to snap or grumble. Jake glanced at his watch. "It's barely ten."

"That's not the late I'm talking about."

"Is Lily home or not?" His own patience was running short.

"Not. I don't know what's come over you, but Lily came home from her time with you in tears."

Shifting his weight from one foot to the other, Jake cleared his throat. He hadn't expected the third degree from Gram. "I came to apologize for that."

"And I'm telling you, you're too late."

A sudden chill went all the way through Jake. "What do you mean?"

"Rick was here earlier."

"I know." All evening he'd been haunted by the image of Rick kissing Lily. He'd considered intercepting their date, but he'd done that before and had promised himself he wouldn't again.

"Only this time Rick didn't come alone."

Confused, Jake shook his head, not understanding Lily's grandmother. "How do you mean?"

"Rick came a-courting with a two-karat diamond ring in his pocket," Gram explained. "He's requested my permission to ask for Lily's hand."

Ten

"I see," Jake said slowly. The words went sour on his tongue. He did indeed understand. Lily had finally achieved her goal. She'd landed herself a wealthy man. Swallowing back the angry denial that trembled at the end of his tongue, Jake buried his hands deep inside his pants pockets. "I imagine Lily was thrilled?" He raised expectant eyes to Gram. The happy, carefree feeling that had been with him from the moment he'd decided to ask Lily to marry him slowly shriveled up and died.

"I can't rightly say. Rick planned on asking her at dinner this evening."

"Lily will accept." She'd be a fool not to, Jake knew.

"It's the best offer she's likely to get," Gram asserted, eyeing Jake in his best clothes. "But I'll tell her you were by."

"Don't." The lone word burst forcefully from his lips. "It wasn't anything important." He took a step back and bumped into the front door. Abruptly he turned around and gripped the doorknob, needing a moment to gather his thoughts. "Actually," he said, turning back to Gram. "On second thought you can mention that I was here. Tell Lily that I wish her and Rick every happiness."

"Do you want me to tell her anything else?" Gram encouraged with her usual astuteness. "You didn't bring these flowers for an old woman."

Jake's gaze fell on the elephant tusks mounted on the wall and the zebra-skin rug spread in front of the fireplace. Herbie, the shrunken head who Gram claimed was their spiritual protector, sat on the end table in its place of honor. Jake would miss all of it, and Gram with her African chants and wise old eyes.

"No," he murmured sadly. There was nothing left to say. Lily's dreams had come true, and his nightmares were of his own making.

The following morning, Lily sat down at the kitchen table with a mug of hot coffee. She needed the caffeine. The evening with Rick had been a disaster from the start. After he'd learned that she'd gone out with Rex, Rick had panicked and come to her with a huge diamond ring and a marriage proposal. She didn't want to hurt him, but she couldn't marry him either.

The morning paper was spread across the table and Lily mindlessly read the headlines. Gram pulled out a chair to join her. "Where'd the flowers come from?" Lily asked, noting the colorful bouquet in the middle of the table.

Gram glanced up from the comic-strip section of the newspaper and grinned. "A secret admirer."

"Oh?" Gram had attracted more than one man. But

to the best of her knowledge, Lily had never known her grandmother to see or talk of anyone except her beloved Paddy.

"Only my secret admirer couldn't decide if the gift was meant for me or you. He finally decided on me."

"And who could this indecisive fellow be? Tom the butcher? Or that new man who's been eyeing you at bingo?"

"Nope. It was Jake."

"Jake!" Lily did her utmost to disguise the wild happiness that shot through her. "Jake was here? When?"

Idly, Gram folded the newspaper to the crossword section and scrunched up her brow as she studied the fine print. "Late last night. It must have been close to ten."

Nearly too overwhelmed to speak, Lily stumbled over her words. "Why didn't you… What did he… Flowers?" She clenched the soft bathrobe at her throat. Jake. Here. Why, oh why, hadn't Gram said anything sooner?

"I don't know what he wanted. He was acting oddly."

Lily jumped to her feet. "I'm going to get dressed. Did he stay long?"

"Five minutes or so. Not long." Gram didn't look up as her pencil worked furiously across the newspaper, filling in the words. "Just remember what I told you the first time we met Jake: you and he were meant for each other."

There was a gleam in Gram's eye that hinted at something more, something she wasn't saying.

"Since Jake came by here, it would only be polite

to return the visit. Right?" She didn't wait for Gram to answer her. "He obviously had something on his mind or he wouldn't have come. I mean, it isn't like Jake to stop by unexpectedly." He did exactly that three or four times a week but Lily was grateful her grandmother didn't point it out.

Hardly caring what she wore, Lily dug through her drawer and found a pair of white linen pants and a floral print top. A quick run of the brush through her hair left it looking shimmering and healthy.

At the marina, the first thing Lily noticed was Jake's taxi with a For Sale sign propped against the dashboard. Lily stared at it with disbelief. The money from the short story sale to the *New Yorker* had been good, but not enough to live on. Jake would never sell his source of income.

Hurrying now, she half-ran down the wooden dock that led to his slip. She spotted him immediately, working on the deck, coiling a large section of rope around his arm. Her pace slowed. Now that she was here, there didn't seem to be anything particular to say. Although he was facing her, he didn't acknowledge her approach or give any indication that he'd seen her.

"Morning, Jake." She stood with her hands clenched together in front of her.

He ignored her, continuing to wind the thick rope around his arm, using his elbow as a guide.

"There's a For Sale sign on the cab."

"I know."

"But why?"

"It's for sale." His voice held no welcome.

Lily could see that this topic wasn't going anywhere. "Gram said you were by the house last night."

"I was."

If he didn't stop with that stupid rope and look at her soon, she was going to rip it out of his arms. "The flowers are lovely."

Jake's mouth tightened. "Consider them a goodbye present."

Her heart pounded wildly in her ears. "Goodbye?"

"Yeah, I'm moving down the coast."

"This is all rather sudden, isn't it?"

"I've been thinking about it for some time."

Lily set her hands on her hips. "You'd move just to spite me, wouldn't you?"

For the first time, he halted and glanced up at her, his eyes a brilliant green. His feet were braced slightly apart as if anticipating a fight. "You're not making any sense. I'm moving because…"

"Because you're afraid."

Jake snorted. Inwardly, he admitted that she was probably right. He couldn't be around Lily without wanting her and the best thing for them both was to remove the temptation. "I've fought in Iraq, tangled with drunks who couldn't afford to pay their fare, and listened to your grandmother sing an African chant over my head. I'd say you have little reason to accuse me of cowardice." That, too, was a half-truth. Just being close to Lily caused him to tremble. What had made perfect sense the day before seemed like utter stupidity now. He loved her, yes. But that didn't mean they should get married.

"You're going away because of me."

"Yes!" Jake shouted, feeling angry and unreasonable. "I have this particular quirk about being seen with a married woman."

"I'm not married."

"Not yet, but you will be. Gram told me about Rick's proposal."

She held up her bare left hand, fanning her fingers. "I turned him down."

"That wasn't a smart move."

"I don't love Rick."

"That's your problem, Lily. You've got too much conscience. Loving him isn't necessary. Rick can give you all the fancy things you want."

"He can't give me what I want the very most."

"Give him time."

"Even that won't work," she assured him.

"And what is it that you want so badly?"

"You."

His dark eyes found hers, stunned and staring. "You don't mean that."

"I love you, Jake Carson."

"I don't have the money to buy you a fat diamond."

"A simple gold band will do." For every argument Jake presented, she would find a solution. She hadn't come this far to let him slip away.

"My home is right here. There isn't going to be any fancy house." *Except maybe one with a white picket fence and a row of flowers at the front.*

"In case you hadn't noticed, I love the *Lucky Lady*. We'll live right here."

"And what about kids? There's no room for children here." He gestured casually at the confines of the sailboat.

"Then we'll buy a bigger boat."

"I told you before that I can't give you the things Rick could." He didn't know why he continued to argue. He loved her.

"No, you probably can't. But I've learned how meaningless diamonds are. I love you, Jake, and if you love me back, I'd consider myself the wealthiest ex-piano player in town."

Jake's defenses relaxed as he let the rope fall to the deck. He held out a hand to Lily, guiding her safely aboard the *Lucky Lady*'s and into his arms. He buried his face in her hair and held her for several minutes, just breathing in the fresh fragrance of her. "I love you so much that part of me would have died to stand by and watch you marry Rick."

"Then why would you have let me?" Even now she couldn't understand his reasoning.

"Because I wanted to give you all those material things you deserved. But in order to do that, I had to let you go."

Lovingly, Lily cupped his face. His strong, proud features seemed to intensify with each word.

Lily sighed as relief washed over her. "The only thing I'll ever want is you."

"I'm already yours. I have been since that night in the attic and probably long before then, only I refused to acknowledge it." His strong arms held her closer as if he feared she would escape him.

Lily's eyes gleamed with happiness. "Gram was right."

"About what?"

"Before I left this morning, she told me that you and I were destined to be together."

Unable to resist any longer, Jake tenderly kissed the corner of her mouth. "How could she be so sure of that?"

Lily's hands toyed with the hair at the back of his neck. "Remember the day we met in front of the Wheaton when Gram chanted over you?"

His mouth found her cheek. "I'm not likely to forget it."

"Gram was sealing our fate. That was a fertility rite. We're doomed to live a long, happy life. And from what Gram said, we're going to need a very large boat in the years to come."

Jake chuckled. "I can live with that," he told her, and then he kissed her, certain that this time he'd never let go.

* * * * *

BARBARA CLAYPOLE WHITE

Bestselling author Will Shepard is caught in the twilight of grief after his young son dies in a car accident. But when his father's aging mind erases the memory, Will rewrites the truth. The story he spins brings unexpected relief…until he's forced to return to rural North Carolina, trapping himself in a lie.

Holistic veterinarian Hannah Linden is a healer who opens her heart to strays, but can only watch, powerless, as her grown son struggles with inner demons. When she rents her guest cottage to Will and his dad, she finds solace in trying to mend their broken world, even while her own shatters.

As their lives connect and collide, Will and Hannah become each other's only hope—if they can find their way into a new story, one that begins with love.

The In-Between Hour

Available wherever books are sold.

Be sure to connect with us at:
Harlequin.com/Newsletters
Facebook.com/HarlequinBooks
Twitter.com/HarlequinBooks

MBCW1475

REQUEST YOUR
FREE BOOKS!

2 FREE NOVELS
FROM THE ROMANCE COLLECTION
PLUS 2 FREE GIFTS!

YES! Please send me 2 FREE novels from the Romance Collection and my 2 FREE gifts (gifts are worth about $10). After receiving them, if I don't wish to receive any more books, I can return the shipping statement marked "cancel." If I don't cancel, I will receive 4 brand-new novels every month and be billed just $6.24 per book in the U.S. or $6.74 per book in Canada. That's a savings of at least 22% off the cover price. It's quite a bargain! Shipping and handling is just 50¢ per book in the U.S. and 75¢ per book in Canada.* I understand that accepting the 2 free books and gifts places me under no obligation to buy anything. I can always return a shipment and cancel at any time. Even if I never buy another book, the two free books and gifts are mine to keep forever.

194/394 MDN F4XY

Name _____ (PLEASE PRINT) _____

Address _____ Apt. # _____

City _____ State/Prov. _____ Zip/Postal Code _____

Signature (if under 18, a parent or guardian must sign)

Mail to the Harlequin® Reader Service:
IN U.S.A.: P.O. Box 1867, Buffalo, NY 14240-1867
IN CANADA: P.O. Box 609, Fort Erie, Ontario L2A 5X3

Want to try two free books from another line?
Call 1-800-873-8635 or visit www.ReaderService.com.

* Terms and prices subject to change without notice. Prices do not include applicable taxes. Sales tax applicable in N.Y. Canadian residents will be charged applicable taxes. Offer not valid in Quebec. This offer is limited to one order per household. Not valid for current subscribers to the Romance Collection or the Romance/Suspense Collection. All orders subject to credit approval. Credit or debit balances in a customer's account(s) may be offset by any other outstanding balance owed by or to the customer. Please allow 4 to 6 weeks for delivery. Offer available while quantities last.

Your Privacy—The Harlequin® Reader Service is committed to protecting your privacy. Our Privacy Policy is available online at www.ReaderService.com or upon request from the Harlequin Reader Service.

We make a portion of our mailing list available to reputable third parties that offer products we believe may interest you. If you prefer that we not exchange your name with third parties, or if you wish to clarify or modify your communication preferences, please visit us at www.ReaderService.com/consumerchoice or write to us at Harlequin Reader Service Preference Service, P.O. Box 9062, Buffalo, NY 14269. Include your complete name and address.

DEBBIE MACOMBER